STILL A RISING TIDE

Still
A RISING TIDE

Still, Race Matters!

DAVID BRUCE GRIM

Palmetto Publishing Group
Charleston, SC

Still a Rising Tide

First Edition

Printed in the United States

ISBN-13: 978-1-64111-137-9
ISBN-10: 1-64111-137-2

DEDICATION

To honor the first freedmen of the Civil War and their descendants.

I hope I have done justice to the strength of their character, the power of their persistence, and the depth of their faith.

ENSLAVED, *NOW FREE*

To be inside slavery and then to be out;
to be under masters and then be without.
Can there be any greater freedom to earn?
Once in bondage, now free. Are there lessons to learn?

A greater injustice no man can do
than to subjugate others in a system so cruel.
To live like kings off the labor of others;
to whip them, kill them, and rape future mothers.

To assume it's one's right to steal humans from home;
to chain down their lives to lift up one's own.
To eliminate hope for a better tomorrow,
and not give a damn at the breadth of their sorrow.

To cut off strong limbs to ward off aggression;
to separate families for profit or lesson;
to live with the fear that their masters would sell them.
These were the slaves' lives in times antebellum.

Such awful treatment would leave anyone seething,
and wanting to be free as long as they're breathing.
Is there any doubt why slaves fought to be free then?
An amazing faith graced that a just God would free them.

Our leaders send troops to fight for our "freedom."
But abuse of that word sometimes loses its meaning.
Being already free, we live as we choose,
our life and prosperity not threatened to lose.

But slave times are lost in our memory bank;
not easy to discuss without being too frank.
We wish not to speak of what whites did to blacks;
no fitting self-image when strapped to our backs.

We cannot square our ideals with this truth,
so we hide it away and ignore the proof.
Is it willful ignorance or desire to forget?
We know that accounting has gone on unmet.

Society worked to keep slave days in mystery.
How can it be muted in learning our history?
That the Civil War ending meant black liberation
runs counter to Southern states' rights education.

Yes, slaves were inside, their descendants are out.
But the facts of enslavement can leave no doubt
that we owe it to those who were trapped in this hell
to remember this story and tell of it well.

David Grim, May 2007 (revised)

TABLE OF CONTENTS

ACKNOWLEDGEMENTS

THERE ARE MANY WHO CONTRIBUTED TO THE COMPLETION OF *STILL a Rising Tide*. First thanks must go to Barb Banus, who edited with patience and care, as she did for *Swift Currents*. Whenever the need arose, Barb conducted extensive research, and whenever my direction or devotion to task was in question, Barb brought her enthusiasm, support, and persistence. It is simply a fact that without her energy and intelligence, *Still a Rising Tide* would not exist. My gratitude is deep and heartfelt.

Then, the reviews and comments provided by Kate Joy, Peg Reider, Lanny Straus, Carolyn Hill, Warren Slesinger, Gary Grim, Marge Barber, and John Barber were so thoughtful, honest, and accurate. I was well advised to follow their guidance, and a substantially improved product was the result. Similarly, I am so appreciative of the cultural sensitivity and grammatical good sense provided by Ron Daise. Burton Sauls has created a reader-friendly website to support my two books and to encourage the necessary dialogue on race the nation needs. Please visit at DavidBruceGrim.com. I am very pleased to thank two talented individuals for the book cover. My wonderful daughter, Kelli Marielle Grim, provided a beautiful painting that was adapted and photographed by the amazing Hank D. Herring.

Finally, I must express my appreciation for the support, encouragement, and work by the fine professionals at Palmetto Publishing Group.

INTRODUCTION

Still a Rising Tide tells the story of an African-American family as it works to survive and find success in the South Carolina sea islands during and after Reconstruction. We first met this family in the historical novel *Swift Currents* when Callie and her brothers were freed from bondage in 1861 by the United States victory in the Battle of Port Royal Sound. *Swift Currents* concluded in 1863 with freedom from slavery established for ten thousand sea islanders due to Union occupation in the region, but with the fate of the nation and the status of enslaved people still in question.

The sequel, *Still A Rising Tide*, is set in 1893 as Callie Hewitt returns home to St. Helena Island, South Carolina, after thirty years working to help sick and wounded people, first on Civil War battlefields and then at the Freedmen's Hospital in Washington. Callie is determined to write a book about the freedom trail she has walked beginning the day she was freed of her master in November 1861. She asks her sister-in-law, former teacher Lilly Bradley Sargent, to take notes as Callie "journeys back" through the Reconstruction Era in the telling of her stories to the family's next generations. For the next week, the past and present collide, but finally, the family reunion Callie has hoped for occurs, and there are even signs of improved racial harmony, despite the setbacks for freedmen in recent years.

For days, wind and rain off the Atlantic Ocean have been increasing, and then the Great Sea Island Cyclone arrives with powerful winds and massive storm surge inundating the islands. In the face of rising tides of relentless racism, as well the unforgiving waves of a surging storm, this family shows the resilience and dignity that have been required of African-American families in search of their rightful place in this country.

AUTHOR NOTES ON THE GULLAH DIALOGUE

IT IS IMPORTANT TO ME THAT THE GULLAH dialogue in *STILL A RISING TIDE* accurately represents the language yet is accessible to the reader. Just as the language is called Gullah, the people are Gullah, and their culture is referred to as Gullah. Connecting with the language even a little bit allows greater understanding of the culture and the impact on the people of the turbulent events described in this book.

Some characters in *Still a Rising Tide* experience great change in their lives that affects their speech. For instance, Callie lived and worked for thirty years in Washington, and her use of Gullah during that time was limited. As she returns to the sea islands, she meets her brother Lucas, who has been a waterman in the lowcountry all his life and has spoken only Gullah except when business required that he speak more standard English to be successful. His wife, Lilly, taught soldiers of the First South Carolina Volunteers to read and write during the Civil War. Though she was raised a black child of the South and could communicate in island patois, she also had a working knowledge of standard English and spoke it with their children and with Lucas to improve his business conversations with white people.

To the extent the reader is able to sound out the phrases phonetically, the richness of the Gullah language of African-Americans on the southeast United States coast can be more fully appreciated. To assist in that result, there is a Gullah Glossary at the back of the book and, in a few select spots, I have provided some standard English translation in parentheses.

SECTION ONE

Chapter 1

Friday, August 18, 1893

Coming south on the narrowing Beaufort River, the steamer slowed, its paddles churning at half their normal speed on its journey from Charleston. Callie felt the vessel ride the river swells created when winds from the north joined the outgoing tide draining southward toward the Atlantic Ocean. She held onto the rail, studying the landscape as the river opened to a wide, looping curve before turning west, where the little town of Beaufort sat on a bluff. She inhaled the warm, salt air as she surveyed acres of marsh grass, resplendent in the bright, lime green of late August. Shore birds fluttered into sight briefly over the spiked cordgrass while egrets extended their necks to sight prey in the low tidewater.

Callie watched a line of pelicans gliding into the steady breeze in their familiar "V" formation. Suddenly, memories of her enslavement on these sea islands more than thirty years before came rushing into her thoughts. Just as Callie began to feel the old fear induced by her master, the steamer rose and fell abruptly from a large rippling wake left by a passing ship, causing her to lurch forward.

An older gentleman, nicely dressed with graying hair, had been on deck enjoying the morning air when he noticed the tall, dignified, brown-skinned woman before she started to sway. He stepped to Callie's side, asking if he could help her to a chair. She was not expecting such kindness from a white man in South Carolina. She felt bolstered by his inquiry as much as by the strength in his arm and yet all the more determined to stand firmly on her own. That determination was matched by Callie's keen awareness of just how unkempt she felt having worn her new gray traveling suit for the entire journey with only one change of her shirtwaist.

Callie smiled slightly while shaking her head "no." The gentleman respectfully took a step back, but he used conversation as a reason to stay near should she falter from the choppy water. He disclosed that he was returning to Port Royal Sound having served here in the Navy during the Civil War, and that he found the region more beautiful than he remembered. Callie immediately responded that she too was here during the war and now was coming back to stay after living and working up north.

In rapid succession, Callie found herself telling him that she was born into slavery on these islands and became free of her master in 1861 when he fled from the US military during the battle of Port Royal Sound. Then she departed by hospital ship two years later on this very same river. She touched on some aspects of her life as a trapped slave woman yearning for freedom, but her descriptions sounded to her more clinical than personal, like stories lived by someone else. She told of the menial tasks and the endless labor required of the enslaved but wanted to share nothing of the indignities and the deprivations she experienced when forced to respond to her master's every demand and whim.

As she spoke, her listener watched her with rapt attention. With every new anecdote of her younger years as a slave, he noticed that Callie grew more animated and her earlier self-consciousness seemed to disappear, making her fifty-five years of life experience harder to detect. Momentum moving her on, Callie continued:

"I learned early on that it was better to pick yourself up when you been beat down. It never helped to tell Massa how many ways I be mad wid him, and I didn't have power to make him change. So, I decided long befo I got my freedom that I had to show him my nice sef, show him how strong I be to take what he give out and move on from it. I even saw how good it made him feel once when I told him I forgive him for how rough he got wid me sometime. Why, you shoulda seen the mean smile that came across his face when he tink he done got ovah on me." She paused with weary recognition. "I just knew my life would be a little less hell if I told him wha he wanna hear."

She turned to the man she had just met, to whom she had just divulged such significant details of her life, to see if he was still listening, slightly embarrassed that she had slipped into some of her natural Gullah dialect as she carried the story forth. When she looked up into his eyes with her head cocked inquisitively, he seemed to understand, shaking his head slowly as he lowered his gaze. Clearly engaged and seeking to understand her pain, he offered softly, "I'm sorry."

Callie quickly shifted the conversation and talked excitedly about her family. "That was more than thirty years ago. Now I get to come back home—be with my family. I love my brudda and his wife. She is like the sista I never had. When I come home ten and twenty yeahs ago, I saw that Lilly brought life to my brudda Lucas, and I thank God for that. But for me, she my sista, plain an simple." Wiping watering eyes, Callie continued, "She raised up my Sunny when I had to go up north—had to leave my daughter during de wah."

That disclosure naturally led to an explanation of how she had first learned about her parents during the war. When she discovered who they were and that they were somewhere near Washington, she felt compelled to go find them. She described her opportunities to learn enough nursing skills to be of service in the US Army Medical Corps, helping the wounded while traveling with Union soldiers in Virginia and Maryland in 1864.

Callie had just begun to tell more family stories when she looked up to see her audience of one, her "rescuer," begin to waver as their boat slowed abruptly. While holding the rail, Callie quickly grasped his forearm. "I hope my stories didn't wear you out, sir. I am sorry to have gone on so. I have too much on my mind, and it just pours out my mouth."

After all, he had only approached her to ask if she felt faint and yet stayed engaged in her telling beyond any expectations she would have had. What right did she have to impose her detailed heartache and heritage on him? And what kept his interest? The gentleman looked up into Callie's face, gently freed himself of her grip on his arm, and leaned toward her. "Your stories are wonderful."

She would have continued, but the steamer came to a full stop at the Beaufort wharf.

LUCAS WAS SO INTENT ON BEING ON TIME TO GREET CALLIE WHEN the steamer arrived that he jumped from the bateau while it was more than a foot from the ferry dock. Leaving his two grown sons to tie up, he hurried to the end of the dock, where two old friends sat taking in the morning. Lucas's excitement was evident to his fellow watermen who, like Lucas, had always fed and supported their families from what they could take from the sea.

Grinning, Santos said, "Ah Luke, yo dahlin Lilly mus mek oona a happy man—fix de mos special breakfas dishyuh day. Oona be crack yo teet (Your smile is) too bright fuh me ol eye." He finished by covering his eyes with his broad, seasoned hand.

Joe Benny chimed in: "Ya man, ih seem fuh sho a extra hop in ih shoe dishyuh monin." And he leaned into Santos to better share their laughter.

Lucas playfully scolded them. "Hush up fo I fuhgit how happy we be. My sista, Callie, come home only two odda time in tirty yeah." Flashing his biggest grin, "My teet stay crack (I keep smiling)."

Lucas was indeed pleased at the prospect of Callie's return. During their too infrequent visits over the last thirty years, and in the many letters that his wife, Lilly, read to him about his sister's exploits in Washington, it was clear to Lucas that Callie Hewitt was still working to help people and to get things done. Though she may have slowed a step, he knew she remained every bit as engaged and duty-bound as their Mama Ruth had raised her children to be.

"Callie been skrong (strong) and true tuh huh Gawd—wukin all huh life fuh hep mek (to help make) sick folk bedda." Speaking almost only to himself, "And now she bringin all huh goodness back home." Realizing anew what Callie meant to him, he turned away before his friends could see the fullness of his emotions. "So, I be too busy fuh mo foolish talk wid de ol men I see right yuh." And with a friendly dismissive smile, he left them on the dock. He had extra impetus indeed, as the steamer was already tied up, with passengers descending the ramp and spreading onto the town wharf.

Callie maneuvered through the crowd on the wharf with an air of confidence displayed by frequent travelers and city folk. She spotted her brother before he saw her, quickly veering behind him and grabbing his shoulders before he knew she was there. Lucas yelped with surprise and then laughter before turning to get the best embrace a sister and brother could share—absolute joy and relief to be in each other's presence once again.

Breaking from their reunion hug, the siblings were on task immediately. "I tek yo bags and de boys tek yo trunk." Callie hesitated briefly before nodding her agreement, allowing her brother to take her big bag, a concession not easy after her lifetime of self-sufficiency. They walked briskly to the small-boat dock where two fine young men, well-steeped in manners, rose from the boat benches to show respect as their revered aunt walked down the ramp. "Douglass, Abram, memba yo Aunt Callie?"

"Yes, Daddy." Abram, the eldest, stepped onto the dock, extending his hand.

Douglass followed his brother. "Yes, ma'am, I memba oona."

Before they could go on with their formalities, Callie reached out with both arms to draw their heads to hers. "You boys are better lookin than yo daddy."

With laughter all around, Lucas interrupted their hilarity, "Boys, soon as Callie's trunk git from up on de wharf," and he pointed back to the steamer for emphasis, "into disyuh bateau, we be floatin down de riba fuh home." Lucas watched his boys jump to the statement as if it was an order.

Callie noted the pride on Lucas's face as his boys, now men in their late twenties, showed their character through their demeanor. As soon as they returned and secured the load, Abram and Douglass, experienced oarsmen, rowed the bateau past anchored vessels back out into the Beaufort River and powered it all the way home to Oakheart in less time than Callie remembered to be possible. "Boys, I memba a time thirty-two years ago when yo daddy and my cousin Will rowed a boat down this river as hard as you two jus did, but they were nevah fast as you."

As they neared the Oakheart dock, Lucas reached for the small, brass bell he kept in his all-purpose sack. Callie smiled, remembering, "That means a big problem happenin or somebody important is arrivin from de sea...tank ya, brudda, but let's just float on in quiet-like." Lucas understood her desire for a peaceful arrival, and after he bagged the bell, the boys' oars pulling through rippling water was the only sound she heard.

Callie breathed deeply, remembering the salty air and familiar fragrance of islands surrounded by tidal creeks and mud filled with nutrients that fed the ocean's living things. As they steadily moved closer to Oakheart's dock on the tip of Constant Island, Callie surveyed the "big house" where she had lived after her master was chased away in humiliation when Union forces invaded on November 7, 1861.

The giant live oak trees had grown even stronger, their limbs reaching around the home and yard like a light-filtering perimeter. In this peak-of-summer heat, their leafy branches provided a grand, cooling canopy. Callie's memories, both terrifying and enriching, flooded back to her as shards of sunlight sliced through oak tree limbs draped with Spanish moss. Suddenly, Callie saw the unfamiliar. "Am I lookin at a bigger house?" Continuing to peer, "Lucas, is that a new front porch? What did you do?"

"We fixed it bout ten yeahs ago afta yo las visit. Got too ol an rotten in places. So, Abram and Douglass wuk to make it skrong and bigga on de front and de sides. Buildin fuh dey future and fuh all de kids you see round yuh."

"Where's the porch roof—supposed to be here on the front facin south, keepin the family cool in the midday sun?"

"Oh, we ain got to dah yet. Dock come fus."

Callie responded, dryly, "It's only been ten years."

"Well…"

The angle of her view changed as their boat slid alongside the dock and she could see all three sides of the porch. "It is beautiful! I can't wait to walk it." Callie struggled to her feet, the boat still rocking gently. Helped onto the dock by her oldest nephew, Abram, Callie looked ahead and then saw that new steps led all the way from the dock up the embankment to the yard. "Lucas, you amazing man!"

"Not jus me, sista. Me wid my boys heah. We keep pretty busy makin use of wha Gawd done gib. I said to my boys, 'Wha all deese big, old oak branch look like to you?' Pretty soon we cut em up and mek deese steps up de bank."

Douglass moved to Callie's side to offer support, and after a feigned questioning look, Callie took his arm to climb up the oak steps. "I say, you boys do real good work. So now we don't have tuh slippy-slide up and down the bank no more. I love these steps!" Once on the bluff, Callie still did not see anyone. She had told Lucas not to ring his little bell, but muttered to herself, "I half-expected somebody, at least Lilly or my gal Sunny, might be heah to say 'Hey!' Maybe I'm too old now fuh folk to memba much."

Suddenly, Callie heard a shout, "Sista!" and looked up in time to see Lilly charge down the front steps and run across the yard with arms wide open. They embraced joyfully, rocking back and forth as the family gathered around. There were at least a dozen smiles and twice as many eyes, all aimed right at Callie.

"So many babies!" Callie exclaimed.

Abram introduced his wife, Amanda, and their sons, ten-year-old Robert and little Saxton, four—Callie managed to hug all of them at once. Douglass's wife, Nellie, reached around Callie's neck with one arm while holding her newborn baby girl, Nichelle, with the other. Douglass presented their daughter, bright-eyed Jancy, for a quick greeting before she chased after two of her cousins—BB's grandsons, the twin offspring of his daughter, Flora June. Callie saw their mischievous grins, noting how they resembled her brother BB's wide smile. She managed to keep up with the family groups fairly well but was totally baffled by the last couple to approach her. Lilly, always attentive to family dynamics, stepped forward to introduce Callie. "We have only recently learned that your brother BB became a father to another daughter in his last year of life."

Lucas smiled through the painful memory of his gone-too-soon brother. "Memba, Callie, BB tol me in his las days bout some research he be doin wid some of de ladies livin roun yuh..."

Lilly looked up at him, declaring, "Husband, don't go on about that." And then she went on, "This is Maybelle, BB's daughter and her man, Jackson, and their infant child, Elijah. This is yo Aunt Callie. Maybelle grew up near Penn School and recently moved to be part of our Oakheart community."

Callie, nearly overwhelmed and still amused by Lucas's reference, extended her hands to Maybelle and nodded, "There is beauty in you bein heah today. Yo daddy was the best big brother Lucas and I could ever want, and we got love fuh you and yours tuh share."

At that, Lilly spared Callie further greetings and called everyone to the west side of the porch, where the food had been set on a side table set for serving. Callie scanned the group and looked at Lilly. "Where is my Sunny?"

Busy getting the family settled for their evening meal, Lilly responded, "I'm pretty sure she will be back here later."

The late afternoon sun highlighted the Spanish moss swaying overhead in a gentle breeze. The hungry children waited just long enough for Lucas to conclude a brief family prayer before they moved as fast as possible to the food table, jostling each other in the effort to be the first to dig into the casserole of freshly prepared chicken and shrimp with rice and chopped vegetables. The adults, talking steadily, ignored their children and stepped aside.

Dinner, mixed with conversation, revived Callie. Promoting interest in her own storytelling, she asked, "Have I told you what I learned from General Wallace?"

Lucas, the nearest and dearest family member seated next to Callie, and within easy earshot, puzzled over whether to admit that he had heard the General Wallace stories several times. But he knew his sister was going to share her "news." She always had some.

Too late, he realized that his delay in responding left an opening for Callie. "I know you heard from me bout General Wallace, but this is new. You know, General Wallace, he and his soldiers fought at the Monocacy River in Maryland to keep de Secesh army busy jes long enough to save

Washington for Mista Lincoln. I was there in 1864 helpin his soldiers when they got shot, and he said if he could ever help me he would." Callie was rolling now. "Then in the very next year, General Wallace was on the jury wha found them that killed our president guilty and fit for hangin. And then, General Wallace was de main judge in the trial of the man in charge of the worse Secesh prison, down in Georgia, where they keep so many Yankee men prisoners durin the war..."

Barely hiding her emotions, Callie said: "I will tell you bout how General Wallace helped me find my daddy another time." She looked up to see the family, seated around her on the porch, listening intently. Then she went on, louder than before, "And so this is my big news." She stood to make it official. "With encouragement of my friend, General Wallace, to write down my thoughts and experiences, I decided ifn my he can write a book about our current president, Benjamin Harrison, which he did, I said, why can't I write a book about my life, wid Lilly's help, of course?"

"Is that de reason you came back, Aunt Callie?" Douglass asked with a smile.

"It's one reason. You know how smart your mama is about readin and writin, so I need her help to write my story. And...!" she said with emphasis, "I'm back here to grab hold of all my family and never let go again!" Callie extended her arms almost long enough to reach around everyone on the porch, now standing with her. Their comfort together made them reluctant to let go.

———◆———

IN THE EARLY EVENING, LILLY, CALLIE, AND LUCAS SETTLED INTO the rocking chairs on the west side of the porch to watch the sun set over the creek and marsh. Lucas said, "Now that you be here wid us, ain no need for Lilly to write de long letters, an she be havin mo time wid me."

Lilly laughed and said, "Husband, she and I gonna be talkin all de time instead."

"Oh Lawd."

"Lilly, you jus got to know how I loved your first letter. I got it three months after you wrote to me. I memba to this day, I got it in Frederick, Maryland, where Clara Barton's people sent me. I was so happy I cried when I read yo words—I wet de pages so much I wrinkled de paper. I clutched it so tight to my haat (heart) when I saw where you got Sunny to write her name—Lord how I cried."

"I been keepin yo letters, too." Lilly laughed, "You be surprised, I got folders full, one each from de sixties, seventies, eighties, and de last three yeahs."

Callie said, "I had at least six letters a year from you—had to jam em in a box in my trunk."

"We talked about so much."

Callie noticed Lucas listening in and got louder. "Good thing nobody else evah saw these letters. Wouldn't want no brudda eyes seein what I say bout him."

"Ain worried bout him. I'm too excited to get started putting the bones of yo story togedda."

Lucas heard the animated voices of his sister and wife of thirty years, smiling without comment as they enthusiastically shared one memory after another, from family stories, to war, to politics. Several minutes later, Lucas could not hold back. "I just have to aks, you ladies gonna write de book, or..." pausing for effect, "are you gonna talk de book?" While savoring his intervention, Lucas was distracted by dolphins out in the creek. He pointed to them splashing in the brilliant reflecting light of sunset.

There they saw fins breach the shimmering waters as a large dolphin and a much smaller one seemed to be engaged in play. Dorsal and side fins and underbellies showed as they rolled across each other.

Together, they drifted slowly with the inbound tide, not seeming to propel themselves in any particular direction. Lucas began to notice a pattern. The larger dolphin came from beneath the smaller one to push it up out of their water home. The movement was so pronounced that Lucas stood up, stating, "She's pushin it up to breathe..." Surely, he was correct. Just then, the calf surfaced but showed little voluntary motion.

Lilly whispered, "Her baby's not gonna survive on its own." Callie could not speak as she watched nature's most natural spectacle—the boundless energy of mother-love when unleashed for cause, to save her progeny. All three stood to admire the struggle of the mother and to urge the baby dolphin to reclaim the life that seemed to be slipping away. Soon, the heartbreaking scene, still stirring the waters, moved out of sight as the inbound tide quickened its drift north from Port Royal Sound.

Callie stood motionless as Lilly and Lucas joined her in tight embrace, leaving no space between them for sadness to creep in further. Suddenly, Callie disengaged, looking first to Lilly, then to Lucas. "Why did you say my Sunny is not here yet?"

Lilly winced. Callie had not received Lilly's last letter. For the moment, Callie accepted Lilly's brief explanation that Sunny and Flora June usually arrived late on Thursday or early Friday, after working in Beaufort during the week.

———◆———

THAT NIGHT, AFTER ALL THE EXCITEMENT OF HER ARRIVAL, CALLIE returned to the second-floor bedroom that she had chosen the first night she was free of her "master" in 1861. She realized that her fifty-five-year-old frame was spent for the day, but her mind was still racing, especially about the news Lilly shared just before going to bed. Rumors spread quickly through the community that an older gentleman had tied up at Will's dock about a mile up the creek. He had entered Will's house with an African woman servant. Callie remembered that she had noticed such a woman on the wharf with her friend from the ship.

Will was no stranger to Oakheart, having been brought there at age ten by his mother when she married Massa Bowen. Callie, as house servant, developed an appreciation of the boy over the next seven years before he left the plantation to attend the US Naval Academy in Maryland. After he returned to Oakheart in 1861 just before slavery on the islands was ended by the Union occupation, he and Callie became good friends. Then, ever since they both learned in 1863 that Will Hewitt's uncle was her father, and that they were cousins, Will and Callie had shared a strong inclination to help each other in every possible way. Only Callie's exhaustion on the night of her arrival stopped her from wondering if the man now occupying Will's house could be the man she met on the steamer who had listened to her stories that day.

Chapter 2

Saturday, August 19, 1893

Callie awoke with a start ten hours later, hungry for food and further news about the strangers in cousin Will Hewitt's house. She remembered how pleased she was that Will also bought property at Oakheart during the tax sale of 1863. It took him until 1867 to build a modest home on the three-acre tract he purchased, right at the point of land where the river split into smaller creeks. When Will first moved into the house, if only on a part-time basis, Callie was thrilled that her white cousin made such a financial commitment to the well-being of the Oakheart community.

When Callie joined Lilly in the kitchen, Lilly's first words were, "Tongues are already waggin bout the new folks in Will's house."

So, naturally, Callie had to go see for herself. "I'll be back for breakfast, sista. I have to check on this for Will, see that everything is in order."

After a quick morning walk down the old plantation's main lane, Callie arrived at the front steps to Will's porch. She looked up to see the kind gentleman from the steamer. He greeted her now as he did then, with a slight, calm smile and an openness Callie had rarely seen in white men during her thirty years working in the burgeoning turmoil of post-war Washington.

"Sir, with due respect, I feel there has been some deception. If you know Will Hewitt well enough to move into his home heah, then surely you know of me, and yet you chose not to say so as we traveled on the boat, nor at all during our conversation yesterday." Callie clearly was in an unctuous mood and intentionally spoke English with unusual precision and little Gullah dialect, consistent with her education and experience. "Did you think that I would not meet you? How long did you think you could keep a secret of your relationship with Will?"

His friendly demeanor remained unchanged. "Certainly, we never wished to be deceptive. We never thought we should keep any secrets."

"We?"

"Will asked that I not identify myself to you until I had to. I didn't have to on the steamer, and I thought it would be so much more fascinating just to let you tell your stories. And it was." Callie began to feel the assurance of Will's involvement through this stranger's manner. He descended the three porch steps and extended his hand, cautiously. Callie accepted the gesture as he further explained, "Your cousin Will and I have remained good friends since the war when he worked under my supervision. He asked me to give you this note when you first raised questions about my presence here. Honestly, Callie, if I may call you that, on the boat, I never intended to keep my associations and intentions secret from you. It's just that your stories were so intriguing."

As she opened the envelope to see Will's handwriting, Callie smiled broadly and responded, "Yes, sir, you may call me Callie, and yes, sir, I do agree that my life...has been intriguing." And then Callie read:

"My dear cousin, I have hired my acquaintance, and former superior officer in the Navy, to repair my house and help look over any pending concerns you may have at Oakheart in the coming days. He is traveling with someone, an African woman servant."

Callie looked up at him, a slight smile breaking on her lips, with a knowing glance at the gentleman before her. She continued to read.

"This man was known in the Navy as a highly creative officer who could procure items needed by any one of his shipmates. I thought I had learned to be resourceful, but my talents do not compare to the zeal that senior supply officer Nathan Gates brought to the sea islands in 1862, and his reputation continues to this day. Trust him as you would trust me.

"You have arrived back in Beaufort, back in the heart of the secessionist South, the very land occupied by Lincoln's Union blues until they disappeared in a political deal that betrayed the freedmen more than fifteen years ago. I love your family like my own, and I won't let you and your loved ones be swallowed by the rising tide of hatred, deprivation, and disparagement that inflict themselves on those who happen to have dark skin. Until I can be there, I have asked Nathan Gates to employ the cunning and ingenuity needed to support the family in any matters as to land or freedom, and to stand by for support as uncertain times unfold.

With abiding love, your cousin, Will Hewitt."

Immediately Callie's partial sense of righteous indignation subsided. Will had always kept his word from the day they first learned they were cousins back in July 1863. His promise to treat her family as his own took many forms through the years, and now that promise was standing before her in the person of Nathan Gates. "Well then, I must say thank you, Mister Gates." Callie gave him the look of warm recognition his presence merited. "I'm pleased to know that the new man, and woman, in Will's house were invited to be here. Now I can return to my morning meal with my family. Sir, I may need your support first thing Monday morning, with a crew able to transport you to and from Savannah."

———◆———

FAMILY HAD ALREADY BEGUN TO GATHER ON THE PORCH WHEN Callie returned. She mounted the front porch steps and sank heavily into the cushioned rocking chair on the east side with the best view down the river. While the "big house" had become home to Lucas and Lilly's family over the past thirty years, to Callie, it still elicited a curious blend of sour memories from days of slavery with the joys of sweet freedom. As she was catching her breath and coping with the exercise and emotion of the morning, Callie confessed, "I seem to be slowin down. Time was I could hop up de stairs two at a time."

Lilly, ever honest, observed, "Well, you ain the same skin and bones as when you did that hoppin! Plus, you got thirty yeah mo...experience...to carry wid you."

"Don't say no more, Lilly, fo you get in trouble. Don't test my love." They both laughed and grabbed hands, looking intently at each other as long-separated sisters do.

The moment ended when Abram and his two boys, Robert and Saxton, approached Callie slowly. With a little encouragement from their Grandmother Lilly, first one and then the other, ages ten and four, greeted the mysterious great-aunt they had never seen before yesterday.

"Good morning, Great-Aunt Callie," said well-trained Robert.

Then Saxton smiled and said, "Hi, Big Aunt Callie." His little arms reached out to hug her as his father's sweeping reach enveloped his boys and Aunt Callie. "Amanda and de boys been talkin dis monin bout how blessed we be that Gawd bring you back to us, Auntie."

"He just keeps doin it for me, Abram. And now, I am mos blessed to see you and Amanda again with your boys. Lilly, you a grandmama of these fine boys? You be proud, girl?"

"Callie, you know I am. Both me and Lucas live to care for the grands."

"Because they are so fine, I'm going to let it pass that these sweet boys called me 'Big' and 'Great.'" She stared at Lilly for emphasis. "I think just Aunt Callie be best."

"Oh, Callie, we all call you that cause you de oldest, not cause you de biggest." Lilly barely contained her amusement while her hand tried to hide a sly smile.

Shouts from the yard interrupted the teasing and announced the arrival of another family.

"Oh my! Look at them!" Callie exclaimed. Pointing at Flora June's twins, Beanie and Bobby, who were already playing in the yard, she said, "I think I saw those boys dashing everywhere yesterday." As a sprightly, fast little girl bounded up onto the porch, Callie added, "And I memba this face. Tell me yo name again, little beauty. Who are you?"

"I'm Jancy!"

"Fancy?" asked Callie, kidding.

"Jancy, Missus. Jancy! I say it start with a J."

Callie clapped her hands. "Why now I know dis family's brains and smart mouth will live on after me!" Laughter erupted all around at Callie's good humor. As he climbed to the porch, Jancy's father, Douglass, chuckled to himself and squeezed his wife's hand. Nellie was carrying their sleeping baby girl.

Lilly gently chided her son. "Almost didn't get here fuh breakfast, Douglass. That's not like you."

"Gah mo fuh do deese days, Mama," gesturing to Jancy as he leaned in to hug his aunt. Birthed just after the war ended, Douglass had learned everything his father taught him about the waterways surrounding their home, and then learned more. He liked to bring his family to the big house by rowboat on the nice days even though their house was just down the road. Everybody knew that, just like his father, he simply preferred being on the water whenever possible.

Lilly began bringing the food to the tables on the west side of the front porch. She paused and nodded to Abram to ask the blessing. With little encouragement from Lucas or Lilly, their son began serving his self-proclaimed call to the ministry when he was only fourteen. Now nearly thirty, he carried himself with solemnity and a certain reverence for others. Since Abram and his extended family had already been subjected to the aroma of Lilly's renowned pork sausages, he demonstrated the sensitivity of an experienced pastor when called to pray before a meal and graced the food with few words.

"Deah Lawd we Fadda Gawd, we tank yuh now fuh annodda day in yo light. We live to praise yo name and ask only dah we people be graced wid de wisdom and de way to live out yo will. By de grace of yo son, de Savior, Jedus Christ. Amen?"

And all gathered answered, "Amen."

Lilly asked Robert to get the basket of hot biscuits from the outdoor kitchen. Robert paraded the biscuits around to all those seated on long benches at the table before placing the platter in front of his own plate. They were still hot, as the children quickly discovered upon snatching them from the basket. Lilly moved the tray with her blueberry, strawberry, and fig preserves next to the biscuits. Amanda, who had been helping Lilly with breakfast, added a large bowl filled with peaches and melons cut to bite-size perfection.

Callie looked up from the splendid array on the table and, glancing at the river, noticed an osprey power-diving onto a hapless fish below. As the large bird climbed, talons already severing the spine of its morning catch, Callie pointed, saying, "It's all part of God's plan. I thrill to see it—such a blessing for me to be back here again."

———◆———

CALLIE HAD NOT FINISHED HER LAST BITES OF FRUIT WHEN ONE OF her great-nephews appeared at her elbow. "Fa true, you be in de freedom wah? Like Grampa?" Abram's oldest boy, Robert, asked breathlessly while pointing to Lucas.

Lilly started to usher her grandson away when Callie gently reached for his arm. "I'll answer this fine boy. Never want to ignore the curious minds of children."

"Or a chance to tell your stories!" taunted Lucas lovingly, giving approval for his sister to swell his children's and grandchildren's imaginations with her wartime experiences. "With your permission, deah sista, you know I love you, but I heah dis tale once or ten times befo." With that, Lucas moved quickly down the porch steps and escaped to the dock, his lifelong place of work and his access point to the water on which his search for elusive peace continued.

Lucas was thrilled that his sister had finally come home to live. He wanted to have more time with her, and he certainly wanted his children to know her and to hear her stories. Lucas also had absolute trust in how she would tell the delicate truths about her days as a Civil War nurse. He remembered that, before the outbreak of the war, Callie always managed, even while in service to Master Bowen, to find ways to help others. Lucas and Callie both knew that increasing the health and well-being of the people of Oakheart would make them a stronger community. That Massa Bowen benefitted from their strength while they were his property was an unintended bonus of Callie's excellent caregiving.

Lilly waved away Callie's offer of assistance as she cleared the table. "Amanda is already washing dishes, and Nellie will help, too. You can just see wha de chirren want to know, and I will be back to listen."

"That sounds good to me," Callie said, rocking slowly, ready to hold forth as the children gathered around her. Robert settled his tall, slim frame on the floor, and Saxton quickly joined his brother at Callie's feet, his hand-me-down clothes from Robert too big for his little body. Beanie and Bobby clambered onto the porch after sprinting across the yard, smiling as they plopped down next to Robert. The twins often slept over with Lilly and Lucas because Flora June worked so many nights away from home.

Jancy raced up the porch steps but slowed before she sat on the footstool and leaned against Callie's knee. Looking up, she asked her great-aunt, "Aunt Callie, my daddy says you been hepn (helping) people all your life. You do dah? Fa true?"

"It's true." Smiling broadly at her great-niece and -nephews who had never stepped foot on the mainland, Callie started to talk about her early years on the islands. "When I was a lee gal bout fifty yeahs ago, I live right down de lane behind dis house. I learn all bout helpin people feel bedda and be bedda. I was not much older than you, Jancy, when I first found out bout de roots wha come from de ground, and how dey can make a body feel good and strong."

Jancy jumped up. "I too skrong fuh be a girl." Flexing her muscle for Callie, she smiled and sat back down, resting her arm and head on Callie's leg.

The oldest boy, always with a questioning look on his face, stood to speak, but waited until Callie called his name, "Robert?"

"Oona see soljahs fightin an gittin huht? (Did you see soldiers fighting and getting hurt?)"

"Honeys, I was helpin soljahs heal from their wounds roun yuh, right in Beaufort, mo than thirty yeahs ago, just after the war got started. You know bout de war, babies?"

Most shook their heads, but Robert shouted out, "Freedom wah!"

"You right, Robert. We people ain have tuh be slave no more." She gave an affirming look to her oldest great-nephew and then looked within. "But what I saw of war was how men's bodies get tore up. How they get hurt so bad some can't go on livin."

"Aunt Callie, wha bout de freedom?"

"Well, I hated what war did to soljahs, but the war stopped slavery. We still got hard times tryin to be free, but we glad we free to decide each day what we do, and plenty of our men and white men fight fuh that."

Jancy said, "My gramma say she teach soljahs tuh read in the wah."

"Lilly sho did, she taught readin and writin to men who never could read before. Just like you chirren learn at Penn School, she taught soljahs of the first South Carolina Volunteers just like yo Grampa BB. We so proud of we people workin so hard to be free."

Again, Robert's curiosity found voice. "Why you go away in the wah, Aunt Callie, ain nebba come back yuh til now?"

"Well, chile, I let that story be for anodda day. I just say I went searchin for my mama and my daddy up north. Then I went to learn mo bout helpin people—I learn bout medicine and how to help doctors and how to nurse soljuhs. Once I start workin in a job that made things bedda for people, fa true, I jus kept workin at it all these years. Spose I jus stayed put up dere..." She thought about that summary description of her past and frowned, but then she remembered her purpose.

"In 1863, when I left home to go north on de steamship, de only home I knew was right yuh. I was so scared, but there were soljahs on the boat been wounded fightin the battle for Fort Wagner, up near Charleston. My job was to help tend tuh their pains and sorrows. My work made me forget my worries. I worked with de soljahs so much on de boat, before I knew, I got to Norfolk, Virginia, without even sleepin. On de nex boat to Washington, I reckon I sat still and slept some.

"Miss Laura Towne at yo Penn School got me started helpin soljahs right here in Beaufort, and she knew a fine lady named Clara Barton who came heah to do the same thing during the war. Well, she had friends in Washington who took me in, let me rest some mo, and then sent me thirty miles north of Washington to a little town in Maryland called Frederick, bout de size of Beaufort. Jus like Beaufort, there were hospitals all round town to take care of de wounded and sick boys in de war. I learned so much in just a few months from many smaat people. Honeys, there are parts inside our bodies we jus don know nuttin bout." Callie began to tickle whatever ribs were in reach, causing great hilarity and distraction, but only for a moment.

"How you laan bout de inside of we bodies, Aunt Callie?" Robert asked, making the question sound as though he really needed to understand how his great-aunt got to see the inside of a person's body.

"Oh, chile, I seen things happen when bullets and cannonballs hit men. I can only say I work with doctors who had to fix the places where bodies get broke open. So, I see too much." Memories, long tucked into the recesses of her mind, began to surface, and Callie began to hear the distant sound of cannon fire.

"I know we are gettin near to battle when I fus start to hear de rumble and roll of de cannons."

"Ooh, why you want to get near de cannon, Aunt Callie?" Jancy's expression reflected the fear she saw in Callie's face. "Stay away!" the six-year-old shouted.

"I ain too near it, honey. It sounds loud even from far away." She uttered those comforting words to Jancy even as she recalled the intense roar that accompanied a fusillade of twenty or more cannons ten miles away, or so the captain said. "It be springtime in 1864, and my job, Miss Jancy, is to follow General Grant and his boys in blue down into Virginny, and if any of em git hurt, I help fix em up." Though Jancy was satisfied with the answer, Callie's own words hurled her back into the horror of those days. She smelled again the foul odors of the injured and the putrid scent of death and decay as her ambulance wagon driver stopped in woods just short of a smoke-filled clearing.

Callie was at once in awe of what she had accomplished back then and gripped by frightful images of the reality she had lived. Was her presence on the battlefields a blessing for others, or was it always to be a curse that what she saw became memories she could not forget? She and those in the other thirty ambulance wagons had recently been taught to move quickly toward the sound of battle, to use their knowledge and equipment when bodies were torn and broken. They had learned from the lectures that they should be very near the battlefield so they could help the wounded as quickly as possible.

"We follow de Union troops pretty close when they be on de march. We wonder ifn all de cannon fire meant Union troops done caught ol Gen'l Lee." Callie paused for a deep breath. "Oh, chirren, we didn't know nothing of the hell, fuhgive me sweet Jesus, we bout to go through."

Again, Robert worked to grasp her story. "Aunt Callie, is dah where you git huht (hurt)?"

"No, chile. We talkin bout injuhed soljahs now..." Her eyes filled with tears, and her hands shook. As Callie bent her head, the children gathered around her, laying on their hands in perfect childlike, human instinct. Straightening her back slowly, Callie composed herself, raised her head, and looked at the children thoughtfully with half a smile before she asked them, "Babies, I'll tell you what I saw, sose you can memba forever how bad war can be. Promise to memba?"

"We promise, Aunt Callie," they said almost in unison.

Looking every one of her fifty-three years, Callie lost her smile and began, "When our ambulance wagon goes over de hill, I see de smoke still risin from de field. Other carts befo me stop, and people jump out quick tuh tend de soljahs. But they be findin only pieces of some de boys. De soljuhs who survive all de cannonballs get taken away quick by their bruddas. Wha be left behind—oh, babies—a couple men are still movin and gettin help. But mostly, I see arms and legs and pieces of blue-coat soljahs. I finally find a man livin. He takes some water and lets me tie up his bleedin leg. He knows how bad huht he be. So much blood let out fo I could help him. He goes to sleep and never wakes up." Looking up from her memory to speak directly to the children, "I knew befo de wah, men can be fools, with their bad, crazy selves. I never knew wha big fools they can be until that day."

Perhaps because Robert sensed the other children had heard enough of real war stories, or because he and his father had already talked about the issue, Robert chose this moment to pose another "why" question. "Aunt Callie, why states in de Nort wan fuh be togedda wid states in de Sout? I heah my daddy and Grampa say de white people down yuh dang sho don want to be wid de Nort. And Grampa say he don know why people up Nort want to be wid de Sout?"

"Got a point there, Junior..." Callie laughed despite the heaviness of her spirit. "How old are you?"

"Ten, ma'am."

But Lilly, who had quietly returned and sat down, did not see the humor. "Lucas know he caint be fillin these young'uns heads wid such ideas." Turning to Robert, "You keep that kind of talk just to family. Yeddy (Hear) me?"

"Yes, ma'am." Looking confused but determined, he said, "Grandmama, we all fambly heah, ain we?"

"Yes, darlin." She gently brushed his face with her hand and explained, "I just meant be careful how you talk about other people. They listen with their ears, too."

"How do I be careful, Grandmama?"

"Practice," said a scowling, loving grandmother.

Robert turned back to Aunt Callie. "Since we all family—I'm jus tryin to figuh—how United States fight so hard just to keep Sout and Nort together?"

"I like your thinking, young man!" Callie meant it. "You can ask me all yo questions. I know Mister Lincoln, as President of the United States, believed we got to keep all states together in one nation. He say we be strong if we can be united." Callie interlocked her fingers and held them up for the children to see.

Although they all attempted to intertwine their fingers, Robert persisted. "Daddy say," and he looked back at Lilly, "I heah people say, when I hang out at de corner stoh, that it ain wukin togedda too good."

"Tell me again how old you say young Robert be?" Callie asked only half in jest.

Again, Lilly as protector spoke. "Don't you be hangin out there no mo." Then, whispering to Callie, "He's ten, but he listens to everything and understands too much." On the substance of Robert's insight, his grandmother said, "Our president didn't live long enough to help the states work together." That was all Lilly was prepared to say, and Callie took her cue.

Holding out her arms to young Robert, Callie asked, "Yo parents named you after Robert Smalls, didn't they?"

Lucas and Lilly had made sure by this point in their oldest grandson's life that he knew of his namesake—war hero, state and national legislator, and local leader through the years. "Yes, ma'am, I name fuh de man wha stole de Confederate boat from Chalston during de wah."

Callie hugged him tightly, and as he moved away, her arms dropped heavily into her lap and her eyes closed. Lilly noticed immediately, instructing, "Come now, children, time for Auntie to rest after her story. Robert, lead the children, please." Callie opened her eyes briefly but settled back into the chair as Lilly lifted her feet onto the footstool beside the little girl.

"Tank yuh now, Fancy!" Callie said with a loud whisper and a tired wink at Lilly.

"Jancy, ma'am."

Nellie, who had joined them, smiled fondly at her daughter as Callie replied, "Yes, darlin Jancy…"

With that, Lilly, Nellie, and the children moved quietly down the porch steps to the expanse of yard between the house and the river bluff that served as the center of operations for most family gatherings. Lilly saw Abram and Douglass about to go down to the dock, and she elevated her voice to reach them. "Nellie and Amanda and I have to do a lot more cookin and bakin to celebrate Aunt Callie comin home to stay. Chirren, yo fathers will help you stay out of trouble."

After the children cascaded down the embankment with their fathers, Lucas and sons secured their favorite places on the dock in chairs on either side of their father, where they could cast lines into the water and then wait comfortably, fishing and hoping. They would move occasionally to pull up crab lines, scooping a net under the greedy ones that stayed feasting a little too long on the rancid fish heads.

When Lilly entered the house, she knew the children would come back to the yard quickly rather than sit quietly with the fishermen. She returned to the porch within minutes to see that Jancy had set up a "tea party" in the yard for Saxton and her doll, talking loudly about Aunt Callie as she served them acorns and "greens." Meanwhile, Robert and his cousins, who had all mastered the art of high flying on the rope swing, were competing passionately for a new record. More than once, Abram shouted from the dock, "Slow down! Don't go so high!"

To supplement the parental guidance bellowed from the dock, Lilly sat down at the porch table near the napping Callie. She placed a large box on it. Acting very much like the organized teacher she had been, and as quietly as she could, she moved her fingers along the top of folders labeled by years: 1864, 1865, 1866, and on. She shook her head, still marveling at the intrigue that accompanied her sister-in-law on her first journey from the sea islands. She pulled a single letter out of the box and began reading Callie's early description of life around Washington during the war.

Just then, Callie stirred, waking enough from her slumber to be vaguely aware of her surroundings. Trying to show she had not lost a step, she began her story where she thought she had stopped. "Yes, children, I ain nebba seen so many ambulance wagons rolling in a row."

Lilly gently touched her shoulder. "Sista, how you feelin? Are you done wid storytellin for now?"

Callie cleared her head enough to realize that she was on home ground, her beloved sea island, and had taken a deeply needed morning nap. "I'm fine, Lilly. I feel stuck in the past, but my head is catchin up. There's one thing I haven't figured out yet. Where is my Sunny? You say she out with BB's girl takin care of supm?"

"That's right, Callie. She knows that you gonna be here this weekend." Lilly redirected Callie's attention. "Honey, your stories got me thinking about all you been through. and it sent me straight to my letter box lookin for all the stories you ain told yet, like when you first went north on the steamer in 1863 with that injured Union sergeant on board? And how did you get to know where your daddy was? And how things went with your mama? And how you saw Abraham Lincoln, and worked with the Union general you talked about, and met with Robert Smalls in Washington from time to time, and, and, and..." While itemizing the high points of Callie's life, Lilly had not noticed that Callie was fixated on the envelopes Lilly had splayed onto the table, all from the "1864" folder, each a reminder of the sights and sounds and smells of the places where those letters were written.

As Callie stared at the papers, she said, "Sista, you got to know how these letters take me back in time."

Lilly reached out to grasp Callie's hand. And with the other hand, she deftly freed a letter from its envelope. "Listen to this.

"'Dear Lilly...I been so tired, sister. This work, this awful, wonderful work. My Lawd, Lilly, you know I got no good sleep in these first months.'"

"It's amazing to hear what I wrote thirty years ago. Can I see it?" Callie immediately started reading.

"'Near here, the biggest battle of de war happened in a little town call Antietam, just over big mountains. Lilly, you and Lucas won't believe how big these mountains be.'

30

"I'm not sayin nothin about my writin back then…" Callie, facing her history in many ways, continued to read her letter to Lilly.

"'Some Union soljahs here still need mo hep, months after the battle. These boys sent the Confederate Army back south. So many are hurt. Too many dyin. So many sad stories.'"

Callie's voice trailed off. Lilly honored the need for silence.

With a deep breath, Callie summoned her strength. "'…and yet you help some boys get bedda and live on. Lilly, do you know ain no feelin in the world like that? To see de boys walk out of de ward an onto de street. Well…'"

Callie started to cry and then sobbed into Lilly's arms as some of the pain of those months of irreparable destruction spilled from her soul.

Lilly pulled back a bit to view Callie's face. "I can imagine the things you saw, the way your heart must have been so full. Maybe we done done all the storytellin for now."

Callie said, "I be all right. It jus all came rushin in on me all ovah again."

"You sure, Callie? I know the chirren can wait. Someday, they do want to hear bout when you got wounded, and Lucas been tellin em bout how you hep save Washington from de Confederate Army. But you don't have to go on about it now. Sista, you still catchin up wid yoself."

"Well, those are stories bout my life I want to share with the children. When they get all played out, send em to me. We may talk about some of the good news from de war, so Lilly, thank you for takin notes if you hear supm important not in my letters. I love you, darlin."

Almost on cue, the tired youngsters straggled up the porch steps, exhausted from their hours of play. Fortunately, and reliably, Lilly had small cups of sweet lemonade ready for all. Their thirst quenched, the children instinctively gravitated to the end of the porch, where Callie rocked in her chair.

She was ready for them. "So, you babies wanna heah mo stories of de freedom war? I'm ready to tell bout some good things—one story where I hep somebody, one story where I get hep, an one story where I hep Mista Lincoln's United States Govmint." Her audience was ready too.

"General Grant made the Union Army the biggest army ever on earth. And he was chasin General Lee and his Confederate Army down into Virginny. The medical wagon I rode in followed de boys in blue to a place, came to be called The Wilderness. It was de first big day of fightin, early in May."

"Wha a wild-a-nuss?" Robert questioned.

"Rolling land so full of trees and vines you caint see where you are or where you goin. I told you about when cannonballs flew, and I didn't see anybody I could help that day. But in The Wilderness, I see soljuhs who got shot in de leg or de arm. We knew we could help em, so we took em to de surgeon."

Jancy hesitantly asked, "How you fix de soljahs' legs an ahms?"

"Well, now, like I said, when soljahs get hurt, all us medical core workers try to be right dere for em soon as we can. Don mean to scare you babies, but think of de noise one rifle make. Now think of a hundred rifles, and now a thousand rifles, all firin ovah and ovah again. Wid noise and smoke all round us, we set up a 'field dressing station.' That be a place where the doctors can work on the boys near where they get shot up."

"Wha dey do, Aunt Callie? Wha oona do?"

"Each of dem rifles fired pure evil. A lead ball breaks everything it hits. It breaks arm bones and leg bones and tears up all de skin. All a surgeon could do to save a man's life was to cut off his arm or leg, mmmmhmmm."

The faces of the children contorted with their imaginations.

"I tell you about dis one man. I rememba him because he was de first man I help wid his arm. My job is gettin him ready for surgery, holdin him still when de cuttin starts, cleanin de wound, and then helpin patch where his limb got cut. And you know wha? I memba his name. He be such a kind man to reach to me with his good arm and take my hand in his, even through his pain, to thank me fuh helpin him." Callie hesitated for a moment, then gathered herself and went on, sitting up straight. "De man, Sergeant Charles Wickware, heal so good he went on to be an Army officer, and I got a letter from him tellin me that, with just one good arm, he led a regiment of soljahs later in the war. An you know wha else? They were black soldiers he led, just like we own First South Carolina Volunteers."

The children's eyes widened in wonder at all they had just heard.

Robert spoke, proudly, "Aunt Callie, you a special lady. You hep de man's ahm en you hep his haat. He be good tuh his soljahs afta you be good tuh him."

As Callie deepened her own understanding in the wisdom of Robert's words, she smiled and said, "Too many men like Charles Wickware be huht bad that day, but at least we were there to fix some of em so they could go on."

"Wha else happen in de wil-de-nuss, Aunt Callie?" Saxton's question showed that Callie had even caught the attention of the four-year-old.

"Babies, it was a terrible time fuh soljahs on both sides. We helped who we could. Fightin went on fuh four days, and then it moved down the road to a place called Spotsylvania. We was jus settin up our work tent, when I heard a whistle and saw a big light, and I didn't memba nuttin. Next I knew, my surgeon was ovah me lookin right in my face, wipin my head. Didn't know it then, but he was wipin blood from my head, right heah." She reached up to her hairline above her left eye, and as she did, each child jumped up for closer inspection.

"I don't see nottin but a little mark!" Jancy observed.

"I was lucky, babies, some of that metal from a cannonball blasted right past me, jus barely touchin my head. My friend, a man nurse, say my whole face was bloody and they were scared I be huht much worse."

"You so tough, Aunt Callie!" Jancy showed her admiration with a two-arm-wrap-around-the-neck hug.

"Well, yes I am, but not so much back then. After they clean me up, I caint stand up or walk without fallin down again. I know de men on that ambulance crew are my friends. They put me on a train wid de wounded soljahs goin back to Washington. They even pin a note on my coat that got me transport back to where our ambulance crew started—Frederick, Maryland."

All the children were facing Callie in rapt attention, jaws agape.

"All I had de nex day was a headache. But there be soljahs on that train needin me tuh fix bandages all the way to Washington. I felt bad to leave those men to go on the rest of my trip."

Lilly interrupted briefly, "Callie, I took some good notes. Are you getting tired?" Callie smiled. Lilly asked, "Have you heard enough stories from Aunt Callie, chirren?"

"NO!" came back a resounding chorus.

"I'm doin jus fine, Lilly. I promised one more story. Memba?"

Robert waited two seconds before responding, "How did you hep Mista Lincoln, Auntie Callie?"

Callie looked at Lilly. "How could I not keep my promise to a smart mind like that?"

Lilly rubbed Robert's head as Callie began again.

"So, the United States Govmint sent me back up to Frederick, Maryland, and I got all healed up real quick. It was summertime in 1864, and a lot of hospital work still to be done. I was able to get settled back into the little room I had before we got sent to Virginny. Just like before, I was always willin to do wha was asked of me, learnin what I could as I went through each day. You chirren know what I mean?"

They nodded to Callie, who challenged them, "What do I mean?"

Once again, Robert was quick to respond, "I tink you wan fuh us to be smaat en to be ready to hep somebody."

"Das right, cause life can ask you questions in a hurry, and you bedda be havin some ansas when de time come. Well, that's what happened when a battle between armies of the North and South came right where I was, right there in Frederick."

Callie looked at each pair of eager eyes, drawing out their anticipation. "And no, jus so you won't be askin, I didn't save Washington. But I was there hepin de boys who did. They be so brave and fight so hard down on dah river, called the Monocacy."

After Callie encouraged the children to let the word Monocacy roll around in their mouths, Jancy asked, "So what did you do, Auntie Callie, on de Monkey-see Riba?"

Callie smiled her appreciation at Jancy's invitation to proceed. "It was in hot July. One day, I be workin in a ward full of twenty patients when orderlies come through shoutin bout de rebels comin in from de west."

Robert was excited by the story but had to interrupt, "Aunt Callie, wha be 'ordery'?"

Callie slowed to explain, "They be hospital helpers, kinda like me. All of a sudden, we rush to go wid de Union Army heading south out of town. We get ready so fas and left out wid soljahs and horses and wagons on a dusty ride down to and across de river. We get our field hospital tent set up in de trees on some farmland. They say a large Confederate Army took ovah Frederick as soon as we left. Chirren, de next morning, fightin starts, slow at first. But then, cannon fire and attacks by the rebels come in waves all day, from de left and de right and de middle." As she pointed to match her words, the children began pointing in all directions, and Callie decided to wait for another day to teach the children all about "right" and "left."

"One time, General Wallace comes riding up, shouting to the surgeons, 'Prepare! More boys are on the way!' Lawd, I know he tellin de trute. When de Confederates push to come across de river, cannons explode closer to where we are, and more soljah wounds come under de surgeons' knives. We patch em up as fas as we can. I workin so haad I fuhgit how scared I be. Afta one of our nurses gets hurt and another gets sick, I have to keep workin on de boys, talkin to em, givin water, jus tryin to make em comfortable. Later in de afternoon, General Wallace comes ridin by again, and he slows to speak wid his wounded men, and he tells them they were in good hands. He is so nice when he thanks all of us for our hard work that day. He looks straight at me and says, 'Young woman, your steady efforts are superb. Please be safe, and keep me informed of what you may need.' I felt so good to heah his words!"

"That is wonderful, Callie. I had not heard about your talk with General Wallace before." Lilly was genuinely thrilled about the recognition of Callie's excellence by the Union general. "Chirren, your great-aunt, my sista-in-law, Callie Hewitt, is a hero, and army generals knew it!"

Callie straightened up as she said, "It made me proud to have my work be praised by such a good man. You know, I learned later that General Wallace was called a hero for slowin down de rebel army that day. They say because of what he and his men did, Washington was protected for an extra day. So, even though de rebels took that ground at the Monocacy River, they got slowed down on their way to Washington."

"And so President Lincoln was safe?" Robert asked.

"Yes, Robert. Later, I saw a picture of him standin on de fort wall north of Washington where de Union Army was strong enough to hold off de Confederates."

Callie stood, extending her arms to the children who had listened so attentively. "So, my lovely chirren, you heah enough bout Aunt Callie durin de war?" They gathered together, all moving to hug Callie at once, her arms and hands able to touch them all.

———◆———

AROUND SUNSET, THE ADULTS GRAVITATED TO THE FRONT PORCH while the young ones went back down to the dock, some fishing, others crabbing with fish heads on a string and net at the end of a long pole. In recovery from an earlier shrimp feast, Callie, Lucas, and Lilly again settled into chairs overlooking the river as the evening breeze picked up, giving them relief from the stifling heat of the day.

Lilly, with folder in hand, spoke loud enough that her sons and their wives gathered around her. "You know, we been talkin to de chirren bout what Callie did during the freedom war. Tonight, we want to lift up all the good that our own friends and family did, especially BB as a soljah in de First South Carolina Volunteers. When he joined de United States Army and git ready fuh fight for we freedom, he said he felt like a man fuh de fus time." Lucas swayed ever so slightly in his chair as Callie reached for his hand, and Lilly continued. "Well, I found an article that tells about that regiment when it mustered out in '65.

"'...the hour is at hand when we must separate forever, and nothing can take from us the pride we feel, when we look upon the history of the "First South Carolina Volunteers," the first black regiment that ever bore arms in defense of freedom on the continent of America.'"

Callie was stirred to say, "My, my...wonderful words. We won de freedom...thirty yeahs ago, mmmm-mmmm-mmmm!"

Lilly went on enthusiastically. "It goes on to urge we freedmen: '...to harbor no feelings of hatred toward your former masters, but to seek in the paths of honesty, virtue, sobriety, and industry, and by a willing obedience to the laws of the land, to grow up to the full stature of American citizens.'"

Lucas had to agree. "We been doin good livin up to wha he say. We be proud of we island people on Oakheart an all roun St. Helena. We carry on jus as strong as Mama Ruth taught us—BB, you, and me." Lucas hesitated, clearly emotional. "Now we be teachin de chirren..." He looked to his wife, who had always been able to keep him hopeful. "But, Lilly, my love, you know we be talkin bout dis too many times. Jus cause the wah is ovah, well, it ain stop men from wantin to fight wid us."

Lilly appeared to know what Lucas would say next. "I know, Lucas. Let me finish. The statement by Colonel Trowbridge to our boys ends with these words:

'...The nation guarantees to you full protection and justice, and will require from you in return that respect for the laws and orderly deportment which will prove to every one your right to all the privileges of freemen. Signed, Lt. Colonel C. T. Trowbridge.'

"When I worked wid de boys in first SC, Colonel Trowbridge stood up as a fair man!" exclaimed Lilly.

"But," Lucas interrupted her rapture, "Miss Lilly, tell Sista Callie bout how we doin on de part, wha you say: 'The nation guarantees full protection and justice...' down heah in Sout Calina." His words hung in the air.

"Callie know wha I'm sayin, Lucas. Back then, before black men were soljahs, top leaders of the Union Army were first to put a rifle in BB's hands and tell him he can stand up and defend himself."

Callie added, "I seen the freedom fight and men involved were of all colors. The United States Army, white men, train our men to fight, ask us to protect forts near the ocean, and let us come back with our families to our home ground."

"And where does that Union protection stand now?" Lucas nearly shouted. Quickly calming himself, "I'll tell you. It stands down, jus when threats and turble acts by white folks happen mo an mo. I tank Gawd ebby day ain no bridge twix de mainland and disyuh islan, or we be in mo trouble fuh sho."

Seeing her effort failed to lift their spirits as they discussed the history they lived, Lilly offered, meekly, "They gave us a chance...a chance to fight for our freedom, and then to be free. We still livin it, Luke."

To move the moment forward, Callie asked, "Well, we bedda decide right now whether we be wantin to work on my book. We lookin back at de past may not make us all happy all de time. Lilly, I don't mean to be upsettin things jus when we come back togedda. It's jus all these ideas keep comin up in my mind—they don't let me be. Figure I gotta get em out by writin my story. But I need help—Lilly, you be my brain, and Lucas, you be my haat."

While Lilly smiled, Lucas showed surprising enthusiasm. "We can wuk wid yo story, an we want de chirren to know bout deese tings. But, or should I say, and, Callie, let's have some fun mixed in. Den we do a bedda job wid yo storytellin fuh de book." He had Lilly and Callie nodding along when he said, "So heah is de word. Tomorrow monin, dishyuh fambly goin on a boat trip out tuh Bay Point."

"Lucas, are you forgettin services tomorrow? It's Sunday." Lilly spoke as if no more need be said.

"Lovely Lilly, we honor de Lawd ebby day by de way we live life. Tomorrow, let we tank de Lawd for all de beauty He done fuh us, and let us go out in de world He made."

Lilly softened her demeanor considerably, saying only, "Husband..."

Without skipping a beat, Lucas planned on. "We tek all we need fuh de day to cook de food we catch. De tide be right fuh shoot us out early in de day and carry us back befo sunset. If we go, an I git to tell my stories to de chirren, too, we be happy, and we write yo book togedda. Amen? Amen." Lucas beamed at his wife, promising, with his hands on his heart, "We tek all fambly tuh church de nex Sunday."

Lilly rolled her eyes over to a smiling Callie.

Chapter 3

SUNDAY, AUGUST 20, 1893

THE NEXT MORNING, WELL BEFORE DAWN, CALLIE AWOKE FINALLY feeling refreshed. Her travels and a day of storytelling had depleted and energized her simultaneously. Though she tried to tiptoe quietly down the old pine stairs, her body and the stairs creaked more than they did thirty-two years before when she and her brothers had claimed the old plantation house after Massa Bowen fled from Union forces. In the still morning darkness on the front porch, she sensed Lilly's presence, quickly confirmed when Lilly said, "I see you finished sleepin early. I knew you would. I said to myself, 'Let me see what Callie wants to ask me today.'"

Determined, Callie didn't hesitate. "You right. And good mornin. I'm up, an you know jus what I'm thinkin bout, sista. Yesterday, when you gave that half-answer about my Sunny, you knew that wasn't enough for her mama. So, what's happenin with Sunny? Is there trouble?"

"She been missin you, Callie, most all huh life! I did the best I could for her when you brought her back to Lucas and me. We all knew that child needed our country life, not the city. You told me all about the sights she seen and the conversations she heard that you wish she hadn't. Sunny came back to these islands as a seventeen-year-old girl thinkin she was twenty-seven."

"Sunny knew she was loved up there." Sounding defensive, Callie quickly added, "She came into your home with Lucas and had that same love. I know it to be true."

"Thank you, sista, tha be a fact." Lilly reached out to hold Callie's hands.

"But that still doesn't tell me where she is now, Lilly darlin."

"I'm gettin to it. You know, she was wantin mo than jus life on this island. We kept her here as long as we could, but by the time she turn twenty, she was on her way. We kept a room for her, and she would come back and spend so much time sleepin I wondered did she ever rest when she was away. She was doin some kinda office work in the day, and then, at night, 'staying with friends' was all she would say."

"And all this is our sad truth, and more, but honey, where is my Sunny?"

"Well, she been stayin downtown right regula. As I said, she knows you arrivin this weekend. But she told Flora that she had to meet someone before she could come out and that once she finished some old business with him, she come yuh."

"Who are we talkin about?"

"You know she's not tellin nothin she don't want to. She is as stubborn as her mama."

Brought up short by Lilly's observation, Callie took a different approach. "Miss Lilly, I know how she can be, and I know how good you be. I just tryin to find out when I'm gonna see my baby…"

"Well now, first off, Impatience, your baby is a thirty-seven-yeah-old woman now. She been a woman almos since she came back from Washington."

Although she received the kidding tone with which Lilly's words were spoken, she knew there was too much truth in them. Yet her question remained before them, clearly evident in the still dark of early morning. "Lilly! Wha Sunny doin?"

She looked beseechingly at Callie. "Can't worry too much if all ain wha we want."

Exasperated, Callie admonished, "Lilly, my darlin sista, you beginning to stir my early morning juices, and not in a good way." Callie administered her famous look, which most sentient recipients knew meant, "Tell me the truth right now!"

"Callie, I wrote and told you just last month that Sunny is stayin in Beaufort mos all the time, and what I understood then, I now am mos sure about, she stayin on de property of a white man. Folk say she done take up wid him."

Callie received the news in her fashion, suppressing her emotions as she looked out over the river, just now starting to glow in the dawn of a new day. Callie always tended to respond analytically and in the way she deemed most helpful. "Well, I guess she and her mama gah some ting fuh talk bout. You not sayin my gal not comin?"

"She say so, but she livin a very...busy life." Empathetically, Lilly rose to move her chair closer to Callie, taking both of her hands. "Callie, she strong, she so strong, but she still hurtin. She reachin out fuh supm she not findin on de islan. I know you know de feelin."

"I don see why she go lookin for mo pain, is all."

"Callie, she ain got ovah huh pain from ten years pass. She livin with the thought that her body didn't birth a healthy baby, without knowin why. Das a lot fuh huh to carry."

"You tink it bes if she knows wha happen with her baby?"

"If she knows wha you did, she may not be able to fuhgive you."

"I jus have to tell huh why and trust the truth. But now, the reason why I took that chile is even more complicated than before."

"Callie, what else you talkin bout?"

"Change comin, Lilly. May be good—may be not so good."

"You know, I am the only one on dis island that knows what you did. Honey, tell me what's goin on."

"Time to tell you more bout Sunny's baby, my grandchile. I didn't want to write about it."

As they leaned in expectantly to share more, they heard Lucas humming his way up to the house from the dock. Upon bounding up the front porch steps, he began to sing exuberantly. Regrettably for him, his elation did not match the time of day nor the somber discussion on the porch. There, the moments of disclosure had ended for the women as they silently rose to greet him. He startled to a stop as he peered at the dimly lit figures in silhouette at the east end of the porch.

"Ladies, you sho nuf scaid a yeah off my life! I was about to come wake you up to get us all movin. Need tuh be goin before de sun come up today to be sure we get de bes tide pullin us out to the big wada." His enthusiasm was not especially contagious.

"Slow down, husband. You know children don run wid de tides same as you, not dis early in de mornin."

"Well, dey bes be down on de dock real quick, or dey won be runnin on any tides at all today." With that, confident and determined to give his family a high-quality day on the water, he called out to his sons, "Abram! Get your people up, and see about the twins. Get down to the dock before the sun come up. Why ain Douglass heah yet? We goin!"

Lilly moved into action with his words. Abram and Douglass had heard the sense of mission in their father's voice on many a morning, and they knew their roles well. For most of their lives, they were expected promptly, and they still practiced the well-learned habit of immediate response, both in their respect for their father and in their understanding of the tides.

While the sons were up and dressed in minutes, their families languished in the lingering comfort of early-morning sleep. The night before, their wives stayed up late to prepare for the early departure. Clearly, the children had not been exposed, like Abram and Douglass, to a lifetime of being ready to rise at their father's first call.

The pace soon accelerated, as the sons of Lucas and Lilly had learned to motivate their children with firm patience. Abram emerged from the front door with the food basket that Amanda had packed in one hand and Saxton's hand in the other. Robert trailed close behind his father with a smaller sack of extra clothing, also packed by his mother. They clamored across the front porch to find Callie standing near the steps, waiting to greet them with extended hands. "Good morning, boys. You ready to go? I been waitin hours to jump on de boat."

"Me too!" Jancy shouted as she ran up the front steps ahead of her mother and father to grab Callie's hand. "You goin out tuh big wada wid us, Auntie Callie?"

"Why, sho I will. Wouldn't let someone as 'Fancy' as you go widout me."

"Aunt Callie, you memba we talk bout my name befo. I be Jancy."

"I memba you, Jancy!" Callie smiled, deciding not to push her game of name confusion onto the earnest young girl this early in the day.

Douglass, though relatively young and agile, was challenged to keep up with the ball of energy that was his daughter. Lilly asked him to go check on the progress of his nephews, Beanie and Bobby. The twins' mother, Flora June, had earned the reputation of being one of the steadiest, strongest branches in the family tree. Just like her father, BB, she was always there when the need arose. Most of her work years were spent in Beaufort on domestic jobs, and the nine-year-old boys were often under the supervision of Lilly and Lucas, but they had not perfected the rapid response to Uncle Lucas's morning call.

Lucas understood the problem of getting his large family on the water before sunrise. He waited on the dock trying to mask his impatience. Staring intently up to the big house and then back to the water line, barely visible as dawn began to break over the lowcountry horizon, he began with a soft shout, "Tide on de way out, men and women,

44

boys and girls." And then he lifted the sense of urgency, "We want to be on the flow. Let's go."

Though the family might complain and mutter as they woke up, Lucas was sure that they would thank him later for his imposition of haste. Very soon, in fact, the sunbeams would sparkle across the water on the warm, humid, August morning, and the movement of their boat would create a gentle breeze. Yes, they would be grateful for the start engineered by Lucas, the patriarch of the clan. He knew that they would all be soothed by the rhythm of the oars on their way to enjoy the gifts of nature waiting on a barrier island next to the great Atlantic Ocean.

Lucas loosened the first of two ropes holding the twenty-five-foot bateau in place as Douglass emerged on the front porch steps, leading the twins down the embankment and onto the dock. Abram helped Jancy and Saxton tuck under the small canvas shelter at the bow of the boat and settled Callie safely on the forward bench as the boat rose and fell with the slight roll of minor waves.

Lilly read the look on her husband's face as she passed him to climb aboard, stopped, turned around, and gently caressed his cheek. For a moment, Lucas turned his head to her and away from a schedule, even if it had been dictated by nature. "Easy, my man," she whispered, "we be there directly. Ain we always get where we goin?" Lilly stretched to kiss his neck lightly and turned to step down into the bateau, still holding Lucas's hand. Callie sensed that they had performed this "dance" a few thousand times before. Lucas pushed aside feelings of urgency as he released Lilly's hand and stood up straight on the dock humming "Amazing Grace," a clear salute to his loving spouse.

As she sat down on the bench with Callie, Lilly playfully bumped shoulders. "We so glad you heah with us! Jus in time to help Lucas and me celebrate being married thirty years."

"I don know how to celebrate," Lucas chimed in, "other than to grant every las wish of my lovely wife. I know das wha keep me healthy an happy. I'm glad I'm so smaat to be wid a woman like huh."

The conversation gave just enough time for Beanie and Bobby to board, dressed in old cut-off pants suitable for wading in the surf.

Douglass pleaded, "Mama, hep deese boys settle in de bow while I get ready to row." Lilly saw his relief as she took their hands. Douglass grabbed the oars and sat on the middle bench behind Abram in one swift and practiced move.

This boat was filled and balanced. Jancy, Saxton, and the twins were tucked into the bow with the tub of fish bait, covered with a temporary canvas canopy. Callie and Lilly were on the bench behind the children with picnic supplies stored beneath them. Abram and Douglass were on the next two benches, each with a set of oars. Lucas sat next to his eldest grandson, Robert, at the stern, ready to provide guidance with a long oar that he also could use as a rudder.

The excursion began as Abram and Douglass pushed off the dock and promptly positioned their oars to row into the tidal creek, joining its southbound flow toward the sea. Even Lucas was impressed by the efficiency of his sons, who quickly synchronized their strokes. Without any more encouragement from their father, Abram and Douglass pulled into their oars with the fresh energy of young men on a holiday with their families. Even the heavily loaded bateau responded to the surge of power and appeared to glide on the surface of Port Royal Sound, carried along by tons of seawater pouring out through the deep harbor as high tide gave way to low.

In only half an hour, they neared Bay Point, the southern end of the island chain where, in 1861, the Confederate fort had crumbled under Union bombardment. Now the tides competed with scavengers to eradicate remaining signs of war. Most apparent were the eroding sand berms, which had failed to keep Confederate troops safe from the onslaught of well-aimed cannon fire.

Scrub pines and myrtle trees grew in clusters along the ridges of the low clumps of sand, providing a little shade for the family on a day made for such an outing. The breeze off the ocean kept the August heat at bay, and when the family climbed up their favorite sand dune, they once again marveled at the expanse of ocean stretched endlessly toward the brilliant morning sun. Peace was evident in all things present, and Lucas asked his family members to celebrate their safe arrival in prayer.

Proudly, he nodded to Abram, who assumed the moment. "Fadda God, we gi tanks fuh anodda day in yo grace, and fo yo son, Lawd Jedus, who gi us new life to start each day. We tank ya now fuh de chirren, fuh we know dah if we do yo will in our time, den de chirren mos surely will be all right. Leh de fambly say, 'Amen.'"

"Amen. Amen. Amen."

Lilly, trying to avoid cranky children, put out their breakfast first. The chicken biscuits were wrapped in one old flour sack dish towel and the boiled peanuts in another. All of it vanished from sight—the biscuits jammed into hungry mouths, the peanuts stuffed into pockets for later snacking. As the biscuits and peanuts disappeared, Lilly handed out small cuts of sugarcane. Each child left the site with cane in hand and legs churning, fueled for the day's adventures down by the dissolving waves.

For the adults, Lilly brought out more flour sack towels holding bigger biscuits filled with slices of tomatoes and smoked pork, all equally well received. They ate quietly, enjoying the rewards of their early-morning exertions while savoring the moments of relaxation. Lucas stretched back against the small myrtle tree that he hoped would shelter him from the rising heat of morning. He asked no one in particular, "When somebody live his life in disyuh perfect place, why be anyplace else?"

Facing the incoming ocean breeze, Callie shared Lucas's daydreaming. "I'm glad to be back, my brudda. Back to stay. Ready to rest." And then, with barely time for a breath, Callie went on, "Lucas, did I tell you I plan to catch a boat into Beaufort tomorrow to meet some people? Should only take a little bit a time."

Lucas gave her a puzzled look, "Your 'only little bit a time' tek my half day." Then he laughed lightly to let his sister know he didn't mind. "Seem to me that you still runnin about like you workin on a schedule. Ain barely been heah a minute, and now you got to git to Beaufort real fas?"

Callie reassured him without disclosing much. "No worry, brudda, I asked Mista Gates tuh tek me when he headin into Beaufort tomorrow at dayclean."

Lucas deflected his curiosity, asking instead, "And now you gettin Lilly all busy writin down stories for your book?"

Callie agreed, "I know fuh fact that you got jus as many tales to tell your grands as I do."

"I got mo," Lucas laughed. "And we made a deal I could start tellin my stories bout Robert Smalls. Our chirren need to know what tha man do fuh we people!"

"Easy, husband," Lilly cautioned. "It's all right to tell the babies, but don't scare em." With a loving smile, Lilly was up. "Who wants to walk down the beach with me?"

Knowing Lucas would prefer to gather the cane poles and gear for those soon to be casting lines in the ocean, Lilly rightly assumed that her only walking partner would be her sister-in-law. Callie struggled up from her sandy perch, and as she walked down the dune with Lilly, she smiled at the realization that more than ten years had passed since she last walked beside an ocean.

They moved down the beach several minutes without conversation, letting gentle waves caress their feet. The shushing sounds of the ocean were welcome after the excited, happy noise of the children on the boat and on the beach. Besides, both women knew the earlier front porch conversation would be continued on the beach.

Callie was first to speak. "Are all your babies at the Penn School risin up to be 'scholars,' as Miss Towne likes to call the children?"

Lilly beamed. "You can see all the things Robert's learning on his face. His parents were good to get him likin books, but Penn School took that eager boy and is doin with him what it's always done—gettin these chirren ready for life. You memba that Laura Towne had a hard time gettin books, new or old? Yet the Penn teachers still get em all to read. Saxton is still too much a baby tuh be a scholar, but he always watchin his big brudda, wantin tuh be like him. The nephews are doin fine, too. Your friend, Miss Laura, has been a Godsend to we people on this island. She been yuh, now more than thirty years, keepin that school goin even when she has to sew books together."

Pleased at the news of her longtime friend and founder of the school, Callie said, "Now that I'm back, I got to see how I can help huh over at Penn." They walked on a while, again in silence, dragging their toes though oozing sand and rinsing them in the shallows. Callie said, "I love the feel of both sand and sea together on my feet. This wada is so warm, and the waves so gentle, the ocean feels like a big bath."

Lilly was next to pick a topic. "Been meanin to ask. What about de man stayin in Will's house. You know he got a mixed lady wid him?"

"We all a bit mixed, ain we? Besides, I ain gonna say nothing bad bout that man." Callie gestured up the beach to the north. "Will done sent him tuh help us with our family concerns. He trusts Nathan Gates like a brudda."

"They sayin he got wood and supplies to fix Will's house."

Callie affirmed, "He a fine man." She breathed deeply. "When I met him at the house yesterday and heard that Will sent him here to help us with some things, I decided to ask if he could take me to town tomorrow. Don't want Lucas to know who I gah fuh see in Beaufort."

Nodding, Lilly remembered how their porch talk had ended. "So we be talkin bout special tings goin on again?"

"Yes, about the future of my girl. But tomorrow, I got to find out more about the past. So, I want Mister Gates to take me and not involve Lucas."

"All I know I told you this morning and in my letter—that Sunny is livin her life downtown in Beaufort on weekdays and seems to be sharin huh time wid a white man."

"You are right. I didn't get that letter."

"Your daughter is a headstrong young woman."

Callie argued, "She being that way forced me to do what I did ten yeahs ago."

"She is determined to live her own life, no madda wha people say."

"Lilly, I don much care no more bout wha people say, but when people tell me they gonna harm my girl and her baby and they mean it, and she say, 'So what?' Well..." Callie reached for Lilly's arm, and they stopped to exchange glances of understanding. "Dependin how the man that threatened Sunny's life answers my questions, he may git a big surprise."

Raising her eyebrows quizzically, Lilly asked, "Is this the man Sunny seein now?"

"I don't know. But I jus got to talk to him and see whether he's any mo a man than he was ten yeahs ago." She looked to Lilly to see uncertainty on her face. "I will know more after I talk to him and git a chance to visit with my Sunny."

Suddenly, they heard a shriek of fear and turned to see the family hundreds of feet away at the waterline, little Jancy running full speed out of the shallow water, the profile of a big fish with a sizable fin on its back following right behind her. Instinctively, Lilly began her grandmother's sprint. Callie followed, not as fast. Jancy screamed louder as the fish moved closer to her.

When they arrived on scene, Lilly and Callie saw the boys and men fall out in laughter, young Robert collapsing breathless and grinning into the knee-deep surf. Abram had snagged a shark for sure, and, unknown to Lilly, Callie, and Jancy, it was on a line being pulled out of the sea. As the maternal figures there to help Jancy, Lilly and Callie tried to stifle their laughter. Jancy, failing to see the humor, stomped up the beach more than thirty feet and stopped, her back turned to the family, her arms crossed. Lilly gestured to everyone to hold down their hilarity and pointed to Jancy. Arms still folded, Jancy looked around, a storm cloud on her face. She stomped twice and turned away again. Only when she heard the last of the laughter did Jancy, her arms still wrapped tightly, move with measured steps back toward her tormentors. Callie opened her arms and embraced Jancy—a momentary cure. As Callie held her close, she remembered holding her own daughter at that age, just before the freedom came.

Robert helped his father subdue the three-foot shark, pressing the wriggling fish to the sand. Abram securely gripped the fish behind the eyes and used a long knife to cut off the head in one mighty slash. He looked up, smiling at his adoring family. "Guess we have some shark meat fuh de stew."

For several hours, the children dashed up and down the beach, seeming not to tire, occasionally sitting with their fathers as they fished in the ocean. In mid-afternoon, Lucas took his cast net to the channel on the back side of the sand dunes. As always, reasons for his fisherman's confidence became obvious. An hour later, he returned to the family's gathering spot atop the dune with a full bucket of squirming shrimp, enough to feed ten. From storage panels in the boat's shelter,

Lilly had brought the large iron skillet, perfect for simmering together vegetables picked yesterday from the Oakheart fields with scrumptious shrimp and bite-size pieces of shark. Mid-afternoon dinner would be as fresh as could be, and after all stomachs were full, legs run out, and family stories told, the incoming tide would carry them back home.

To that end, Callie had corralled the young ones as they came up the dune to collapse on the blankets she had spread out upwind from the fire. While the shrimp and shark meat began to sizzle in the grease with vegetables and seasonings, Callie began preparing the way for more storytelling.

"Afta we eat our fish, you gonna heah your Grampa tell the most amazing tings, true tings, about a man we roun yuh know and love. Even folk up in Washington and New York City know about dis man and all his brave deeds. Who am I talking about, babies?"

Robert was first to shout out, "Robert Smalls," followed by the others, who chimed in with different degrees of certainty and decibel levels.

"What did Mista Smalls do?"

"Stole de boat outa Chalston Haaba," Robert said with pride.

"That's right, young man," Lilly said, proud of both Roberts.

Callie added: "What could be a more audacious show of courage than to take that boat, named the *Planter*, away from the Confederates and give it to President Lincoln's navy?"

"Aunt Callie, wha mean 'awd-a-shus'?" Beanie asked, showing more comfort with his great-aunt.

Callie responded. "Au-da-cious...bein brave, chile...bein so bold and determined that no one can stop you from gettin what is rightfully yours."

"Not even them wha hate yuh?" Robert asked. "Not even them that got de power?"

Callie spoke from the heart of her defiant spirit. "Specially standin up to them that hate you and got the power!"

"Now, now, Aunt Callie." Lilly showed an amazing ability to carry on her tasks and keep an ear on what her flock was doing and hearing. "Be careful not to fill these young heads with ideas that will get them in trouble."

Callie added, "Of course, chirren, you got to be smart and figuh out what's best for you and your family." She looked at Lilly, hoping she moderated enough for the safety concerns of the loving grandmother.

"That's right, chirren. Listen to Aunt Callie." Her praise preceded a quick change of subject. "I got some sea-stew heah!" Lilly started banging her metal spoon on the frying pan, a sign to her loved ones that good eating was sure to follow. On such a family beach outing, niceties were encouraged but not required, though all were provided the option of one spoon or one large oyster shell, made perfectly for scooping the fish stew that Lilly had conjured up in that big skillet. As soon as the stew hit the bowls, the family dug in, discovering that the heat was worth fighting through for the taste.

Everyone had a second bowl of the sea-stew except for Jancy. She looked sadly at her grandmother while rubbing her midsection. "My tummy too scaid to eat mo fish."

With her pre-dinner words to the children about Robert Smalls, Callie had already tilled the soil for Lucas. "You know, chirren, Aunt Callie's stories be important for you to heah, to learn bout her time in Washington. But what happened down on deeseyuh islans be jus as big."

Lucas stood up and sang the first few bars of "America." "My country, tis of thee, sweet land of liberty, of thee I sing...land where my father died..." And then, as his voice trailed off, he stood, walked around the group one time, and stopped at a spot on the sand dune where he would be illuminated by the sun. His eyes already wet, he began, "You chirren may wonda why we keep tellin the stories of past times—you know, bout my brudda, BB, your grandfadda and great uncle. You know, chirren, when de freedom come, and we no longa be propety of

Massa Bowen, I change my name to honor my brudda. The US Army was gonna mek BB a sargent, so since I ain gonna be name Bowen no mo, I took de name 'Sargent' fuh me and my family. Ebby day I keep his memry an oddas who die fightin fuh freedom, at de front of my brain. They lead me on, even now."

When Lucas paused slightly, Jancy, who seemed to be recovering her moxie, impetuously shouted, "Wha you do in wah, Grampa? You be like Aunt Callie?"

"Ain nobody be like Aunt Callie, darlin." Smiling now, Lucas continued, "I could tell you about the night I helped guide Moses—thas right, we people call Harriet Tubman 'Moses'—up the Combahee River. Thas right, she was a leader of three Navy boats and Union soldiers. Local watermen like me hep her visit all de plantations tuh set de people free. Mo den seven hundred folk get on de boats tuh Beaufort that one night." His voice booming, Lucas looked around at each child. "I saw deese new free people wid deese eyes thirty yeahs ago."

"Grampa!" Jancy seemed to speak for the group.

"But that story ain bout me xactly. Wha Robert Smalls done, steal the *Planta*, mek me see how I can hep Miss Moses, Harriet Tubman, do what she do best—git folk free."

Again, pausing for reflection briefly, Lucas held his hands out over the children. "I gonna tell four quick true facts bout my friend Rober Smalls. I give you a big prize, maybe two, if you can tell me de stories tomorrow. Ready?"

Of course, Jancy had to ask, "Grampa, what's the prize?"

"Later fuh dah. Now listen goot. Fus fact. Like Callie say, Robert Smalls steals a boat from Chalston in 1862; brings it through Beaufort, where I see him wid deese eyes; and he teks de boat right ovah dere." Lucas pointed south across the Port Royal Sound to Hilton Head's north end and stood taller at the telling. "And here's de new fact bout dah. He has his wife, his chile, and other people's families, and dey all be ready to blow de boat up if dey gonna be captuhed (captured). Dey be willin tuh die to git an keep dey freedom." Lucas let his word echo in the breeze, the roar of crashing waves growing louder as the incoming tide brought the water nearer around the dune.

The children did not move.

"Fact two: After Robert steals de boat, dey take him to see President Lincoln. Robert says how much de African man want to fight fuh his freedom, just like yo grandfadda BB." Lucas paused, holding both hands over the twins' heads and cupping them gently. "Right afta meetin Robert Smalls, President Lincoln decides to set de slaves free. Das fact two."

Still, there was no movement from the children.

"Fact shree: In 1863, when Robert Smalls serves on a Union Navy boat durin a battle, de man in chaage be too afraid to lead. Robert Smalls takes ovah as captain. Afta he show dah courage, de US Navy mek him de fus African man to be captain, and he lead de fight in seventeen Navy battles durin de wah. Seventeen! You know how many dah be?" He proceeded to count one to seventeen on his fingers, while grandson Robert stood to join in the count. When done, Robert yelled and clapped his hands, the other boys shouted, and Jancy got up to dance.

The excitement came to an end as Lucas boomed, "Fact four: Afta de wah, Robert Smalls went to de Sout Calina convention to hep write de new state constitution." Lucas realized the words sailed right over the heads of his audience. "Lemme mek fact four simple, Robert Smalls hep mek de law so all chirren can go to school." While the children who were old enough enjoyed their status as scholars at Penn School, fact four did not set off a wild celebration.

Callie observed, wryly, "Shoulda stop wid fact three, brudda man." She laughed all the way back to help Lilly with the last of the dinner cleanup.

Lucas recognized Callie's truth and looked over his beloved family, tears of purpose and pleasure glistening in his eyes. "In the name of BB and all those who came before and lifted we people up, rememba all Robert Smalls do fuh you! Class ovah."

With an admonition from Lilly to stay dry, the children were off for one more run on the beach before piling into the boat for the trip home. The gulls started to pick over the scraps of food as Lilly and Callie shook out the quilts and folded them into a large sack. With cooking tools rinsed in the sea and packed into the boat, Lilly shouted for the children to come. They left their play without a whimper and dragged their hot, tired, little bodies into the bateau. They would never admit it, but with legs sufficiently run down, they were ready to fall asleep in this gently rocking cradle.

While most of the family could relax on the journey home, the oarsmen had work to do. The expected incoming tide surrounded the boat where it had once rested on exposed sand. Expecting to ride in on the last hours of the rising tide and be pushed by a southerly breeze, Lucas offered to take one oar and, with a quick look at his grandson, gestured for young Robert to take the other and sit down beside him to share the rowing bench. Abram looked on proudly, if slightly doubtful that his young son's body could match his will in taking on the long wooden oar. Trusting his father and his son, Abram took his place at the stern, watching attentively.

Lucas assured Robert, "We gonna bring de fambly home togedda, wid a lee hep from yo Uncle Douglass." And with that, Douglass shoved the boat out into the shallows, lifted his trim body over the gunnel, sat down on the main bench amidships, and, with powerful strokes, pulled the vessel into the homebound current. "Watch and do what I do." With that simple instruction to his grandson, Lucas began rowing while Robert watched and imitated him as best he could, dipping his oar and pulling with difficulty and determination. Soon, he was in rhythm with his grandfather. The tidal swells rolled up behind them and, with a whoosh, pushed them forward. Robert beamed. Callie and Lilly sat back to back on the front bench with eyes closed, both grateful to rest on each other with no tasks to complete.

After only twenty minutes at the gentle pace chosen by Douglass, Abram steered them near the bank for their turn into Chowan Creek. Unexpectedly, Lucas hesitated, held his hand up, and peered toward a marsh creek in the late afternoon light, studying the part of a bateau he could see, aground on the bank, partly obscured by thick spartina grass.

"What is it?" Abram asked, noting the concern on his father's face.

"That bateau be from de Capers family, an dey not gonna leave one aground like dah. We check it tomorrow—I ain like de look."

As Lucas concentrated on the mystery, Robert struggled to catch his breath. Abram moved up to hug his son, tapped his father on his shoulder, and said, "Let me row us up de crik." Lucas was as grateful as Robert to relinquish the oars. In minutes, Douglass's and Abram's smooth, powerful strokes, combined with the push of the tide, let them chase a dolphin pod all the way back to Oakheart's dock.

The tired children and adults wearily climbed from the boat and had made their way up the steps to the bluff when a figure jumped out from behind a live oak tree emitting a high-pitched shriek that made everybody jump. It was Flora June, as sturdy as her father had been with the same wide a grin.

"Mama!" the twins shouted. Without falling over, Flora June managed to catch her two sons as they leapt into her arms.

"You boys be too big now," she said with a hearty laugh.

Jancy, Saxton, and Robert screamed with delight, "Auntie Flo!" and quickly joined the welcoming embrace.

Flora June saw Douglass and Abram advancing toward her, and she backed away, "Naw, cuz, no jumpin." They both caught her in a heartfelt hug.

"Missed you bein wid us on de big wadda, cuz,"

"Awww, Douglass, we got heah dis morning an found out you all lef fuh de day."

"Sunny heah too?" Abram asked. "Whey she be?"

"Good to see you, darlin!" Callie stepped around the brothers for her own greeting. Flora June hugged and rocked Callie with effusive words to match. "Oh, Aunt Callie, I'm so glad to see you again. You mek it all de way back to us. So happy, so happy-happy."

"Yes, darlin, I'm happy, too, looking at my brother BB's little girl. Before I get too happy, do you know where Sunny be now?"

"No worry, she be back directly. She was so sorry to miss you this morning." As they walked arm in arm up the path to the house, the children being herded ahead, Flora explained, "When we learned you be gone all day, Sunny decided to visit wid farmers tuh git fruit and vegetables we need tuh mek our pies." Reading Callie's inquisitive look, Flora continued, "Yes, ma'am, from what I heah bout you, she jus de same as you be. She figuh she could get supm done and not sit roun all day waitin, so she jus go."

"Yes, that's my Sunny. She got too much energy and grit..." With Flora June's testimony, Callie's wariness receded. "Please sit with me, Flora June, and tell me more about you and my girl."

Chapter 4

SUNDAY EVENING, AUGUST 20, 1893

THE COMMOTION STIRRED BY THE FAMILY'S ARRIVAL SUBSIDED WHEN the children were ushered into the house. They were too spent from the day's happy exertions to do anything but rest or go to sleep for the night. While their mothers were settling their children, Lucas pulled Douglass and Abram aside for a brief word in the yard. In an instant, they went off in three separate directions. Lucas immediately lit a fire in his stone pit, using well-dried pine logs from the wood pile. Douglass lugged the biggest cookpot on the property from the old kitchen house and clanged it down on the iron grate. He then hefted the nearby bucket of fresh well water and dumped it into the pot. With the fire sputtering from the splashing drops, Abram hauled the old wooden crate onto the dock, clattering with the grasping claws of angry blue crabs fighting for their freedom.

On the porch, Flora June was still telling Callie about her daughter. "She a steady girl, Aunt Callie. She got a deep haat (heart), but dah mean she can git huht (hurt) deep." Callie listened quietly, not wanting to interrupt the loving descriptions told by Sunny's cousin and close confidante. "You be so proud fuh huh, de way she wuk. An de way she care fuh odda folk." It was as if Flora had studied the

59

exact words Callie longed to hear. "She want to see you so bad, Aunt Callie. She plannin to spend all day tomorrow wid you befo we go back tuh town."

"Yeah, baby, but I got plans to go to Beaufort tomorrow mornin. Ain that jus the way?" Callie's casual tone hid her great disappointment. She leaned in toward Flora with a steady gaze, determined to understand more about her daughter. Callie consciously softened her expression to avoid frightening her lovely niece in their first moments together, but her look was one that waited for an answer. "So, you think Sunny comin back heah tonight?"

Flora June understood the body language of her elders and had heard enough stories about Callie's iron will to know that she expected answers. "Yes, ma'am, I do. She out wukin today to have more time fuh visit wid you. You don't know, but de pies me and Sunny make fuh sale in Bufut are de best around. Ebbybody say ih so. We always use de fresh food from islan people, an de folk up de riba in Bufut know our pies be de bes, and dey pay top dollah. Ebby week we use a little kitchen we pays fuh in town to mek our pies. We cook em up on Tuesday an Wednesday, sell em out by Friday. We been doin right well now fuh mo den a yeah."

"I'm so proud you both be workin fuh good money and cookin fine food, too. Thanks for the word about my girl. I see how you care about her." Then Callie shook her head. "I still got to be in to Beaufort early tomorrow. I have a man ready to take me at slack tide before it turns us back out to sea."

"Sunny be sorry, but we be back. I mek sho we git our pies sold quick so she git back out heah quick. I still tink you be seein huh tonight. That be okay, Auntie?"

Flora June's efforts to assure Callie about Sunny's schedule were effective. Callie felt BB's kindness and love emanating from his daughter. She was about to respond when Abram brought the bucket of boiled crabs to the table and turned it over, crabs clattering to their last stop before being crudely dissected.

Lucas grabbed the crab cracker and gently crushed one of the succulent claws. Almost simultaneously, his nimble fingers exposed the meat for a second before he dipped it in melted butter and popped it in his mouth with a great sucking sound. Lilly arrived on the porch in the faint light of sunset just in time to see the final act of her husband's crab conquest and shook her head. Callie had forgotten the routine and looked on in wonder, as Lilly murmured, "There is nothin that can keep that man from enjoyin his crabs." It was not something that others at the table could easily watch, though they had seen it all their lives.

Lilly worked through only one crab before she moved to the box she brought out to the porch. "Pay attention, family. You grown-up children of ours know, all life-long we been tellin you about your history, tellin what your mothers and fathers and grandparents did to help mek yo way to freedom bedda. We told little stories to the kids on the beach today, and we back talkin it agin now with you." She pulled out a large book with papers peeking out of the edges at many angles. "But this be a special night togedda. On dishyuh porch, we got BB's brudda, sista, and one of his big baby girls, and we gonna give tanks that our BB served in the wah in the First South Carolina Volunteers. BB is ours, and he cared for us all, even them not born yet."

The eating proceeded though Lilly had the family's attention. "Ebby night and day dis week, Callie and I will be talkin and makin notes. We gonna need yo hep when you have de time. So we gonna be puttin notes into an outline, like General Wallace advised Callie to do befo she writes her book. Yesterday, we talked about all the good work done by our soldiers from deese islans during the war. BB was so proud of his regiment. Turned out he couldn't go wid em, res his soul, but his men fought on and marched into Charleston in 1865. We praise them fuh what they did thirty yeah ago, and most especially, we praise what BB did."

Callie heard again about her brother's kind heart and brave spirit, and despite her joy at the gathering of family, she dipped her head slightly at Lilly's words. She claimed a little more privacy for her own grateful, painful memory of the night her brother died acting in her defense.

Lucas stood abruptly during the lull in Lilly's storytelling, crossed the porch to Flora June, and reached out to her with both arms. She stood to receive his embrace, and shortly, he pulled back to hold her face in his weathered hands. "Florie, I see you, and there be my brudda, and darlin, it's not just yo outside put me in mind of BB, it's yo haat. You look at problems people have an you fix em. Jus like yo daddy."

Lucas kissed Flora June's forehead and stepped back to his chair, wiping tears as he went.

"I live simple, Uncle Lucas. My Gawd say love odda folk jus like you love yo own self. He say prepare yo sef, laan yo letters, and get some facts bout de worl, and den go choose how to live yo life hepin others." A chorus of affirmation greeted the wisdom of BB's daughter.

Callie's spirit had not received the lift that Lilly intended. She glumly reported, "Got to say, Lilly, you know how proud I am for BB. And I'm so glad the First South Carolina Volunteers got to march into Charleston at the end of the war. But what I saw when the war ended up in Washington made me so sad. Wrote about it in a letter to you at the time, I memba."

No one moved or spoke.

"All them big parades up in Washington to celebrate the Union victory? Ain no black regiments to be found. Line afta line of white boys in blue, and we cheered em, cause they died to make us free too, but we didn't understand why we didn't see black men marchin in Union blue. We knew they got shot up, bled out, and buried just like white men."

Shaking her head slowly at the memories, Callie went on to fill the silence on the porch. "Black men weren't the only folk missin in the parade. Ebby battlefield I been on during that time, I saw women, mostly black women, comin from the forest or up from the river, helpin hurt soljahs best they could. Womenfolk carried their own load."

Abram smiled. "I hear how you feel for the people, Aunt Callie. You been takin care of needy folk from way back when. And tellin stories when you visited us ten yeahs ago, and even when I was little—when was that, twenty yeahs back? It excites me to hear it to dis day, and I want my boys to hear it, too."

"I love that you feel that way, Abram. You be my first nephew, and I loved you the longest," Callie joked, trying to keep a straight face. Abram started to laugh with her. "Go ahead," she urged, "my longest-loved young nephew. Seem like you got supm on your mind."

"Aunt Callie, you mos always talkin bout things you seen, but you not talkin so much bout yo own history and how it mek you feel." Frowning, he tried to explain his thought simply. "You talkin bout history of odda folk, but not how you lived it. Wha can you say bout yo own life, and how it fit in de history?"

"History is personal," Callie asserted without hesitation. "And our whole lives are part of the chain of livin—people passin along their hard-earned stories." Then Callie slowed down and nodded at Abram, encouraging him to go on.

"I just been wonderin, you went up nort lookin fuh yo mama and yo daddy. I memba hearin you found em, an...well." Again, Abram hesitated. "Mean no disrespect, Aunt Callie. Afta de wah ended, why you stay up dere in Washington? Why you not come back yuh fuh live wid we? Yo fambly miss you."

Callie had just finished off her second crab and was ready to respond. "Well, there are too many reasons, Abram." Callie appeared energized by the flash of memories she could share.

Lilly scurried from the table and her plate of crab debris, saying, "Let me get my pencil and paper."

Callie barely skipped a beat. "The reasons go back to President Lincoln. I came back to Washington afta the battle on the Monocacy River, when they close down mos hospitals up in Maryland. They told me they got too much work at the new Freedmen's Hospital in Washington, so I went there to keep helpin the boys..."

Callie stood, walked toward the corner of the porch, and grasped the railing tightly. Though still facing the river, she spoke loudly enough to be heard by everyone as they finished off the last of the crabs. "In those first months in Washington, I began to pay more attention when people talked, specially bout our President Lincoln. I read news accounts of the war and how that good man worried so much over it."

Abram decided to do the unadvisable. "Aunt Callie? About your daddy..."

Callie turned quickly, remembering that she loved her young nephew. "Young man, I be talkin bout the president you named for." Considering that to be enough explanation, she continued, "That man fought so hard to end slavery by gettin Congress to approve the thirteenth amendment—you know what it say?" Callie didn't wait for an answer. "'Neither slavery nor involuntary servitude...shall exist within the United States.'"

A chorus of "Praise Gawd" followed her pronouncement, with Flora June crying out, "Tell it, Aunt Callie!"

Callie stood erect, directing her gaze into the distance. "I be so joyful when Mister Lincoln wins the election in 1864, so very joyful. I thank God for the life of that man who tried so hard to bring justice to our land through that terrible war. Standin with my feet in deep mud at the US Capitol building when Mister Lincoln swears on the Bible again, I be proud just to be breathin the same air on that cold day in March. From what he says in his speech, and I remember to this day, about the war bein needed 'until every drop of blood drawn with the lash shall be paid by another drawn with the sword.' I know that Abraham Lincoln honors the black man's sacrifice on the battlefield and in the cotton field."

Realizing she had digressed slightly, Callie made eye contact with each family member on the porch before she continued. "When Mister Lincoln died, I know a part of me did too." Though she hesitated, her family knew they were not at the end of the story. "Through the weeks after we lost him, I spent what little spare time I had readin newspapers about those who conspired to kill him, and that's where I began to find my daddy."

"In the newspaper?" Lucas asked half in jest.

"Brother, I learned that my friend General Lew Wallace was on the military commission that found President Lincoln's killers guilty. He told me at Monocacy that if he could ever help me, he would." Callie, startled at sounds coming from the yard, looked but did not see anyone. She continued, "You all rememba that my daddy was reported lost at sea? I begin to hope that smart man, General Wallace, can help me find my daddy. So, I go to see him, and, true to his word, within weeks of my visit, he sends a carriage to pick me up and bring me to his office in Washington. He tells me that my daddy has been in Salisbury Prison in North Carolina and will soon be released along with hundreds more. General Wallace gives me a list that shows my daddy's name, Harris Hewitt."

As if to tie the bow neatly on the package, Callie concluded, "So, my admiration for President Lincoln, and my mourning for him, provides the answer to my prayers. My reading leads me to my great friend, General Wallace, and my search for my daddy is over." Though tired from her telling, Callie knew from her family's inquiring looks that she needed to conclude this chapter of her story. Somberly, she quickly added, "Will decides to escort me to North Carolina, and with General

Wallace's influence and connections, we are able to arrive in Salisbury on the day my daddy is released. I greet him and hold him in my arms. He is just a sliver of the man I remember from our meeting on the pier in Beaufort before the war. Yet, I see through his vacant stare that he recognizes me, and..."

Callie started to sway just as Lilly reached her side. "That's all for now, dear heart. We'll hear more of your father at another time." Again, they heard the sound of movement on the ground below the porch, perhaps a small animal grunting, or perhaps a sob.

Abram focused fully on Callie and, clearly distressed by the story, apologized. "Aunt Callie, I didn't mean to bring a bad memry to yo haat."

"No worry, Abram. I'm too sad about it, but so happy to answer your question." Callie stood taller and lifted her chin. "I'm glad that my love for Mista Lincoln helped me find my daddy, but it will always weigh on my heart how sick that prison made him. You know, thousands of men died there?" She paused and looked to Abram for understanding. "On another day, I will say more about my father's fine life and how it ended too soon." She reached a thin but deceptively strong arm out to Abram and drew him to her by the neck. "Don't be sorry to ask about our beautiful family history. Be proud to tell the stories. They brought us here today." Callie's smile lines deepened as she beamed lovingly into Abram's face.

Again, some shuffling down below, closer. As Lucas took one step off the porch, someone small and quick jumped up, darted up the steps, and touched his arm lightly while dashing straight to her mother.

"Oh, Mama!"

"Sunny!"

As Lilly herded the family inside, Callie and her daughter silently embraced and cried as one. With space lovingly granted for their reunion, Callie and Sunny pulled back to look at each other. Through tears still streaming into the corners of her smiling mouth, Sunny whispered, "Mama, I'm so glad you're here."

"Me too, Sunny. Let me hold you some more." After another brief embrace, Callie said, "You know I been heah since Friday."

Sunny immediately responded, as if ready to counter, "Mama, I got wuk I do, things to tek care of, people to see. It's part of me, my life, Mama." She slowed her cadence. "Not used to comin out yuh tuh see you."

Callie threw another jab. "Even so, boat ride from Beaufort can be quick. Don't take too long."

"Some time it do."

"It DO?" Callie asked in her best mother-teacher voice.

"Mama...it does. Sometimes the boat trip back home last way too long."

Callie understood her daughter's well-earned right to reference her mother's absence for most of the last thirty years. Still, Callie challenged her again. "Take a lot of time if you got some current running against you—some force of nature—some wind in yo face. Then maybe it can take, how long I been yuh? Been yuh shree days...!"

"Been yuh shree days?" Sunny held up three fingers. "You talkin like an islan woman now, come yuh jus deesyuh shree days?"

In Sunny's tone, Callie recognized that the mocking words were born of hurt caused by too many years apart. Her mother's love kept her from responding gruffly, though the words were poised on her tongue. She said instead, "Well, I am glad you be heah now, my lovely daughter. I'm ovah my feelins bein hurt a little bit. You?"

"Sometimes you ask too much, Mama. I been missing you fuh too long." Sunny did not lift her head to face her mother. Callie turned away to hide her emotions and her regret at being so contentious during their first conversation. Seeing that she had had impact beyond her intent, Sunny, like her mother, moved to comfort the other.

"Mama, you know I love you, and I live to meet yo standards. Just don't try to mother me too much right away. I got some serious things on my mind." She hesitated, turned away, and then spun right back to hug her mother again.

Callie remained quiet, so Sunny brought her face within inches of her mother, then rubbed noses with her. With a wide-eyed expression, Sunny said, "Maybe I can share deese worries bedda if I...if I can talk togedda wid you mo as my friend than as my mama."

Sunny's close proximity, silly expression, and nose-to-nose rub broke through to her mother. They exchanged identical smiles that expanded into grins. Callie, always one to push into tender territory if she perceived it to be needed, asked, "Then Sunny, as a friend who has loved you the longest, may I ask you a personal question?"

Exasperated but amused, Sunny's "Mama!" gave permission.

"When I ask your Aunt Lilly what my—friend—Sunny is doing, she says Sunny got a man in her life, ummm-hmmm, and that he lives in Beaufort. She say dah wha folk say..."

Left hanging, the phrase turned into a question that Sunny did not intend to answer. "Mama, my amazing, too-long-gone friend, I ain ready fuh share bout that part of my life right now. Not tonight anyway." Instead, Sunny diverted, "I was downtown Beaufort on de corner, you know de one where dey let us sell our vegetables down pass where de white folks sell theirs. So funny." Sunny stopped to laugh, still covering her refusal to talk about her man. "Florie en me, we mek some fine pies, Mama. You be proud. De people know wha we fix is bedda and cheapa. MMMM-mmmm!"

Sunny's response had the intended effect. Visibly sagging, Callie said, "Well, baby, I'm tired and my tired is tired. I got plans to go up river to Beaufort tomorrow to take care of some business. Got to go early, right afta dayclean, befo high water flow back to sea." Then Callie went one step too far, again. "When can I find out mo bout dis man?"

Sunny was quick. "Ain none my friends, cept Florie, know dis man, and she don't know much." Having had enough of the friendly inquisition, Sunny asserted, "Besides, tomorrow, I had plans to be out heah visitin with you and takin care of things with Florie." Looking as tired as her mother, "Mama, why you goin to Beaufort?"

Not able to say truthfully, Callie deflected, "Some business I got. Won't take long. Be back by afternoon."

"Well, Mama. That's when Florie got her friend, Ed, to row us back to town with all our fresh pie fixins." Realizing how they would be missing each other, Sunny shook her head. "My...my...my, ain dah jus de way? Mama, friend, ain dah jus de way?" Wanting to sound more hopeful to her mother, Sunny hastened to add, "I will be back late in the week to spend time wid you."

"Please come back by Thursday, fa true!" Her mother's plea was heartfelt both due to the yearning for more time, at last, with her grown-up child, and because that is when Callie planned to share some hard truths with her daughter. Even as she wished to be closer to Sunny, Callie knew she did not have the perfect words, and had not yet mustered the courage, to tell Sunny how she lost her baby ten years before.

"Yes, Mama, promise we be togedda by Thursday night, and if not then, fo sho sometime on Friday morning." Sunny laid a gentle hand beside her mother's cheek, and Callie leaned into it, knowing their fragile connection remained, not to be further tested for now.

They climbed the stairs to the bedroom they shared in the early days of freedom and during Callie's two visits home. It was still Sunny's room. Sleep found them instantly, first Sunny, as Callie gently rubbed her forehead, and then Callie, satisfied that her child was at rest.

Monday morning, August 21, 1893

SUNNY NOTICED HER MOTHER RISE FROM THE BED JUST BEFORE DAWN but did not stir. Callie went downstairs and out on the porch where Lucas sat every morning to welcome the first light.

Callie greeted her brother, "Ah, bruddaman. Good dayclean to ya."

"Monin, Sista. Wha you gah fuh do?"

"Not wantin to wake my baby, I'm goin out to my reflectin spot. Is it still there?"

"Yeah, Callie, it's still yo spot." Lucas, once again, pressed her about matters not his business. "Wha you gah fuh do in Bufut dis monin, and why fuh you ain ask me fuh hep?"

"I'm needin to do some private business, and I'm not wantin to trouble you. I asked our new neighbor, Will's friend, Nathan Gates, to take me in. Thas all."

"You ain no trouble, sista. Don want you findin any trouble yosef." Lucas grew stern. "Callie, it ain like it used to be roun yuh. It ain safe. There be too many white men actin like dey did befo de wah."

"Not my worry dis mornin, bruddaman. I got to get down to my reflectin spot to see what the water show me befo the wind starts stirrin my view." Descending the porch steps, she smiled back at Lucas, knowing that his love followed her every day. "I need tuh figuh out a few tings."

Soon after, Sunny moved quietly from the house and started down the porch steps in pursuit of her mother. She passed by her uncle without seeing him on the porch. "Heah come yo shadow!" Lucas shouted loud enough for Callie to hear and for Sunny to be completely startled.

"Unca Luke, you scared me," she stammered as she stumbled down the last steps.

Callie waited, laughing, "I see yo uncle still like to help the young people get off to a strong start in the mornin." They walked off together arm and arm.

The morning air was laden with moisture, the August sun and daily breeze not yet having their drying effect. Callie led Sunny to the bluff where two old live oak trees extended gnarled branches in all directions and where, just over the bluff, roots reaching ten feet down to the marsh were exposed above the waterline. This morning, as the sun rose, Callie stepped down the bluff carefully, holding onto damp roots as she made her way out to perch on the very branch that she had settled on during the first quarter century of her life. Instinctively, Sunny followed but found her own roost out beyond her mother, made special by the two branches that formed a chair for those agile enough to get to it. Hanging over them, improbably twisted branches supported large strands of Spanish moss and long vines that reached into the marsh.

Callie was quiet for the first minutes they were there, peering into the still waters below and lifting her eyes through the tangle of wood to the brightening sky above. And then she spoke, in prayer. "Please God, light the paths my daughter and I walk, fuh us to see that where there is light, there is love, even after done red fa down (darkness). And let the light shine for all of us who seek things we have lost, so that we may find peace."

As her mother bent over to study the water, Sunny looked on curiously, respecting her mother, not knowing what matters caused her intensity. When the prayerfulness had ended and Callie looked up to see her daughter, Sunny asked, "When I see your life, Mama, I see how you done done so much good work, and now you got no mo worries. And yet, you be lookin fuh ansas to questions from our water, our mornin sky, our God. Why, Mama?"

"My chile, sometimes you may see those with the biggest bounce in their step got the most reason to be weighed down. Don't get me wrong, Sunny. I am pleased with my life and the work I have done for others. And yet, there are more problems that need solutions."

"You got some stories you wanna share, Mama?"

"All God's chirren got stories to share, my love. And they all will be shared, in time. Fuh now though, I got to get to the dock. Got my new friend, sent here by your Uncle Will, to take me to Beaufort. His name is Nathan Gates, and he will be waitin for me."

"You gonna take care of those problems up de riba in Beaufort?"

"Still trying to figure out what the problems are fuh now, chile." And, holding up her long skirt, she slid off the branch-seat onto the embankment leading up to the bluff, her booted shoes getting caked with marsh mud. "You comin?"

"Naw, Mama, gonna sit here decidin whether I got any problems needin solutions."

"Please save your answer til we talk again Thursday. I may have a story or two for you by then. I love you for comin out with me this mornin!"

"You know I love you, Mama."

Callie smiled and touched her hand to her heart as she turned to make her way to the Oakheart dock, where she found Nathan Gates waiting with a crew of two young men from the community. She acknowledged each one with a nod and a greeting. "Good morning, sir and young men. I trust we will be compensating these fine oarsmen for their services over the next few days, Mister Gates."

"Yes, indeed we will. Your cousin briefed me well before I left Annapolis, including your strong commitment to paid labor. Will also advised that my duties may involve an immediate trip to Savannah. So here we are, me and my wage-earning crew."

"Thank you, Mister Gates. First, we must be off to Beaufort for a meeting that may be important to your Savannah mission. If all goes well, you can bring me back to Oakheart by noon and set out on your short trip from there, still on the outbound tide."

"I'm impressed that you would consider thirty-five nautical miles by ocean and tidal creeks a short trip."

"Well, I meant for men such as yourselves." Callie realized anew the benefits of having Will Hewitt as her cousin. She was feeling increasing gratitude for Nathan Gates, the man Will had chosen to bring Sunny's child home.

As captain and crew began to make the twenty-foot row boat move through the water, Callie once again marveled at the magical quality of the rivers and creeks that snaked through the islands. Without knowing it, she had missed the peace that these surroundings could instantly provide. Having worked most of her life in Washington, the return to island life required Callie to make multiple, simultaneous adjustments. As she relaxed physically onboard, moving with the power of the oars and the slight roll of the river, Callie's mind engaged fully. She focused on the love of her life—Sunny—and how they had arrived at this difficult moment.

Callie reflected on her extended visit to the sea islands in 1883, when she learned how strong and independent-minded her daughter had become. She knew that Sunny used her "knowledge" of the world in various ways, some productive and some not so much. Specifically, after Sunny moved back to the sea islands in 1873, she began a quiet relationship with a young white man whom she knew as a boy on the island before the war. His father had moved the family away during the war and then back into Beaufort, where he found wealth and moved up in society. But the young man seemingly did not aspire to his father's lifestyle, as he was a waterman who blended easily with other watermen, white and black. Over time, Sunny and the young man maintained and matured their relationship, to the extent that, upon Callie's return to Beaufort in 1883, she was presented with the gift of an impending new title: grandmother.

Of course, this was cause for concern, and Callie asked many valid questions. At first, Sunny declined to disclose the name of the father. But when she did, Callie's worries multiplied. She knew from long ago that the males in this particular family were willing to keep close company with the women of Africa, but they would never own up to it in public.

Callie remembered her fear that day in 1883, on a similar boat ride up the river to Beaufort, when she visited this young man to discern his intentions. She was sorry, but not surprised, to learn that her worst fears were justified. Not only would Brent Landon not admit to fathering the child, but he also warned Callie never to tell anyone he was the father. Callie took careful note of the dark seriousness in his eyes as he ushered her to the iron gate of the backyard at his family home. He was blunt. "If my daddy ever hears of this, he won't let Sunny or her baby live long enough to tell the story again."

After that threat, Callie had gone back downriver, ignoring the beautiful sunset and the soothing rhythm of the boat as the oarsmen rowed her home to Oakheart. She had to get back to her daughter and to a problem that knew no easy resolution. When Sunny told Callie about other threats the father had made to her, and that Sunny planned to defy this family and carry her baby openly in Beaufort, Callie knew she had to act—to protect Sunny and her child. The expected baby could not grow up anywhere on these islands.

Splashes from a mishandled oar jolted Callie into the present and the reality that she was on her way to another visit with Brent Landon. Callie had set the sequence of events, now unfolding, days earlier when, upon arrival at the Beaufort wharf, she sent a messenger to Landon informing him of her intended visit first thing Monday morning. She had invited him to meet her at the town dock or at his home, whichever he preferred. Of course, she had no expectation that he would meet her in a public place, so she left Mister Gates and crew at the boat. She walked one block from the waterfront and had just turned down the street where she last saw Landon at his backyard gate, and there he stood.

Brent Landon, ever mindful of appearances, pretended not to notice Callie as they approached each other, until Callie spoke. "Good morning. I know I'm not so old that you don't remember me."

Looking surprised, he said, "Miss Callie?" And without waiting for her response, he pointed toward the end of the road at the edge of the salt marsh and redirected their walk accordingly. Callie suspected that she would be greeted with rudeness or a brief and definite repudiation of any shared business or relationship. Instead, Landon walked silently, both beside and slightly in front of Callie. She was used to sizing up situations promptly and making immediate, objective analysis of white men, as to their trustworthiness. She was not sure what his neutral, yet polite, manner indicated.

Callie wasted no time in taking charge of the conversation, informing Landon, "I am grateful that you have come out to meet with me. Though I hope you have been well, I can't talk about that. I have to tell you first thing that your family's threat ten years ago forced me to do an awful thing."

Landon withdrew his hands from his pockets, dropped his arms by his side, and then clasped his hands tightly. His head and shoulders drooped perceptibly, making him look much older than Callie expected after just ten years. As they arrived at a wooden bench overlooking the marsh creek, he sat heavily. Callie watched closely. He did not look at her directly. Instead, Brent Landon covered his face with his hands.

"No, young man. I did not end the life of my grandchild, I saved it."

His quizzical look at Callie was as compelling as his shaking voice. "How, please?"

Standing above him, Callie declared, "I tell you soon enough. First, my spirit haffa leh me know if it can live wid de spirit inside of you. Tell me. Do those threatening words you spoke to me ten years ago still anchor the boat you sail through life on?"

Callie was prepared for the worst of responses. And for at least five deep breaths, Brent Landon said nothing. He wiped his teary eyes and let his hands fall to his knees before looking at Callie. His words spilled out. "Miss Callie, when we last talked, I was a younger and more stupid man, and I was scared of my father and my mother. I ain't never forgive myself for how I scared you and Sunny."

That was all Callie needed to hear. "When you was a boy on our island, I never knew you to be the kind of evil person I heard that day. Yo words sounded like yo parents' hatred, threatenin the life of my girl and my grand."

"I let my family's feelings control me back then. That was before I got to know about true Christian love. Now, I got to stand up for myself, account for my mistakes, and accept my responsibilities."

Callie sat down beside him, placing a comforting hand on his shoulder.

Brent turned toward her, looking into her eyes. "And, Miss Callie, I been prayin for years that you didn't hurt the baby cause of me. Is he...? Did he...?" Brent struggled to speak.

"Your son is alive. He has been living safely for ten years down in Savannah."

Brent stood abruptly, emitting an anguished, moaning cry. The relief came across his face in an instant, followed by realization that he was a father—of a son. So shocked by the news was he that he sat down by Callie again and gave her a brief hug. "So, I'll be there when that boy needs me. Tell me what to do, ma'am. My daddy and mother are gone. I'm ready to stand for right."

"Well, he needs a new home now, and we are gettin him from Savannah and bringin him to his mama on St. Helena Island."

"Does Sunny know about her boy? She ain't never said nothin."

Callie hesitated, uncertain what Sunny would want and wishing that she had shared this story with her daughter already, but she had feared the conversation too much. "Let me talk with Sunny first before we make any plans. Nothin for you to do right now. I just needed to find out what I needed to know bout you."

Callie told him that she had a boat waiting to leave immediately for Savannah and that perhaps they could arrange for him to meet his son sometime soon. That seemed to be sufficient for Brent, whose eyes had dried and whose back had straightened such that he resembled a different man. He had not forgotten where he was, however, and so, he thanked her politely without further contact, while looking at her with a smile and new life in his eyes.

Callie watched him walk back up the street before she left the bench, pleased that the young man had shown his kindness and not blindness. She could not have imagined a better result. With this good news came the reality that Callie's plan had been set in motion and that the journey to Savannah and back would be completed by the weekend, God willing. Callie's plan also meant that soon she would share stories with her daughter that might not be believed...or forgiven.

SECTION TWO

Chapter 5

MONDAY AFTERNOON, AUGUST 21, 1893

CALLIE, STILL THINKING ABOUT HER TALK WITH BRENT, QUIETLY SAT in her porch rocker after the brief, loving welcome from Lucas and Lilly. Looking quizzically at Callie, Lucas opened his mouth to start the interrogation about her trip to Beaufort when Lilly, knowing the sensitivity of Callie's mission, interrupted.

"You get back with enough jump in yo step to do some work today? You know you told the family we would finish your outline this week? You still mean to be that good?"

Tired, Callie's affirmation, "Sure sista, when you ready," did not sound so convincing to Lilly.

"Memba you told your girl to come back here by Thursday—leaving what's left of this day, Tuesday, and Wednesday? I say let's get to it. We got lots of daylight. I bring you some food and we start in. You ready, fa true?" With gratitude, Callie looked at her dear sister-in-law, whom she judged to be more enthused than she was. Lilly piled it on. "I got real excited lookin ovah yo letters while you went to Beaufort. Either you gonna help me fill out your outline, or we gonna call it my book."

With a weak nod from Callie, Lilly moved into the house, reappearing in minutes with a plate of fish, vegetables, and a biscuit like she and Lucas had consumed. "Yes, your brother did just catch these this morning while you were away."

Lucas, genuinely interested in the proceedings, asked Callie, "Wha you do in Washington afta de wah, sista, that you ladies gonna put in a book?"

"My Washington life was nothin but work, mos all the time. Even on my time off, I still got asked to work. My first two years, I slept in a rooming house, ate hospital food, and learned supm every day from smart people all round me." Shaking her head, she frowned. "But my heart was with my Sunny back heah. When I looked up from my work, I thought about you and Lilly, and Sunny, and..." Callie slowed to a stop.

"How she was doin at Penn School," Lilly suggested.

"I did worry bout that. You know from readin my letters."

Smiling broadly, Lucas took the cue. "I tell you de trute. Sunny almos talk my ears off when I row huh to and from school. I ain nebba seen a lee chile mout move so fas."

Lucas's evident pleasure at the memory warmed Callie. "I can see her little self now. She trapped you in the bateau where you had to listen."

Lucas nodded. "Dah she do. Dah she do."

Lilly jumped from her chair and dashed into the house with her finger up, saying, "I almost forgot our drinks. Dohn say nothin important."

Callie recalled, "I memba Lilly writin bout Sunny's school work bein so good. I smiled so much at work people asked me why. I say my girl Sunny's an excellent scholar, like they call the children at Penn."

Lucas said, "Yo Sunny always took huh school wuk tuh haat."

Callie responded, "I have been so proud of huh. Oh, brudda, I missed huh so much for so long. But I had to go on with my work. I knew you and Lilly and this place was zactly what my child needed then...and what I need now."

"Sweet lemonade for a sunny August day."

"I say Lilly has a way of knowin wha people need. Tank ya, sista." Callie took a satisfying gulp before getting back on task. "Brudda, a big part of my life was right yuh. I had sadness in my life, workin where I was needed in Washington and wantin to be back yuh where I needed to be. Back then, I needed yo hep to raise up Sunny, and now I need yo hep again. As this book idea gets in my head, I got to figure how these two parts of my life come together to tell the story."

Lilly allowed several seconds to pass before saying, "We all try to keep balance tween tings. You did what was right at de time. You were in de right place then, and you in de right place now. So, go inside to that mirror on the bureau. Go on."

Callie moved uncertainly as Lilly continued, "When you get there, tell me what you see." Callie peered at her reflection as Lilly asked, nearly shouting, "What made Callie Hewitt turn out so good? Now, thirty years after she left, what brought Callie back yuh?"

"You know, Lilly? You are a good teacha! You get me thinkin..."

Lucas, knowing of his wife's determination and remembering his sister's strong will, teased, "You ladies sho is cookin up a mighty big dish. Stirrin in dis, stirrin in dah. But I sho ain kno who de stirra is."

Callie suddenly was feeling the spirit of her work. "All thanks to Lilly, ticklin my memry bone. You know I been tellin you bout General Wallace? How he be writin some books? One famous book he wrote was called *Ben Hur*. You hear of it?"

"Girl, I don be readin all that much any way, but I mos sure ain no book crossed my eyes by a man who say he 'been her.' That don't sound familiar," Lucas concluded with mock seriousness.

"Silly bruddaman. *Ben Hur* is the name of the book. B-E-N H-U-R, *Ben Hur*. Not B-E-E-N-H-E-R. His book tells all bout Moses and Bible stories about partin the waters. You know?"

"Still ain nebba yeddy (hear) nuttin bout dat."

"That don mean it not so." Callie recognized that she had had similar conversations with her dear brother before. "Anyway, this man, General Wallace, who also wrote *Ben Hur*, told me I can write a book if I decide that I can. Like I told you first night, if he can write a book to tell the president's story, I can write a book to tell my story."

"Well, my sista, my wife," and Lucas bowed deeply to both, "ain no way I gonna argue wid you both. Befo I go down on de wada, I wanna know what happened dis moning in Bufut. You say you had business? You okay?"

"Brudda, jus fine. It was mostly personal; maybe I tell it sometime."

Lucas shook his head and started down the front steps, then turned back. "Soon as I'm outa hearin range, I know you be tellin it. Mmmm-hmmm. I know dis. Das all right tho. Lemme jus step away sos you ladies git on tuh yo talk." True to Lucas's words, as he moved away, Lilly leaned forward, staring intently at Callie with raised eyebrows, her head cocked at a questioning angle.

Callie responded, "Yeah, I saw the young man. Ain seem to be filled with hate like ten years ago. He seem almos like a good person. I don't know if he and Sunny talk or even know each other."

"You don know if they be togedda now?"

"I couldn't tell from wha he said. And I didn't feel right askin." Shaking her head, "Sunny wouldn't want me askin questions about her life."

Lilly summarized the lack of information. "So, you don't know who she seein?"

"No, you?" Callie responded quickly.

"No. Reckon it's not him cause she woulda say supm."

Callie questioned Lilly's presumption. "Lilly, when you were younger, did you tell yo business to your parents, or your aunts and uncles?"

"No!"

"Well then. She could be seein this man or not. All I say fa true is that the young man showed me a good-hearted person that I didn't see ten years ago. I reckon that must be the side Sunny used to like."

"Maybe still do."

"Maybe still do," confirmed Callie.

After a deep breath, Lilly turned in her chair to face Callie more directly. "So, let's go!"

"Say where," Callie muttered, not wanting to sound too enthusiastic.

"Goin back in time. It's our job to find the big news of yo life." Lilly rose to the occasion, leaving her chair and shaking from the toes to the nose. "Clear out that mind, dear sista, and let's see what we can see."

"You sure you ready to get back into it?"

Holding up her pencil, Lilly said, "I'm ready to write. Keep me busy. Maybe you can tell me supm bout your search for your mama and daddy."

Accepting Lilly's challenge and her gift, Callie began. "Maybe I'll start with my mama, since that story won't last too long. Right after the war, I found Mama, and I would see her some. She worked in a food place on the first floor of an old Washington hotel." Callie's tone indicated that the memory was not a pleasant one. "She told me that she loved me, but she told me that I reminded her too much of her life as a slave. Each time I went to see her, she was reluctant to talk and more distant than I hoped."

Lilly offered, "Maybe she didn't want to get attached to you."

"I reckon, Lilly, cause she never wanted me to stay around too long and didn't invite me back to visit, not once. I made a mistake one day in the room she kept upstairs from de restaurant. She asked me ifn I had a man, and I shuddered at too many hard times wid de massa. As I thought, I looked round her place, makin a face bout my own life. All of a sudden, she got real mad at me, askin why I judge huh. Who am I to judge huh life?"

"She was ashamed."

"Maybe, but I know I was thinkin bout the bad things happened to me. She took the look on my face to be a comment about huh."

"I got to think there was mo to it," said Lilly. "Maybe she felt guilty bout not evah bein a mother to you."

"Maybe, Lilly, maybe. I got my own sadness on that subject. We talked together a couple more times...about things that didn't matter much. She asked me if I have children and I lit up tellin her about my Sunny, her granddaughter. But she didn't smile or anything. I don't understand to this day. Made me feel like my mama didn't know me."

Lilly tried to find truth. "You reminded her of her life as a slave. Sounds like her hard life made her unhappy and tough."

"We couldn't share the freedom of that time, even though we had it in common."

"It seems like her mind ain able to be free."

Callie shook her head slowly. "When I left her for the last time, after Harris died, I turned back to look at her. I saw her watchin afta me, with a sad smile on her face."

Lilly, writing furiously, said, "Tell me some mo bout your daddy."

"You know, he stayed sick afta bein in that Salisbury prison. I don't think he drew a good, deep breath the rest of his life." Slowly, Callie added, "But he was such a nice man." Callie beamed at Lilly, who looked up from her notetaking as Callie clapped her hands. "And for the rest of my days, I'll be glad my Sunny got to know her grandfather. Through her, I got to see his gentle ways, the different times he would explain things to her, the walks they took beside the Chesapeake Bay. Even though he lived a day trip away from Washington in Annapolis, my Sunny and me would go see him if I had just a few days off from work. I know Sunny loved to get down close to the wada in that town, but, even more, I know she just liked to be in the presence of her grandfather. From who he was with us, we learned more bout who we were." Callie looked at Lilly expectantly. "Does that make sense? I feel so close to him...like he's still with me."

"Tell me more." Lilly drew out her phrase to make way for Callie's words.

"Our days with him be magical. You know he reads everything and he be into all the politics of every new day. He talks to everybody he meets, and then he shares with me, and Sunny too, about every little thing that fills his head. I thought I been places and seen a lot, but my daddy, ooooeeee! He has so many facts. And the more I listen to him, the more I realize how much I don't know and how much I love him. Sunny came to me after spending a day with her Grampa Harris, and she say, 'He like a walkin, talkin book.' Hah! She was right."

Callie stopped talking long enough to pour some more lemonade into her glass, then hurried on. "Will Hewitt joins us when he can. He even brings Daddy to Washington for overnight visits to stay at that fancy hotel near the president's house, the Willard Hotel. Sunny and I walk into that hotel and tell the guards at the door that we are to see Mista Harris Hewitt. They carefully check their papers, look up, and pass us along. Lord, have mercy, I feel like I be liftin my baby girl up in special ways I never could do before. Just like my daddy does fuh me."

Lilly interrupted briefly. "Callie, you should see how your eyes be dancin."

"Daddy be so happy to cause a stir by bringin his dark-skinned family members in to such a high-class place. I memba in his first year outta that prison, 1866, he talks so excited bout the United States Congress and how it passes a new Civil Rights Act that gives citizenship rights to all, and he quotes the language of the law to us, sayin, 'without distinction of race or color, or previous condition of slavery or involuntary servitude.' He say the United States is supm it ain never been before—equal for all members of his family."

Lilly added, "That sounds like a great day, sista, but that law is just for menfolk, right? And Lucas would be quick to remind us that the law been reversed nowadays."

"You right, Lilly. We can't get too happy bout de way it was back just after the war. We got work to do yet, women and men." She raised her finger, as if to have the final word on the moral merit of Harris Hewitt. "Long ago, my daddy supported rights for black men AND women. He really believed that and treated people that way."

Callie paused, looking to Lilly for understanding. "I don't know how to say my feelins bout my daddy in a book. Lilly, I never knew I had Daddy until that day in 1863 when Will said fa true his uncle was my father. And then, to sit and talk with him, share stories and laugh…I loved to watch him be happy. He couldn't shout about it no more, couldn't get enough air in his lungs. But his face could light up and, with effort, he could share his joy in a forced whisper." Callie had to stop and cry. "It's the purest piece of good I ever knew, cept for havin my Sunny. To see him, even for those few yeahs, and to share him with Sunny…well, it be the best blessing, ummm-hmmm, best blessing of all."

"Speakin of blessings, I wrote my next question down, if you done bout your daddy." Callie nodded for Lilly to proceed. "In a letta to me, you said that you been in that nice big house in Washington with that old white couple for a year when you decided that you wanted Sunny to join you in Washington. What made that happen?"

Just then, Lilly heard her son's call from within: "Mama, Jancy just got sick all over the room, come back heah now." For Callie, left waiting on the porch, the urge to close her eyes overwhelmed her thoughts about her past. The next thing she knew, she was waking up from her nap with Lilly sitting ready, notepad in hand.

"Girl, you been sleepin more than an hour. I guess you got an early start with Sunny this mornin."

Her mind beginning to stir, Callie added, "And then took a boat ride to meet the father of her chile. You been workin my brain too haad, sista. So, I got a right and a reason to res." Then remembering, Callie asked, "How is that sweet Jancy?"

"She doin fine now, restin. Supm soured her stomach. It gave you a chance to sleep a bit. You ready now?"

Before Lilly could get back to her question, she spotted Lucas on the dock, moving laboriously with shoulders slumped, arms at his side, fists clenched. She pointed him out to Callie, who nodded her head and remained quiet. Lucas had no spring in his step. He stared at his feet silently as if in a trance, not even humming.

"What is it, Luke?" Lilly demanded and reached for him as he ascended the stairs. He looked at her without reaction. "Talk to me, man!" She hugged him insistently.

Callie stood abruptly. "Bruddaman, what?"

"I went back to de bateau we saw comin back from de beach. Still in de marsh. I could see it was a boat from the Draper family. So, I rowed up to put a line on it, and de stench get so bad. Well…" Lucas hesitated. "Man in de bateau look like old Uncle James Draper. You know, de old crabber?" Lucas assumed that would be all the identification anyone would need.

"You see anything?" Lilly asked.

"Lilly, he been shot through his chest—big bloodstain on his old yellow shirt." Lucas held his hands about a foot apart and then gestured as he spoke. "As I grabbed de line on de bateau, a voice holla from de wood, 'Leave de boat be, boy!'" Lucas looked to both women, then down at his hands. "I was mos sure I was gonna tek my friend's body wid me, so I lean ovah agin to grab de rope. A ball rip past me and splash in de wada. I stop, look to de source and heard a shout, 'Bout to shoot me anodda nigger.' I had to leab James be and sat down to row, come straight back yuh."

As Lucas's weight sagged toward the chair, Lilly tightened her hold until he was safely seated. They sat quietly for several moments, absorbing his angst and the loss of an old acquaintance.

"Who do these things?" Callie asked, hoping for logic to explain the circumstances.

Lucas, recovering his equilibrium and inhaling the moment, muttered, "Always been hate—hate too easy fuh some—and now, some deeseyuh buckra folk be too open bout de hatred in dey haat."

Lilly added, "And they actin out mo and mo."

Lucas looked at his sister and his wife. "Dey called me a nigga—shout it across de marsh. There I was tryin to hep my friend's body git tuh his fambly." He shook his head slowly.

"Ain been called da name in a long time."

Lilly hated to admit to herself and her husband, but said out loud, "Bedda get used to it. That way of thinkin comin back right now."

"Ain nebba goin way!" Lucas barked. And then, "Got called a nigga today! We put money in de bank we save from our wuk, and yet still we a nigga. We mek money from de boat and build we own boats, and yet still we a nigga. I got my own bidness sellin my hard wuk and my know-how, and yet still I be a nigga. Got my fambly and my chirren that I care fuh good as any buckra father and yet still I be a nigga. We tek dishyuh fambly tuh Sunday worship tuh pray tuh we Gawd, and yet still we be a nigga fambly."

Callie offered, "Got to have somebody to blame for what they ain got."

"It's the way people be," Lilly added.

Lucas responded, "Maybe, but de white man blame us fuh dey poor lives. Trute is, dey been de one keepin us down all deese yeahs."

"Not all of em," Lilly added with certainty, receiving Callie's nodding affirmation. "Miss Towne and her kind be favorable in dey belief and kind in dey manner."

"We'll see a bedda day," said Callie, searching for optimism. "I ain given up on em, not yet anyway. Brudda, I know it don't make today bedda. That damn word stink and sting, and when whites say 'nigga' there ain nuttin worse. I can't tell you how many times people in hospital, people knowin I'm hepin to fix em up, use that word toward me. Those were times when my belief in my God and my on-the-job good sense forced me not to say supm somebody needed to heah."

"Good you can deal wid it sista, cause I sweah, I caint." Then Lucas uttered the unthinkable. "Sometime it mek me so sour, so down on de worl, I don wanna go out on de wada, don wanna get in a boat."

"What you feeling like doin now?" Callie looked at him with genuine concern, not having seen her brother this despondent since their brother was killed.

Lucas took in a deep breath. "Sometime I tink I can jus smile and get by." He pondered Callie's question for a few more seconds. "You know wha I gah fuh do? I gah fuh wuk on de boats. Not my boats on de wada, but my boats in de trees." Lucas saw Callie's puzzled expression and pointed to the trees down near the creek. There, as improbable a sight as any around, were three bateaux up in the live oak trees. Callie had seen the number increase over the years and was always impressed. She had not thought about what maintenance the tree-boats would need. "Yeah, sista, boats don't just get up in de trees by deysef, and dey sho don tek care of deysef."

Callie was both amazed and relieved by the modulation of her brother's emotions. "I love you, my brudda. You are such a strong man, for yourself and for your family. They are lucky."

"Callie, I be huht in me haat. I caint spread de sadness to my sweet chirren." He reached out to Callie, hugging her for a few seconds before backing away and saying, "Now lemme git my crew to wuk on deese boats. Sista, we may need yo hep wid de boats, too." Lucas called out, "Douglass, Abram...and Robert. We gah some wuk fuh do!"

Lucas's sons and oldest grandson soon gathered in the front yard below the porch. Lucas began, "You know we ain wuk on de treefleet fuh a while." Smiling, he pointed at the lowest branch. "De low boat been sittin in de same spot fuh mo den twenty yeah. Time we tek it down en put up de big bateau we ain usin no mo, the one we dragged up on de bluff to mek mo space at de dock. We gah fuh put a bedda boat dere so de lee chirren an dey friends be safe." Reaching for Robert and grabbing his shoulders, "You old enough to hep mek de low boat de bes it can be."

"Yes suh!" Robert answered, standing straight and tall.

"You got two jobs—do wha yo daddy and yo uncle tell you to do, fus, and second, tell em wha you tink bout dey wuk. You in chaage of hepin deese old men know what de chirren want fuh de low boat in de tree."

For two generations, since Lucas put the low boat up for his boys in the summer of 1873, the children around Oakheart found it irresistible, the way it sat cradled in the branches of the old oak tree. In fact, children of all ages could be found there most any time. All agreed that you felt higher than just four feet off the ground when you were in that boat, especially when a strong wind caused the branches to move ever so slightly.

Then, when his boys were around fifteen, Lucas decided it was time for a second boat, twice as high as the first. It took long days and nights of planning, since the branches were not as thick at that level, but there was a perfect fork on the sturdiest limb, and they figured out how to anchor the rowboat with ropes and with wooden braces nailed together. Lucas put the third boat up in 1884, after Callie last visited. It was highest and sat on a branch just like the one at eight feet, located directly over the low boat. Both of the high boats had the same bracing, as well as block and tackle to hoist up willing guests on a wood seat and buckets for lifting food and supplies.

"And now, boys," addressing his own sons, "afta we put up de new low boat, we gah fuh get de high boats fix right. And...," elevating his voice, "we gah fuh mek sure de chair can carry de weight of yo mama and Aunt Callie." Abram and Douglass looked surprised, as Callie, who had been engrossed in conversation with Lilly, shouted down to her brother. "Why you say my name?"

"We need to get you and Lilly up and in de boats. You been sittin on de porch too long already. So, we gonna git de boats ready dis week fuh you two. You gonna like it."

Callie was skeptical. "You know I don't like goin up on high places, Lucas."

"Sista, mos ebby time I got a problem fuh figuh out, I get out on de wada in my boat. But lately, I been pullin me old bones up to the high boats and sittin. Ifn I go up dere, I tink bedda."

As he pointed to his head, Callie knew that her brother was serious. Laughing, she promised, "I'm ready for the boats when you boys say they are ready for me. I need a place to, as you say, bruddaman, 'tink bedda.' Don know about the high boat up there," she said. "It looks like it could use a little work, fa true."

"Well, de men of dis fambly will git ih done. You be mos satisfied and safe. You see." With that, Lucas and his sons turned back toward the fleet in the trees.

Douglass volunteered, "Daddy, I been wantin to fix de braces on the two high boats, so I'm ready to get to it."

Patting Douglass on the back, Lucas masked instruction as inspiration. "Gonna be yo babies en Abram's usin deese boats mos so, Abram, you in chaage fuh get de big boat ready to set in deese low branches."

Observing from the porch, Callie told Lilly, "That was something special your beautiful husband just did. I was sure his spirit was broken, and yet, he just lifted himself straight up and turned his own self around and gave his family some jump in their step." Shaking her head in mock disbelief, "I say I'm too impressed. He is a strong man and a most fine daddy."

"You know, sista, they say a high tide lift all boats. For Lucas, any time a tide is liftin his boat, his emotions carry along in a positive way. Any time he real down, you know he always head out on the water. Lately though, I been seein him sittin up in the top boat lookin out over the river. He gets peace bein up in the trees."

"Well, I'm willin to try it I guess. You go up, too?"

"Yes, darlin, I'll hold your hand."

They laughed briefly, but Lilly was quick to remind Callie of their project. "So, let's get back to Callie's story. We got a way to go this evenin before we sleep. The kids are playin, the men got work to do, the new mamas are mothering, and we be makin good progress on your outline. I appreciated hearin about yo mama and daddy today, and you were gettin ready to talk bout bringin Sunny up to Washington."

"You sure, Lilly? After all we heard from Lucas tonight? You want to go back in time again? I can heah him sayin, 'Why it madda wha happened twenty-five yeahs ago, when my friend get shot dead out on de wada right now? What it madda bout da freedom feelin back den?'"

Lilly reassured her. "Through the strife, honey, we got to live. Speakin of which, while it's just us on de porch, if you want to talk about relationships you had wid any special men in your life, we can cover that ground now. I know you wrote about a man or two in your letters through the years."

Callie did not seem inclined to respond to Lilly's fishing expedition masquerading as a book question. "Well, that's personal—don get in the book!"

"Why not, because I thought this was the story of you, what you did in Washington, including what you saw and who you met?"

"Here's what I will say—for your outline. I lived with that good sergeant from the Massachusetts Fifty-Fourth for more than a year after the war. We loved each other, Lilly. So much. But he had to tend family back home, something about his father I think. I understood, but it hurt pretty bad. Oh, I loved him, Lilly. Mmmm-hmmm. After him, no more loves, not during that time anyway."

"Really, sista?"

"Oh, I could get a man around me mos any time I wanted. I don't mean to sound vain, but, you know, men. I could keep em too—jus didn't much want to. I was too busy with my hospital work to have time for such." Shaking her head, "But that's really all I got to say about my relationships. And then my Sunny came to be with me for five years."

"All right then. I heah you. So, back to what you want in yo book. Got my notepaper. What made you decide to bring Sunny up to that big city?"

"You mean besides me missin her too much? I memba it was the way everything felt at that time. We dark-skin people were gettin the right to live and have rights protected by law—like my daddy wanted for us. Bein in Washington afta de war, I read and heard how the United States Government was gonna make it safe for my child to grow up in it."

"Isn't that de truth. I felt good about my chirren bein free to run around in de yeahs afta de war, but now, I worry about my boys and my grandbabies."

"Lilly, it seemed like a time when common sense was takin hold. I laughed when you sent me a letter about black folks getting ready to vote for the first time here on St. Helena Island. Things seemed right to me in Washington, and then readin about people votin down here, that made me feel certain that things were going to be all right."

Lilly said, "I know you kept that letter, too, but we won't look for it now. I remember to this day the way our folk sounded. In one meeting, a man said he didn't want to work with white men in politics. A lot of people argued with him. One of em said, 'I would stand beside a white man if he acted right.' Another man spoke so kindly, 'Come, my friends, we mustn't judge a man according to his color, but by his acts.'"

"I know, Lilly, our people were bein reasonable, and most all God's children were actin right back then. We were learnin how to use our freedom. I memba one man you quoted at that meeting made me laugh so much I told my work friends. He said, 'If dere skin is white, dey may have principle.'"

Lilly cautioned, "Of course, the US Government wasn't letting the bad actors get control then, either."

"See what I mean? Regla people were making good-sense decisions back then."

"So, things in the world were gettin bedda. But what about your life made it good to bring Sunny to live with you?"

"I had been working so hard but then got a job working in surgery most all the time and teachin new people how to assist with surgeries. My hours at work got a little easier for me to think of having time to share with my girl. Then I found a nice place in the basement of the Grangers' house. They were so good to me, Lilly. It was a time when we thought all things were possible."

"We felt that way down yuh, too. The way Robert Smalls went to the South Carolina convention representing us, and he helped make a new state constitution with voting rights and for free education for all chirren."

"Education was part of my decision about Sunny too. Missus Granger said she would be willin to teach Sunny. I was so excited to have made friends with this good woman."

"Didn't Cousin Will introduce you to the Grangers?"

"He did. I love my cousin so much. I told him how bad I wanted to bring Sunny to live with me, but my work was too busy and my room wasn't right fuh huh to live there. Just when I got a new job with a little better schedule, Will told me he knew an elderly couple who had too much space in their home and could use my help.

"They were as kind as could be when we talked, asking me if their basement was good enough for me. Can you imagine that? They said I should bring my baby-girl to live in their house. God is so good, Lilly. Of course, by that time, Sunny wasn't a baby anymore."

"You right about that. When Sunny left de islands to live with you in Washington, she was twelve goin on twenty and acted in a hurry to get there."

"That was her. Between Missus Granger, and her granddaddy Harris Hewitt, and me, we gave her lots to think about. Washington was just big and busy enough that she saw she had things to learn. But she still was a little hard-headed, thinkin she could go out and walk about town on her own."

"Well, I'm sure you didn't expect your daughter to stop bein who she was, which was, by the way, bein just like you."

"I ain hard-headed. I'm jus determined when I think I am right."

"Which, from what I hear tell from Lucas, was pretty much all de time."

"All right, sista, let's get back to the subject of my little lady comin to Washington. You know, the very first night she was with me, I was gettin her into her new bed in the Grangers' basement, and she asked me, 'Mama, why didn't you come back to live with me?'

"I said, 'Honey, you know why I went away—to find my parents. Then when I found my daddy, and he was sick, I needed to help him get well.'

"Then she said, 'Mama, I was just so sad that you stayed away.' And she had these little tears in her eyes, and I knew she wasn't lookin for a detailed answer. She just was wantin to know that I loved her. I hugged her to me and said, 'Honey, I missed you every day, so much that I had to bring you here with me now.' That seemed to be enough talk for the night, as Sunny went to sleep in my arms."

Lilly understood. "I saw that sweet chile learn to live without her mother and grow stronger for it."

"Oh, yes, she is a strong little lady. We had some other tough talks too. You know, I'm sure, when you give your child an answer that just ain good enough?"

"Yes, Lawd, and grandchirren be the same way," said Lilly, who had become something of an expert on the subject.

"Sunny really got angry one night a couple weeks afta she arrived. I had spent a lot of time takin care of the Grangers' needs upstairs before comin down to the basement. Soon as I sit down with her, Sunny gets after me, in her strongest island language, almost screamin. 'How kin oona do fuh huh all you do? How you respek yoself? We dun been slave fuh too long tuh be actin like dah! I can't believe you be so meek in front of a white ooman.'"

Taking a deep breath, Callie continued. "You know, Lilly, what she saw me doin that night didn't fit Sunny's memory of me. Not the strong mother she remembered from when the freedom came to Oakheart Plantation five years earlier. Not even the mother she knew from listenin to you read all my letters to her.

"So then I told her, 'Sunny, I been workin with this good woman, Missus Granger, for more than a year now. Thas right, I said workin with, not workin for. I take care of her two grandbabies sometimes, and I do what I can to help her. You know what I get in return? Our house right here, and the gratitude and friendship of a fine person.

"'Honey, you got to understand that Missus Granger ain no way like a missus from back in slave time. She is so much nicer and good than my old missus, Julia Bowen. Missus Granger got a kind heart fuh all people and will help them no matter the color of somebody's skin.'

"I got right around in Sunny's face to make sure she understood. 'Some days I have to tell Missus Granger to settle herself, or even tell her when she be wrong. And you know what? She listens to me. Yes, she asks me to do things around here, and I do it gladly cause they let us live here fuh no money. Fact is, Sunny Day, I love her, an I take pleasure in takin care of her and her sick husband.'

"So, Lilly, I got to say Sunny and her mama, we had our little spats. But we learned about each other, and we loved each other stronger. Mmmm-hmmm. We had some sadness, too. One day, one of your letters told us about a minister on St. Helena who got into politics. You told us that one night while he was travelin on the mainland, he was chased down by night riders on horses who shot him dead. Sunny was very upset that such a nice man tryin to lead our people got shot. She heard him speak at Penn School a couple times. When she found out the men who shot him was white, she lost her temper in our basement home that night, cryin and screamin so loud I finally had to hold her tight and talk to her. I remember it as if it was yesterday, even though twenty-five years done pass. I said to her: 'Chile, you believe you the first one who ever been bitter about the way the world is. I been workin, scrapin, servin my Lord, and helpin my friends the best I know how to do all my life, and it ain all been easy.'

"Sunny's eyes stopped wandering around the room. She sat up straight and looked right at me. I went on. 'Long before I ever had the sense to think it, I done what needed to be done. I knew how to keep still with my mouth shut, if I thought it would help me and mine. And you best believe, if I see fit to run my mouth to right some wrong, I do that and more. You ain your strong self for nuttin. You runnin around with my blood in you, don ever forget that!'

"I had to turn away from my daughter to keep her from seeing me cry. But, Lilly, please tell me why folks have to be better than somebody else?" Lilly just shook her head and kept writing. "I ended up tellin Sunny—'Don't make sense that somebody thinks they be better because they are light-skinned, when it's what's inside that skin that counts?'"

Lilly was spellbound by the story. "Oooh, Callie! You told your girl some truths. Never heard it said better."

"So, Sunny and I figured out that night that the last thing we wanted to argue about were problems other people caused. We decided we didn't need to compare how tough we were for walkin our different paths, just to see who was stronger. Sunny told me that night, 'Mama.' And she leaned up against me. 'Mama, I know it ain neva been easy.'

"I said, 'That's right, Sunny Day, life be hard. But many days turn out fine.'

"As her eyes were closing, Sunny asked, 'Mama, we gonna find de way togedda? Even if we don't always agree bout supm?'

"You know I told my sweet daughter, we always would do that. Lilly, I couldn't hold her close enough that night when she went to sleep."

Callie stood up and with teary eyes declared, "Dear Lilly, I am done done for this day. Let my daughter's words bring storytellin to a close. You already done git water from a stone."

"You ain no stone, dear sista. You a fount of love, heart, and inspiration. I'm honored to be hearin your stories."

"You the same, Lilly, you know that. Tomorrow, we find supm to get us off this porch."

Chapter 6

Tuesday, August 22, 1893

Tuesday dawned cooler, with a freshness in the air that invited action. Inside the house, the few that were up moved quietly, nibbling on biscuits and pecan pie while sipping sassafras tea. Outside, nature had begun to stir; early birds were singing and feeding while squirrels chased one another up, down, and around the trees, even jumping between the branches.

Adding to this serenity, Lucas came down the stairs and through the front hallway on his way to the porch, singing in his pleasant yet challenged baritone, "Wade in de wada, wade in de wada, chirren, wade in de wada, we gonna trouble de wada."

Once again, his work crew recognized their father's rallying call. Though Abram shared the excitement of his sons, Robert and Saxton, about the day's plan to work on the tree boats, he was slow to move. His boys bolted from the house following their grandfather down the front steps. They especially wanted to work on the lowest bateau, which they considered their own personal fort. Douglass was trying to finish off his biscuits and gravy while wiping Jancy's face. Unfortunately for Douglass, Nellie had chosen to stay at their small home down the lane from the big house, leaving him in charge of their energetic daughter.

"Abram, Douglass, I know I don need fuh sing bout de trouble on de wada again. Somebody get the twins goin." Flora June, as usual, was working in town, so her sons were staying with Lucas and Lilly. Amanda volunteered, as she was up early and out of the family's nest in the downstairs bedroom, preparing food for her husband and sons. She had been conscientious in her efforts to lighten the load on Lilly while their family stayed in the big house—Abram was slowly making extensive repairs on their own house.

Within minutes, all called had assembled out in the yard under the live oak trees that cradled the three old bateaux. Lucas raised one hand to get their attention and, with his other hand, lovingly patted the lowest boat which was only four feet off the ground. "Dis boat been up yuh mo den twenty yeahs. I put it up when my boys were lee chirren bout same size as you, Robert. At firs, I wanted tuh mek a skrong tree house, like a boat. Den I said, why not use an old bateau? Dey still in good shape but not fuh da wada. I knew dey cud tek mos any abuse from de chirren and still stay put on deese live oak branches."

Lucas stopped talking, staring into the distance. "I memba de day we raised de fus boat. Uncle James Draper rowed ovah with a bushel basket fill up wid crab, and den he stay to help. We a lot younger den..." Frowning, Lucas shook his head as if to clear away the memories and turned back to his young work crew. "Now, we gah fuh pull down de low boat and put up a bedda one. And we gah fuh fix up those high boats. Now..." Lucas paused several seconds to consider the tasks ahead and the instructions he needed to give to his young crew. His delay was unfortunate.

In a flash, the twins had entangled legs, Jancy had her hair pulled from behind, and a bee had landed on Saxton's shoulder. It was swatted off by his big brother with enough force to cause a brief howl, a kick, and the first steps of a chase before Lucas yelled, "Stop! Now!"

At that moment, as if in answer to Lucas's unsent prayer, Lilly and Callie emerged from the house onto the front porch, fresh from their prolonged morning tea and biscuits. Callie had just started toward the table with a small platter of benne cookies when Lucas noticed her, chuckled, pointed, and announced, "Look who up on de porch, chirren, wid a plate of good-tastin tings." His ploy worked as intended to cause the young ones to race away while their fathers remained behind for instructions.

First to reach the porch was long-legged Robert, with Jancy close behind. Saxton tried to keep up with his brother but couldn't, and when he arrived at the top of the stairs, he plowed into his big brother, knocking over Jancy. Flora June's twins, still partially entangled, were several steps behind. En masse, they nearly tackled Callie. In one motion, she plunked the benne cookies onto the table, spread her arms wide, and bent forward to engulf the busy bodies and avoid a calamitous fall. "Whoa now, chirren, good morning. I love you too, babies. Don't love me too much."

Jancy was quick with a question full of expectation. "You been on lotsa boats, Auntie Callie?"

"Now before I ansa yo question, Miss Jancy, can I take a minute this mornin to ask a special favor? Can I ask supm?" Callie looked searchingly into each pair of eyes, gaining nods and "Yes, ma'am" from them all. "That favor is..." And she leaned in to her listeners. "You see, Lilly and me have to go on a mission on de river. We have to leave now." She looked over to Lilly, who was suppressing her smile behind a napkin. "Sista Lilly, don't we have to go directly, to take care of some business? Lilly, you got yo pad and pen ready to work?" Lilly nodded yes, lowering her head to hide her amusement. Turning back to the youngsters, Callie continued. "So, while we be gone, I need you to make a special promise to me and Lilly that you be good chirren." They nodded. "That when you go out to run and play, you stay away from the work on the boats, unless they ask for your help."

Robert started to protest, and Callie quickly understood, "And that you help Robert to help Grampa Lucas any way he can? Can you promise all that?" Again, her lingering looks at the children drew affirmation in response. "Good young'uns. You be doin a special favor for Gramma Lilly and me."

"So," Jancy persisted, "you been out in boats as much as my grampa?"

As Callie began her answer, she ambled toward the porch steps, arms outstretched to the children around her, and talked as she stepped down. "Children, I been on too many boats, boats bigger than any you seen on this river. I took injured soljahs away from Beaufort during the war on a big steam paddle boat. One steamer took me to Savannah, and another bigger boat took me all the way to New York City." When Callie and her entourage reached the ground, she guided them over to the side yard, where Lucas was organizing the effort to replace the low bateau and secure the high boats mounted in the live oak trees.

"And that's why it so hard to have to go out on this special mission on de boat, but," and she held a finger across her lips for all the children to see, "memba, don't tell secrets and memba your promises to help Grampa Lucas." As she said the last words, Callie's voice grew loud enough for Lucas to understand that Callie was up to something. Callie looked at the children once more with a smile and a finger to her lips. As she and Lilly passed the construction area, the children magically stopped walking. Lucas turned to watch, his hands on his hips and a perplexed smile on his face. Lilly and Callie walked serenely, unaccompanied, down the steps to the dock. "Lilly? Callie?"

Jancy tugged on her grandfather's belt, saying, "Auntie Callie told us not to tell." Lucas immediately realized that the ladies had given him the slip and that care of the children when they were outside would be in the hands of the men for the morning at least.

Callie giggled as she efficiently freed the lines from the dock cleats, climbed into the small bateau after Lilly, pushed off as she sat down, and, without rushing, picked up the oars. Lilly watched in wonder at

Callie's display of nautical skills learned in her youth when she and Lucas, still enslaved, traveled more by boat than buggy.

In no time, Callie's small, but strong, strokes propelled them away from the dock on a water surface smooth as glass. Callie stopped rowing to let the boat float with the tide and looked at Lilly, smiling again. "We surely left the family behind today. I had to laugh how fast you grabbed your notebook and stuffed it in your pouch."

"You nevah know, you jus may say supm that fits just right in your story, so I got to be ready when de author speak."

"You are too sweet to me, sista," Callie said, meaning it.

"You deserve it, Callie. You worked hard to serve others. If you got supm you wanna say, I wanna help."

"You mighty easy goin, sittin there, leanin back over the stern, not holdin on."

Lilly smiled at the water. "Well, it be so calm. And I trust you, Callie. You been up an down dis river so many times, I know you ain gonna dump us in de wada. And if you do, I know you gonna get me out. But it ain true that I'm calm. Yes, I trust you, and yes, I live with a waterman, but I still got worries. Worried bout my Lucas, that wonderful brother of yours. What he told us last night bout people actin up cross the river." Lilly dismissively shook her head. "No, ain even worried bout what they do—we can handle it. I worry bout how it settle in his heart and mind. He carries so much inside."

Callie had to praise Lucas as well. "You saw how he handled it. He went from all worried and down, and then, snap, just like that, he turn it into something good for the babies."

"And for us," Lilly said proudly.

"And what he does for us makes me feel a little bad about takin off..." Then they looked at each other, laughed, and rocked the boat a bit. Callie kept on rowing.

Lilly tried to settle onto her bench after the boat's movement. "Nah, we be all right. Ain gonna lie. I fear de wada. You know dah."

"You talkin to me or you talkin to you?" Callie asked, part in jest. "You said it once in a letter, but you never told me why you got so afraid."

"Oh Callie, one day back when the boys were little—maybe six and eight years old—they jumped in a bateau at the dock and somehow got de rope untied. De boat was still in shallows, but floatin on the outbound tide down to Chowan Creek. I just took off down de bluff and into the oozing mud as the tide go on out. Da muck grab at my feet as I kep movin out to my boys, de wada gettin deepa, tuh where I could jus grab de edge of de boat." Lilly was reaching toward that unseen boat with a mother's worst worries on her face. "I had de boat, Callie, but I could barely touch my feet tuh de mud below. De wada was at my neck.

"Praise God, my motherhood gave me strength of arm and leg to push and pull de boat full of my greatest treasures, de beats of my heart, to safety in shallow wada. I memba bein so tired, knowin I got em to safe groun, I didn't notice I was standin in mud up tuh my knees wid mo wada comin in on top of de mud. I gave de boat de biggest push evah and told de boys to jump out to de odda side and get out to dry land. Sista, wid my las push, I was stuck in de mud, couldn't lift my tired legs from de hold of it. It just suck onto my foot. I kep talkin to my boys, mek like ebbyting all right. But my legs wouldn't work for me, and I fell forward, tryin to catch my breath, hands diggin in the mud.

"I wanna keep de chirren from seein I was in trouble, jus when I began to know how much trouble I was in. I started leanin my hands down in de wada again, and shiftin from side to side, and little bit at a time, I felt my legs comin loose of de mud. A big wave came rollin in an I just dove forward and as I landed in de wada my feet popped free. I splashed my way to the boys, as another wave knock me down. Oh! Did me and my boys have a long-time hug. Callie, I couldn't let go of em for so long, lookin back where I was caught up in de mud.

"That night, as the boys and Lucas sleepin, I got up and wrapped up in Mama Ruth's blanket that had soothed many upset babies, including Lucas, and I just cried, Callie, I just cried. Ain nevah thought I might not be strong enough, might not be good enough, to take care of my babies. I pulled de quilt round my neck, shivering as if it was all sea wada. Since dah day, I had dreams bein caught in de mud, wada comin all aroun. I always wake up though befo bad tings happen."

"I can't hug you from heah, but I can say, Lilly, you were strong enough, you were jus as good as you had to be—to save your boys and to save yourself."

"I know, you right. It just scaid me so bad. I told Lucas that all my future trips to town will be on calm wada or not at all. But I ain told him how scaid I was that day or why...just told him supm bout chokin on salt wada in my mouth made me mo fearful."

Pressing Lilly to recognize her ability to handle that and any other situation, Callie said, "And don't I rememba from one of your letters that you forced yourself to learn how to swim and then kept practicing at it to get ovah all fear and to get stronger? True?"

"Fa true, Callie." Lilly answered with a smile. "Jus cause I can handle supm don mean I ain scaid of it. You know, I been workin with men for many yeahs. Back durin the wah, I was teachin troops, and since then, I been hepin Lucas wid his business by doin most of his bookkeepin. I ain jus been home with the babies though I like to do that best. Lucas and me, we partners, and he knows it work bedda that way. But some of these men, from right afta de wah, they did not want any women in dey business or in dey politics. Some say not to leh women work in dey fields either."

"But they sho don't mind when they see the row been dug, do they?"

"That's fa true. So now I'm tryin to help the mamas in our community learn to read, to know how able they can be, and to know how pleased their men will be at all they can do."

"We love our men," Callie observed, "but why aren't some in favor of freedom for their women afta they got freedom for themselves?"

"Lovin my husband and my sons as I do, I can only tell em the truth. I respect what they can do, and they got to respect what I can do. Men and women are de same in wanting such. If I try supm and it don succeed, I will accept help, though I want to know how I can help myself. That's the feelin I want to give these women."

"Everything you jus said are reasons why I was glad to bring Sunny back here to live with you. She was ready to be a strong woman, and I wanted her to see how you handle yo life."

"Tank ya, sista. Nuf bout me. Now you talk."

Callie demurred, saying, "I been doin a lot of talkin lately. Ain you had enough?"

"You gonna be an author. You got supm to say. Tell yo stories, my sista. Stop yo rowin an jus let this high tide turn roun and carry us on back to Oakheart as it flow to de sea."

Silence fell between them, as Callie pulled in the oars and looked over the water, clearly not focused on the present. Lilly finally said, "I turn it back to you to say what make you afraid?"

Callie focused on Lilly and smiled. "All her life, I worry bout Sunny growin up too fast and standin up for herself too much. And I worry bout too many bad men watchin her do it. Ain dah funny? You think women got to stand up more on these islands, and I worry bout my Sunny standin up too fast."

Lilly said, "You know what I mean bout how women can be round here. And I know how headstrong Sunny can be. But, be serious now. What else make you afraid, besides bad men?"

"Oh, I don't mean it that way, sista. Most of em can't help the way God made em. They plenty good ones been roun my door too, sista." She smiled at the distraction, then began to consider her fears. "You ask what makes me afraid? Nothin like yo story bout gettin mudstuck. I can't say afraid really. But I know I dream about it and get upset. Startin back in the war when I worked on so many wounded boys. I dreamed about em, the young soljahs, waitin to have their legs or arms cut off. In my dream, it was an endless line of soljahs, their eyes all lookin fearful at me, like they askin for help. And years later, when I worked in Freedman's Hospital, my dream changed some, but really stayed the same. See, one of my jobs was talkin to people when they came in for treatment and again when they got ready to leave. My dream then, and to this day, no matter how good we fix em up, more people jus keep comin, lookin for help."

"Callie, I know you helped those people so much. You can rest easy knowin you did all you could to make their bodies the best they could be."

Shaking her head, Callie responded, "You know, when people have disease or an injury or a wound, maybe we can fix the problem with their bodies. But they also have hurts to their hearts and souls—they are hardest to fix cause people keep such hurts deep inside most times."

Lilly pulled out her notebook and started writing. "While we driftin here, let me write a little. Keep talkin, Callie. Keep talkin bout your hospital days, en how you could help de people, outside and inside."

"Lord knows, Lilly, there was no end to bein busy. No end. For thirty yeahs, my work was about the next person I have to help get well. But now I stopped work, finally ready to come home."

"You said you had dreams lately that upset you. What were they about?"

"Yeah, I be dreamin that the men on the ward wake up in need at night, and they are lookin for somebody, and they ask for help in their search. I realize they are lookin for me to give em help in the night, but they can't see me because I'm not there. It's a dream I been havin for many yeahs now, more lately since I left hospital."

"Oh my. That's a dedicated heart you been bringin to your work."

"That ain the half of it, Lilly. I told you bout the battlefield injuries in the war, and we all know the war was about whether we gonna be slaves forever or be free. And when the Union won, we all became free. But I was so sad to see so many freedmen come to the hospital who were livin such unhealthy lives. Many of my hospital friends said the same thing—bein free made so many people get sicker."

Lilly looked up from her writing, surprised. "You sayin it was tougher to stay healthy for dark people after they get free? I nevah woulda thought it."

"Think back to when we were trapped in slavery. At least, we had some chance to get medicine, maybe see a doctor when sick or make our own medicines from plants in the gardens and the wood. That's what we always did at Oakheart before freedom came. Now, freedmen who are off the plantation ain got medicine, doctors, healing herbs, and usually not enough food, unless they can pay. Wherever they lived, conditions were crowded and probably not too sanitary.

"During the war, military people didn't want to take time or give supplies to help free people, even if they were sick. Afta, no one around Washington knew what to do to help, but they knew the Freedmen's Hospital would take in those in need. Do you know that, after the war, some Virginia planters refused to give medicine to the people who worked for them who got sick with smallpox and instead sent em to my hospital in Washington? For those years right after the war, we still took care of wounded soljahs, but just as many were sick with some disease as were hurt in war."

"I ain nevah thought of how many people lived they freedom like that."

"Lilly, sad as it was, that's why I couldn't leave. As mo and mo folk got free, too many mo of em got sick. I was right in the middle of the fight for how we take care of the free people. Seemed like nobody much cared about the woes of the colored people, and my hospital, the last Freedmen's Hospital, was one of the few places still workin to help em. You know when I decided I had to stay in Washington? It was 1872 when Congress gave money for the Freedmen's Hospital to stay open, and it's still open to this day. I was so proud to be right there to help."

Lilly looked at her sister with admiration. "My, my, in your letters, you told some strong stories about all the people you helped, but just now, I see how you feel bout it all. It's in the middle of your heart. Instead of dreamin or thinkin bout more people comin to you for help, you got to memba all the good medicine you gave to so many and all the smiling faces because you help em."

"Did my best every day, sista. And missed you all down heah every one of those days."

"You were in the right place. Every person you worked with would say so. Don't let anybody say different, including Sunny."

"I know she understood what I was doin and why. But when I decided to bring her back here in 1873, she was hurt that I planned to keep workin in Washington. I wished it wasn't so, but she needed to come back to these islands, and I needed to keep workin at my job."

Callie started rowing again as their bateau was drifting with the current near the creek bank. With the conversation so focused and the water so calm, neither noticed the overhanging branches of a live oak tree until its leaves started brushing their hair.

Pulling back into midstream, Callie asked, "You know what I learned in all those hospital yeahs? I saw it in so many people. The people were in a process of becoming free. Maybe by law they say we were free, but by the way some had to live their lives—to suffer hunger, and lack shelter, and not get fair wages, and not have good medical treatment—harvestin the fruits of freedom was slow, and some never did get a good taste."

"My, my, I jus nevah knew such was happenin."

"Not only that, and after this I'll shut up, cause I see you writin faster than I'm workin the oars."

"You doin fine, Callie. This is answerin a lot of questions in my mind. Your medical work is real important to your life, and to your book."

"Oh, I most forgot about the book. I was just tellin how proud I am of my work. But I was going to say one more thing about where I worked. Early on, back in the 1860s, after the Freedmen's Hospital moved to the campus of Howard University, the hospital began training black students to be doctors. I was so pleased to get to know some of those boys as they learned to be doctors, hundreds of em now out servin the people."

"So proud for your work, sista! But somebody else steppin in to help yo patients?"

Callie smiled broadly. "Just like somebody stepped up today to take care of your grandbabies." They caught each other's glance and burst out laughing as Callie settled into a smooth and easy rowing cadence that carried them right up to the Oakheart dock.

They returned to find that order had been maintained. Most of the children were up on the porch, quietly drawing designs on paper under Amanda's loving eye. Robert had been joined by a crew of one, Beanie, in putting a quick coat of white paint on the bateau destined to replace the first and lowest one in the trees. Most of the paint actually made it onto the boat, though the painters were speckled white. Lucas and sons prepared to remove the old boat that, for two generations, had stirred the imaginations of Oakheart children.

Callie and Lilly were admiring the progress of the paint crew, from a safe distance, when they heard Douglass's voice. "Good afternoon, ladies." They did not see him until he stood up in the highest bateau, waving down at his mother and aunt, who were properly astonished. "I've almost got the pulley system fixed just right. You jus sit in de chair, and we bring you right up. We may be ready for you today."

Callie muttered, "Did we say we were in a hurry to go up in that boat?"

Lucas helped answer the question. "Yes, ladies, you so nice tuh give us dis good time to wuk on de boats wid all de chirren runnin round. We finish fixin all de braces on de high boat. So, we decided that you two would be perfect to test de weight limits on de new pulley system."

"Be careful, husband," Lilly said, mostly joking.

"So, sista, it appears that you and Lucas are finished with your anniversary celebrations," Callie wryly observed.

Sensing his offer may not have been well received, Lucas added, "We want to share the joys of dis new, safe, tree-boat chair, fixed jus fuh you two fine ladies."

Lilly quickly rejoined, "That's much bedda use of your words, dear Lucas."

"I'm serious. Tomorrow, your children and grandchildren look forward to you liftin up into de top boat. Chirren been talkin bout it while you two were up de crik."

Just then, Jancy stopped drawing, clambered down the steps, and made a beeline to her grandmother and aunt. In mid-hug, Lilly asked, "What did you learn today?"

"I learned that drawing with Aunt Amanda can be lots of fun and... and...and I learned that Grampa likes secrets, too, jus like you and Aunt Callie do."

"Oh, what secrets?"

"I can't say, but I wanna see you get up in de top tree-boat."

Smiling toward Lucas, Lilly responded, "I believe I understand, and yes, I would love to ride up in that silly chair. I mean that fine chair. Now, what is someone fixin for us to eat? Have you started yet, Jancy?"

"No, ma'am, I'm busy drawing. I tink my mama been fixin food for all us chirren. Maybe you can have some, too."

To the relief of all, Jancy's mother, Nellie, called from the side porch as she pointed to the table where she had laid out the food from her favorite big sweetgrass basket. There was a pork and egg salad, a chicken still hot from being reheated in Lilly's oven, and a tall cake with chocolate icing. Amanda brought out another basket full of fresh greens, ripe tomatoes, freshly picked corn, and peaches gathered that morning from the small grove of trees Douglass had planted.

The children raced to the table and, with Grandma Lilly's urging, waited respectfully while the elders filled their own plates and made plates for Saxton and Jancy. For sure, the chocolate cake in the center of the table elicited the children's best behavior. Their few years of experience had taught them that the quickest route to such a reward was by being a patient child. To emphasize that lesson, Grandmother Lilly announced that no one would have Nellie's cake until they had eaten a healthy blend of meat, vegetables, and fruit. The small sounds of discontent quickly subsided as the urge to fill hungry stomachs took over.

Lucas downed his first plateful before speaking. "Lilly and Callie, I know you both mus be too tired from gettin out on de wada today."

Callie said, "Brudda, it wasn't so bad, specially cause the tide pushed us up and back."

"Oh, I ain worried bout the rowin." Lucas hesitated, to let interest build. "I was fraid you both be exhausted by all dah talkin. From what I hear, your jaws did not rest fuh one moment while you be out dere. I worried you both gonna...gonna...run outa wuds." He looked up, his face full of mischief. "Den I say, nah, dah ain gonna happen." He looked on with mock concern, his theatrics unappreciated.

"Oh, brudda, you know you don't want me to get outta this chair and get afta you."

Lilly chimed in. "It's good for you, husband, we already celebrated our anniversary."

"I know what you two discuss is important..." Lucas hesitated just a second too long to make his point, allowing first Callie and then Lilly to complete his sentence.

"So that's why you sorry to make fun of yo sista and yo wife?"

"So that's why you gonna let yo wife talk whenevah she wants?"

Trying halfheartedly to recover, Lucas offered, "I just worry that you either be out of stories or out of air and water so you couldn't carry on tonight. Wha would we do?"

Looking at the children, Lilly jumped in with, "Fact is, Aunt Callie and me were right at the place in our talks where she ready to tell wha she and Sunny did when they were in Washington. I thought maybe all you chirren wanna heah Aunt Callie's stories bout Sunny?"

Callie proceeded on as if introduced. "It was twenty-five yeah ago when your Aunt Sunny, my sweet daughter, came to live with me in Washington. She was just a lee bit older than you, Robert. You ten? Yeah, Sunny was twelve. We got to do so many things while she was there with me, all the way up to her having her seventeenth birthday. One of our favorite things to do was to take long walks and climb up hills."

"What are hills?" Jancy asked.

"Well, now, I guess you would not know that. Your little eyes only seen what they seen. Hills be land that get big and tall, bigger than trees and almost as high as clouds." Exclamations came from the children. "And Sunny and I, we would walk up trails to the tops of hills and look out over everything. There was one place where we could see a river going on down into the valley below like a snake." Callie led the children in making her hand, wrist, and forearm wriggle like a snake.

"We walked everywhere, from one side of Washington to anodda. We saw so many trees we never saw down here, and then we looked in those trees and we saw birds we never seen in our trees at Oakheart. We saw so many people up in Washington, you jus can't believe, and they aren't all black people or white people, but they have skins of all different colors."

Suddenly shouts of colors showered Callie.

"Blue?"

"Dey red?"

"Are dey green like trees?"

"I like purple—dey be any purple people?"

Callie smiled and lifted both hands palms down as a signal to calm the children. "Chirren, chirren, Aunt Callie needs to say what she means. There are people from lands all round the world. Different faces, different eyes, different hair, different ways of walkin and talkin. They have skin that is yellow or brown or a lee red or black as night, like some folk on these islands. I never did see and never will see so many different kinds of people as I see up in Washington."

Color curiosity satisfied, Callie continued. "One of our walks took us to Ford's Theater in Washington; you know, where our President Lincoln was shot. That was a sad thing, chirren, to be right there. They took him from the theater across the street to a house, where they lay him on a bed, and he passed the next morning, God rest his soul."

Any lingering hilarity settled because the older children knew the reverence with which the adults talked of Abraham Lincoln, and the little ones imitated them. Callie continued, solemnly, "Sunny was old enough to understand the importance of the man, Mista Lincoln. She jus wanted to sit there for a long time, first lookin at the theater building and then crossin the street to stare at the death house. He was killed three yeahs before we visited in 1868. We was all still gettin used to it, but for Sunny, bein in the actual place for the first time and bein at an age when she was feelin things deep in her heart," and Callie clutched her heart. "Well, we stayed there at that place for a long time."

After a few more seconds, Callie shifted toward lightheartedness. "Jancy, you asked me bout bein on boats. When my father got better afta the war, Sunny and I would visit him in nearby Annapolis, right on the Chesapeake Bay. We would take long walks with him down by the wada to see all the sailboats. One day, Sunny was surprised when he led her onto a boat, and she acted worried about them gettin caught. He said she should ask the owner for approval. She said, 'Where is he?' After a while, his smile gave her the answer. 'Grampa Harris, we on your boat?' She could barely contain herself. After that, my father took us out in his boat on the Chesapeake Bay five times. I thought Sunny's face would stretch too wide from her smiling all day on that boat. One time, we dropped some crab traps in shallow water and pulled em up a few hours later. Oh my goodness, the white meat from crab claws steamin hot an dipped in butta—my Lord. Oh, we had some sweet days on that wada.

"I memba one time, my cousin Will brought Grampa Harris over to Washington, and Will rented a boat ride across the Potomac River." Callie held her arms wide apart. "I think the Potomac River is almost as wide as the Broad River we got here. Anyway, afta we crossed the river, our first step out on the land put us in Virginia." Callie raised her hand to point above the imagined tree line. "Right there, looking up on the hill, we saw a big ole house Grampa Harris said belonged to General Robert E. Lee, head of the Confederate Army. As we walked up the hill toward General Lee's house, we saw all round it they be buryin the Union soljahs who died in the war. So many graves, chirren, you couldn't count em all. From this hill where his house looks out on Washington, we saw the city spread as far as you can see over into Maryland. Down below us, we saw houses, little shacks really, hundreds of them spread out between the Lee house and the Potomac River. My, my, I thought, how times change with Mista Lee out of the house after losin the war."

Lilly affirmed, "Sunny talked about your boat trips all roun de Washington area. She loved getting out on de wada. She said it put her in mind of her home back in South Carolina."

"Did you ebba git tired?" Saxton asked through a yawn.

"Well, we didn't do all that I been talkin about in one day, baby. But I do get the gist of your question. The last thing I'll say about my daddy and Sunny's grampa is that he tried hard to make up for the ye- ahs we never had together. He was one of the kindest gentlemen I ever knew, even though he was a tough sailor. He was a decent man, and he showed us his soul during the years we got to know him. We loved him, and he loved us back."

Robert raised his hand and asked, "Aunt Callie, can you tell mo bout your wuk, and why you stayed up in Washington so long and not come back yuh wid us befo now?"

"My, my young man, I see how you been thinkin bout things."

Callie gave Robert a hug and said, "One of the things Sunny liked to do most was to visit me at work in the hospital. She liked to see the doctors and nurses tryin to help people. She didn't know so many peo- ple had problems in their lives or in their bodies."

One of Flora June's boys spoke up enthusiastically. "Wha you do in Washington, Aunt Callie? You be a nus or a doctor?"

"Beanie, good question. I learned how to help people early in my life, right here in Beaufort during the war. The hospital in Washington hired me right afta, and that's where I worked until just last week. Durin that time, the hospital directors wanted to use my skills in different ways, kinda like a nurse. When I first started to work there, they asked me to assist with surgery, since that's what I was doin in the war—helping doctors do surgery on the soljuhs. Then, the hospi- tal manager found out I knew how to 'triage.' You know that word? Triage means how to determine how badly people are injuhed so you can decide what patients to treat next. I learned about that when I got to work with Dr. Letterman in Frederick, Maryland, and then we used it when travelin with the Union Army afta the battles. The medical corps followed the fightin, and we used triage methods all the time. So, the hospital directors decided I could do good in the 'first care' room, you know, where injuhed people come first? And, yes indeed, that was work I could do. It felt so good to be helpin people as soon as they got to hospital. And then, they decided to move me to where all people come in the front door, to talk with em about what they need and, if I couldn't help em, tell em where in the hospital they need to go."

Callie looked around at the quiet audience held in awe by her words. And she continued, "We had a chance each day to give the best medical care for black people anywhere. I worked with a lot of very smart people, and they were nice, mostly. They wanted me to help them do their jobs, and I was honored to do that. They gave me two things: they gave me money for my hard work, and, most important, they gave me respect. I gave it back to them, and it felt good.

"Chirren, I was blessed to do work at a high level, doing things to help our people. I been tellin Lilly how much I missed not bein heah with all you, but God put me where I was for a reason, and I served His purpose. Though I love you all and our family, I had to be on my job in Washington."

"You heah now!" Robert declared.

"Yeah, Aunt Callie, stay with us, please?" Jancy pleaded.

"With my work done, and I see how beautiful you all are, I can jus sit back and let all this love wash ovah me. I'm not goin away again." The children cheered, and all found a place to hug Aunt Callie at once.

———◆———

THAT EVENING JUST AFTER SUNSET, THE FAMILY ADULTS—CALLIE, Lucas and Lilly, Abram and Amanda, Douglass and Nellie—gathered on the porch as the first hint of cooler air came in on a northwesterly breeze. Lucas was sprawled in his favorite chair overlooking the length of the front porch, the yard, the dock, and the river. Callie had settled nearby when Lilly joined them with an armload of folders and a box she had stored in the house. She spread the folders neatly across the table and showed Callie at least one hundred envelopes packed tightly in the small box, ready to spill their secrets.

"Oh Lawd," said Lucas with a resigned smile. "I see you ladies are goin back in time agin."

Intensely into the project, Lilly either actually missed or pretended not to hear the sarcasm coming from her husband and instead gave him a short briefing. "We still talkin bout things that were happenin back when Sunny was up in Washington. That's why we lookin through all these letters again. Lookin for what caught Callie's eye back then."

Callie added: "You know, Lilly, we need to add more family news. We just been talkin bout what happened in Washington."

"We will get there, sista. I found letters where you tell bout takin Sunny to Congress to see important things happen—I think it was 1869."

Lucas made himself a factor. "Now wait! You can't be skippin ovah 1868 and the South Carolina Constitutional Convention and what Robert Smalls did there."

"Brudda, we already talked about some of those good things, like how the blacks and whites at the convention worked together to vote for free education for children ages seven to fourteen."

Lucas added, "Robert Smalls made South Carolina the nation's first state to require it."

"That is amazin, brudda. And, thank you, Robert Smalls."

"And protectin the black right to vote came from his leadership in that convention."

Lilly exclaimed, "And praise be for that, too, even though no women get to vote yet."

"Well, no." Lucas shrugged, recognizing Lilly's strong feelings on the subject.

Callie added, "I remember back when my Sunny had been with me a few months, and my friend from the Maryland battles, General Wallace, arranged for us to watch Congress on the day the Fifteenth Amendment passed, given voting rights to blacks," and she looked at Lilly, "to black men. We be so proud, Sunny and me. That day, standin wid my daughter. I thought of you, Lucas, and all the work you do for us and de community. And I think of BB's life here at Oakheart as a farmer, and yes, I think of his dyin here, too, tryin to protect his family from an evil slave trader. He was so proud to serve in the United States Army. No doubt, our family and thousand more black people just like us, we earned de right to vote in this country."

"Dah beautiful, Callie, truly it is. I feel yo emotion." Lucas shook his head. "An you know, in the next yeah or two, de same Congress had to pass mo laws to fight against de terrible tings people doin down yuh in Sout Calina to keep black people from dey right tuh vote." Lucas stood up, animated. "Hard to belieb. We fight and die fuh rights as citizens, and then we need mo soljahs to protect us as we try to use de rights."

"Yes, brudda. It's one thing for the law to pass and another thing to enforce it."

"Callie, in de fus yeahs afta de wah and into the 1870s, de whites kill six of de men we vote to represent us in de state legislature."

"I'm sincerely sorry, Lucas. I was too far away to feel the pain and the fear that those murders caused."

Lilly said, "You know, I been afraid for the life of Robert Smalls for the last thirty yeahs. He been so brave, from bein captain of the *Planter* and other military boats during the war, and then bein up in front of the political fights. I'm surprised they ain tried to kill him."

Lucas nodded. "He been jus great fuh we. An he ain been shot down yet."

Lilly's response gave cautious praise to Smalls. "I worry about my own good men—my Lucas, my boys, my grands—if one day they try to stan up like Robert Smalls, proud as I am of him. I fear that one day they may stan up too fast or too tall and be too big a threat to some white man who decides to shoot em down. All my men would ever do is stand for family or for their own land, and for that they could be killed. I fear that every day."

"I know you right to worry bout the bad acts white men do." Callie chose her words carefully. "Our brudda was killed by a white man in a Yankee uniform, while tryin to stop a Southern white man from tryin to hurt me. But, I can't say all white men guilty for it."

"Aunt Callie," Douglass spoke up, tentatively, "it been haad growin up hearin stories from Daddy bout how his brother, BB, got shot. I want to agree wid wha you say—most white folk be good in dey haat. But, when I see how bad some folk be...I ain sure."

"I say don't doubt. There are plenty fine white folk, my daddy and Will Hewitt, to name two. Most white people be good that way. They just need leaders to set em on the right course."

Lilly affirmed, "I liked what you sent me about Robert E. Lee right after de war ended." Lilly spoke quickly as she rifled through her box of envelopes. "It's on my list from one of your letters, quotin General Lee from 1866—when he was asked about settin up monuments about de Civil War. Here it is. He said: 'I think it wiser not to keep open the sores of war, but to follow the example of those nations who endeavored to obliterate the marks of civil strife, and to commit to oblivion the feelins it engendered.'"*

"Mmmm-hmmm!" Callie moaned, voice rising, "War ovah. Take off de uniforms. Lower de battle flags!"

---

* Letter from Robert E. Lee to David McConaughy, 1869 August 5. David McConaughy Papers, Gettysburg College, Musselman Library Special Collections & Archives. And https://leefamilyarchive.org/9.../861-robert-e-lee-to-david-mcconaughy-1869-august.

"Nevah thought I'd say sech a ting, but General Lee be a smart man," Lucas offered in earnest. "When he ain fightin to keep us slave."

Lilly agreed. "I hope the good folk rise up and stop the ones still tryin to hate us." Lilly's shoulders drooped from strain. "Then I can stop worryin bout my men."

"Lilly, memba when General Grant visited we islanders afta de wah—he stay ovah on Hilton Head? He talk bout how de white man gonna treat de black."

Lilly went back to her files. "I kept a newspaper about that, too. Wait. Yep. Grant said that 'the racial attitudes of the former Confederates could not be changed in a day.' He also said freedmen would need protection 'for a few years.'"

Lucas recalled, "So when he got to be president, Grant did wha he say to protect we folk in ten Sout Calina counties—he sent de US Army to stop terrible violence gainst freedmen who jus tryin to vote." Lucas stood up abruptly. "That was twenty yeahs ago that Grant tried to protect black folk in de Sout. And I hate to say," Lucas was almost shouting, "tings be gettin wus fuh we people, not bedda!"

The after-sunset conversation came to a stop with Lucas's uncharacteristic outburst. Lilly rose quietly and suggested there was work to be done in the house, even though the children had settled. Some were sleeping already. Abram, Douglass, and their spouses also stood to leave the porch when Lucas asked Abram for a brief word. In passing, Callie heard him say, "I need you then," and Abram nodded. Seeing that the gathering had cleared but for Callie, who was staring right at him, Lucas said, "Sista, let's us tek a walk." They moved down the front steps, across the yard, and down to the water. Lucas gestured to the dock. "See dis yuh."

"Yeah, brudda, I see our dock. What?"

Walking slowly, Lucas put his arm around her shoulder and said, "Sista, do you know people roun yuh tink we be rich? We know we ain, buh dey tink we be rich, jus cause we were able tuh buy dis land back in de freedom wah."

"Who you talkin bout?"

Lucas gestured across the river to the western side of St. Helena Island. "Dey some brothers bought land ovah dere bout ten yeahs pass. Dey been mad at we people from Oakheart fuh a long time. One of em be a Confederate soljah. He seem upset tuh dis day bout de wah."

As Lucas led Callie farther out onto the new portion of the dock, he explained, "See where you walkin on de newest wood? Right afta yo last visit, we built dis dock up. It took a lot a hammerin fuh mo den a week. We finished wuk one day, and I saw a boat comin from de plantation wid de buckras. Sho nuf, de boat came right up tuh dis dock. I chased de kids inside and came down from de yard, askin what I could do for em.

"De leader came onto my dock fus, while annodda man stay in de boat. He walked slow, watchin me, his long barrel pistol holster strapped to his leg, like he was lookin fuh trouble. 'We want to meet de owner of de land.' When I splain I own it wid my family, he walked real slow right up where I could punch his face, and said, 'Boy, nigga landowner don't sit well with me.'

"Right afta he said that, I heard Abram's voice speak loud and clear. 'You men should know I'm a God-fearin man, a God-lovin man.' Nobody seen him or his rifle til he stepped out from de tree, still talkin. 'And disyuh rifle is a tool of my God, and he say I can protect my daddy. So, I will ask you once, before you meet your maker. Do you believe I will kill you?' And he pointed the weapon directly at the man who called me 'boy.' Callie, I was so proud of him, and I was fraid he might have to shoot.

"The man turned and moved back down de dock near his boat, bout where we standin now, and turned to face me. 'Mighty fancy new dock, boy.' He looked to Abram and back. 'If you really do own all this land, the owner heah, which I'll find out, you best commence tuh worry bout yo property.' Then he signaled, and they got into their boat and rowed away quickly."

"Why you tellin me dis now?" Callie asked, with more tenderness on her face than in her voice. "Why you askin Abram fuh his help, tellin him, 'I need you'?"

"I'm tellin you cause you own dis property along wid me. And dem buckra boys were threatenin our land."

"Ten yeahs ago?"

"Well, dey been showin disrespect on de wada and in odda ways. Times round yuh got serious, sista. Dey be some bad-actin folk. Wid de politics of de day an de new government heah in dis state, de hateful people tink dey can act any way dey want."

"What you plannin to do with Abram?"

"Just so you unnerstan, Callie."

"Brudda, wha you hafta do?" Callie's voice demanded an answer.

"Dem boys de ones wha shoot at me yesterday when I try fuh git de body of James Draper. Tomorrow, befo dayclean, when it still dark, Abram and me goin fuh git de boat and body an tek em back to his fambly on St. Helena." He looked at her with a mysteriously settled smile. "We be back by noon." And with that, he took several steps up the embankment, saying, "Sista, I want you tuh know, but not tuh worry. We be fine."

Silently, Callie followed Lucas into the house, where the family had settled for the night.

Chapter 7

WEDNESDAY, AUGUST 23, 1893

THICK EARLY MORNING FOG BLANKETED THE OAKHEART COMMUNIty. When it began to lift, Callie awoke to the smell of baked bread and the sounds of cooking in the kitchen. She dressed quickly and went downstairs to find summer fruits cut up into bowls, as well as cornbread and butter, sitting in the center of the table. "Goodness, Miss Lilly. I hope your people appreciate you as much as they should."

"Well, they know ain nuttin I wouldn't do for em. I do run down sometime though."

"Lucas up already?"

"He's gone. He and Abram went out early, while it was still dark."

"He went ahead in fog like this?" Instantly, Callie knew she had said too much.

"You knew he had plans, too?"

Callie nodded. "He told me last night."

"He told me this morning jus before he left. He said they were gonna get old Draper and his boat, take em on home."

"You know, sista, Lucas and your boys know how to take care of themselves."

"Yes, honey, I know." Lilly looked up at Callie through moist, tired eyes.

"I got an idea. You done done in de kitchen this morning. I take ovah from here." With a resolute smile, Callie offered, "You rest yourself now, and afta the chirren eat, we gonna go for a long walk outside."

"Ain gonna argue, Callie."

"Wouldn't do much good, anyhow."

Within the next half hour, Callie advised Amanda that she could have a free morning, too. Then she woke up Robert and Saxton and Flora June's twins. Jancy and her father arrived from their nearby house just in time for her to get the biggest piece of cornbread and a slice of juicy peach. "Ummm, peaches," she cooed while managing to smile, chew, and rub her tummy simultaneously.

Douglass looked around, noticing the absence of his mother, father, and brother. "Well, I was thinkin I was late to get back workin on de boats, but in all this fog, I guess folk are sleepin in?"

"Your mama is, and Abram went with your father to go get Uncle James Draper's boat." Though Callie's words did not hint of danger to the children's ears, Douglass immediately went out of the house and down to the dock.

After all the children had eaten, Callie seized the moment. "Let's go, chirren, time to get outside on the porch." She waited a few seconds and when they were a little slow to assemble, she elevated her voice and deepened her tone. "Aunt Callie say get movin!" All pairs of feet shuffled into place quickly, eyes concentrated on their great-aunt, mouths generally agape.

Callie softened. "Since you just ate good food, your day is ready to start. Chirren, we gonna have some fun." Attitudes changed immediately. The children looked at each other, chattered, and giggled in anticipation of what their Aunt Callie had in mind. "We gonna have fun learnin bout ourselves." With puzzlement surrounding her, Callie clarified, "That's right. We gonna have a field trip, and on the way out to the field, we gonna see what new tings we can see. When we get to the field, supm tells me we jus may learn even more bout ourselves. Let's go!"

At the bottom of the porch steps, Callie led them into the backyard and down a footpath that she walked daily until she went to Washington. It was bordered by live oaks and tall pine trees until it reached the former slave quarters. Callie noticed that all the shanties were still there, though many had been expanded with a front porch or extra room, and most had been painted or whitewashed recently.

Callie had decided that this was a good day for the children of her family to hear more about the history of Oakheart when it was a plantation with its crops tended by slave labor. She did not share her purpose with the tour group. Callie slowed to a stop outside the first shanty, set off from the others. "Chirren, in the early part of my life, I lived here as a slave. I had a massa who lived in the big house where we had our good food just now. Then, almost thirty-two yeahs ago, Union soljuhs brought freedom to these islands, and we people didn't have a massa to tell us what to do. We could choose how to live our lives." Her words were distinct and spoken passionately, such that the children heard the reverence their Aunt Callie held for the word "freedom."

"Sunny was born right here, and she played all around our cabin." Smiling, Callie remembered, "Just up the road from here, under de biggest oak tree, is where my brothers, Lucas and BB, chase massa away from Oakheart. Das right. Yo grampa and yo uncle tell him to get out cause he ain gonna be massa no more. From that day to this, we be free!" As Callie envisioned the scene where her brothers embraced after leading friends and family in celebration, the children moved closer to her, laying their hands on her arms and shoulders. "And because of that freedom day, chirren, you be born free, part of this new Oakheart community."

Callie spread her arms round the children and then started moving them on down the path past all the shanties. Once the path opened up, the close-knit group unraveled, diverted by the squirrels looking for acorns, the chattering birds, or a tree that begged to be climbed. After a few minutes of this mobile hilarity, Callie called, "Chirren, come here!" They quickly complied.

"Look back where we come from, see how small that big house looks? I'm so glad you sweet young'uns had fun on that walk, cause back in slave days, twenty or thirty of your friends' parents and sisters and brothers took that same walk without any jumpin, or singin, or playin, or bein free. You see, they were slaves, walkin to start workin a whole day in this field, digging up sweet potatoes. Ain no choice. Ain no pay. Ain no freedom. They had to work, or they would be whipped."

Callie allowed moments of silence to pass...the children stood very still or just slightly shuffled their feet in the dusty soil.

Robert asked, "Aunt Callie, did you wuk in de field?"

"Yes, Robert, on many a day. I didn't get any pay; I didn't get to keep what I picked. Massa gave us some food back fuh us to eat, but then he sold what we grow and pick, and he keep all the money for himself."

"Ain right," Robert muttered.

"But today, we free to do what we want." Callie uttered this as if leading a cheer, and the children responded accordingly with heartfelt joy. Then she added, "What we want to do today with our freedom is dig some sweet potatoes from this ground." She pointed down the row for the children to see that Aunt Callie was asking them to dig sweet potatoes for a very long distance. The youthful exuberance audibly declined.

"Today, my lovely young ones, you get to feel how satisfyin a little hard work can be, if you do it by choice. Yes, I am choosing it for you today, but it can still be a good thing to do, even when you didn't plan to want to do some work. And the best thing about it is you get to eat what you dig up." Callie dumped the contents of the basket she asked Robert to carry. "I've got small shovels for each of you, and we, as a group, have to work our way down this row."

With that, Callie bent over at the waist, stretched a bit, and placed her shovel where she knew there would be a worthy root. A few quick strokes around and under the leafy plant exposed the target, and a quick swipe with the side of the shovel cut it free. Callie tossed it into the basket with the casual air of a seasoned worker, just coming back from break. She looked up at the children. "So, what day you plan to start workin? Where you see a plant, dig in about a hand or two away and see what you find."

Finally realizing that their amazing great Aunt Callie fully intended them to become a work detail, the children moved slowly to their tasks, with greater and lesser degrees of enthusiasm. With sustained effort, each took to the work with his or her own brand of diligence, because Callie was working down the row in front of them. Before long, the basket was filled.

Callie stood up, more tired and pained than she would ever let on. The workers were so engaged they did not see her stop, and so she let them work on before saying, "You have done very well. Think what you got done in those twenty minutes." Then she smiled. "Now think of doing that work all day and bein punished if you don't." Her words were greeted with silence.

"Let's head back across the field and through the woods. Down by the river, I got supm to show you before we go back home." The work detail was considerably more restrained on their hike away from the field. Leading the children single file through a freestanding pine forest, Callie emerged near the creek in a location well known to her. "You see, down heah, babies, this is my flectin spot." Callie pointed with pride to the large live oak trees overhanging the tidal pool just off the river. "You all know what I'm talkin about? Flectin spot?"

"Where you flect jus as much as you wan to!" Beanie shared enthusiastically.

"Well, yes, that's right. And, this place heah is where I still go when I got important decisions to make. You know, sometimes, we got to think real hard just to figuh supm out, and we pray to God, and we try to feel what our heart says is the right thing to do.

"Now, let me teach you supm. When I say 'flectin,' it means reflecting. Say it with me. Re-flect-ing. Thas right. R-E-F-L-E-C-T-I-N-G." And then she spelled it out a second time and asked them to repeat the letters with her.

"Wha it mean, Auntie Callie?" Jancy sounded impatient.

"Different things. It means first sunlight reflectin on wada at day-clean. It means in my head, when I am reflecting about what I will do about supm important. Long time ago, I come down yuh, and jus like this, I walk out on these big old oak branches."

Robert spoke up with a caution. "Caful, Auntie Callie! Be caful!"

"Robert, thanks for worrying about me. I'm just gonna sit right out here." And she settled at the fork of two branches. "I can sit here, look down, and if I look real hard, I see my face reflectin back at me in de wada. When I see my face lookin back at me, it helps me know what I need to do." The children stood transfixed, mouths agape. "So, this is the best flectin spot in the whole world for me. And you got to find yo own."

Jancy spoke right up. "Wha if I like dis flectin spot?"

"Well, young lady, fine with me. But don't you think you wanna look roun the world a lee bit befo you decide on this spot as your one and only?"

"Maybe, Auntie, but if you like it and it wuk good fuh you, I know I like it already."

From her roost on the branch, Callie peered up the creek to see Lucas and Abram rowing the family bateau up to the dock. To end further exploration of the "flectin" spot, Callie declared, "We will come back to this tree when the water is smooth as glass and the sky clear, so you can see your own flections in the wada. And rememba, nobody walks out on these branches like Auntie Callie did without a parent around. Everybody understand?"

Though disappointed, they nodded agreement.

"Let's head on back and see bout fixin these sweet potatoes up nice for tonight." Walking with Aunt Callie, Robert and Beanie carried the heavy harvest basket back home, as the others ran ahead, arriving just in time to greet their grandfather and uncle coming off the dock. Before they even spoke, Callie could tell that the men were somber but unharmed. She walked up to Lucas and gave him a special sisterly embrace. "Worryin bout you boys in all that fog. I'm so glad you back safe."

Lucas responded without expression. "We cut through all right. Helps to know where you goin in the first place." He looked directly at Callie. "We tuk de boat and its captain back to de fambly. Dey were sad and grateful as Abram offered prayer."

"Abram, you and your father did God's work today."

"I know it, Aunt Callie. I know it."

Lilly waited in the yard for the travelers and their welcoming party to arrive. When she and Lucas met, they held each other for the longest time without speaking. They remained there, not moving, as the others ascended to the porch to begin the midday meal.

At the table, it didn't take Jancy long to remember yesterday's secret, intended for today. "Auntie Callie, Gramma, do you want to go up in the tall boat today?"

Although Callie was hoping the offer had been forgotten, Lilly quickly accepted for them both. "Why, yes, Jancy gal, we are excited about it. Right, Callie?"

"Oh, yes, sista, too, too excited." Callie's half smile was several teeth short of convincing, but Jancy heard all she needed to hear.

"Our plan is on, Grampa!" Jancy's words brought Lucas back to the present.

"All right, Jancy. We gonna put em in the top boat, ain we?"

Robert, so sensitive to the feelings of his family members, saw that Callie was less than enthused. "We hep you, Auntie. You be happy. You see."

Douglass picked up the refrain. "Yesterday I fixed de chair so it can't dump you out, Aunt Callie. No worry. I tighten up de braces and made de boat real nice too. Gonna do same wuk on de middle one soon. Once you get in de high boat, you like it jus fine."

The words were reassuring, but Callie filled her plate with more fruit salad to forestall the pleasure a bit. It didn't work—the children were more than ready to hoist the women of the family to new heights. Callie was asked several times, "Have you finished eating yet, Aunt Callie?" Finally, she surrendered her lunch plate defense.

The project had become a family affair. Lucas and Douglass untethered the pulley system and secured the wooden boson's chair, which hung at the ready two feet above the ground. Surrounded by youth, Callie edged her way across the yard at a measured pace, though small hands pulling her forward urged more rapid progress. Of course, the children did not know that their Aunt Callie feared being in high places.

Lilly stepped forward, quietly encouraging Callie. "You know, sista, your nephew and brudda not gonna let you fall."

"Then you go ahead."

"I will, and you will too."

Lilly sat on the boson's chair, and, with modest effort, Lucas hoisted her up the eleven feet to the high bateau. Lucas instructed, "Lilly, see de rope handle Douglass tie jus ovah yo head? Pull yourself ovah de gunnel and onto de back bench."

Lilly executed the instructions with relative ease. Then she leaned over the edge to ask, "Can I stand up?"

"Yes." Douglass reassured them both again as the chair was lowered in front of Callie. "I set it myself with new wood braces around the tree limbs. You can stand, you can jump. It's not goin nowhere."

Callie saw that the time had arrived to sit down and go up, and she did, with hands clutching the ropes and eyes closed tightly. As she reached the level of the top boat, Lilly's soothing voice opened Callie's eyes. "Reach up and grab that rope, swing your legs over and land your feet right in front of me." Trying to remember how she trusted her family, Callie quickly thrust up one hand, grabbed the rope, swung her legs over to plant her feet firmly on the bottom of the bateau, and slowly looked up to Lilly, muttering, "Am I here?"

"It's all right, dear sista. I got the ropes steady, so you just sit down easy."

With a grimace, Callie slowly slid off the chair and sat with a thud. Startled and breathing rapidly, she gasped, "Oh, the boat's not rocking. I didn't fall. We're safe."

"I swear, Callie, to be such a worldly wise lady, you sho can be a baby."

"I'm happy to be here, with you, Lilly. Just let me settle down." Indeed, when she began to look around, the panoramic view from that height was thrilling. With the changed perspective, she looked through gaps in tree leaf clusters to the Atlantic Ocean about five miles east. She could see south down the river to the northern tip of Hilton Head Island. To the west, across vast stands of marsh grass and the Beaufort River, Callie spotted Parris Island, property owned by the United States Government due to the legislative leadership of Robert Smalls. Back through the trees to the north, behind the house on both sides, she could see and appreciate the scope of the Oakheart community property.

They were so captivated by their surroundings, neither Lilly nor Callie spoke at first. At eye level, Lilly pointed to squirrels chasing each other from branch to branch in the neighboring oak tree. Callie gasped and put her hand over her mouth as a line of pelicans flew by just over the branches above their heads, wings flapping together before they glided down to cruise above the creek.

"Auntie Callie, Gramma Lilly, are you okay?" Jancy screamed from the ground below.

"Oh, yes, darlin, we gettin settled," Lilly assured her baby's baby.

"Are you scaid? Or do you like it?"

"Yes, we like it. Thank you, Lucas and Douglass and Miss Jancy, for wanting us to be up here. It is beautiful with all these birds."

Callie peered over the edge of the bateau at Jancy and the others. "And you are beautiful down there, too."

Lucas added, "Glad you happy, ladies, cause we got a problem with the pulley right now. You might be up dere a lee bit."

Lilly responded, "Husband, don't you try to act funny."

"I'm fa true, Lilly, we got a twisted bit in this rig to fix. It ain be long."

"Best not," Lilly warned. "You doin all right, Callie?"

Callie looked serenely at her brother's wife. "My dear sista, we have just been given a gift. Let us enjoy this as long as we can."

Lilly shouted down to Lucas, "You bedda get that fixed, but we be fine fuh now."

In the privacy afforded the women by their elevated perch, Callie and Lilly reached out and clasped hands, giggling with delight at their predicament. They maneuvered the cushions Douglass left them for maximum comfort on their respective benches. Callie said, to no one in particular, "My, my, we got a beautiful day today."

While Callie was feeling the moment, Lilly reached into the leather pouch she managed to sling over her shoulder for her afternoon aloft. "Before you go off too far in your head, let me try to guide yo thinkin a lee bit. Tell me some more Washington stories."

"You really want to start in on my life notes again?"

"We got us a project, an if I'm not mistaken, Sunny is comin back home by Thursday evenin. That's tomorrow. There may be some other tings on your mind bout then. So, let's do this now. We can stop to sit back any time we want. We up heah for the afternoon." Then she leaned toward Callie. "Hope you ain drink too much befo comin up yuh." They touched hands again and laughed out loud.

Lucas was still below, but the others had gone on. "You ladies sho you still doin fine up dere? You sound a lee touch in de head. We bedda git you down quick."

Callie said, "Take time for now, Lucas. I'm likin bein up in the trees." And then she turned to Lilly's question. "Naw, not quite done with the Washington stories. Got to say a little more bout my mama and daddy. I been sad and got over bein sad, ever since I realized my mama wasn't wantin any life with me. I made my peace with it. But I didn't want it to be a sorrow for my daughter, so I didn't take her around."

Callie looked out across the water and somberly shared a deeper memory. "One day, when Sunny and I are in Washington near the White House, I see Selena just as she sees me and Sunny. Sunny gets distracted talkin to a young man, so I walk toward my mama. She nods toward Sunny, askin, 'Is that yo baby? She look like you with that thin frame and strong face.' And I told her yeah, and she says, 'She pretty. I'm happy fuh you both.' Then she drops her head and wipes a tear away. She says, 'Don't want her to see me an be ashamed. I got to go.' Then she turns and hurries behind some bushes before Sunny can see her."

"Oh, Callie." Lilly reached out to touch her arm. "Seems like she thought she wasn't good enough to be wid you."

"I'm sorry that day to this that she didn't know we had no judgments to make. I just wanted the time to have a friendship with her and to love her." Callie wiped first one eye and then the other. Then she sat up straight, as if turning the page. "Now bout my father...

"Way back in the war, you know, I found out from Will Hewitt that his uncle was my father. All my life, I never thought my father was a real person. Then, suddenly, he had a name—Harris Hewitt. Before I knew him to be my father, I met him once on the dock up river in Beaufort, when he brought Will home to Oakheart. That was 1861. Two years later, after I learned he was my daddy, Will also told me that he was 'lost at sea.'

"General Wallace helped me find him in that Confederate prison camp in North Carolina. But when he came back to Maryland, he was sick and weak. He never got his lungs workin right again. Will compared his uncle before the war and afta—he said that his uncle's voice was softer and his jokes not as quick, but he still had the same twinkle in his eye Will remembered.

"You know what else I saw in his eyes? I saw the light of his love for me. And, if I thought he loved me, well, there ain no way to describe the love he showed for my Sunny. He loved that girl and couldn't spend enough time with her. The three of us would just talk and talk and talk some more. Me and Sunny, we mostly listen. Even though he walked less each year, he talked mo and mo. He seemed to have new stories he needed to tell. Maybe he knew his time was comin short. I tell you one thing sure. Even though he was slowin down in his last year of life, he got really mad when Congress voted to close the Freedmen's Bureau in 1872. He was so upset, he said, 'If I felt better, I would go right over to Washington to tell Congress what's so.'

"Lilly, I loved that man. I just wish I had more time to give to him. We never shared days when he was healthy, but we knew each other well by the time he passed. Sunny and me, we visited him so many times in his last months. The leaves were fallin in 1873. We were so sad to lose him. And so glad to have him."

Callie lingered for a minute with memories of her father and then tried to surmount her sense of loss, declaring, "I know you got some good notes from me there—I was talkin bout my heart." And she clasped her hands over her chest, and with tears seeping from closed eyes, she smiled up to the sky above.

Lilly allowed the quiet to surround them and then realized that it was not quiet at all. No less than four different bird calls passed through the branches they shared. They looked over to the next live oak tree and saw a squirrel's nest built down in a fork of the tree. Out on the creek bed at low tide, egrets stalked and speared their prey in the shallow streams left behind by a receding ocean.

Soon, Lilly asked, "Can we do a little mo work? Should we? What about your return to the islands with Sunny?"

"It was so hard, Lilly. She questioned me, wonderin, 'You gonna tek me back home and then leave me again?' I couldn't deny it, Lilly. I had made my life and my life's work up North. But I knew that area was not best for her, specially since she got to be such a grown-up young lady. It was time for Sunny to get outta that too-busy town. You know, we were gonna come sooner, in the summer of that year, but then my daddy got weaker and we decided to wait. Took us a while to get ready to go afta he passed."

"So sorry, Callie. Maybe your daddy helped you one last time, hangin on like he did. He delayed you comin back heah until after we had that big cyclone hit us in September. I wrote you bout it. I memba sounds I ain nevah heard before. Wind so strong, tried to tear ebbyting down. It shook dishes outa de cabinet. Tings breakin all ovah de house. So much rain fell, wind blow tall pines down when de wet ground can't hold de roots. Big pine tree smashed a shed out back, and we had branches all round de yard. Couple more trees fell in de fields. And Callie," Lilly pointed down to edge of the yard, her eyes wide, "I'm tellin you, wada almost topped de bluff right here. One mo foot higher, and we be wadin in wada up near de house. Course, ain nobody out walkin in de terrible wind."

Callie nodded. "I remember reading the letter you wrote to Missus Granger up in Washington. She was askin me about the storm, and I showed her the newspaper drawing. It looked like the worst of it came on land east of Savannah, headin north, sending wind and water up our creeks as it spun. Missus Granger showed how winds of a cyclone always spin this way." She made her finger go in a circle, over the top, right-to-left. "She said that made the winds worse right here on these islands."

"Well, let me say, the lady done tole de whole trute!" Lilly testified. "The way the winds pushed all that wada round scaid me so."

"Now that I hear your story bout gettin mud-stuck, I'm even more worried for you in such a bad storm. Glad you survived it. Let's make some magic to keep big storms away."

Lilly laughed and shook her head, almost able to enjoy the memory. "I gonna see about that. I know some people who can channel dey energies to keep storms away."

"Up in Washington, I learned that scientists can measure storms' real energy. One of my doctor friends told me bout cyclones and how air pressure goes down in a big storm. I told him my bruddaman needs to be able measure what the weather is doin. So, I gave Lucas that barometer when I came back home in '83."

"Callie, he check it all the time. I mean, at least once a day. I ask him once, 'You really lookin at that ting for air pressure or you jus tink it's pretty?' He looked at me like he was insulted, sayin, 'I'm checkin it so I be bedda fisherman, keep my family fed.' So, please know, he loves his barometer. He always tell his friends bout it, that he gonna know bout big storms comin before they get here. They ask him, 'If a big stohm come, what help be a weather machine?' Lucas was offended, but he still loves it."

Callie said, "I'm so happy it helps him be a better waterman!"

"I reckon it's good to be ready for the storms—all the damage they cause. I don't like to talk about it much though. Those storms in 1873 and 1883 scaid me too bad."

Callie responded, "You know, when you say you don't talk about the big cyclones, that sounds just like how we don't wanna talk bout slave days. It was such a fright for so many years of our lives, we don't want to rememba, and we don't want to tell our children."

Lilly said, "But they need to know! People sometimes be bad to dark-skinned people, just cause they are dark-skinned people. It been that way all through the years, through history."

Callie responded, "And sometimes big storms come into your life and turn things around."

"So, you say it good we talk about the past with the family?"

"Guess so. It's our job to make the children smart."

Lilly nodded in agreement. "But not make em afraid."

"Gramma, Aunt Callie!" They heard Jancy call from below. And they both poked their heads over the gunnels to see the little girl squinting up at them. "There you are. I been feelin bad, Gramma Lilly, real bad."

"What's wrong, honey?"

"Got a secret." She shuffled her feet in the sandy soil as if the secret could not be contained.

"Honey, keep yo secret ifn you want," Lilly said.

Jancy shook her head. "Gotta tell it, Gramma."

Callie encouraged her. "Sweet baby, tell us what's worryin you."

After only a few seconds delay, "I'm sorry, Gramma. Dey tell you de pulley rope broken but it not. It wukn. Dey jus wanna leh you stay dere in de tree-boat."

Suppressing amusement, Lilly said, "You are doin jus right to tell us, honey. We help Grampa figure this out. Run on now, so we can talk."

No sooner had Jancy run down to the water, Lucas started up from his shack at the base of the dock, tools and pulley parts in hand. "Well, my wife, my sista, I tink we gah disyuh ting figuh out right." He looked up expectantly, hoping to find some sort of affirmation, or even gratitude. Instead, silence.

"Say huh!" Lucas called out. "How you doin up dere?" Still no sound. "Lilly, honey?" said Lucas with tinges of concern and suspicion.

"Don't honey me, husband."

"All right now, wha bee done got wrapped up in yo head scarf?"

"Jancy-bee loves and respects her grandmother and her auntie enough to tell it. Ain no problem wid de pulley. You jus keepin us up yuh."

Callie added, "And don you get after Jancy about her bein honest, brudda."

"Believe me," Lucas sounded pitiful, "we talk bout keepin you up dere, jokin wid each odda. We ain gonna do it."

"Oh yea, brudda," Callie said, "dah dog won't hunt up dis tree."

"Fa true, de pulley need a fix, an I done done it."

Lucas's protests of innocence fell on deaf ears. Lilly continued acting the role of the wounded party, even as she started to smile. "You done done it all right."

Lucas decided the only thing left to do was install the fix, which he did, and said, "Ladies, you come down now?"

"Husband, we gon stay awhile, we enjoyin this too much." Callie and Lilly leaned from their benches to hug each other.

Callie added, "We gonna watch the sunset next hour or so, so please use your little pulley chair to send us some food and drink. And those fine binoculars you always using."

Lilly, continuing to exercise her superior position, said, "And, honey, you can jus give us supm from whatever dinner you fixin de chirren."

It was not ten minutes later, Lucas sent the functioning pulley chair up with a sack that had a jar of tea, two peaches, some cornbread from the morning, and their new binoculars.

"You be forgiven, Lucas," said Lilly.

"Tank ya, brudda," said Callie. Their praise barely reached Lucas's ears as he headed back to his work shack on the dock.

"Now, where were we?" Lilly asked while still chortling gently at the predicament Lucas had found himself in.

"He really is a good man, sista," Callie offered. "He just needs to be careful who learns his secrets. Our little Miss Jancy was feelin sad bout helpin him be the fool with us." They shared a good laugh before Callie added, "And if you are talkin bout all those notes you been writin down, the last thing we talked about was Sunny and me comin back here in late 1873."

"Yes, ma'am," responded Lilly as she picked up her notepad from the bench.

"Simple fact was, I knew that I had found my place in Washington, and I was almost sure that it was not right for my Sunny. Besides, you and Lucas and the family were settled in just fine right here. I knew it would be a safer place for Sunny to keep growin up than livin with me, sorry to say."

"I know we did our best for her."

"I knew you would, sista. One reason I wanted her to be back here was to return to Penn School. Tween me and Mrs. Granger and her grandfather, we did pretty good to keep Sunny up with her studies in Washington. She got good common sense from bein with us, but she needed more work in books, and Penn School was the right place for her then."

Lilly nodded. "I memba when you two came back and the three of us went over to see Laura Towne at Penn. You know I been so happy for my boys to be at that school. When you came back with Sunny twenty years ago, they were around eight and ten years old. They thought their cousin was so smart about the world. Since they loved Penn, they wanted Sunny to go there with em."

Callie smiled in gratitude for Laura Towne, who had run the school for more than thirty years. "Miss Laura has been a strong force for good in all our lives. I rememba she was so glad to see Sunny again. Soon as we finished sayin 'hello,' Miss Laura took Sunny to the classroom where she was workin and invited us to join her. Memba what she was doin?"

"I do. We spent the next couple hours tryin to patch up books for Penn School. Things like that are why I love her so much. Look what she does for the children, her 'scholars,' as she calls em. She told us she makes as many as one hundred patches in a book usin real thin paper and paste. She said sometimes she puts pages from two half-worn books together to make one book good as new. I memba tellin her that's what I felt in hospital work, specially with surgery. We patch people when their body isn't workin and help em so they use it again." A mischievous look came across Callie's face. "As Miss Laura Towne would say, 'There is satisfaction in making a neat, nicely bound, patched book from a horrid old pair of covers and many ragged leaves.'"

Lilly burst out laughing. "You got her just right, but you know there's a lot of love in that woman. She does all that work to help the children learn their lessons. You know, Penn School got courses for beginners, other classes for children that learn well, and even a high level for those that really take to it. Got a different teacha for each. The grands, Flora June's boys, just moved up to the middle level, and every time they talk of Miss Laura or Miss Ellen, you see the light in their eyes. Penn School is not just teachin readin, writin, and math and such. They are teachin em how to live their lives, dignified and respectful."

"Lilly, you go write that into your notes, cause it's true for me and Sunny, too. Every day I'm thankful for Penn getting my Sunny and hundreds of others on the islands ready to work in the world just when chances to work were opening up."

"Especially in these years since the war, Lucas and I sit heah and watch out on de wada, and we jus caint believe how many boats keep comin into Port Royal Sound. And the railroad started up, bringin business to the boats and more work for people."

Callie added, "And mos everywhere I look when I come back, I see they been cuttin trees and puttin up mo buildins."

"Yes, and you know, Abram says that cotton farmin has stayed strong, so much that they can't find enough workers for the field."

"Well..."

"Good news fuh we island people is that since the wah, folk can get work. The more education people get, the bedda paid they be. Our people be educated and willin tuh work."

Callie said, "From what you say, seems like Beaufort County been one of the best places fuh freedmen to be."

"I know it's been good for my Lucas, too. He could support our family doing what he liked to do on the water, fishin and ferryin people round the islands. But you know him. Sometimes he get too worried bout things. You know how hard he always works. Add to that, he been in the middle of organizing farmers and fishermen to sell their products for the best price."

"You can keep worryin bout Lucas if you want, but you know he's doin what he wants to be doin. I know you are proud."

"Sho am, Callie. Proud and grateful. It's hard for me to believe that those little boys born at the end of the wah are nearly thirty years old. Lucas and me, we give thanks to God."

"Me too, me too. Yet, I've seen freed Africans havin hard times, specially in my hospital work, but I know there lots a people like you and Lucas and me who made progress afta slave times end. We got a fair chance to get some education and work for money, and even to buy the land we worked as slaves."

"That's all true, but hard times been comin thicker and faster lately," Lilly said, sounding a bit like Lucas. "You rememba when the Freedmen's Bank failed?"

Callie shook her head slowly. "I memba too much about how tough that time was."

"The year afta you brought Sunny back to stay with us, the Freedmen's Bank in Beaufort closed with our money in it. You know that happened to more than a thousand other people livin round here?" Lilly spoke softly, despairingly. "I talked Lucas into puttin money in the Freedmen's Bank to show others how to build up our community and to support what the United States Government was tryin to do to help we freedmen. So, Lucas finally agreed and put jus a part of our saved money in there, along with part of what you sent for Sunny."

Callie nodded. "I know losin that money made him even madder at the government. Between our brother BB dyin by the shot of a Union soldier and losin our money to greedy bankers backed by government, sometimes I wonder why Lucas is not even more bitter than he shows."

"You know, sista, I can say, he's too smart to lose his head when times get hard. Oh yeah, he get mad, but it don't last. He stayin strong for his boys, for his grands, for his whole family, and even for BB."

"I know you have heard the stories from Lucas bout how Mama Ruth raised us up." Callie looked down to the outdoor kitchen where she and Mama Ruth spent so many hours together. "She lived a righteous, God-lovin life, and she learned a lot while servin as old Bowen's house servant. She made sure her children knew right from wrong, and she also made sure we were smart enough to save what little money we could earn afta workin our tasks for a day. Her teachin, and the money we earned afta freedom come, led us to be able to buy all this beautiful Oakheart land during the tax sale thirty yeahs ago."

"Speakin of not getting our money back from the Freedmen's Bank," Lilly said, "I was so afraid we would lose this land. You know, when Robert Smalls bought a big, fine house in Beaufort town, the case against him went to the Supreme Court. Mister Smalls worked hard to win his case, and that decision was good for all the rest of us who bought land down here."

Lilly added, "That's right. I ain nevah forgot that day we learned that the court decided that freedmen bought their land fair and legal during the wah. Lucas said it felt almost as good as buyin it in the first place."

Callie affirmed the thrill of that decision. "I remember jumpin up and down and hollerin when I first heard about it. I was workin in the hospital, and people wondered what came over me, so I had to settle down and explain. I memba when I saw Congressmen Smalls at a party fuh South Carolina folk in Washington, I had to give him a hug and thank him for makin our land safe for us and our children. I could tell how proud he was."

Picking up the binoculars to peer to the east over St. Helena Island, Lilly said, "It does my heart good to know we who bought this land and worked it through de years, can now keep it and pass it on to our chirren." Panning toward the south, Lilly smiled and nodded her head. "Mmmm-hmmm. There got to be hundreds of families on just this island." As she pivoted in the boat facing west, "Oh my, look at the colors on de wada. They don't even look real."

"Please," Callie asked, reaching for the glasses and, not willing to stand up, twisted slowly to look around. As the sun disappeared beyond the water line, colors in the clouds flared to brilliant pastels before fading to the dusky grays of early evening.

Lilly spoke softly. "Yes, my dear sista, we have tried to use our freedoms for good. As a people and as a family. Praise God."

Callie added, "Give Abraham Lincoln his due. But as Mista Lincoln found out, there was a reaction to the actions that we love him for, and it was not all about love."

As Lilly retrieved the binoculars from Callie, she said, "We even seein mo of a reaction round here, even though we think these islands are too special, there be some problems just like we saw cross de water." As she steadied her view to that very location, she whispered in exclamation, "Oh my God, tell me I am not seeing this!" Lilly sat upright, her senses attuned, leaning toward what she saw in the lenses. "I'm lookin at one big bateau comin from the area of the riverbank where they live. I'm seein two sets of oars drawin a straight line from them Southern boys' property to right here.at Oakheart." She handed the binoculars to Callie.

"They do seem to be keepin a straight path and a regular pace. Ain stopping or turnin."

They exchanged a quick look, and Lilly immediately called, "Lucas!" Next, she whistled several notes easily mistaken for bird calls by the unknowing, but were the emergency calls that Lucas and Lilly had planned years before.

Lucas moved out of his dock shack quickly to see his sister and wife pointing excitedly across the wide river. "Lucas, they comin across de riba from de buckra place." She leaned over and dropped the binoculars to Lucas, who looked and began to act.

"We don't have time to get you down. You both stay put up dere out of sight wid heads down. I'm not playin bout dah. Stay put and stay quiet." Lucas ran up the steps to the porch, where his sons' families were eating and spending the early evening. "I need ebbybody inside right now. Abram, tek em all tuh backside in de house and tell em to stay. Den you and young Robert be lookin out de front window. I may need to call on you."

"Douglass, get your rifle and come wid me." They quickly walked away from the big house to the side yard, where the boats were in the trees. "Douglass, you the best shot in the family, so hide in this low boat; don't do or say nuttin. Dis ting ain gonna end wid a bunch a gunshots, but I want yo cover in case I need it." Lucas gripped his son by both shoulders. "Son, you either gonna aim fuh a weapon in somebody's hand, or you gonna shoot their dock line. You good either way?" Douglass nodded and hoisted himself into the bateau. "If I need you to shoot, I'll call out the target. You stay down and raise up just enough to shoot."

With that, Lucas looked out on the river to see that his visitors had made it about two-thirds of the way. He carried his own rifle down to the dock shack and leaned it just inside the door. Then, he pulled up a crab line, netted three irate crabs, and dumped them into the nearby bucket. Seemingly unhurried, Lucas pulled one more line from the water—it held the mullet he caught that very afternoon—and hung the fish on the nearest dock post. The catch was so fresh that gills were still pulsing in a struggle to sustain life.

Lucas looked up, saw that the boat was still aiming directly for the dock, now close enough to see three figures clearly, two pulling on oars and a third standing in the bow. He strolled to the end of his dock so he could be seen watching their approach, and then he turned to walk back to his shack. Passing it, Lucas took a few steps up the embankment, rotating slowly to face the bateau as it pulled in along the dock. The man in the bow stepped off and dropped a line to the dock, motioning for his mate to tie up. He walked deliberately down the dock, a pistol holstered at his side, watching Lucas all the way.

"We come to take our boat back."

"What boat you talkin bout?" Lucas responded crisply.

"Been sittin out in our marsh for a couple days. You probably seen it there, ain't you?" Lucas didn't respond. "I seen you there jus a few days back. I took a shot at you." After a menacing pause, he took a few more steps and turned directly toward Lucas. "Imagine my surprise when we look afta the fog clears this mornin, and ain no boat. We figuh you got it, and we aim to tek it back."

"Well, boys, I hate tuh be de one tuh tell you, but you figuh wrong. De boat you talkin bout ain heah. Ain neba been heah. My son and I, we good Christian men, an we took that boat, wid de body of our friend Frank Draper, back to his family. De boat was his, just so you know."

Lucas's directness caused the leader to pause. Then Lucas stepped up the encounter. "You got a problem with what my son and I did? Return a dead man to his family, along wid his boat? Actin unda de teachins of our Gawd?"

The leader was silent as he turned to look at his friends. One started moving slowly up the dock away from the boat about ten steps when he stopped and turned, scanning the steps up the bluff where Lucas stood, and beyond toward the house.

Lucas continued, "I hate tuh tell you. Look like you mek a boat trip fuh nuttin."

That prompted the leader to say, "Boy, you mighty confident to be talkin that way. Standin out all by yoself, facin three guns. Don appear to be any family around."

"What mek you tink I ain got fambly roun yuh? De las time you boys made an unwelcome visit to dis dock, you didn't see any fambly roun either, until my son showed himself and convinced you dah yo lives been in danger."

Lucas stared at the leader of the group as he dropped his hand to his holster. "Tell you what, so we don have to pull out our guns," the man said, "you just give us one of your boats and we'll go away happy."

"First, lemme aks—do you tink yo lives in danger now?" Lucas quickly added, "No need tuh ansa dah. Here be my best ansa bout de boat you want. Dis be yo lucky day, cause I'm in de boat business. I caint jus giv a boat away. I wouldn't do that for a friend." Lucas paused a few seconds. "But I offer to build you a boat and only chaage what I charge my friends."

The leader did not know quite how to read this black man, clearly a risk taker. But he wasn't ready to up the ante on the gamble either. Lucas sought to resolve the man's dilemma. "How bout dis, so we can settle yo concerns in a peaceful way." Lucas smiled, nodded first at the leader and then at his two associates, and shouted, "Abram, send Robert down yuh with one of them peach pies." Lucas returned his attention to the leader. "You know, yo land like mine, it grow plenty crop, trees burst wid fruit." Robert came running down the porch steps, across the yard, and down to the dock, an action that froze all the men in place.

"In de name of Christian love, and neighborly courtesy, take de pie from my grandson." The leader took it and passed it behind him. "Run on back now, Robert." Then Lucas stepped down the embankment, moved just onto the dock, where he lifted the fresh-caught mullet line from the post. Extending the fish with his left hand to the holster side of his visitor, Lucas stepped forward. "Heah. We got us a mighty big riba; no reason we can't share it. I don have tuh like you; you don have tuh like me. Ain no reason fuh us tuh worry each odda. If you let me, I can be kind to you."

The main antagonist took the fish and stepped back to pass it on. "Ain been expectin to git kindness an food from a nig—negro. Ain expectin any slave man to own property."

Without hesitation, Lucas spoke clearly. "You can be sho you ain lookin at a slave man now." Lucas looked the man in the eye without blinking. "My Gawd tell me tuh give a man a chance to prove that he ain worth much befo you treat him that way. You ain gib me a big enuf reason to not be kind—not yet."

Lucas paused to look into the faces of his three visitors, then focused on the leader. "Gah fuh say, ain no reason fuh threats, but you already found out, we will act to defend what we done earned. You defend yown. We defend our own. Been doin it right yuh on dis lan fuh mo den thirty yeah, ebba since my sista and brudda an me bought it wid our own money." Lucas pointed to the house. "Up in de attic be de deed fuh disyuh land. I may show it to you some day. But not dis day." The visitors still did not step back.

"One mo ting. In case you didn't know." Lucas elevated his voice slightly. "We black folk all roun yuh fought fuh de Union in de wah. We been train fuh hold back when we be provoked, and we been train fuh be very accurate wid our rifles." He paused briefly and then said, "Fuh now, we havin a fambly day, and it's time fuh you to go."

The leader could not allow himself to be dismissed by a black man and stepped forward. "I'll take yo kindness but befo I go, I intend to see that deed. Either that or we'll take a boat."

Holding his hands up and smiling, Lucas spoke loudly, "Man, since you wanna warn me bout my property, bein neighbors, I feel I bes warn you bout yours. You see how you tie up yo boat? Dah don look right." The three visitors turned to see the rope holding the heavy rowboat to the dock as it stretched against the pull of the outbound tide. Lucas shouted, "Douglass, boat line." One sharp shot ended the boat's tenuous connection to solid land, and it immediately started sliding down the length of the dock with the current.

The visitors startled, looking around but unable to locate the source of the shot. Their leader, having the longest distance to go, turned and moved quickly down the dock, urging his friends to do the same. The party arrived at the end of the dock as did their boat. The leader, swinging his line of fish, jumped in just ahead of the man awkwardly clutching the peach pie, who fell on top of the first, rocking the heavy bateau. The third man jumped for the stern just as the boat drifted past, hit the water instead, grabbed the gunnel, and dragged himself aboard.

Lucas watched after them as Douglass joined him on the embankment just above the dock. They smiled broadly at the sight of their unwelcome neighbors still drifting away, fighting over who got what portions of peach pie.

Chapter 8

WEDNESDAY EVENING, AUGUST 23, 1893

IN THE BACK OF THE HOUSE, AMANDA, NELLIE, AND THE CHILDREN froze with alarm at the rifle shot, listening intently for a retort. Instead, the first sounds they heard were Abram and Robert laughing loudly as they hustled up the front porch steps. "Did you see how your grampa made that man take the fish line with his gun hand?"

Robert exclaimed, "And Daddy, what a great shot by Uncle Douglass! He made that boat float away!"

"Hey, I'm too proud of you. You did yo part—deliverin good peach pie to de bad men."

Recognizing the voices, the children screamed with relief and raced into the hall, followed by the two tearful women. They surrounded the storytellers, avidly listening to every word. Slowly, the celebration moved back outside, where they saw Lucas and Douglass dutifully operating the pulley system for the bosun's chair. As quickly as possible, they lowered two important ladies from their exciting afternoon aloft. They hugged and briefly praised the remarkable shooting of Douglass and calm control of Lucas before making a beeline to the outhouse to tend to matters of personal hygiene.

After Callie and Lilly were refreshed, Lucas gathered everyone in the front parlor of the house. "Now, Douglass been practicin all his life tuh mek dah great shot. Tank you, Douglass! You see, chirren, sometime you gah fuh use what you know to hep yo fambly. You done done yo fambly proud, son."

Lucas explained further. "I'm real sorry ifn anybody got scaid dis evenin. We didn't invite de men tuh come heah, and soon as dey walk on de dock, dey ain friendly. Befo I came down tuh meet em, I asked Douglass to be ready to shoot de tie-line on dey boat. De shot was not fired in anger, but fuh a purpose. I want all we people heah togedda to unnerstan and rememba dah." Lucas smiled. "When dey saw de boat floatin pass de dock, bout to be in de crik, dey knew it be time fuh go." Laughter rippled around the family as they smiled at the success.

Lilly frowned. "Wisht you didn't have to shoot a gun. Robert Smalls didn't have to use one when he waded into the rice worker strike."

"Not even gonna compare de two situations, though tank you for de reminda of Robert Smalls's bravery and skill in talkin a problem through to fix it." A little peeved, Lucas quickly said, "You know, I coulda jus walk onto de dock and said, 'Scuse me, gentleman, while I untie your boat, cause you gah fuh leave right now.' But I thought doin dah might not wuk." He relented, "Lilly, honey, I love you. I unnerstan yo worries bout guns. Please be sho de white men who came yuh tonight, left heah knowin we are skilled shooters who hit dere mark. Dey also know we meant em no harm. We jus meant tuh be in control of tings and mek em leave." He looked around at the family. "It was a good shot to settle tings down, not mek tings wus." Smiling broadly, "Beside, we be generous folk—we gib em fish and pie."

Lucas walked a few steps around the circled family. "We been through an excitin time, an we gonna be settlin down now. Lilly, Callie, you got supm to shayuh?"

Lilly quickly added, smiling at her offspring, "If chirren ready to settle, me too. Sun go down, I go down wid it. We talk mo in de morning."

Callie rose and walked to Lucas, kissing his cheek and rubbing his shoulder with one hand as she talked. "My brudda, you impressed me today. You got my highest praise fuh how you turned worriation to goodness. You didn't turn the other check, no sir, but you used your brain and strength to get your way with kindness. I'm a proud big sista how you kept yo family safe. You too, Douglass." She walked back to her place in the circle, brushing her nephew's cheek with her hand as she passed him.

Lucas acknowledged her love with a nod. "Please, Abram, give us a prayer to take us toward tomorrow."

Abram stepped forward to the moment. "We ask deah God that, jus as you looked down on disyuh fambly on dis day, that you look on every other righteous fambly with the same love and abiding protection. We know, fadda God, that however strong or wise we be, and you showed us the best strength and wisdom in our father heah on dis earth today, that we are nothin without you, and through you there always gonna be a bedda day. Amen."

And with that word of faith on what turned out to be a blessed day, the women and children retired for the night. Lucas and his sons decided to take shifts watching the dark water through the night.

Thursday, August 24, 1893

THE NEXT MORNING, TRUE TO THEIR WORD AND THEIR STORYTELLing ways, the family gradually assembled on the porch with their plates full of fruits, breads, and leftovers from the night before. The children, energized by a good night's sleep and breakfast, quickly disappeared down the porch steps to play, laughing loudly as they went. On the other hand…yesterday's conflicts with neighbors forced the adults to face the immediacy of racial strife in their lives.

Callie reached for the joy from the children's laughter, starting off the adult conversation with levity. "I got to say Lucas, the more my achin backside thought about yesterday, the more it asked me why I sat in a rowboat all afternoon, and then be in de line of fire last night?"

Lucas saw the mischief in her eyes and responded more seriously than Callie intended. "Got to say, at times I had the feelin that I might be lookin at supm I couldn't handle. I didn't have time fuh git you ladies down safe and still git ready fuh whatever. We didn't want no violence, so had to force em away. It wuk out jus fine."

"And what bout my back all day in a tree?"

"Aw, sista, you know you two had de bes time up dere, fa true. Don't even try fuh say yo back be huhtin."

Lilly's face showed worries that stayed with her through the night. "Lucas, you know how proud I am of you for standing up to those men. Please, next time you meet danger, leave our grandson out of it."

"Lilly, I knew if I called fuh food, dey ain gonna start nuttin. Even mo, I could tell dey wouldn't act if de boy was bringin it."

Callie added, "I know it felt safe to you, brudda, you are in the situation, but I'm with Lilly on keepin our babies from harm."

"I know it may sound strange. But I belieb bringin Robert out when I did help settle de whole thing down and keep ebbybody safe."

"I unnerstan, Lucas. You had to do what you thought right."

"Sista, das all you do when time come tuh act."

"Seein what you had to face from across the river, I got to say something on my mind."

"Speak, sista."

"You know what I'm seein bein back here at Oakheart? I'm seein more of the real life, and it ain lookin too good. Could be Lilly and

I are spendin too much time on what happened in the past and not enough on the real things goin on around here."

Lucas took a deep breath, looking to the water and then the soil before him. "Callie, honestly, de way tings be today mek me a lee down in de mouf. I been too glad tuh heah you and Lilly talkin bout progress we made since de war. It hep me rememba why fuh be grateful."

Callie persisted, "I got to say, the hate from your neighbors surprises me."

"Worl changin now real fas, fa true, jus like back in de wah, except backward. I still say, it right fuh you and Lilly tuh look back to our good days afta de wah. We should talk bout how we got from slave days tuh dis day. Hep us see ting more clear."

"I appreciate that, brudda. I want to heah more from you to bedda understand wha changes you been goin through."

"Ain special. We all dealin wid it." He looked into Callie's face, and their glance spoke to them both about the universality of being born with dark skin. Lucas shook his head from side to side. "So how far you ladies get wid de storytellin?"

"Brudda, we talked ourselves all de way to 1876."

"You talkin bout 1876 when the US Navy brought its biggest fleet right here to Port Royal Sound? When we got so much wuk tekin fish and crop to Navy boys and private boaters too? We couldn't keep up, we had so much wuk fuh do. Is that the 1876 we talkin bout? Or are we talkin bout 1876 when de damn election let people staat stealin our freedom away agin? Fuhgive me, Lawd!"

Lilly explained, "Well, Callie and me talked through the bedda days and yeahs after the wah, and we just now got to the point where bad changes start to happen. But we can talk more bout that when we not havin family time."

Lucas conceded, "Since we got Confederate men comin cross de riba wid guns on dey hip, I guess we bedda be honest bout folk who hate cause we hab daak skin. We gettin back to white men bein in chaage of ebbyting again, and it ain pretty."

"Dis where I'm not sure how much to say around our babies," Lilly cautioned.

Lucas asked, "De big babies? De boys, Sunny, and Flora June? Well, Douglass and Abram been in the middle of it—dey know wha dey be fightin fuh—Sunny and Flora June do, too."

"Maybe we save some talk of it for when the little ones aren't around."

Callie saw Jancy bounding onto the porch and offered, "Then we can talk about how good education has been for all our babies since freedom come. Right, Jancy?"

Jancy smartly asked, "What about the chirren right now?" And then she repeated the phrase, and then again, louder. To her great joy, Robert, who often sought to be the dignified child of the family, joined in. Their decibel level growing, the children were not to be ignored.

Lucas responded, "You two mekin too much noise. Go get my toolset fuh wuk on da scrap wood pile in de yard. You can use old screws and bolts and clamps and levels in my box." Before they could move, he leaned forward and said, with whispered enthusiasm, "Go mek supm de worl ain nebba seen befo." Their eyes opened wide at the prospect, and, turning quickly, they dashed down the steps.

Lucas saw their joy and was satisfied with his redirection. So, he turned back to his wife. "Lilly, I been wantin to say, last night you said Robert Smalls had no gun when he hep de rice workers in de fight wid de growers. I agree wid you in praise fuh how he walk between men ready tuh fight, and fa true, he went in with no gun fuh protection. But, honey, you know why he can act da way?" Lucas paused long enough to see that neither Lilly nor Callie were going to jump in. "He succeed doin wha he did dah day, and ebby day, cause he built his reputation wid de people and dey trust him. And it help him to be brigadier general of a state militia."

Callie added, "And he was serving his first term as a US Congressman then, too."

"Honey, I tink de peaceful way is de bes way ebby day." Then Lucas pointed east across the river. "But dem buckra boat boys, well, dey ain lookin fuh a relationship wid me, an dey don know bout my fine reputation." He looked to them for affirmation. Callie nodded, and Lilly's head sunk a bit. Lucas continued, "So, we gonna be prepared fuh what dey bring, and be ready tuh stand up tuh danger, and even do it wid mo fish and peach pie. But we gah fuh be ready all de time."

"Shhhhh! Husband, I am trying to protect all my men and babies and have them not stand into danger, ever! I only spoke bout de rice worker strike cause Robert Smalls did good work without havin to use a gun. That's all." Lilly looked up at him, fear combined with hope on her face as they sought to perfect their lectures for their offspring that could keep them safe in an increasingly threatening world.

Lucas responded quickly but gently, "And that is what I do too. Been always teachin my chirren when to stan up, who to stan up wid, why to take a stan, when not to stan into danger, as you say. Dere be a time to stan." He reached his arm around Lilly's shoulder. "Robert Smalls knew dis; how you tink he still alive today? Wha you tink happen if we not stan up last night?"

Lucas gazed out over the river. "I decided in all tings I gah fuh act base on wha I know fuh be true. Den I be ready to respond, smaat, skrong, and friendly-like. I'm mos sure Robert Smalls felt good when he be up wid de rice workers on the Combahee River fields, tryin to hep folk get pay in cash fuh de wuk. When de strike first started in May, Robert had to wade into groups of men ready to start shootin each odda. When de strike broke out again in September, he went out to Gardens Corner to stop anodda bunch a men with weapons ready fuh fight."

Callie just remembered, "You know, I saw him in Washington that same summer, but it was in July. I had been to a couple of his events since he came to Congress the year before, and he was kind to offer a chance to watch the House of Representatives meet, just like Harris Hewitt helped me and Sunny to do a few yeahs before, and just like General Wallace did, too. My, I was lucky sometimes.

"Well, there I am in the gallery lookin down to see our friend, Congressman Robert Smalls. The issue they are talkin about is whether or not to take United States troops out of the South. I hear his name, and the big voice of Robert Smalls starts to fill that amazing room. He tells Congress, No! The United States Army can't leave the South just yet, because there are so many people wantin to do harm, especially the Red Shirts militias—South Carolina's version of the Ku Klux Klan. He says the Red Shirts would 'make war on the government and on the freedman.' He says we need the US Army there to 'cut off those rotten parts all round South Carolina...which are troubling us.'"**

Lucas added, "Tha was mo den ten yeahs afta de war ovah. We still needin de troops fuh protection."

"Lucas, memba when de wah came to these islands bringing freedom from Massa Bowen?" Callie smiled at the memory. "Well, we worried every day bout what if de Union soldiers leave us alone without protection—what would happen to our people."

Lilly could not contain her passion. "Robert Smalls certainly told the truth to Congress. Startin later that summer, Lucas and me hear bad stories bout what be happenin to people, mostly Republican supporters of Mista Smalls, who want to go to meetings or try to speak fuh our freedom. Fa true, even though we all jus learnin about democracy and voting, I ain heard men be scaid to be a part of it befo that year when white men in South Carolina started comin in to folks' homes and churches to beat, and destroy, and threaten em if they try to vote."

** *history.house.gov/People/Detail/21764* [7]*Congressional Record*, House, 44th Cong., 1st sess. (18 July 1876): 4705. https://leefamilyarchive.com

"I talked to Robert Smalls afta de election," Lucas said. "He was happy he got elected fuh Congress again, but sad de Republican candidates got beat bad all ovah de state. He say de violence be wurs ebbywhere else. I tole him we ain feelin safe heah either."

"And that was with the US Army still here to protect us." Lilly continued to rage against the memories. "And you know what those Democrats did, the ones tryin to fight back against our freedom? Forget the beatings and violence for a minute."

Lucas asked, "Wha you say?"

"Yes, it was awful, but during those same months in 1876, they sent letters and reports around our island communities tellin folks how many hundreds of freedmen were switchin from the Republican Party to their party. It wasn't true, but they told folks it was—flat out lied bout how we people weren't supporting Robert Smalls. I'm still amazed that a liar thinks he can win people's favor. They won't evah get my vote if they tell outright lies and call em truths."

"So, Mama, Aunt Callie, Daddy," Abram spoke up tentatively, "you be teachin me things. You know me and my brudda an our wives be too young to know about dis. What happened bout keepin the Army here and in the rest of the South?"

Callie was ready for the question. "The whole country was divided between Republicans who supported freedmen like us and Democrats who wanted to stop the progress of black men...and women." Callie nodded to Lilly. "The national vote was in favor of the Democrat, Samuel J. Tilden. Yet, a deal got made that allowed the Republican candidate, Rutherford B. Hayes, to become president."

"What?" Douglass said. "I thought the vote decided who won."

Callie explained. "I learned all about it because the Grangers were very well connected in Washington circles. Even though most people voted for the Democrat, the Democrats, including some of em from South Carolina, gave their votes to Hayes in the strange process known as the Electoral College, and that made Republican Hayes the president."

"All right, my smart sista from Washington," Lucas asked impatiently, "why would de Democrats do dah?"

Callie took a deep breath. "Here's what is so bad about it for us—for all us people who been slaves and got to be free. The conniving Democrats, mostly former Confederates, said they would allow Hayes to become president if he agreed to take the United States military out of Southern states. And, sure enough, Hayes agreed, and then as president, in the spring of '77, he issued the order to do exactly that. United States soldiers, who had protected freedmen on these islands since 1861, were removed from here and from across the South."

Lilly said, "We feared, but couldn't even know back then, just how awful the results of that deal would become for all of us. I memba tryin to be hopeful. One night, talkin to Lucas, I saw the look in his eye—the doubt, the lack of belief." Lilly shook her head and wiped both eyes.

Lucas added, "I knew wha movin the troops would mean fuh our safety. Made me feel as bad as when my brother, BB, get killed. And then..." Lucas hesitated.

"What is it, Daddy?" Abram asked.

Callie urged, "Tell it, brudda."

"Right afta de president ordered US troops outa South Carolina, de Democrats in power arrest Congressman Robert Smalls, sayin he took bribes when he was state senator. Dey put him on trial, found him guilty, and sentenced him to shree yeahs in prison." Lucas then said, "And somehow he got out afta shree days, but they still try tuh keep him from goin back to his job in de Congress."

Lucas sighed heavily and shook his head. "Das de odda ting bout politics. Robert Smalls try to git supm done, so he talk wid one man dis week, den he meet wid mo men de next week, den he have a big meeting two month lada, and by next yeah he hope dey git to vote on it." Lucas looked around, utterly astounded. "How can anyone do de wuk an not be crazy from it?"

Lilly agreed, "Nobody say they ain crazy up in Washington."

He tried to laugh a little. "I say, Gawd mek me a fisherman, I throw line in wid hook, hook wid bait, soon fish come." Lucas clapped his hands, startling the listeners who weren't watching him. "When I be fishin and boatin people from one place tuh notha, hepin people sell dey food and dey fish, it all feels like we git supm done. But politics? Scary to me. People wukin to git nuttin done. I honor Mista Smalls, he be so excellent at getting wuk done wid and through odda people. I tink I bedda tuh wuk wid fish."

With that, Lucas stood. "They callin to me right now. And since you ladies took your sweet day out on de wada already, I bleib I do de same befo de afternoon heat get up too much. Sides, I got no time and mind fuh give to what old and new tricks de white man use fuh mek my life haad. Got to leave all dis worriation alone fuh now."

They smiled at his determination to soothe his soul with his favorite pastime. Callie watched her brother walk down to his dock. His sons went to check on their children. Lilly spoke confidently from their years of familiarity. "My husband knows when he needs to take a boat on the water."

"Lilly, I rememba always bein happy for Lucas, and maybe a little jealous, cause he could find what he always seemed to be looking for out there, at least for a little while."

"Yes, sista. The water gives Lucas his sense of purpose. He thinks the fish are waitin fuh him to git em in hopes he will feed em to his family and friends. That's the way he lives." She turned to Callie. "How we going to find our sense of purpose today."

Callie returned a blank stare until she burst out laughing, leaning into her brother's wife, as would lifelong confidantes. "Sista, I don't rememba asking myself that question in my life. I been actin with purpose as long as I can rememba, but I didn't have to plan too much for it. 'Gah fuh do dis, gah fuh do da. Shud do dis by den.' You know what? I have never been without supm to do."

Still chuckling, Lilly said, "Not to interrupt your thoughts, but, I just meant we need to get some food ready fuh this weekend—gonna be some hungry mouths at de table. Either that or I thought you might want to talk bout Sunny comin tonight."

"Whoa, Lilly, you say what you thinkin. Thank you, darlin. You know she's on my mind—wonderin how we gonna get through these days."

"Ain every day, a ten-year-old child gets to meet his mother for de first time."

Callie added, "...Ain every day a mother gets to hold her baby, now too grown up. And it sure ain every day that a mother needs to be forgiven by her daughter."

"No, Callie, don't be thinkin bout it that way. You know you did what you thought was right ten years ago. You thought you were saving your daughter's life and her baby's life, too. That young white man and his parents, and your daughter, created a situation where you had to act. That's all. Your family was threatened, and you protected em."

"You see it that way. I know it to be true. We will see what Sunny says."

Lilly spoke of the Sunny she helped raise. "She may have strong opinions on things, but she knows what direction she supposed to go. She knows the hard right from the easy wrong."

"Which means it might be a little excitin roun here for a day or two when she comes."

Lilly decided not to pursue it. "Since Sunny is expected by dinner, we won't have to guess much longer bout her reactions to learnin that she has a ten-year-old chile. Now, about that food, Callie."

Showing that family tendency to speak her mind quickly, Callie said, "I thought Nellie and Amanda were fixin some of their fine dishes for today."

"You right. They are. But you know what? We need more sweet potatoes—only twice as many as before."

"I know you ain askin me to take the children back to the fields?" Mocking offense, Callie turned and hollered, "Children! Everybody gather round. Boss Lilly got supm to say!"

Ever obedient, the children arrived within a minute, in various stages of readiness for whatever came next. When Grandmother Lilly called, they were seldom disappointed, and their creative Aunt Callie had brought new energy to their supple minds. Callie spoke first. "I called yo lovin Gramma 'Boss Lilly' cause she just gave me a task to do. But I need the help of smart children like you to get it done. And I already know that you can do this job really good."

The youngsters were so full of themselves that their Aunt Callie could hardly have pumped them up further.

"I smaat."

"No, I smaat."

"I mo smaat."

Callie turned to her sister-in-law and said, "Gramma Lilly?"

Noting that Callie said nothing about digging sweet potatoes out of the ground, Lilly realized the setup was complete and forged ahead. "Yes, you are good at this, and we need you now." She paused to look at each eager pair of eyes. "We need you to dig some more sweet potatoes with Aunt Callie."

Reaction was immediate and not overly positive. In fact, the best you could say about the childish muttering was that it was subdued. Robert, clearly pondering the request, asked, "I thought you need the help of smaat chirren?"

"Yeah." said Beanie, offering rare outward resistance. "Don't gah fuh be smaat fuh dig taters. Gah fuh be smaat fuh ketch fish."

Callie said in a monotone, appearing not to address them directly. "Smart children know when to say, 'Yes, Gramma, I will help you with the chores.'"

Since they indeed were smart children, they slowly resolved to help, except for Beanie, who said, "Gramma, kin I ketch fish fuh fambly and not dig taters? Please..." Permission was granted.

With tools gathered and attitudes adjusted to the task, Callie's work crew was, once again, hiking down the lane. Callie started singing an old work song, making up verses as she walked. "I be happy, Aunt Callie be home..." A little laughter followed as the children repeated her sing-song words. Then Jancy shouted out, while sprinting just ahead, "I be happy, to run to de fiel..." And Robert lead the group response. Saxton, who had been holding his great-aunt's hand all the way down the lane, projected his little boy voice above all: "I be happy, Aunt Callie like me!" The response was loud and enthusiastic as the crew arrived, laughing, at the field they had worked. Yet, looking down at the long row of potato roots waiting to be pulled was discouraging.

Callie persisted, "I be happy when de taters are pulled; eat em tonight when dey be so good." All the children joined in the verse and began to dig into the field.

Inertia overcome, Callie challenged the small diggers to use what they learned a few days before and to be smart about how they tried to fill their buckets. As she cut one free, Callie sang again, "I be happy, tater lookin at me."

Soon the scrabbling was on, up one row and down another, some sweet spots found, each child having dug up at least one quickly. A small voice sang, "I be happy to put in de pot." In just minutes of hard work—Callie and the children, singing boisterously, "I be happy to eat em up"—the buckets were filled. The children stood at their collections proudly, some breathing hard.

"Children," Callie said gently, "you see how good you feel? Don't ever be afraid of a little hard work. Makes you feel good to do things for yourself and others. Get good food and earn a little money too, maybe." She looked at them, holding out both arms and sweeping the field. "But don't ever forget there was a time, right yuh, where yo grammas and grampas were forced to work haad, as slaves, no money for the work, no smiles on their faces, no freedom in their hearts."

The words echoed on the field. Then Callie said, "A wonderful old man named Hezikiah drew his last breath right yuh, thirty-two yeahs ago, while he was pickin taters. He was eighty-two ears old. Let's say, 'Tank ya, Mista Hezikiah,' and then take a nice walk back."

When they left the field, as their voices and lips allowed, each said a form of "Tank ya, Mista Hezikiah."

"I love yuh, babies!" Callie sang.

Just like before when they worked the potato field, they stopped by the cool waters of Callie's reflecting spot. She let them climb out on the branches with only the admonition to "be careful." Robert did slide off one branch and fell five feet to the ground but bounced up laughing. Even though it was low tide as they scrambled about on the limbs, a fall from branches farther out meant a splash in the water rather than a plop in the mud.

There were no more falls, allowing Callie to worry less about the children and more about the evening ahead. She was squinting into bright yellow reflections off the creek when she saw a bateau in silhouette out on the river as it headed toward the Oakheart dock. When her eyes adjusted and the boat moved just beyond the brightest reflections, she could see two figures, Sunny working the oars in a final authoritative pull and Flora June standing in the bow, reaching out to secure the dock rope.

Callie announced, "Now, chirren, I want you to be careful comin off your branches. It's time to go home."

"Why, Aunt Callie?" Robert quickly asked.

"Keep comin down now, and when you are all here with me, I'll tell...everyone here? Sunny and Flora June are on the dock." The children started to run, but Callie stopped them. "Rememba your taters." Bobby lifted his heavy sack and ran ahead, anxious to meet his mother.

Sunny and Flora unloaded six small boxes and then two more the size of a large hatbox. A long slender box remained in the boat. They lifted it out carefully, with coordination borne of many hours working together on land and water.

By the time the boxes were resting on the dock, Bobby had raced to join Beanie, the fisherman, who had three small ones on a line to offer for the dinner. Their mother gave each a large box which they handled with extraordinary care, for they knew that good box carrying led to good boxed-cake eating. Their noses sniffed what their eyes would see inside, one of the peachiest cakes ever made.

As Jancy, Robert, and Saxton rushed into the yard, Lilly redirected them to the well to wash off the sticky, stubborn smears of creek mud. This allowed the landing party time to walk up the embankment steps to the yard.

Sunny and Flora June warmly greeted the children. Lilly shouted, "We're so glad you are back!" as cheers from the children rose and fell. Despite the busy joyfulness, Callie realized that Sunny continued to stare at her. Callie's words of welcome, "We've been anxious to see you again" told more truths than she intended. The arrival group moved up toward the house as Sunny lagged behind, continuing to look directly at her mother.

Callie looked back with concern. "Are you all right, Sunny? You look like you worked too hard comin down de river."

Callie moved tentatively to embrace Sunny, who stepped away but still stared at her mother. "Oh yeah, I wuk pretty haad rowin all de way from Beaufort gainst an incomin tide. That's how bad I wanted to be here, Mama, just like I promise. I come yuh dis evenin, cause I know you got supm you wantin to say to me. Yes, I certainly want to be here to hear the news. It surely must be something!"

It was clear to Callie that Sunny was intentionally switching from Gullah words like "yuh" and "supm" to the standard English "here" and "something." Then she was saying each English word with perfect pronunciation, as her mother had taught her while they were together in Washington. Whatever her point, Sunny was undeniably angry. "Calm down, honey," said Callie as Lilly, watching from the porch steps, turned to follow the children inside, shaking her head slowly.

Sunny declared, "I am calm, Mama!" With that, she stared at her mother with a look that only her mother could have taught her, just as Mama Ruth had taught Callie fifty years ago.

Callie began to suspect that Sunny knew her mother's secret. "Let's go on down to the dock, Sunny."

"Oh, Mama. I'm not sure I can wait any longer to hear the stories you been waiting to tell. Fact is, I can't. Got questions bustin outta me. You did what with my baby? Why did you make me think I didn't have a chile? You didn't tell me my baby was alive. Why? My baby didn't get to know his mother. Why?" Sunny walked briskly away from her mother and down to the dock. When her mother followed a few seconds behind, Sunny continued, "And now you show up heah ten years later and go tell the man that made the baby before you have the guts or respect or love to tell me? Don't I deserve to know that I have a baby, Mama? That I had a live baby?" Sunny began to sob. "Oh, Mama, Mama, I said I would not be this way but..." She sank against the dock railing. "Mama, how could you? How could you live with it?"

"I respect you got to say all dis to me." Empathetic and open to whatever direction Sunny needed to go, Callie asked calmly, "You want me to answer you at all?" Nothing more came from Sunny, her silent anguish suppressed by deep, short breaths. "I had to protect you at all cost. The look of race hate in that man's eye ten years ago made me know I got to protect my own."

"What about my own?" Sunny looked up. "Ain my baby my own? Not yown?"

"I was scared that awful man, the father of your...friend, would try to kill you the first time he saw you in Beaufort with the baby. And you rememba, you promised me that you would live free with that child no matta what." Sunny dropped her steady gaze at her mother. "You were the one I had to protect first. I didn't know your baby, though God knows I wanted to. First, I just wanted you and that baby to both live. Daughter, fa true, I did it for you."

"How you expect me to believe you? You been lyin about it fuh ten years?"

"I ain been lyin. I let a sleepin dog lie down until we could deal with it. I had no reason to think it was safe down here in South Carolina for your child to come back home, especially the way people be actin out their hate, just like slave days before freedom come. And, you made it clear to me that you had no intention of coming up to Washington with your baby. Now that I see your ongoing relationship with Brent, I understand."

"Mama, even if I believe your story, why you did it, how can you not tell me about it from that day to this?"

"The threat against you lived on in my mind right up to the minute I talked to Brent Landon three days ago. I had no way of knowin, so I had to see him first. If he is still the hateful man that scared me into believin he would kill you and the baby, then I may not have told you at all. That's how scared I was til now. Ain nobody more relieved than me that he has seen the light about his parents' ungodly ways."

"And that raises another thing. How can you visit this man and not tell me, since I been with him all this time?"

"Honey, daughter." Callie paused to digest the news. "How am I supposed to know who you spendin time with? I was pretty sure he had no intention of ever seein you again. You ain been tellin me much about your life. How am I to know about him and you? He didn't tell me when I talked with him. I didn't know that you took up with this same man until just now when you told me."

Sunny emitted a sigh of recognition and looked for eye contact with her mother. "You got a point there, cause we ain been knowin each odda's business most of our lives, have we?"

"No, my daughter. I ain been writin much—you ain been no prize writer either. At least I wrote to your Aunt Lilly to tell huh what I was doin so she could tell you."

"Well, Mama, I know that's not the best we can do."

"Oooh, Sunny, you sound like me when I'm tryin to teach somebody supm. Listen to that. My chile talkin to me like a chile." She looked up at Sunny and then smiled. "You right, you know. We could have been and should have been doin better for each other. Partly, me comin home now is to find a way back to bein close with you."

"You off to a pretty tough start, Mama. I been on that river rowin fuh nearly an hour to see you Sunday night, and when I get heah I hear all this history talk. Meanin no offense, but how bout dis chile of mine? How bout wha happenin to me?" Sunny started tearing again. "What about my history, Mama?"

Callie realized there was no more room in either of them for conflict. Her daughter's plea moved her straight back to the child. "Let's change it right now and talk about your boy! He's been in Savannah."

Sunny moved from victim to mother. "He's safe? He's a he? He's comin home? Whose home? When?"

And they both managed to laugh a little. "So much to tell. If the connections are successful, I have a responsible man, a friend of your Uncle Will, pickin him up and bringin him here. They left Monday after I talked to Brent. Will's man said he and his crew should get back by tomorrow."

"Mama, you mean I may see my boy tomorrow? Mama?"

But Callie was distracted by something on the water, in about the same location where she and Lilly had seen a rowboat coming across the river the night before. "Lucas!" She reached a protective arm to Sunny, who clasped her hand as they moved up the steps from the dock. "Lucas!"

As he hurried down from the porch, Lucas began instructions. "Get on inside now, ladies. So glad you're here, Miss Sunny Day; take your mama to safety. Douglass, Abram, get on either side of the porch with your rifles and wait for my signal to do anything."

"Only one man in the boat, Daddy," Abram reported as Lucas moved rapidly to his position atop the bluff. He walked down the steps to the dock as the boat drew near.

Waving from well out on the water, that man shouted, "It's all right. I'm comin to visit, comin to be peaceful like."

Lucas walked onto the dock, and as the boat pulled up, he saw no weapons. So, he leaned in and pulled the visitor onto the dock. "Young man, what brings you back heah?"

"You rememba? I was one of the men last night, stayed back and didn't have a gun then neither."

"I rememba. You wearin de same shirt." Lucas gave nothing away, including his curiosity.

"Some of my people feel bad about what happened last night."

"You mean you getting shot at?"

"Nah, no, sir. Bad that my uncle keeps botherin you and yours."

"Seem to me I gah fuh know why you were heah wid em las night?"

"We, my daddy and me, didn't know what he was gonna do when he told us to come with him. We don't think it's right to be worryin another man and his family, no matter what color he is."

Lucas looked on, wondering where this conversation was going.

"Anyway, my sista and me decided, and my mama agreed, we could bring ovah some of our crops for you. Notice you ain got corn dis yeah, so I got some bushel baskets full, and my momma made some cornbread she said I could bring."

"What your daddy and uncle think bout dis?"

"They ain know nuttin. My daddy be all right. My uncle, he's still mad, you know, bout the war, Yankees winnin, the Confederates losin, and…"

Having left the sentence hanging, Lucas finished it for him. "And slaves bein free."

"Well, yeah, he don't believe in that. But my mama say trash come in all color."

Shaking his head in wonder, Lucas offered, "She right."

The visitor jumped back in his boat and lifted out the baskets of corn. "Well, I got to go, but I wanted to ask. We need a new boat; my uncle been wrong to try take one if it ain his. My mama says, if we pay you and if I get to help work on it, we sure would like to buy one you make at a fair price. I truly want to help, cause I want to learn how to build a boat."

"How old are you, young man?"

"I'm bout to be fifteen."

"Well, come back annodda day and we talk some bout makin a boat. Maybe my boy Douglass can teach you a little supm."

"I will, yes, sir, I will come back next week. Oh, and I wanted to say, I'm sorry."

"What's your name?"

"William," the boy shouted as he pushed off and jumped into his boat.

"Well, William, you a credit to yo family."

"Thank you."

"We have a William in our family, too. He be jus bout your color." William didn't speak again, but Lucas detected confusion on his face as he began to pull on his oars.

Lucas hadn't noticed that Lilly, Callie, and Sunny had come down toward the dock and witnessed the last half of the conversation. When he turned to see them watching, he said, "The Lord works in mysterious ways, and I just witnessed something like a miracle."

Lilly responded, "Such a brave thing to do—to reach out across the water, and with such kindness, in opposition to his uncle's way."

Sunny added, "Actions by young folk give me some hope."

"Yes, they do," Callie affirmed. "And that includes you, too."

They were watching William row across the river when it began to pour. They had been distracted by their visitor when the small storm approached from the southwest, screening out the hot afternoon sun. Lucas and Lilly moved with haste up the porch steps and into the shelter of the big house. Callie and Sunny joined hands and stood on the bluff, motionless. The rain drenched them before passing into the river where it caught up with William as he reached the far bank.

Callie and Sunny walked down the steps to the dock and sat, dunking their feet in the river and watching the storm until it disappeared.

"I still have bunches of knots in my gut, and it feels like you caused em, Mama."

"I did, honey, and I'm sorry. Maybe there were other ways to avoid the danger I felt."

"I don't know. Right now, at least, I got to think about bein a mother. You tellin me the truth that this ten-year-old boy, my little boy, is comin here tomorrow? From Savannah?"

"Yes, daughter. The family he stayed with for the last few years came on hard times and had to move to a one-room place. They wrote me tellin of their problem, and I asked them to let me make some arrangements. I told your Uncle Will about it, and he said he would have help for me here in Beaufort, and he did."

"Mama, I got so many questions."

"Me, too," said Callie cautiously. "I didn't tell Brent about any plans, since I didn't know you two were involved, and before we go on about that, can I ask, Sunny, are you sure you want to raise this boy with Brent? You think that is the best thing to offer the boy?"

"Mama, that is too hard a question for you to ask right now."

"It's just that in these crazy days with so much bad change happenin, you got to think bout people's skin color."

"Mama, when ain we been made to tink bout dah?"

"I'm talkin awareness, Sunny. Seein where problems might come from."

"Oh Mama, I'm gonna be gentle heah. You ain been livin my days, one at a time, to try to tell me about the right time to do things in my life. I know you ain got that knowledge, but I respect your opinion. And, I know you really not tryin to tell me nothin bout race and pickin a man to be with. You know as well as me that it depend on de man. And no, jus like I ain askin about what you been doin with your body de last twenty yeahs, you ain gonna be askin that bout me and mine. But since you are askin, I can tell you this much. Just like with you probably, I had my chance to love people with different color skin, dark and light. I'm glad for it and couldn't claim no difference. But right now, this man who is a light-skin man, this man who you now say is the father of my son, well, he is pretty important to me. And it is very important to me how good a man he is. And the color of his skin is not."

"I'm jus sayin you never know when the next surprise gonna come. Don mean to be sayin I know best. I just say you always got to be ready to be surprised, again."

"Mama, I know. I know it now from my own life. Don forget, I was born a slave, too. And though I didn't understand then, one of the biggest changes ever for me was freedom. Now, you brought me the biggest surprise, and it's about a life, my child's life."

"Well, honey, if you think about it, what happen heah is due to race hate, fa true. I ain sayin bout the young man—his parents had the problem and they made it his, and yours, and mine. From what I see, he is on his way to fixin it, even before we had a talk in town on Monday. Once I found out he a good man, I was proud to tell him he had a child, cept that I shoulda told you first."

"Do you really like him, Mama?"

"Yes, I do, and I let him know that. Even before I knew he was your man. I knew what he said ten years past came from his parents, not from him."

"Um, hmm. That's beautiful, Mama. Thank you fa sayin so."

"I ain never stop carin bout what be bes for you, honey. You my only child, my only daughter. I ain been around you enough, and I don't know you like I should, to be your mama." Unsuccessfully, Callie tried to wipe her eyes without Sunny seeing.

Sunny said, "Mama, I love you too much to let you go on not knowin me bedda. I wanna show you what the heart you put in me feels." Sunny stood up, took her mama's hand, and led her to the house, where she reached up under the front porch to get a lantern. "Follow me please." They walked over the wet ground in the yard and out behind the house about one hundred steps to an old shed, used years before to store meats.

Callie said, "You know I ain hungry fuh meat."

Sunny could only smile at what her mother didn't know. She lit the lantern, pushed the shed door open, and began to show the walls of the shed, all four adorned with paintings.

"What? Sunny! Oh!"

Sunny held her lantern so that light shown onto the first painting to the right. In it, a young African girl with natural hair holds her arms outstretched to the sea. Beneath it, neatly lettered, a word: "Waiting."

Next around the wall, Sunny stopped in front of a painting a little smaller than the first and framed—a view of the ocean from the beach with city buildings in the distance resembling the skyline of Washington. "Oh, Sunny! This is the view we saw the day we crossed the Potomac River and hiked up the hill to Robert E. Lee's house in Virginia. You remember?"

The next three paintings, all smaller, were of fruits and vegetables, and the last one an overflowing piecrust with steam rising from it. Callie followed the light cast by Sunny's lantern, her mouth agape. "Uh-oh," Callie said. "I want to eat that pie."

Sliding around the far wall, Sunny led her mother by the arm to the next painting. Callie caught her breath and covered her mouth. She was seeing small dark children so skinny that their ribs showed, with their hands reaching out to the viewer, the whole image cast in shades of blue.

"Sunny, my lovely daughter. You have such talent, and even more heart. Can you ever forgive me for not knowing?"

Sunny smiled slightly without showing her teeth and turned her lantern light toward the third wall in the room. On it, Callie saw herself. "No one has ever painted a picture of me," she said, mesmerized by the image. "I got my uniform on—a black skirt and long-sleeved blouse with white apron—and I got papers in my hand. Look at that room full of hospital patients." Callie leaned against the wall near the painting. "Oh, girl, young lady, my daughter, I can't say."

The lantern moved on. Clearly shown was a full representation of Brick Church, where Penn School started and where Sunny, as a seven-year-old, was first called a "scholar." A line of young people is coming from the church door beneath an overhanging American flag. The title under the painting, neatly written, said, "Scholars Out." Callie puzzled over it but did not question.

Next was another portrait of Brick Church in a frame the same size. The light showed adults, lined up to go into the church, with decorations of red, white, and blue bunting hanging everywhere. At first, Callie did not discern the connection. The first painting showed students leaving the church; the second image showed adults entering. Callie saw that the second painting was titled, "Voters In."

"Oh, again, this is too much, Sunny. The two paintings are titled 'Scholars Out' and 'Voters In'—I would never dream of painting anything like this." As she looked in wonder, Callie put her arm around her daughter's waist. "You are so smart to make those thoughts connect." Wavering slightly, Callie leaned into Sunny. "I got to sit."

"Just three more, Mama."

On the fourth wall, the first image was a black and white sketch, framed, showing a babe in arms. Though the lines were inexact, the shapes seemed to be young Callie and a very young Sunny. Tears burst from Callie, uncontained, in such a torrent that the artist moved quickly to hug her mother. "Mama, it's hard for you to know me, you been gone so much. These pictures tell part of the story you maybe missed."

They moved together as Sunny held up her light. Callie immediately saw the likeness of her father faintly in the upper corner of the painting looking down on a woman in a nursing pose at the bedside of a patient, with a long row of beds yet to be visited. "Is that...my father?"

Sunny nodded. "I always knew he was lookin down on us."

Callie moved on reluctantly, as Sunny led her to the final image. It was a young woman, Sunny, holding just a blanket, emptiness in its folds. Callie gasped. "Sunny, it's too good, it hurts. Thank you, but I must leave now. Oh, daughter, how I love all you have become."

And on an easel, the lantern briefly lit an incomplete painting, seemingly a portrait of Callie, with regal bearing, waving to a crowd of persons leaving the hospital, each smiling back at her as they departed. The background around Callie was not filled in yet. Then the light was gone from the easel and focused on the door.

Outside the shed, Callie looked back and gestured to it. "You are wonderful. I have looked at you many times, still too few, but I feel that I have never seen you as I do now. You are so many good things."

Resting her head on her mother's shoulder, Sunny smiled. "And, according to your report about my boy, I'm about to become supm else."

SECTION THREE

Chapter 9

FRIDAY, AUGUST 25, 1893

"GOOD MORNING, GOOD MORNING!" CALLIE AND SUNNY REPEATED cheerfully as they walked down the stairs, through the house, greeting family, and out onto the porch. Sunny stood quietly with a dreamy smile as Callie raised her voice slightly to ask those still lingering in the house. "I wonder, can we get everybody together this beautiful morning? If you are awake and fed or just now eatin, can we just gather roun, please?"

Baffled, the family began assembling. Amanda called Abram and the boys, still rubbing sleepy eyes, from their room. Douglass and Jancy had already walked over from their house, leaving Nellie at home with baby Nichelle. Flora June had just completed early morning deliveries of fresh pies to Oakheart customers with the help of her boys—they were finishing breakfast on the porch when Callie and Sunny summoned the surprise family meeting. Sunny hugged Flora June as Lilly ushered Lucas out to the porch, a look of anticipation on her face and confusion on his.

The family, eyes fixed on Callie and Sunny, realized that the deep stress between them upon Sunny's arrival the night before had diminished.

They puzzled over the cure as mother and daughter stood with arms around each other, glistening eyes, and barely suppressed smiles.

Callie spoke first. "We have some news. Today is a big day for our family."

Sunny continued, "We gonna get a new fambly memba. Well, not new exactly, he's my boy."

Jancy screamed, "What?"

Robert said, "Where yo boy been, Cousin Sunny?"

Callie answered first. "Well, let me try to tell it. When he was born ten years ago, he wasn't breathin, and we thought he was dead, and we told Sunny he died. Turned out though, he had a problem so that he had to go away, and the problem was so tough it took nearly ten years to fix. Sunny didn't know until this week that he could come back home!"

Sunny, as a practical new mother-to-be, actually answered Robert's question. "A man hired by our Uncle Will gonna bring him up from Savannah today sometime. So, if I'm jus a little crazy, you know I'm too excited. We all get to meet my son, startin today."

That rapid set of facts was received by the family at different levels of understanding. The youngsters jumped up and danced around. The menfolk looked thoroughly confused. When Lucas raised a finger and started to ask a question, Lilly stopped him cold with quick and exaggerated throat clearing. Abram and Douglass took a cue from that. Amanda knew not to ask, seeing the look of joyful concern on Lilly's face.

Jancy was not deterred. "Sunny, you ready fuh be a good mama?"

"Yes, baby. My mama taught me all bout mother's love, so I already know supm. I'm ready to learn more. You want to help me, Jancy?"

"What you wan me fuh do?"

"You just crack yo teeth when you see me and my boy." At that, Jancy smiled broadly, while accelerating down the porch steps to the yard.

Robert stayed behind to ask, "You say he's ten yeah old?" Receiving a smiling nod, Robert said, "I wanna hep him when he git heah. Aunt Sunny, you tink maybe he hep me, too?"

"We will all be workin togedda, Robert." Sunny received Robert's youthful query with a whole new perspective, motherhood reborn. "I love your ideas fuh hep each odda."

Amanda rose and, taking Robert's hand, led her family back into the house, stopping with Sunny for a close embrace. Abram lingered long enough to offer his cousin whatever help she needed for her boy. After Douglass followed Jancy and the twins down to the dock, Flora June, with a grin on her face, walked over to Sunny. Soon they came together like magnets, rocking in their hug until Flora June lifted Sunny up and whirled her around. "Little Mama, your boy comin heah today. I been prayin fuh him each day since you told me dis might happen. Is he de same age as my twins?"

"He's Robert's age." Sunny beamed. "He gonna have bruddas to run wid him."

Flora June danced off the porch, eagerly following her sons.

Lucas remained silent, still seated at the table with Lilly. Without looking at her, he leaned toward Callie with a smile on his face that didn't match the furrows on his brow. "My, my...some secret been kep roun yuh."

"Uncle Lucas—" Sunny started to explain, before Callie interrupted.

"Brudda man, let me explain some things." She looked to Sunny and then to the river, flowing out on a strong northerly breeze. "I won't be able to say I'm sorry enough times to my Sunny fuh what she just found out. Because someone threatened my girl, and her baby, back ten years ago, it seemed to me the only thing I could do to protect my Sunny and to protect her chile at the same time was to take that baby away from here. I was too scared to think what else to do cause the threats from that family seemed strong and real."

"Da mek some sense, Callie. Now, bout de threats. Flora June just said she found out a few days ago. From you, Sunny?"

Sunny explained, "Well, I told her what I learned from Brent."

"Brent?" Lucas was still confused and newly energized by the pursuit of information.

Callie and Sunny started to respond simultaneously. "Brent is my friend in Beaufort," Sunny said as Callie stammered, "I met Brent... when I was trying to find Sunny."

Sunny clarified, perhaps. "So, Brent learned about this from Mama when she visited him Monday, and then he told me."

"I tink I wan know how you know dis Brent person, Callie, but de question might lead to ansas..." Lucas hesitated as he watched Sunny and Callie. "Ansas I might hafta tink long an haad fa like."

Callie swallowed, looked to Sunny, and started to speak as Lucas continued, "You tellin me Brent is de man you know today, an he de man who threatened you ten yeahs ago, Sunny? Ain I right?"

They could both see that Lucas was assembling his facts into more questions. Sunny, a stronger woman than either her uncle or mother knew, asserted herself. "On this busy good mornin, the day when my son be comin home, that be enough bout me and my man." Redirecting the conversation as if she were steering a wayward child, Sunny declared, "I'm too nervous bout my boy comin home to me. I love you all, and want to share my joy, but I ain wantin mo questions bout how it came to be right now." To ensure her intended effect, Sunny said, "So, last night when I came up and changed the evening fuh ebbybody, what were you all doin?"

Lilly, with her quick response, helped Sunny change topics. "We been havin fun with the chirren and eatin too much. Mostly, yo mama and me been talkin bout her life—makin notes for her book. We talkin bout big things that happened up in Washington and not so big things that happened down yuh on deese islands."

Callie added, "Seems like when we start talkin bout some 'historic' things, we end up sayin how it affects lives of real people—like how the election for president in '76 caused the US Army to leave the South and take away our military protection."

Lucas, trying not to be offended that his interrogation was cut short, offered, "An if all de history talk ain excitin enough, we got some good an bad ting happenin wid de neighbors cross de riba. Das what we been doin...talkin bout de past an tryin to live each day."

"I liked the way that young man talked to you yesterday, Unca Lucas. Mama told me how you offered him fish and peach pie the day befo when they came to our dock wid guns on dey hips." Sunny enjoyed the moment in her imagination, laughing. "Reminds me of some young white men who came up to our table lookin at our pies. I tol em how fruit and vegetables grow on deese islands an we put em in our pies. They questioned what 'a gal' could know bout crops and such tings." Sunny looked around at her family audience, anticipating. "They did not know who they talkin to. I said, 'I'm proud to be one of the first people freed from bein in slavery in the United States! Happened way back in 1861 when the Union military took ovah deese islands!'" Her family stirred with pleasure on hearing the origins of their freedom.

Sunny held up her hand. "And then, the nastiest one of them said, sneering at me, 'I knew there was somethin about talkin to you I didn't like.' Rather than say supm nasty back to they evil selves, I said, while gettin a cup, 'We also have a special today on sweet tea. It go perfect wid yo sour personality. An ifn you don have enough money, I reckon I could give it to hep yo problem.' And I said all dah wid a nice smile."

And then, eager to reach out to her revered uncle and to reestablish their status, Sunny said, "Unca Lucas, you would have loved to heah an old man in Beaufort talk bout what a great man Robert Smalls was."

"Is!" Lucas responded.

"Is! You right, fuh true. Anyway, I could tell as I watched him, de old man knew Robert Smalls well and had defended him against the false charges and all else." As Sunny spoke, she hitched up her skirt to look like pants, pushed her hair up under her oversized hat, picked up the old cane by the door, bent down, and leaned on it, assuming the posture, somehow, of an elderly man.

Callie, mouth agape, watched her daughter transform herself. Lilly and Lucas began to smile. Apparently, they had seen Sunny "act up" before.

Sunny continued. "Let me try to tell you wha it like to vote fuh Robert Smalls, tuh represent me in Sout Calina an den up in Washington.

"Fus, I know de man, met him, talk wid him, look in his eyes and he into mine. Feel like he gonna do wha he say. Gonna hep we people mek progress in deese parts. Was ebbyting he done tuh git de vote always perfek? No. Hab ebbyting done by de white man tuh get vote been perfek? No, and agin no! Has ebbyting done tuh us by de US Govmint afta freedom com been perfek? No. But I know Mista Smalls is tryin to do wha he says he gah fuh do. He git folk togedda to support him and his ideas. So, if Mista Smalls git a crowd togedda, ain no different den any white politician eber done. You can quote me on dah as a natural fact."

Sunny paused to scratch under her hat and hoist her trousers like any old man would.

"De real confusin ting I try fuh figuh be how da buckra man came tuh be in chaage ebbyting all ovah agin? How come dah be? Din we git de vote? Ain it in de Constitution of the United States dah we hab de right fuh vote? How deese boys try fuh tek supm away thirty yeah afta thousands of men died in de wah fuh mek African men and oomen and chirren free. 'Free' mean many ting, but fuh me, ih mean ebby man git to vote. Women need fuh vote, too. We be skrong people if dah be so. Simple as dah."

When she stopped, there was silence as her audience thought about the message. Pointing toward Sunny, Lucas said, "That man talks good sense. Too bad folk don wanna live by wha he say."

Callie couldn't stay serious another minute. "That man," pointing to the figure in the large hat still leaning on a cane, "is my daughter. Girl, when did you learn to do that? Last night I learned that you are a skilled painter. Today I see you act—an actor talkin sense through huh character." Smiling all the way to a hug with Sunny, Callie said, "Daughter, you are supm else."

Lilly reflected, "Sunny, my beautiful niece, you so good at bein that old man, you got me thinkin again about all the hate Robert Smalls faces every day, knowin people round deese parts be wantin tuh see him dead. You know he started that Republican party right here in Beaufort after the war? Mmmm-hmmm, Robert Smalls and some other men. It was the party in charge til Confederates grabbed power back afta the 1876 elections."

Lucas also was stirred up by memories carrying him back. "De damn Redshirts already killed six of our leaders tryin to git elected—all black men, all Republicans, killed. And dey scaid off voters all across de state. Folk jus wanna be free and vote, jus like govmint promise."

Lilly had picked up her notebook and was scribbling furiously— she looked up to see everybody watching her. "I'm makin notes on Callie's outline afta what I hear just now."

Callie added, "And down heah, I'm learnin from you all, it seems like white men are gettin to do whatever they want to take freedom from the black man."

Lucas asserted, gently: "Well, I ain wantin to add mo strife dis breezy monin, but I got supm to say bout that. I see dis wid my own two scaid eye. Befo de '78 election, Robert Smalls aks me fuh tek people to a politics meetin up on de mainland. We have two big rowboats and a barge in tow, full of people. Take em up tuh Bull Creek landin, where dey ketch wagons tuh de meetin. When I get there, saw so many people under these big old oak trees. I see Robert Smalls down front, talkin wid ebbybody, lookin like tings bout ready to start, when we hear dis noise comin up from de little town. Horses, hundreds of em, wid de riders in red shirts, swarm into de grove, smashin where all de people be laughin and talkin jus befo. De horses knock ovah tables of food and trampled on people's sittin places. De men on de horses use dey whips to strike men on dey head, tryin to start a fight, but Robert Smalls said, 'Don't give em wha dey want.'

"Den I hear words of de leader, a colonel, dey say. He get in Robert's face, demandin tuh speak. He say if Robert Smalls speak, den he gonna speak or else watch out. Smalls said no, he ain plan tuh speak, and no, dey ain no meetin. And by Smalls decidin to tek a step back, de Redshirts finish actin evil an went away." Shaking his head, Lucas stood up, "Lawd, I learn too much dah day. I was too close to too many angry white people wid guns. Dey carry a mean look in dey eyes and dey stop our meetin, darin we stand up to em. One friend I know get beat so bad he ain wake up fuh days."

"I know if Aunt Lilly wasn't writing so much," Sunny added, nodding toward her aunt, "she would want somebody to say that, by keepin a cool head, Robert Smalls kept a lot a folk safe dah day."

"Yes, indeed, my lovely niece!" Lilly looked up from her notetaking. "You right though. Sometime bein a hero means steppin back. Can't say it enough."

"Yes, she could, say it enough, I mean." Lucas was quick to express himself with a joke. "See wha you started, Miss Sunny Day, bein yo old man self?"

"Unca Lucas, I'm glad you stop helpin wid politics." Sunny reached out to grab his hand.

"Yes, brudda, it's sad to heah what you and so many more went through when the change came fifteen years ago, and it scares me to hear about things happenin now."

Lilly had to add, "Let Robert Smalls's peaceful way that day be a lesson to us all."

Lucas responded directly. "Don't you tink dah when I give de buck-ra from cross de riba fishes an a peach pie dah I acted in de peaceful way like Robert Smalls?"

"Yes, my husband."

"All right den."

Abram declared, as he and Amanda joined the conversation again, "I know you a smaat man, Daddy, but dah was one of yo bes days. And funny...," he said, jostling his wife.

Sunny joined the praise. "You did the right thing, Uncle. And so did Robert Smalls. I still cain believe they arrested him when he won his seat in Congress again. Still mek me mad."

Lilly recalled how she counseled Sunny to hold in her anger. "You worked to get him elected and got so upset."

"Sure did."

"And you believed in how democracy was supposed to work?" Lilly asked.

"Right up to that time. And then I stop, specially when de new government of mostly white folk started doin wrong things again. They said that people on St. Helena Island couldn't raise their own tax money to pay for their own schools. I didn't understand how people could be so mean to the children—to deny them books and schoolin."

Callie clapped her hands and exclaimed, "That's my daughter."

Sunny continued, "We knew we needed an education, if we sup-posed to grow up and be good citizens. Everybody knew that."

Lilly asserted, "I hate to say this, but the men that made those de-cisions didn't want us to get educated. Jus like the men that ride horses to whip people and keep them from voting—they didn't want us to have our right to choose our leaders."

Around the porch, spirits were down, some shaking their heads. No one spoke until, true to form, Lucas interrupted the dour mood he had helped create.

"Dah mek me laugh even in de face of it. Dey don want us to get education. Dey don't want us to vote. Dey want us to be propaty, not people. Wha mek me laugh is, not only we be free, and we get education, but Supreme Court say we git tuh keep our propaty. In that tough year, 1878, de court say we be de owners of de land we bought back in de wah. Even while some so busy treatin Robert Smalls and de res of us so bad, de Supreme Court say we have de right to dis land we bought wid our own money."

Lilly said, "Thanks, Lucas, fuh seein de good in it. An again I say, 'Thank you, Robert Smalls, for takin our case all de way to de top.' We keep our land, and we be grateful fuh de victories we git. Yes, we are!"

Others were adding their thoughts when the conversation was drowned out by a ruckus from the yard below. The children, tiring from chasing games, started squalbbling enough to draw the attention of their parents and grandparents. Abram and Amanda quickly rose to the call of their boys. Douglass, who had been listening from the bottom of the porch steps while keeping an eye on Jancy, hesitated until his energetic daughter ran over to pull him up.

While Lilly moved down to the yard, Callie stayed behind, declaring, "If it's gonna be so hot, then I'm gonna be stayin right here in the breeze." Returning to sit with her brother, Callie said, "Looks like we got good duty right now. We got to hold this porch down."

Lucas ignored Callie's humor as he concentrated on the sky, head titled up to direct his gaze. "Looka de long bands of clouds high in de sky. Each one got a lee curve, like dey be part of a big circle." Lucas stood up and slipped inside the front doors, where his prized possession hung. "You know I'm checkin yo bromedda—bes gif I ebba git from you, sista. It hep me know each day ifn de wind and wada gonna mek de day be success."

He returned, pensive. Callie asked, "And so?"

"Oh, air pressure down jus a lee bit." Suddenly enthused, Lucas asked, "What if I tell you dere be a much bedda breeze ifn you go out on de wada, and at de same time you hep yo bruddaman?"

Callie could tell that he had already decided for himself, and probably for Callie, that it was time to empty the crab traps that had been on the bottom of the river through the night. "Come wid me." He looked directly at her and said, "My sista, I need hep wid de crab."

Callie resisted, "You don't ever need help with your traps."

"I need yo hep, an I need some ansas to some questions. Come wid me, yuh?"

In his early life, Lucas had seldom been so insistent with his older sister, and Callie absorbed his request. "Brudda, if I do what you ask, is somebody gonna pick my crabmeat for me?"

"I'm glad you decided to go. De day not gonna get cooler. Good we be gone now." And when Callie started down the steps behind him, Lucas said, "I pick two crab fuh yuh, and, ifn I like yo ansas to my questions, I pick two mo."

Callie saw Jancy heading her way. "Aunt Callie, you wantin to run wid me? I'm too fast, you know."

"Oh Jancy, I'm gonna say yes, but let's do our runnin later this evenin. Got to go hep your grampa bring in some crab. You can ask him."

"I wanna go. I really do. I wanna go." Jancy was the very essence of enthusiasm.

Lucas looked at Callie as if to say, "Tryin to slip my questions?" Intending to have the discussion Callie was trying to avoid, Lucas disappointed his granddaughter. "Little honey, we go boatin tomorrow. Aunt Callie an me be doin wuk now."

Lilly, overhearing the end of the conversation, recognized this tactic, having just deployed it days before. "Where you both off to? Leavin these youngsters on the run?"

Lucas repeated a line familiar to them. "Crab callin me, love."

"Lucas tellin me I got to go, sista."

Lucas called over his shoulder, "We gonna miss you."

Callie suggested, "Sunny and Florie are here in the yard. You can do what you want."

"I like it. You heard Callie. While they out on the crab hunt, I'm headin in to de house to fix some things."

Without delay, Sunny stepped up. "We'll do it. And I know just how. No worries, Aunt Lilly." Sunny's cooperation sprang from a deep well of gratitude for all the love Lilly had extended to her niece.

"Chirren, gather roun. Florie an me, we got good news. Tell me what you like best."

She watched their faces change from wrinkled foreheads and pursed lips to wide open eyes and big grins. Animated, one after another shouted, "Blueberries!"

"Nah, dem peaches, bes fuh eatin an fuh pie."

"Best ebah is a pecan pie, wid maple syrup on top," declared Robert, with no doubt.

"Chirren, I know you each got a different idea what you want. Florie and I got two extra pies, an we gonna keep em fuh you. How many are you? The twins, Robert, Saxton, and Jancy. You five can split these two pies." The children exploded in delight, their faces filled with amazement that this had become their lot in life that day.

After exchanging glances, Florie started to fill in some details. "Fus, befo we get to eat pie togedda, we gah fuh get fixins fuh mo pie. I heah you be real good at diggin sweet potato." The youth began to rebel. Florie was quick. "But we don't want you to do that, nah. We need buckets of blueberries and strawberries."

"And pecans," urged Robert.

"We gah fuh wait til afta de trees drop dey nuts befo we mek pecan pie. Sorry."

Like a good partnership, Sunny then shared the good news again. "And after all that work, you get to eat some mystery surprise pies."

Jancy asked, "Wha you mean mystery surprise pies?"

"Caint tell. It's a secret," she whispered to Jancy. "We say mo bout de pies afta we get some work done. Hey, Robert, get your baskets and some sacks from round back of the house, please?" Turning to her cousin, "I'm gonna get em started and then come back to get ready for my boy. That be fine wid you, Florie?" A short smile gave Sunny permission to leave the expedition as early as she wished; such was their friendship.

Sunny took a few quick steps from the yard to the path, singing, "Okay, chirren. My mama say she teach you some good work songs. You ready?"

Callie turned to watch them go and smiled. To spur them on, she sang out, "I be so glad Aunt Callie be home." After they repeated back to her, they went off singing under the live oaks. Sunny led them: "I be so glad when de berries be pick" and "Sweet berries in de basket smilin up at me." Flora June followed behind, bolstering the work crew's enthusiasm and adding her booming voice to the softening responses of the marching children.

Descending the embankment behind Lucas, Callie sang quietly, "I be so glad to go get crab." Lucas barely smiled as he ushered his sister into the old work boat, holding her hand as she sat on the passenger bench at the stern. With a slight push, Lucas expertly dipped the oars and began to row, quickly encountering the tidal current.

"Lucas, what's on your mind? You ain been that polite to me since I don't menba when."

Although working the oars hard to pull against the tide in the early going, Lucas stared at his sister. "Honest, I jus today laan bout Sunny's baby, yo gran chile, and wha you say happened back ten year now. Don't even know wha must be like to feel yo burden. I'm sad fuh you an fuh Sunny. I'm sad you couldn't tell me bout it, and, fuh true, I cain unnerstan you not trustin me."

"Well, brudda, don't hold back, tell me wha really botherin you." Not getting a reaction to her attempt at humor, Callie became very serious. "I can't create for you the fear that I felt from this man and his family ten years ago. I can't make you know the worry I had for my daughter and my grandchild after those people threatened to kill them both. So, I made this my decision, and I think I saved their lives. Sunny and me got a ways to go to understand and accept what each of us feels about it. But we got a good start last night."

When Callie paused, Lucas said softly, "Hep me unnerstan supm. Why you git Will involve? Why you not aks me fuh hep?"

Callie felt her face warm and lips tremble, seeing her brother's hurt and confusion. "I didn't tell Lilly what I planned to do until the day before, and I did not want to ask you to do something I knew you couldn't support. I knew how you loved Sunny, and you would want to fight fuh huh and the baby, and I jus wanted to protect them."

"And Will?"

"You remember he was down here for short visits the summer of '83? He had been so busy, we hardly saw each other after his uncle passed—it had been more than ten years. So, when we traveled down here together by boat, we had time to talk through many things. One was all my worries about Sunny. I asked his advice, and he offered his help, not knowin what it might be. When finally I decided to move the baby to a safe location and to deceive my daughter about the life of her child, I didn't want anyone else to know."

Lucas looked up after staring at an oar dripping water into the river. "Mmmm!"

"Please, Lucas, I didn't want to do it. The threat of the boy's father in combination with Sunny's headstrong determination to have the baby out in the open, and even take it downtown, well...I was sure she and the baby would die. I didn't know the best way to do it when I decided to go forward. I took the burden myself. But now, I ask for your understanding and support, jus like you always do."

Hesitating only slightly as he guided the boat up to the next crab trap, Lucas pulled his oars in and smiled. "Sista, you know you got de fambly support, an I lead de fambly, most of de time."

"Lucas, I know you look to do right all the time, and I know how well you provide for your family. I trust you for that, always have. But ten years ago, I didn't want my baby and huh baby to be a fight about race hate. I had to stop it."

"I see, sista, I see. I be too happy to have yo grandson comin home. Leh de fambly love you an yo babies."

"That's why Sunny and I called the family togedda this morning."

As Lucas hooked the wood trap and pulled the rope, bringing it up level with the top edge of the boat, Callie grabbed the other end of the trap and helped direct it into the bateau. The crabs climbed over one-another, trying to escape from the trap as Lucas lifted it over the open tub. With strength and efficiency, he opened the trap door to let ten sizable blue crabs tumble out. "Only seven mo traps to pull."

"You gonna pull em all today?"

"Feel dah extra breeze I be promisin you out yuh?"

"Yeah, it's bedda on the water."

"Wind gettin up a little mo, comin off de ocean. I see high clouds pushin up from de south, lookin like outside rings of a stohm. So, yup. I wanna empty all eight traps now an set em out again. We be eatin crab fuh de next few days, den we eat some more. Hand me de big jar unda yo bench."

As she did, the top opened, revealing a terrible stink. "Aughhh!! What is that?"

"Fishheads from last week. Crab love em."

Callie shoved it toward Lucas. "You do the baitin, right?"

"I do. If you do yo own crab pickin."

Callie took that wry, incentivizing statement by her brother as a challenge. "I will bait your crab trap if you keep your promise to pick my crab meat, four crabs." Lucas nodded—it was settled, so she dipped a hand in the fish head jar.

As she planned, Sunny left the young work crew harvesting fruit to fill future pies. She walked slowly along the river path back to the big house, between live oak trees spread majestically along the embankment and stands of tall pine trees that bordered the fields. She spotted her mother and uncle way up Chowan Creek, emptying and resetting the crab traps. They did not see Sunny wave both arms over her head as they labored side by side, pulling traps while carrying on their debate.

Sunny continued her measured stroll all the way into the house, where she found Lilly in command of her kitchen. Lilly looked up to see her and smiled warmly, praising her niece. "You been a beautiful young woman today, sharin with your family in the best way, and I know you are a tied-up bunch of nerves inside. I was wonderin when you were gonna settle down and think about all that is comin your way."

"Aunt Lilly, you know me too well. I stay busy to keep from worryin."

"I know how strong you are, just like your mama, thinkin you can take it all on at once by yourself."

"Let me help you." Sunny stepped up to balance a large bowl as Lilly poured from it.

"You see, that is your nature. You see things needin to be done to help people. And now, all of a sudden, you gonna be a mother—of a ten-year-old boy."

"Hearin you talk makes it sound a little scary. But I feel it's gonna be all right, maybe because I know how our family is and how good we will be for him."

"That's true, honey. We always gonna hold each other up, and that boy of yours will be one of the pack that runs across this yard, any and every day."

"That's why I decided it would be good to have the boy's father come out from Beaufort tomorrow afternoon on the outbound tide."

Lilly paused, surprised that the boy's father was still involved. Yet she posed a gentle question: "Don't you think that's rushin things a bit, honey?"

"You know, Brent questioned me on that too."

"Brent? Yo man is Brent? All right. Sound like Brent may have some sense."

"Lilly! It may be quick for Unca Lucas. But Lilly, we love each other, and I need him now to be with me when we meet our son."

"You told anybody else about your plan to have this man come out?"

"Just you."

"Mmmm-hmmm. Just so I understand, Brent is the man that scared your mother so bad ten years ago?"

"Aunt Lilly, you gotta understand, his parents made him act that way. He feels terrible about what happened."

"And he should, mmmm-hmmm."

———◆———

As Callie pulled out the last stinking fish head to bait the eighth crab trap, her clothing reeked from the putrid odor. Lucas chose this time to focus on Sunny's new loved ones. "Now, what about dis young man Sunny found?"

"Well, Lucas..." Callie pondered. "That is a pretty broad question. You are good at askin exactly what you want to know."

"Sunny ain wanna talk bout dis man befo when I aks huh. Afta yo visit tuh Beaufort tuh see em, seem like Sunny and he be talkin bout dey baby boy?"

"Yes, Lucas, let me stop your wonderin. Brent is the white man whose family threatened me back then. Now, Brent and Sunny are together, and they have just learned that they are parents."

"Oh." Lucas remained quiet as he hurled the last trap, fully baited by Callie, back into the water. The crab harvest had grown to fill two tubs, more than four dozen. Lucas looked up from the crabs. "Can Sunny an you guarantee dis man won't cause problems wid we fambly, we neighbors, or we friends?"

Callie laughed at her brother's serious face. "Brudda, I can't guarantee you that I won't cause problems for you with family, neighbors, or friends, specially smellin as I do." Still laughing gently, she continued, "I doubt that anyone could pass your test. But Lucas, I know that this young man loves Sunny and that she loves him, and I could feel his joy when I told him that his child is alive. I can't predict the future though. What more you wanna know?"

"If Sunny care fuh him enough to stand fuh him, and if he stand fuh doin de right ting, which mean he gonna suppote Sunny and her boy wid his time an his money, den I be nice tuh him, mostly." After looking down in the boat as he spoke, Lucas refocused on Callie's searching eyes. "If she stand up fuh him, I will too."

"Tank ya, brudda. You gonna make Sunny real happy." Callie's smile turned to a frown as she tried to get the fish head smell off her hands by dousing them several times in the hot salt water of August. Looking around the bateau, she asked, "You got anything to clean with on dis boat?" Seeing the blank stare on his face, she moaned, "Of course you don't. You got good labor out of me, and now I'm a stinky woman, so I bedda be havin that crab meat drippin wid butta on my plate tonight."

"We see. Still gah fuh git deese crab up tuh de fire. Yo may have mo wuk to do."

"Brudda, you pushin grace. For me to smell this bad so far from where I can get clean, you best move a lot of water wid yo oars and take me home."

IN THE KITCHEN, SUNNY HAD FINISHED CUTTING UP TOMATOES AND cucumbers and then had helped Lilly fill the big fruit bowl with peaches, grapes, and peanuts before going upstairs to the bedroom she now shared with her mother. To accommodate her son and allow her mother to continue to sleep in the bed, Sunny stacked three old quilts on the floor to create a pallet for herself. Looking around the generally tidy space, Sunny glimpsed herself smiling into the mirror before she noticed the tears welling up and trickling down her cheeks. "You have a son!" she whispered to herself, at once feeling the joy and fear of impending parenthood.

With that thought, Sunny sat on the bed and then lay down, almost instantly drifting to sleep. She barely moved until Lilly called from below, "Sunny, can you come help me spread icing on this cake?"

Confused at first, Sunny quickly recalled the importance of the day and bolted upright. She laughed at the shouted question that awakened her, for she knew it was her Aunt Lilly's standard practice to cure any ailment with a spoonful of extra chocolate frosting. She said to herself as she hurried down the stairs, "On dis day, my Aunt Lilly is motherin me."

Lilly inspected her cake for proper coverage of her rich peach icing, noting, "Seems like we may have too much icing left over. Can you fix that?"

"Yes I can! Bout as good as you always been able to fix my troubles."

"You know, your mother is real good at it too."

"Aunt Lilly, don't worry. Won't be easy afta missin my boy's first ten years, but I got to accept her reason for doin it. Brent knows he was wrong."

"You sure, honey?"

"Yes. I know the kind man he is now. He ain nothin like his parents raised him."

"So, did you and Brent get a chance to talk about what you want for your child?"

"We did, and we want to make him happy, first. We want to find out what he likes and give it to him. I know that sounds bad, but..."

"No! It isn't. You want to love your chile and make up for missed years."

"And we really do want him to get an education. From what I see, people who learn bout de world can do all right in it."

"Sure seems to work fuh you."

Sunny said, "I thank God and good fortune ebby day that my Mama and you made me go to school and that Laura Towne and Penn School helped me learn so much. Then, in Washington, Mama and my grampa and Missus Granger taught me bout de bigger world out there. I'm wantin to give all that to my boy."

"Sounds like you thinkin jus like a mother."

With the bowl and spoon licked completely clean, Sunny's hands were free to hug her aunt. "Oh, Aunt Lilly, life just keep on movin. Thank you for keepin me on the right path."

"Sunny, you been knowin the right thing to do for a long time now."

They heard Abram call from down on the dock, "Boat comin up de river from Port Royal Sound. Look like two sets of oars makin good time."

Lilly and Sunny pulled apart and looked at each other with alarm, despite the very recent calm words of reassurance. "He's here! Am I ready fuh be his mama?"

"I know you are ready!"

———◆———

ON THE BACK CREEK, IN THE BATEAU WEIGHTED DOWN WITH CRABS in water-filled tubs, Lucas pulled slowly on his oars. "You trust this man to bring your boy back on time? He gotta a name?"

"Nathan Gates is the man Will chose," Callie explained. "Will knew him from their time together in the Navy and got to know that Mista Gates can take care of most anything. And he knows the waterways between here and Savannah from bein here during the war."

"They been gone since Monday, wid only two oarsmen, you say? Somebody betta know wha dey be doin."

As he rowed around the last bend in the creek before the Oakheart dock came into view, Lucas heard his oldest son hollering. It became clear, Abram was shouting, "Welcome!" He waved to a large rowboat as it neared the dock with four oars in the water and four figures in the boat.

"Oh my goodness, praise God! Is that the boat? Is that my Sunny's boy?" They were still quite a distance away watching as the boat slid up beside the dock, Abram throwing a dock line to the man, Nathan Gates, standing in the bow. Callie shrieked, "Noooo! I'm gonna meet my grandson smellin like fish heads!"

———◆———

HAVING BROUGHT THE LONG ROWBOAT TO THE DOCK AT A PERFECT speed and angle, the two oarsmen withdrew their oars just in time to grab two more dock lines from Abram, which they efficiently looped around the boat cleats. Both men appeared spent from the rigors of their journey but held the dock lines tightly to stabilize the boat as Nathan Gates stood, gently lifting a slender boy to his feet. With the boat rocking and Nathan Gates holding him tightly, the boy stepped on the bench, bent forward, and on all fours scrambled onto the dock. Abram immediately lifted him up and gave him a man-size bear hug.

Sunny moved so quickly from the house to the dock that Lilly was left on the porch in wonder. When she arrived, Gates was just stepping from the boat and he greeted her while looking for Callie. "Hello, I'm hoping to see Callie Hewitt today. Is she—"

"My mother," said Sunny as kindly and calmly as she could. "She is coming in on the crab boat out there. See?" Sure enough, Callie was waving from several hundred yards up the creek. Nathan Gates turned back to see Sunny's hand extended. "I'm Sunny, Callie's daughter, and I want to talk to you. I do, and I thank you so much for what you have done, but...can I see my boy?"

Gates smiled and stepped aside, waving to family members gathered on the bluff with Lilly. When Sunny saw her son in Abram's arms, her hands flew to her face. She lost her composure—she could only stare at her son; she couldn't speak. Forcing herself to breathe deeply, Sunny concentrated on this long, thin, exhausted little boy. Moving close to him, she asked, "You want to get down?" No response. "Abram, please bring this very tired boy off the dock." Sunny put one hand on Abram's shoulder and the other on her son's back, guiding them to the sanctuary of dry land.

Abram set him down as Sunny kneeled to embrace her child, and just as quickly, she leaned back and said, "Let me tell you supm that's real important. You come a long way to be yuh, and I am happy happy! You know why? I be yo mama!" Shaking her head up and down ever so slightly and gently biting her lower lip, Sunny worked to keep a calm demeanor. "I won't tell you the story now, but ifn you want to, we talk about it later. I been wonderin when I'd get to meet you. You been away too long." Sunny touched her chest, "My name is Sunny. What is your name?"

"You sure you my mama?"

Sunny nodded.

"Ain you sposed to know my name?"

Sunny turned sideways to her son, stopped a tear from moving down her cheek, and then reached for his hand. "My son, I ain ever had a chance to be yo mama—ifn I coulda been wid you, I woulda. I can now."

He allowed her to embrace him again, and when they pulled away, the boy looked around. "Dey called me Woody where I been stay." He took a step away from Sunny and looked up to Abram and then around at the water, finally turning to see the group up on the bluff, all looking at him, some waving as he tried to lift his arm.

"It's purty heah. So purty. Feels like heabn. Ain nebba seen supm so purty." Woody appeared faint, threw up into the nearby creek, just missing the dock, and started to collapse. Abram grabbed him by the shoulders just as Sunny caught his head in her hands to cradle it from harm for the first time. Then, knowing that her son was not watching her, she began to cry.

Callie witnessed the scene from afar as she and Lucas arrived at the dock, and cried out briefly on seeing Woody fall, but consistent with Lucas's guiding hand urging calm, she restrained herself. Hurrying from the boat, Callie arrived at her daughter's side, fish head scent and all, in seconds. Woody looked at Callie through half-opened eyes and smiled. Other than saying, "I'm so glad to see you. I'm your grandmother," Callie remained quiet and deferential to Sunny.

"Abram, Mama, let's get him to de house, fuh food and rest."

"Go ahead, I'll be right there, let me thank these gentlemen." Turning to the three men responsible, Callie offered, "You must be exhausted from such a trip. If you want food, please stay. Or come back later this weekend. We will feed you and your family. You have brought my grandson home. Thank you, thank you!"

The oarsmen gave Nathan Gates his small seabag and another bag for the boy, nodded their appreciation for the invitation, and declined before pushing off. "They want to get to their homes, as I do, where we can stop moving. I will be back to receive your kind offer, perhaps tomorrow."

Lucas heard those words and was not surprised. "Mista Gates, I am Lucas Sargent, Callie's brother, an we are too grateful."

"Ah, Will's brother, Lucas." Gates's smile showed his awareness of the deep friendship Will and Lucas had established. "Will's maps helped us follow the inland waters on the tides and avoid the challenges of a rough sea."

"I wondered how you could mek dis trip in four days without doin what you just say, followin de incomin and outgoin tides through de creeks. Good wuk."

"Well, Lucas, I have heard of your exploits from Will, especially leading Harriet Tubman on that plantation raid up the Combahee River. I cannot possibly know these waterways like you do, but during the war, I had to make quite a few quick trips with the flow of the tides. I have a lot of respect for these rivers and creeks, the way they fill and empty with ocean water on the rise and fall of the tides." Gates spoke with the same affection that Lucas felt for the surrounding saltwater.

"I can tell you be a man of de sea." Lucas did not often extend himself with such praise.

"Thank you, Lucas." Gates nodded and reached out to clasp Lucas's hand.

Lucas, noticing the rough and open blisters on his hands, looked up to Mister Gates, "Suh, you be one of de crew, too. Yo hands tell de story from bein on de wada."

"We all were crew." Changing the subject, "And as a man of the sea, I must say I've shouted across the water to many a boatman the last two days. The word is that a mighty big storm is coming up from Florida."

Lucas looked up. "I been watchin clouds today, jus like you. Sho look like supm down sout comin dis way."

"That's what they say, riding up the Florida coast."

"Ummm-hmmm. My barometer been goin down a little all day." Extending his hand again, "Glad you got yuh befo de stohm. I know you wanna get to Will's house. Can we help? Abram, can we git a buggy ready?"

"Not needed, Lucas. Thank you. I want to feel the land and stretch my legs. A ten-minute walk is exactly what I need."

"God bless you, Mista Gates. We see who you be an what good wuk you do."

"Thank you, Lucas."

Callie decided to walk toward Will's house with Gates as Sunny and Abram carried Woody right up to the bedroom, past all the children on the bluff waiting to meet and touch their new cousin. Abram gently placed Woody on the bed, where he fell into a deep sleep. Sunny settled next to her son and, for the first time, watched his face, like any new parent would. Soon, she had to pick up her sketch pad and begin drawing. She held it out, comparing her work to the angelic face sleeping next to her, and then returned pencil to pad. Perhaps the movement awoke Woody, allowing him to watch Sunny draw. He reached for the biscuit and peach that Sunny had brought up. He watched Sunny draw some more. He ate. Sunny finished and smiled slightly at the picture she had created, and then she turned to Woody, her grin widening.

"You really my mama?"

Barely able to stop smiling to speak, Sunny affirmed, "I'm really your mama."

At that, Woody reached for the pad of paper and pencil that Sunny had been using. He looked at her sketch of a sleeping young boy with curly, dark hair and a pleasant smile on his light brown face. "That me?"

Sunny nodded.

For several minutes, Sunny watched as Woody worked the pencil on the paper, looking up at her several times. Woody stopped, put the pencil down, and handed the pad of paper back to his mama. Sunny took the page and was stunned to see a likeness of her that was as good as any she had ever seen, even catching the dimples around her slight smile, and the folds of the scarf that reined in her hair. It wasn't detailed, but it was clear evidence of special talent.

Woody looked on, enjoying Sunny's wonder. "I ain nevah draw my mama befo."

Chapter 10

Friday evening, August 25, 1893

Long after Friday evening supper, Lilly cautiously questioned Callie. "You been so quiet since you came downstairs peekin in on Sunny and her boy. You said they were sleepin. I know you got to be happy, so why you lookin worried?"

"You're right, Lilly. I keep thinking about them and wondering if Woody is all right...that was a rough boat trip from Savannah to Constant Island."

"I'm sure he is fine, Callie. Sunny would come and get you if there was a problem. After all, Grandma is a nurse."

"Well..."

"Go up and see them, Callie. It's just about sundown. Woody may be too hungry to sleep tonight."

"Oh, Lilly. I really just want to see them together. I have yearned for this day."

"Go!"

Callie hesitated, climbed the stairs, and quietly opened the door a crack, expecting to see a sleeping mother and son. Instead, she was surprised to see them sitting on the bed, looking at papers. Sunny waved at her to come in. "This is my mama, Woody. She is your grandmother."

"You feelin better, young man?" Callie reached to touch his forehead gently and smiled, pleased there was no indication of fever. "I thought you both might be asleep."

"We slept and ate a little, Mama, and I drew this picture of him." Then she flipped the page to show Woody's drawing of her. "And look what he did!"

"Oh my goodness. Did he..." Callie turned to Woody. "Did you draw this?"

"Yes'm."

"This is so beautiful. You must be very smart to draw so well."

"Not too smaat. Jus try to mek wha I see."

"Well, I can't wait to see what you can do when you get a good night's sleep and some more food. Can I get supm for you?"

"Thank you, Mama. Not now. Please come back here tonight. I can sleep on the pallet. We will move a bed up for you tomorrow."

"Sunny, you and your son take this bed, and maybe I will come back to the pallet later tonight." She leaned over to kiss Sunny's forehead, an act that Woody watched intently. When she moved toward his head, he leaned slightly toward her with a smile that widened.

Callie fairly floated out of the room, stopping at the hallway window to see shafts of light piercing dense cloud cover as the sun dipped low on the horizon. She whispered to herself, "I am a grandmother!" Coming down the stairs, Callie noted that the house had become so quiet she could hear the muffled sounds of work and conversation in the kitchen between Nellie and Amanda. As she emerged from the house, she heard Lucas and his sons talking animatedly on the porch. Douglass pointed to his father and said, "Be happenin mo ebby day!"

Lucas saw the strange, satisfied look on Callie's face and asked, "Sunny an de boy doin all right?"

"They been sleepin some and eatin a little up on the bed. Touch my heart so."

"Praise God!" Abram said.

"You would not believe...Sunny drew a picture of her boy, and when he woke up, he drew one of her." At peace, yet genuinely interested in what drew such heated discussion, Callie asked, "So, what's happenin more every day that got you pointin at yo daddy?"

Abram spoke up. "We talkin bout how some white folk still treat us bad, you know, cause our skin color is daak."

Lucas said, "You know, not bein sure who you can trust. Dey may be some good white people, but de system is set tuh keep de daak man in his place."

Lilly added, "It really is the old slavery mindset. Started seein it again back in '76 and '78 when they beat up African men tryin to vote."

"Rememba, Daddy?" Douglass inserted. "You tole me how de laws be changed to mek new votin districts in Sout Calina, makin it so a black man could only win right yuh in Bufut County, but whites win everywhere else. Memba? You knew all bout politics back then."

Lucas agreed. "Politics ain pretty any time, especially when evil folk take ovah."

Callie sighed heavily. "I thought I had found a place, up in that bedroom just now, where the worries went away. Wasn't thinkin about how tough things can be." Shaking her head, "I know I been the one talkin bout my past and all the important things that happen long ago."

Lucas nodded his head and then shook it side to side. "Well, there been some great change come from de freedom wah. Good ting happen fuh we people. But, jus seem like dey ain gonna leh us hab too much success fo dey try to knock us down agin."

Callie remembered, "One night when I was working late at the Freedmen's Hospital, after the bad changes started coming, all my friends were upset, even sounding scared. They were talkin about a bad decision from the Supreme Court that makes the Ku Klux Klan legal.

From that night on, we talked about not feelin safe walkin around, even in a city like Washington. That was back in '82."

Lilly agreed, "People ain felt safe down yuh needuh."

Callie added, "It's true, race hate seems to be happenin everywhere."

"Das what I'm tryin to say, sista." Lucas became more intense. "It ain de same ebbywhere. It be different down heah, an you should be rememberin dah an not be believin all you heah a white man say."

"We talkin bout Sunny's man now, ain we?" Callie responded quickly.

"Das wha we talkin bout." Lucas looked directly at Callie, "Can we talk togedda jus a minute bout wha went on in '83?"

Callie, knowing Lucas wanted to continue their talk from the boat that afternoon, kept the conversation on the increased racism in their lives. "I won't forget that year, cause right after the court gave that terrible Klan decision, another court decision made the Civil Rights Act of 1875 unconstitutional..."

"Callie...," Lucas tried to redirect, unsuccessfully.

"Startin right then," Callie asserted, "all these Confederate states started changing laws to make it legal to keep black people out of public places or hotels or buses or trains or boats. Seemed like they wanted to encourage more hateful acts against us."

"But that's not what we aks—" Lucas tried again.

Callie continued. "That decision made every trip I took on trains and trolleys harder. Wherever I stayed on those trips, people were more hostile, or at least unfriendly and disrespectful to me and my friends, sayin and doin whatever they pleased. So, don't minimize that. That's what was happenin in 1883."

"Callie!" Lucas used a rare commanding tone. "Dah ain what I aks bout. You know it."

Abram interceded. "Aunt Callie, I think I know what my daddy is sayin. We yo fambly, an we want to understan bedda how this blessin came to be, how Sunny got huh boy back. We tank Gawd, he be here wid us, and if it ain for us to know everything, we all right an happy fuh Sunny. So, please, tell us what you can." Abram ended his comment with a smile and his hand extended to his aunt.

"Oh!" Callie understood that they deserved to know more than just the logistics of the matter. "I will tell you what I can, if I think it be all right with Sunny." As Callie waited to begin, the day's breeze welled up into a moderate gust. Callie pulled her chair in closer. "Don't want to have to shout across the porch on this breezy evenin.

"Ten years ago, I had to take an action that I question to this day, yes, even to this day, when my daughter is finally holding her son." More emotional than she expected, or could control easily, Callie took a deep, nervous breath. "I came down here to visit then, cause I loved my daughter so much, and you all as well. So, I came back in '83 to visit for three months, I even got Will to come. Memba?" Lilly and Lucas nodded, he with evident impatience.

"You know I ain been able to spend too much time with Will after his Uncle Harris, my daddy, passed. He got his family started and moved out of Annapolis and across Chesapeake Bay. So, Will decided to come with me, because he knew I needed some special help." Inquisitive looks surrounded Callie as she stood and began taking small, meticulous steps in the open space at the center of her gathered family. Looking down, Callie proceeded, "I'm a storyteller, and I ain keen to be tellin this story. At least not today, now that we have an end to the pain and a good, new beginning."

She looked up and turned toward Lucas. "I found out from Sunny back then, when she was pregnant, that there were some problems with the family of the man involved. They weren't happy with their boy, the young man Sunny took a fancy to. And they told him to solve the problem or they would. They threatened Sunny's life, and the life of her baby." Again, Callie couldn't seem to take in enough oxygen to support her words. "I didn't tell you, Lucas, because I knew how much you loved

Sunny—she been yo special niece for so long, and you raised her, you and Lilly, when I couldn't." Callie started her small, measured steps again. "I decided to find out what's so bad about that family by myself, and I went to visit the boy's parents...and found out they were as awful as could be. They repeated what they told Sunny." Callie imitated the tone of the father's words, spoken with slow meanness. "'If you want yo daughter and that grandbaby to live, take em away from heah, away from Sout Calina.' Then the old man came right up to me, whispering, 'Nigga bitch, I always defend my family, and if killin anotha nigga or two is how I do that, it ain nothin to me.' Then they made their boy come out of the house and take me into the backyard with orders to repeat their threat to Sunny and her baby before he rushed me out the gate.

"Later, just before Sunny birthed her baby, she told me that she would take her child downtown any and every day she wanted to, and that those old white people couldn't stop her." Callie delicately wiped a tear from her cheek. "I told her to be serious about their threat, and she say, 'Who are they to tell me where and when I can go?' You know how strong-minded our Sunny can be."

Looking to the darkening western sky, now an hour past sunset, "I knew what you would do, Lucas, if I told you. You would rise up and fight. But I decided all I wanted to do was protect my child and her child. So, I asked Will to help me do that. On the night Sunny's baby was born, after nearly a day of labor and in severe pain, Sunny was almost asleep when the baby arrived. I gave her a mixture of natural things that make a body sleep. And sleep she did as I cleaned up that little boy. Seeing he was healthy, I prepared him for travel before giving him to Will, who had a crew and a wet nurse for the baby ready to take him down the coast to Georgia. The boy been livin in Savannah from that day to this."

Callie stopped abruptly. "That is the story. We can all have our discussion bout what I did, but I did what I thought I had to do to protect my babies. I kept track of the boy all this time, first puttin him with an old couple, then three years ago, I put him with another family—this one with children. But they came on hard times, and they ask if I could take him away. I decided it was time to make things right. And the last thing I'll say is that, my beautiful Sunny," and Callie could not hold back the tears, "my daughter, didn't deserve to lose her child at birth. And I got to spend every day of my life, startin yesterday, to make it up to her and her fine, young son."

At that, the family rose as one from their chairs on the porch to surround Callie with love, all arms engaged in hugging someone. "Praise Gawd that we have made it to this blessed day when we get a new fambly memba to love," Abram concluded as if leading a service.

Seemingly on cue, Sunny emerged from the front door, and the group opened to enfold her. "My goodness, family, what you been talkin bout. Don't know whether to laugh or cry." With joyful tears falling all around, she joined her mother at the center of the family hug.

Sunny asked, "Mama, would you go stay with Woody while I get some food? I be right back up there," and she looked around, "if these people let go of me." Sunny was fully engaged as a mother and didn't allow herself more than a few minutes to share her joy with the rest of her loved ones before retreating again. "Please, please, I love you all, but I love love my boy."

Most of the family followed Sunny's lead and retired for the night. The steady, cooling breeze and its pulsing, wooshing sounds induced sleep, despite the low rattle of windowpanes pressed by strengthening gusts.

Saturday, August 26, 1893

ALWAYS ATTENTIVE TO THE WEATHER AND ITS EFFECT ON HIS HOUSE, Lucas was awakened well before dawn on Saturday by stronger and more frequent bursts of wind. Anxious to assess the conditions, he dressed quickly and quietly tiptoed down the pine steps, avoiding the places that creaked, and went out the front door thinking he was the lone family member on the move.

Lucas was not easily startled, but Callie, standing just outside the front door, whispered, "Bruddaman," and Lucas gasped and jumped several feet away from the ghostly voice. Giving herself away as the cause of his fright, Callie chortled at the reaction of her brother, who did not share her levity.

"Callie! Wha oona tink?"

"I'm thinkin you got to settle yo nerves, my dear bruddaman." Stifling more laughter, she explained, "I just whispered loud enough so you could hear me over the wind. You know I'm an early riser. Betta get used to that, at least while I'm still a guest in your home."

"Well, let me tink bout wha odda choice be fuh you." Lucas paused, appearing to be in deep deliberation with himself, while Callie waited. "Ah, sista, I may be crazy to say so, but dis house always be fuh you, too."

"Awww, brudda."

Lucas quickly added, "I might have to leave, when you move in tuh stay, but..."

Callie had to dig a little deeper than their playful banter. "Lucas, anything we not talkin about heah that we need to get said?"

"We all right long as you tink you can trus me," Lucas offered with a slight laugh.

Callie knew exactly what Lucas referenced and responded quickly, "Lucas, even though I been gone most of thirty years, I always know when you laugh that way, you sayin supm serious, too. Ain nothin bout wha I did because I didn't trust you. I said why yesterday, but I say again, I didn't want you to feel like you had to stand up to the threats from that damn buckra colonel who was still fightin the war." As if to erase the image of that possible conflict, Callie moved in front of Lucas and smiled. "You know it's true. It's been better you thinkin Sunny lost huh baby. You didn't have to hide what you knew from Sunny all this time." After brief, reassuring eye contact between them, Callie said, "I always trust you, brudda. Always. So does Will."

Still struggling with Callie's explanation, Lucas asked, "If Will and I be like fambly wid each odda, how he keep me from news like dis?"

"I'm sorry to say, my brother, I asked him to keep what we did quiet, to keep it to himself. I asked for that favor to protect the secret, to keep it from everybody. It was easier for Will because he doesn't live here and see you all every day, especially Sunny. Please don't blame Will for doin what I asked him to do."

Lucas turned slightly away from Callie as first light began to rise despite thick cloud cover. He looked up with arms outstretched. "Got mo wind dis monin. I thought it be rainin by now. But them clouds just keep circlin, comin in from ovah de ocean."

"Well, that's good, isn't it? No rain?"

"It don't mean rain not comin. It mean dey supm pretty big still spinnin on de wada. It jus takin a little time to get yuh. Wish we knew where it gonna go."

"What your barometer say?"

"Ain seen it yet in the daak, but I know wha it gonna say." Looking directly to Callie and then up to the clouds, "I know fuh fact it be lower now. It say de stohm gettin bigga and closa. We may need fuh change our plans today. Right now, I gah fuh see how our dock did las night wid de wind an de high tide."

"Memba those traps we put out yesterday?" Callie asked. "If you bring em in this mornin, whatever fresh crab and shrimp you get, I'll add em to my fixins today. I'm gonna get goin on that pile of vegetables and fruit the children brought back yesterday. Florie must have really worked them. It's no wonder they went to sleep so fast last night. Well, let me get busy to see if I can keep Lilly out of her kitchen today."

"You gonna have tuh hurry some. Look." As Callie declared her intentions, Lilly quietly carried the first bowl of fruit for the morning to the porch table. Taking a peach from her collection, Lucas ambled down the steps. "Bye, ladies. I gah fuh check de dock and pull some traps befo disyuh stohm decide to git serious. When Abram and Douglass git up, send em on down."

Callie playfully admonished Lilly. "You up and busy too quick. I'm gonna take over the cookin today. Since I got back, I been wantin to use the fancy new oven you got downstairs under the porch. I cain't believe you can bring it into the kitchen in the winter and cook yo food indoors."

"Well, I appreciate that, Callie, but don't you want time with yo family?"

"I want to give them time together. They need time...time I took away. So, the best I can do is just stay clear."

"You sure you don't want to be with your babies, Callie? I know Sunny won't agree with you. That sweet girl will share her son with you."

"Thank you, Lilly, you right bout her. But I just want to give em room today anyway. Besides, she says her man is comin here on the risin tide sometime late this afternoon. I just told Lucas I'm gonna be a good new grandmother and spend all day fixin food."

A worried smile broke across Lilly's face. "Oh my, I figured Sunny would want to get the three of em together. She must like that man a lot. Question is, is this family ready to have that white man here, especially after what they learned just last night?"

"Well, I reckon they can just get ready before he comes," Callie asserted, "because Sunny tells me she is pretty sure they gonna raise this boy together."

"My, my! Nature movin in mysterious ways. I hope Sunny is ready fuh some mixed responses in the community."

"Really?" Callie asked.

"Mmmm-hmmm."

"Really?" Sunny's voice echoed back from the front hall as she led her son by the hand onto the porch, declaring, "Sunny and Woody had good sleep, and we are ready for today!" With an inquiring glance at both her mother and aunt, Sunny asked, "Is there supm I need to know bout now?"

Callie quickly shifted direction. "No. Uncle Lucas just said we might have to get our family meal earlier in the day in case we get some rain, especially if we plan to cook up some crab, shrimp, and other good eats on the griddle over the fire pit. You like shrimp and crab, Woody?"

"Yes'm—don't eat it much."

Sunny offered, "Mama, I know you keepin supm, but that's okay. Woody and me goin out to see the yard and the trees and the river. Then we gonna get some of that bread and butter and jelly from the table inside." Woody tugged on her hand as he leaned toward Lilly and the peaches. "Can you tell Aunt Lilly, 'thank you very much'? Woody seems to love peaches."

While reaching for his peach, Woody parroted, "Tank you, Ain Lilly."

With that, mother and son were off down the steps, still holding hands.

"I'm too happy, Lilly. I never dreamed this day could come, fa true. You know what you said about Sunny bein sweet? She already invited me to share the room with them, and she asked if I wanted to share the bed or get a daybed brought up, so I don't have to sleep on the floor, as I gladly did last night. But you know, I think we should leave the daybed downstairs."

"Looks like you and your girl are finding your way through another storm."

"Well, with this man of hers arriving later today, I wouldn't look for clear skies too soon." Callie looked up at the lowering clouds. "Who knows when these skies may open up with some rain. For now, I'm lovin this morning wind."

"Callie, does Lucas know bout this man comin?"

"Sunny whispered it to me just this morning when I was gettin up. I didn't tell him yet. But I think he will be all right with it since both Sunny and me see him as a good man."

Lilly advised, "Talk to him about it, Callie. Let him know what's in yo plan, so it can be his plan, too." They smiled knowingly.

"I will. Thank you! You know your man so well!" Callie looked around. "It's so quiet in the house. Are those chirren still sleepin in?"

"Only Robert and Saxton were here last night, and I know if they sleepin, Abram and Amanda ain gonna rush outta bed."

"I just figured as soon as it was light, no matter where they sleepin, they'd be here to see about Woody."

"Well, you know why they so bushed? Flora June got them to do extra work in the fields yesterday. She had em out there pickin for hours and got back jus before Woody got here. What you saw on the kitchen counters ain half of it. Yea, those peaches are luscious, and with the buckets of figs and blueberries, we are well stocked. But check the crates at the bottom of the back stairs—full of apples and cantaloupes. They even rolled up some ripe watermelons. I mean, those chirren worked. Flora and Sunny will be making pies all weekend."

While listening and nodding, Callie's gaze was transfixed on the bluff below. "I'm glad Sunny and Woody are havin this sweet time. Look."

Sunny was pointing down toward the dock and talking when Woody looked up at her, squeezed her hand, and pulled her to the side yard, heading straight toward the tree-boats. In seconds, Sunny helped him climb into the low bateau.

Callie laughed. "You'd think he'd had enough of boats for a while.

"Anyway, that's enough gazing at my grandson. He is here and safe, and I need to get to work on all that food the children brought in fresh from the field. Ready to wash, cut, and start cookin…also ready to take orders. Lilly, tell me what you want done first."

"Start cuttin what you want to serve with your pork stew later today. For now, I'll get another platter of biscuits and jelly ready for the hungry chirren—big and little."

"That sounds good. I'll take the fruits and vegetables I need to cut up out to the porch and catch this cool morning breeze.

Almost on cue, Robert materialized from the back room rubbing his eyes and, before they were fully opened, questions tumbled out of his mouth. "Where is he? Where's Woody? Is he up?"

Lilly pointed to the tree-boats, and her grandson was out the door in a flash and down the steps. Without even trying to catch up, Saxton shuffled out behind his brother, followed closely by Amanda, who was urging him to eat before going out to play. Before Abram could even sit down with some food, Lilly told him, "Your daddy needs you and your brother to help get the dock ready for bad weather."

Abram took the news with grace. "Yes, Mama, as long as I get to take two ham biscuits with me." Without waiting for permission, Abram stuffed one into his mouth, grabbed another, and hustled down to the dock.

In the distance, perhaps hundreds of feet away and getting closer, Lilly heard a high-pitched sound which she thought was a wounded animal or perhaps an osprey screaming while in a power dive. But as the sound grew nearer and louder, it became clear that Jancy was running toward the house, yelling, "Wood-eeee! Wood-eeeeeeeeee!! Wood-eeeeeeeeeeeee!!!"

Lilly waved Jancy away before she reached the front porch, both to redirect her to the tree-boats and to stop the ear-splitting screech. "Darlin, be happy, be calm."

Jancy did not hear the admonition as she turned in full stride to her new destination.

Woody's admiring cousins were arriving. No sooner had Jancy been lifted into the low bateau with Sunny, Woody, and Robert than Flora June's clear, strong voice rang out from the wooded path as she arrived with her boys. "What's all this I be hearin bout a new cousin in these parts?" The twins rushed up the porch stairs and delivered their mother's just-baked sweetbread with honey and her platter of pork sausages. Without stopping, they dashed down the steps into the yard, sprinted across it, grabbed the gunnels of the bateau, and pulled themselves up and over. Delighted screams welcomed their energetic arrival. Sunny may never have been so happy, as she protected Beanie's head from hitting a bench and prevented Bobby from crashing into Jancy. "Boys!" she yelled amidst the wiggling and giggling. Douglass, with Nellie and the baby, trailed far behind Jancy, walking up to the boat just in time to encourage all children to pick a bench and settle on it. Then Sunny led introductions all around, with each child reaching out to touch or shake Woody's hand. A better orientation to his morning on Constant Island could not have been planned by a welcoming committee.

Laughing out loud, Lilly and Callie watched the event from the porch as they began to operate on the fresh fruit and vegetables surrounding them. Still chuckling as Flora arrived, Callie said, "You must have a special way of gettin these children workin so hard to pick all this. Those two crates of apple and cantaloupe. Where? How?"

"When we got to Mista Johnson's place and saw all he was growin out there, we aks ifn he had any to shayuh. He said, 'Tek wha you can and leave de rest.' So...Bobby ran home to get our little wagon, and we brought back three watermelons and what is that, fifteen cantaloupes? And just down the way on Ben Farmer's plot, they had some fine grape arbors full of the best. Jancy got up on Beanie's shoulders, and she just kept pickin and dropin. She was goin so fas, de boys had trouble keepin dey sacks in de right place."

Callie said, "Oh, and figs, Flora June. Where did you find the figs?"

"That kind lady down the lane, that teacher lady, she just planted the fig trees a few years ago and was so proud. I see her smilin next to em sayin, 'Please come take some.' She gave us mo than we expected, and she say, 'Lucas always gib us his catch from de wada. Ain no nicer man.'"

Lilly added her thoughts: "You'd be pleased, Callie. Jus like you said when the freedom came in the wah. We all work together, and by sharin our gifts from God, we make this Oakheart community strong. So, you can be proud of what you started here, sista!"

Callie hid her pride and exclaimed, "Mercy, just look at the four boxes of peaches!"

"It was good we had the cart, Aunt Callie, though I had to help the boys pull it." Flora June explained, "Those peach trees were just about done, peaches ready to go. You know the kids be singin de songs you taught em while dey worked a few days ago. I had to laugh. Dey jus wanted to see who could get de mos."

Callie said, "You did the whole family a service, Florie. I know you got plans for all this fruit—makin some great pies and, I hope, jars of jam and jelly. My mouth is gettin ready for my big pig stew, throwin some sliced-up sweet potatoes and apples, and some onion in the big old pot. Maybe add some juicy, sweet peaches at just the right time. What you say, Miss Pie Maker?"

"Sounds delicious! Is it a stew or a pie fillin?" Flora June asked. As they laughed, Sunny dragged herself up the steps, having left the children running in the yard, dust flying. Woody had looked at her once as she moved toward the house and then returned to the chase. Suddenly, she was no longer essential to his sense of security.

"Oh my, got to love those children!" Sunny gasped as she fell into the chair near the peaches, one of which quickly disappeared from the bowl. "Florie, these are perfect for our pies."

"If we ever get around to makin pies wid em. Look at you."

Peach juice squirted out one side of Sunny's mouth. "I was thirsty."

"Are you happy?" Flora asked with a knowing smile.

"Oh, Florie. I can't begin to say. To see my boy with your boys." Sunny looked over to her mother, who shared her daughter's exuberance as she wiped tears wth her sleeve.

Callie said, "Every time I have ever looked at you, I thought you were pretty, but never more than right now. What you feelin bout your boy?"

"I just know I want his happiness, Mama."

"I know the family he stayed with in Savannah were good people. They were poor church folk Will found through a minister friend of his family. He felt sure they would take good care of him."

"And I see he's got a little quiet strength in him," Sunny said, almost boasting.

Callie turned to Lilly as if her daughter were not on the porch. "Well, I know he get the strength from Sunny, but the quiet part must come from someplace else."

Sunny interrupted the hilarity. "And, I want him to read, so he can find his own way, just like I did and just like you did."

"Well, we had help, too, all along the way."

"Mama, yes, and we were born pretty smaat to staat out." Sunny stopped herself. "Hopin that didn't sound too...too...much. I'm just sayin, we can learn, and we did."

"And we had help." Callie continued to supplement Sunny's statements. "I had Mama Ruth, and Old Bella, and my brothers—they all taught me things every day. Then havin you, baby, taught me things."

"And I had you, and Lilly and Lucas to help me grow up, and Grampa Harris, and the Grangers, and the teachers at Penn School."

"So, do you want Woody to go to Penn School?"

Sunny started her answer, "Sure do. I give Penn School so much credit for making me confident and able to think."

Lilly added. "And it's been doin that for all the kids—Robert, Beanie, Bobby—and now Jancy gettin started there."

Lucas arrived on the porch sweating profusely despite the steady wind. "Ah, do I hear praise for Penn? Can't say enough good ting bout what Penn done done fuh dis family!"

Flora added, shaking her head slowly from side to side, "It's sad to say, but one of the most important reasons fuh schoolin is to know when people are lyin to you."

"Amen to that," Lucas affirmed while casting a nervous look at the clouds.

Sunny echoed his enthusiasm. "Memba, Florie? Jus like wha happened last week. We had some people stop at our table and buy pies, nice white folk we been seein for a while. They were talkin to themselves about the wah and how the Confederates left the Union to defend states rights. They were standin right in front of us and said nothin bout slavery."

Flora chimed in, "Das right, like it wasn't even real. Later, we were tellin Brent about it, and he say, 'Well they say it's states' rights, but I say, states' rights to do what?'"

"Keep slaves!" shouted Sunny.

"Oh my," Callie said, smiling. "I got hope for the future when I hear the young'uns understandin where they came from."

"Sound like yo man Brent knows supm bout how ting be," Lilly said, nodding at Sunny. "I know we are done for now, talkin about your book outline, Callie, and all the history you have lived through. But now, thirty years later, when I heah people still say the war was caused by some idea about 'states' rights,' I got to say supm." She went into her satchel, the repository for all her notes about Callie's story and her newspaper clippings. "I been waitin to talk about this with you, Callie, and right now is the time. What I got here are the exact words from the mouth of the new vice president of the Confederate States of America about what caused the war." Lilly continued to unfold the paper.

Still chopping the fruit, Callie glanced at the Spanish moss getting blown about in the live oak trees and interrupted, "Hold those papers tight, Lilly. The wind is pickin up."

Lucas could not resist asking, "Lilly, you be talkin bout when de Confederate States mek treason against de United States?"

"That too," said Lilly. "You see I'm readin the newspaper, *The Savannah Republican*, from March 1861, quoting Alexander Stephens: 'The new Constitution has put at rest forever all the agitating questions relating to our peculiar institutions—African slavery as it exists among us—the proper status of the negro in our form of civilization. This was the immediate cause of the late rupture and present revolution.'" Lilly looked around at the faces of her family. "Mmmm-hmmm." Nodding her head, "Case closed bout that." And then, "Listen heah, that man, Mista Stephens, went on to say the United States was wrong to believe in equality of all people. Here he go again in that same speech written down in the newspaper: 'Our new government is founded upon exactly the opposite idea; its foundations are laid, its cornerstone rests upon the great truth, that the negro is not equal to the white man; that slavery—subordination to the superior race—is his natural and normal condition. [Applause.] This, our new government, is the first, in the history of the world, based upon this great physical, philosophical, and moral truth.'"***

Lilly concluded, "Now ain that just about clear? And yet, if our children can't be educated to read those words, they won't know enough to correct somebody who says the war was about the issue of states' rights."

Sunny's pleasure in Lilly's pointed fire was evident as she shouted, "That's my Auntie Lilly, the truth-teller!"

*** Cleveland, Henry. *Alexander H. Stephens, in Public and Private: With Letters and Speeches, Before, During, and Since the War*. National Publishing Company: Philadelphia, 1886, 717-729. And the Alexander Stephens Corner Stone speech (Savannah, GA, March 21, 1861) *teachingamericanhistory.org › Library › Civil War Era › Alexander Stephens*

Lucas, fidgeting in his chair, was pleased with what he was hearing and the serious purpose that had drawn the family's focus. But he interrupted, "Listen yuh. I know we havin a good talk an a good time—I know we havin a day fuh strengthen our fambly wid food an fun. I see de chirren lovin young Woody, an I know we all grateful fuh all de good when we be togedda. But God may have a different plan fuh dis day." He paused. "We may need skrent from high places, praise God, because we got a big stohm gettin too close. Ebbyting I see in de cloud an de wada an de wind tell me dis stohm gonna keep gettin stronga. De rain is gonna be startin any time. Fact be, we may even have a little salty mist right now in de air. I'm about to go check my bromedda to see how much de air pressure be droppin. I know it be sinkin. I feel it."

He looked around at the women in his family as they pushed back their chairs, stood up, and surveyed the sky. Lilly and Callie began to gather the cut fruits and vegetables. Sunny frowned, showing the greatest concern, as she walked to the edge of the porch, first looking at the children in the yard, then studying the wind's effect on the surface of the river.

Lucas spoke again. "Sunny, I hear what you and Florie say bout yo man. He sound like he might be smaat enough fuh you. Someday, I be happy to meet him."

Callie abruptly stopped cleaning off the table. She gasped, "Oh, I was supposed to talk with you today to tell you that Sunny wanted to have him come visit. She wanted your blessings."

"Sho. She can invite him anytime."

Sunny, as quick as her mother, turned to face her uncle and smiled. "I'm so glad you feel that way, uncle, because I invited him already. And that 'anytime' you speak about, well, it will be on the outbound tide today."

Starting to frown, Lucas caught himself, then looked out on the river where a little white water topped some of the waves, and back to

Sunny. "Well now, ifn he willin to jump on dis windy riba today fuh visit you an yo boy, then I gah fuh gib him respeck, and I welcome him."

"Oh, Uncle Lucas, thank you!" Sunny delivered a powerful, joyful hug. As she went down the porch steps, she said, "I love him, you know, and we are gonna be a strong family. You'll see."

Flora June added, "Uncle Luke, I been knowin dis man fuh some time now. I tink you an Lilly, an you too, Callie, will be findin out, like I did, he be mos worthy of our Miss Sunny."

"All right, Flora June, I know you lookin out fuh Sunny." Lucas shifted back to the impending weather, now his primary concern. "Ladies, can we get to cookin wha gonna be cooked and stored? Soon, Douglass and me gonna bring in some full crab traps an buckets of shrimp. We even got some oyster we rake and been soak till we ready. Abram gonna tend de grill. When we get done fixin food, we can all turn to makin sure we be safe an ready if dis stohm keep comin."

Callie asked, "What about the chirren?"

Lucas cautioned, "Let em run now, not near de wada though."

Lilly offered, "They are havin the best time with Woody now, and Sunny be watchin em. It's just windy and not even wet yet. Let em play until we get some food ready." She turned to take her fixings to the kitchen. "As Lucas says, the weather may tell us what to do with our plans anyway."

Lucas returned to the dock where Douglass was loading gear into the workboat for pulling crab traps. Abram stayed ashore to heft the remaining boat gear up to the storage shed under the house. Lilly soon urged him to light the kindling between the stones, so the iron griddle could be laid over the fire later and be sizzling—ready to cook oysters, shrimp, and fish. Callie shouted out the kitchen door that her pot of pork stew needed to simmer on it for a couple hours.

Sunny had exhausted her supply of youthful exuberance after thirty minutes of running with the children from one exciting adventure to another. She had just settled on the front steps when the children started shouting, "Buckra man comin up de crik." Sunny took one quick look and recognized the familiar form and rowing style of her man.

At once thrilled and frightened, Sunny called out, "Florie! FLORIE!" Callie came out on the porch first, followed closely by Lilly; Flora June rushed from the backyard. "Brent's here, oh my goodness, he is here." Turning to her cousin for a quick hug, Sunny asked her to hold all the children on the bluff so she and Woody could meet Brent on the dock. Without waiting for an answer, she raced to her son's side.

Sunny gently steered Woody away from the other children, who were being corralled by Flora and Lilly. "Come with me, young man. I have a good surprise."

"Wha it be...Mama? De kids. Dey be callin you my mama."

"Is that all right with you?"

"Not if it ain true." When Sunny knelt in front of him to hold his hands, his eyes fell to the ground between them and she felt his small shoulders sag.

Sunny lifted his chin with the most gentle touch. Eye to eye, she declared to him, "You can always call me yo mama. You are my son, and I will take care of you."

Righting himself slightly, Woody said, "One of de boys say, 'It too good to be true.'"

"Oh, Woody," Sunny smiled, "that's just supm people say, a way of talkin. He didn't mean it wasn't true—he meant it was really, really good! You see?" Sunny wrapped her arms around her son, who sighed heavily as he leaned into her embrace.

"And now, you wanna hear supm else that's really, really good? Supm true?"

Woody spoke from a life of uncertain promises. "Yes'm. If it gonna stay true..."

"I know. This is yo mama talkin. I know, this really, really good thing will stay true."

"Wha it be?"

"If you turn around and look out on the river, you can see a boat." And as she spoke, she straightened up a little taller so that she could see something really, really true, too. "In that boat, there is one man workin very hard, rowin toward us. You see him?"

"Yes, ma'am."

"Oh, Woody, I love how polite you are."

"I see the man...he just turn round to look at us."

"Yes, honey, he's coming to us. That man, his name is Brent. Woody, he's your daddy."

As Woody saw his father for the first time, Sunny stood behind him, hands on his shoulders, rubbing softly. "Mama? That's my daddy?"

"Yes, he and I, we are your parents, fuh true. We are gonna take good care of you." Woody reached up and grabbed Sunny's hands tightly as they watched Brent draw near. Sunny shouted, "Hey, Brent! Look who is waitin for you!" Brent turned to see Sunny and this small, skinny boy intently looking at him. On the bluff behind them, the adults and children were doing the same.

Appreciating one more moment alone, his back facing his destination, Brent fought through his emotions and the last persistent waves as they finally diminished near the dock. He powered his craft with one last pull on the oars before casting them aside to grab the bow rope and secure it. Sunny normally would have helped but did not feel she should leave Woody standing alone on the windy dock. Brent struggled a bit with the stern rope before he looked up. After brushing his matted, brown hair out of his eyes, Brent saw his son staring at him.

The boat rolled up with a particularly high wave as Brent stepped onto the dock. Sunny's steadying arm embraced Brent's shoulder as she kept her other arm around her son. "Brent, this is our son, Woody."

First Brent reached out his hand, and the boy responded in kind. Brent immediately went to one knee and embraced his son as Sunny cried into the wind, light rain now joining her outpouring of grateful tears that had waited ten long years.

Chapter 11

SATURDAY AFTERNOON, AUGUST 26, 1893

As Woody greeted his father, Florie persuaded everyone to stay up on the bluff to give the new family a little privacy. Soon after, with a light rain beginning to fall, Lilly urged them to return to the house, granting Sunny's family more time and space to get acquainted.

Sunny, in turn, stepped back and gave father and son a chance to make first impressions with no interference. When Brent stood and quietly clutched Woody's hand, Sunny guided them up from the dock and through the side yard to the old meat shed.

Watching from the window, Callie smiled at how oblivious they were to the rain. She was glad they went into the shed first, Sunny's sanctuary where, through her art, she conveyed her innermost feelings about her life.

Callie fixed a glass of sweet tea and a big plate of gumbo with rice and fruit for Sunny's man. She was heading down the back steps when she saw them emerge from the shed and start toward the house, Sunny and Brent each holding one of Woody's hands. Callie returned to the kitchen, deciding to give them a little more time before they were engulfed by the rhythms of the family.

Indeed, it was a whirlwind. No sooner had Sunny entered the kitchen than the women of the family lined up. Sunny, being raised right, took her cue. "Everyone, I would like you to meet Brent, my best friend and Woody's father. This is Nellie, she's married to cousin Douglass, and Amanda, she's married to cousin Abram, and my Aunt Lilly who been so good to me." Sunny hesitated long enough for Brent to smile warmly while greeting the younger women.

Then he extended his hand to Lilly. When she responded, he said, "I've heard so many stories about you."

"Well, that's good, I hope." Lilly smiled back to Brent, saying, "I look forward to hearin that much about you. Yes, I do."

"Yes, ma'am." Brent showed his heartfelt respect to her and nodded his understanding of her meaning.

Woody pulled on his mother's hand, and when she leaned down, he whispered, "My daddy polite, too."

"Yes, he is, Woody. Good for you to see that." Through her mother's proud smile, Sunny continued, "And Mama." Sunny moved close enough to place her arm on Callie's back. "I know you met Brent a time or two before, but I want to introduce him to you as the man I have chosen to be with me—worthy of bein my son's father, and of bein your son."

"Well...," Callie started.

"Brent, this is my Mama, Callie Hewitt, the most amazing woman I know."

"Yes, of course, Miss Callie, Miss Hewitt, uh...," Brent stammered to a stop and then looked up to see Callie's hopeful face. "I'm just glad to meet you in these circumstances. And I have to say, thank you." Brent lifted his arm, showing father and son holding hands. "Meeting him and knowing Sunny as his mother, these are the best things that ever happened to me."

Callie leaned forward, one hand extended to touch the side of his face. "Me too," was all she could utter before tears told why words would not come out. Callie fanned her face and regained control enough to remember the food. "Brent, here is a plate for you; I know you must be hungry and thirsty after all that rowin from Beaufort. Since we won't have dinner for a while, why don't you just sit down here and take a moment to get your strength back before meeting the others."

Sunny smiled at her mother's thoughtfulness and sat quietly, just watching her son and his father, amused by Woody's polite, yet firm, "Daddy, look like you got too much gumbo." Brent moved his plate closer to Woody, nodded, smiled, gave him another spoon, and held out his palm in signal to proceed. They took turns dipping spoons until they finished.

After the three new family members sat for a few more moments sharing sips of the tea from Brent's cup, Sunny asked Brent, "Are you ready to meet the rest of the family?" Sunny took Woody's hand and led Brent out of the kitchen and through the dining room, saying, "Where are the little ones? It's too quiet for them to be inside, but it's rainin outside." There they were in the living room, playing pick-up-sticks and marbles.

"Okay, Florie, how you do it?" Sunny asked, pointing to the kids.

"Oh, I told em they get a piece of candy from you if they stay quiet and play nice with each other until you come back."

"Oh, thank you." Sunny spoke the familiar sarcasm of good friends. "I'll get you back."

At that, Jancy could hold it no more, shouting, "Hey, Woody!" And then, not quite as loud, "Hey, man. You Woody's daddy?"

Nellie and Amanda followed Lilly and Callie from the kitchen, carrying platters with a variety of fruit to the dining room table. The quiet period engineered by Flora June ended abruptly as each child took the quickest path to the table through the open double doors of the living room. The action drowned out Brent's proudly stated response to Jancy's question, "Yes, I am."

Robert was first to circle back to the visitor with a plate of grapes, pecans, and a fig. Directing his question to Brent, he said, "You know what, Mista Brent? You look a lot like Woody."

Brent bent down level with Robert's face. "Or do you think Woody looks a lot like me?"

Robert thought for a moment, then looked more closely at Brent's laughing eyes. "Ah, Mista Brent, you know he do." Robert decided that Brent was all right, evidenced by his next comment made through a grin. "Woody be a little bedda-lookin dan you!" Then he pushed on Brent's outstretched arm and scampered out of his reach.

Sunny overheard the conversation and stepped back from Brent, taking a good long look. "You know, I think Robert is right." Smiling her way back to a hug up under Brent's chin, Sunny said, "You are both good-lookin to me."

Soon, Flora June was surrounded by requests for the candy she promised. She said, "Eat all dis healthy food first. Den you get a small piece from Sunny like I say."

Sunny, now motherly, cautioned, "You know, we still got dinner comin."

Callie pointed excitedly. "There it is. Dinner arriving just now on the dock." As the children gathered to look, Callie said, "Those men have been working hard out in the rain to get our food. Look in the back of the boats at all those empty crab traps stacked up."

Robert joyfully told Woody about the scene that he had witnessed often. "Looka my daddy liftin em out to Unca Doug. They got crabs in de tubs, and buckets full o shrimp."

Lilly encouraged the kitchen help to return. "Ladies, we are gonna be servin our fixins with all that fresh fish. Callie, how's your pork stew?"

"Been simmerin for a whlle—got more to go before it be just right."

Suddenly, after looking out the window, Brent turned to face Sunny. "I should be out there."

Without words, Sunny stared at him with raised eyebrows, quietly questioning his decision. Brent nodded "yes" as he hurried out the front door.

Brent carefully descended the front porch steps, now wet from a steady light rain, crossed the yard, and then went down the bluff to the dock. Squinting into the easterly wind and facing the improbability of his circumstance, he said, "Gentlemen, I'm Brent. How can I help?"

Lucas was seldom surprised, but he hesitated long enough for Douglass to say, "I'm Douglass. Thanks for helpin. You can carry dis tub o crab to de brick firepit outside de house, and come back fuh mo." Brent grabbed one, turned quickly, and headed up to the firepit.

Lucas and his sons exchanged looks as Abram said, "We see how fast he movin afta one or two mo tubs." They laughed, probably not loud enough in the wind to be heard by Brent.

Abram and Douglass each grabbed two buckets of shrimp and made their way from the dock to the top of the bluff, almost colliding with Brent as he was returning for more. It took him three more trips with full tubs to empty the boat of crab. Without asking, Brent stepped onto the dock and hefted a crate full of oysters that had been harvested days before, but just pulled from the water. As he turned, Lucas spoke up, "Tank ya. You Sunny's man, right?" Brent nodded, still holding the crate. "While I appreciate yo wuk, it ain gonna be that easy."

Nodding again, as if he understood, Brent said, "Yes, sir," and stepped from the dock.

With the arrival of the day's catch, activity around the firepit immediately picked up. On his first trip up with shrimp buckets, Abram added dry logs to the fire. Despite the light rain, the fire started readily atop the smoldering embers. Steady wind stoked the fire and in minutes the water-filled crab pot, set on the grate which covered half the pit, began to boil. Sunny and Flora June sprinkled Lilly's special seasoning blend in the pot, joyfully anticipating mouthwatering, spicy crab meat and melted butter which, they knew, would please all palates. Once in the pot, the hapless crabs quickly turned from their ocean blue-green colors to a bright peach-orange. They were ready for eating.

The other half of the open firepit was covered with a steel plate that was steaming hot and sizzling with each raindrop. Lucas spread dozens of oysters on it, quickly covering them with damp burlap sacks. Though he had to be exhausted from the labor required to bring in the catch, Lucas was a man whose mission was clear—to cook this food up for his family as quickly as he could.

Brent noticed how involved Lucas was in all aspects of the seafood preparation and, trying to be a grateful guest, went down the porch steps and back to the large firepit, angling toward Lucas. "I just want to say thank you for receivin me heah on your property." Lucas said nothing as he pulled the crab pot away from the heat. Brent tried again, saying, "In all my life, I ain arrived at a place and have such a meal prepared..."

Brent's small smile was not noticed, and his comment hung in the air a bit, but not long. Lucas paused his labor to look toward Brent. "I fish this out today befo de stohm, so I can feed my family. We fixin fuh shayuh wid dem we love. I say welcome, Ben, but honestly," and he looked purposefully into Brent's eyes, "I ain know you was comin." Lucas turned away, then slowly turned to face Brent again. "But now you standin right yuh on my land, I gah tuh aks you supm. You know, fuh mo dan ten yeah, it be gainst de law in Sout Calina fuh white folk tuh marry colored folk. Cost you five hundred dollars an dey put you in jail fuh twelve mont or mo." You know dah?"

Brent sighed heavily. "Mista Lucas, I know what you say is true." Hesitating, "I want to take care of Sunny and our boy. We feel real strong bout each other."

"Reckon dah gonna be enough?" Lucas turned to spill out some water on the grill, creating a great plume of perfectly seasoned seafood steam, carried by the easterly breeze up, over, and around Brent into the trees beyond. Brent's face showed that he considered carrying the conversation on, then reconsidered and walked away toward the river. Minutes later, the crab and oysters were ready for tasting.

Amanda had taken the first bucket of shrimp brought up from the dock and spread them out in the largest frying pan available. They already sizzled with melted butter, garlic, and several pinches of Lilly's special crab seasoning. Flipped once, they would be ready in no time.

Meanwhile, Douglass had fulfilled Lilly's request to set up temporary tables under the porch on the west side of the house, to let the family get some relief from the steady, misty breeze on the east side. He used miscellaneous planks left over from building projects and cobbled them together on top of sawhorses. Then he brought chairs for the adults and benches for the children down from the porch, wondering all the while when his father would choose to replace the porch roof that was destroyed by the cyclone of 1883.

Lucas continued to move seafood around on the griddle and, when cooked, to its edge where it waited for takers. Needing no invitation, family members filed by his "kitchen stove," filled their plates, and gravitated to the makeshift tables set by Douglass. Just when Lucas allowed himself to do the same, all chef duties performed for the moment, Nathan Gates walked up through the yard. "Mista Gates, good timin, suh. Grab yosef a plate."

"No, no, thank you. I just wanted to check on the young man. You know, Will is going to expect a report from me on the mission."

"Step round yuh an you will see a happy boy." Lucas led him around to the west side, where Woody was sitting on a bench between his parents.

Sunny immediately stood to greet him. "Mista Gates! Oh, sir, I got to say sorry."

"Why?" Gates was smiling.

"You and the other men worked so haad to bring my boy heah, and I barely spoke a word when you were standin in front of me."

Still smiling, Gates said, "Well, I could see you had other business on your mind. In my few days with him, Woody was a very good boy."

Realizing who Gates was, Brent stood and extended his hand. "Yes, sir, please let me say thank you too." Seeing Gates's confusion about the man in front of him, Brent continued, "You brought our son back to Sunny and me."

"Of course, well, yes. I'm glad to help the family get together. Hello, Miss Callie...good that all of you are here." Callie nodded, waved, and smiled through sealed lips, bringing her hand down to cover her mouth as she finished a chewy oyster.

Gates, sensing the importance of the family moment, said, "My good friends, I just wanted to make sure all was well with Woody." Gates looked over to him, smiled, and waved. "I see he is quite happy with his fine, new family. I'll leave now and wish you all well in the approaching storm."

Callie rose. "Please sir, take some food for you and the others with you. I been hearing all the hammerin and bangin by you and your crew down at Will's house."

"I will. Thank you all." Gates waved again and turned to walk back to the firepit with Lucas. Placing his hand on Lucas's shoulder, Gates said, "You know, we have a situation out on the water."

They both turned into the easterly wind, looking toward the creek, its surface now choppy in the gusting winds. Lucas shook his head. "Wind buildin all day. Now, gusts from de sea gettin right stout."

Gates added, "I've been watching the swirl of the clouds. See how they are coming in lower now? There is a big storm center somewhere off Florida and coming nearer."

"We been clearin de dock. Mo to do when we finish our meal. I heah all your hammerin today, too. You ain givin yo hands a rest?"

"I promised Will I would strengthen the deck outside his cottage and over the marsh. I figure better get to it before this storm arrives. I have some help too, so we're going to keep at it as long as the weather allows." He laughed, holding out his blistered hands to receive the large basket of seafood Lucas had hastily packed. "Thank you and yours."

"You a hard-workin, good man, Nathan Gates. We appreciate you so much."

As the pace of family feasting subsided, heavy humidity in the atmosphere moistened the faces that looked up to see the cloud movements Gates had described. Even the children sat still. Lucas brought his plate to sit with Lilly and Callie, their chairs tucked well under the porch.

Sunny, who had been blissfully ignoring everyone but her new family, glanced at her uncle, finally sitting, but not at ease. When he finished eating, Sunny walked over to him, quietly asking, "Uncle Lucas, afta all you do fuh us, wha can I do to help you?"

Lucas focused on her earnest face. "Darlin, I gah someting worryin my head, is all."

Knowing her uncle and knowing better, Sunny persisted, "Uncle, say."

Lucas couldn't hide his concern. "I tink bout ting we gah fuh do bout dis stohm." And then, his face brightened. "And, I tink bout how happy happy I be fo all yo joy." Lucas leaned in. "You know, Woody be a fine boy."

Sunny giggled her response, "You tink?"

But that was all Lucas said.

Sunny pressed her luck, asking, "Wha bout his daddy?"

"I'm figurin on da, too."

"What is it? Say, please."

"Maybe later, niece, maybe later."

Woody jumped between them, redirecting Sunny's attention. "Say 'excuse me' to Uncle Lucas."

"Scoozmeee, Unclukus."

"And excuse me," Lilly stood and said quietly to Lucas, "you know, we best move inside while we still got light."

"Yea, wife, you right, I was just tryin to steal a minute. Let's get movin. We gah mo fuh do tonight ifn de stohm gonna wind up."

Lilly used her teacher voice with the family. "We know we want to be easy at the end of dis day, but Lucas say we gonna get more rain any time now. So, all hands carry supm up to de kitchen. Men handle de meat and big bowls, women and chirren clear off de rest. Afta we get inside, we gonna have dessert in de parlor and decide wha we need to do." With that, everyone grabbed something and marched up to the kitchen in a somewhat orderly fashion, newly energized in their task and talking loudly with one another. Plates, bowls, platters, and pitchers filled countertops and tables, mixing with meal preparation debris, making cleanup quite a task for someone.

Nellie, dutiful since the first day Douglass introduced her to the family, quietly asserted herself. "It's my turn to be in chaage a supm. De kitchen mess is mine. Ifn I need hep, I say so." Amanda briefly questioned her decision but, getting rebuffed, followed Callie, Lilly, Flora June, and Sunny as they ushered the children from the kitchen to the living room.

Outside, in twenty minutes, the men had broken down and stored the "tables" on the west side of the house under the porch and began moving other random items to the back storage shed, per Lucas's instruction. When Lucas put more wood into the firepit, he saw Abram's questioning look and simply said, "Wid de weadda comin, we gah fuh cook it all up tonight. Right, boys?"

Abram understood and called out to Douglass, "Let's git to cookin, brudda."

"I have a question, Lucas," Brent spoke up.

"All right. I'm listenin."

"I thought it best to ask you while we were down in the yard." He kicked at the wet grass briefly, then proceeded. "With respect, sir, I'm askin if I can stay in your house tonight, or on your grounds. The weather bein so rough, seems I better not try to row back to Beaufort tonight."

Lucas hesitated, looking out on the water just long enough to make Brent believe he should prepare to leave. "You got a job to do?"

"Yes, uh, I work every day, but this is a Saturday, sir, and the shop closed at noon."

"No, I asked ifn you got a job down heah in de yaad. Seem like you oughta go inside. Mek sense you wanna be wid yo boy an his mama, I spose." With that, Lucas turned and climbed up the back stairs.

"Yes, thank you, sir." Knowing better than to ask if the brothers needed help with the grill, Brent followed Lucas into the house. They passed through the kitchen and dining room to find the children just settling on the living room floor. Sunny, Amanda, and Flora June were milling about, talking louder than the youngsters. Lilly urged, "Gather here, big chirren. Sit down and behave like these young'uns; you still our chirren, you just bigger. Go find a seat. We got a few things to talk about with you, Lucas and me."

Lilly began. "Now we just finished up a fine meal, and we thank God, and we thank all the hands that prepared it. Amen? We lucky people to be beside these waters, to be able to have fresh fish, crab, and shrimp whenever we want. Ain we? And to have fields that grow all the food we can eat? I love bein heah. I see you be smiling every day since comin back, Callie."

"You right, Sista Lilly. Love bein back with you all again, and I mean, all of you."

Lilly continued, "Sometimes this place we love get some tough weather. Well, we tough too, ain we?"

Waiting for her answers, they came back. "Da right."

"Tough."

"We are."

"Sho be!"

As a former teacher, Lilly immediately knew that her question invited oral cacophony from the children, so as it started, she stepped up, hands out, and said, "Hey! We are tough, and we are respectful."

"Yes, ma'am!" came back the chorus.

"Well, tonight, we probly gonna have some rough weather, so wha we gah fuh do?"

"We be tough!" shouted Jancy.

"And respecal," offered little Saxton.

Laughing for all to see, Lilly echoed, "Yes, Saxton, we be respectful, and we be special."

Robert asked, "We goin to pray meetin tomorrow?"

"We may not get to go to church services in the morning. But we will be worshipful, and thoughtful, and quiet. We may even have our own service right here." That statement provoked frowns and whispering among the children. Lilly began walking around, looking at each child. "So, I need to ask a big favor of each of you. You know how much we love you, right? The best way we can love you tonight, is for you to stay in one place, right here in the living room while we adults are busy takin care of things around the house. We gonna have paper and pencils and we askin you to help each other have fun, be safe, and stay right here. We gonna always have somebody in here wid you. We need you to be extra special good tonight. Everybody understand? We gonna be good together, and we'll have dessert after our meeting."

Jancy's voice rose above the other voices. "We love you, Grandma Lilly! We be good."

Lucas stepped up beside Lilly, laughing with everyone. "So, my chirren, you know I love it when you mek a joyful noise, but, like Lilly say, we need yo voices to be right fo inside de house. All right?

All right. Flora June, you an de boys be welcome to stay right yuh. Amanda, you and Abram are all set. Douglas and Nellie know they can stay, too, or go back to dey own home an come back tomorrow, dependin on de stohm. Dere be rooms an blankets fuh ebbybody. Dah right, Lilly?"

She nodded, and Lucas continued, for all to hear, "Lilly, we got someting tuh do heah befo we res. Right now, de boys be cookin all de fish. We gah fuh put all de food in crates and boxes. I jus want ebby-body in de fambly to know, we look out fuh ourself, and we proud of it. Memba wha my big sista Callie tell me? We may not be able to see wha comin roun de bend in de riba, but we can get ready fuh it."

With that, Amanda headed into the kitchen to help Nellie clear the way for the evening's food preparation and storage. Lucas looked out the window to see the firepit operation proceeding, so he started toward the front door. Before Brent could offer assistance, Lilly asked, "Sunny, can you two stay with the children first?"

"Brent, did you hear that? She called us 'you two'?" An occasion for a longer hug was cut short with the rumblings of seven children.

Callie dug into one of her pouches and pulled out some pencils and a notebook filled with blank paper. "Here, daughter, I was saving all this for a special occasion, like this. I know you and these children can do something with these."

"Can I!" Sunny held the papers up for all to see. "Looka heah, young'uns!"

Flora June shouted to Sunny from across the room, "I'm gonna git some dry clothes fuh de boys and mo blankets. I may stay heah too if dis stohm git wus. Anybody usin dah daybed in de room across de hall?"

Callie responded, as she disappeared into the kitchen, "That one in the parlor? I don't think so, darlin. It's yours."

Sunny turned to the excited little people in front of her. "Children, listen yuh! We got a good ting happenin right yuh. See, we got paper and all deese nice pencils. Brent, I'm havin an idea. Let us adults help you kids, each one of you, to make a special project."

Brent asked, "Do you children know what a project is?"

"Supm to git done done," Robert offered, while others shook their heads, faces blank.

Sunny crouched down to the children's eye level and in a loud whisper said, "Doin a special project is like makin magic happen." Looking each child in the face, she had claimed their attention. "But, you got to have supm special. You got to have supm special that we all have." The children looked at one another and back at Sunny. "You all got...imagination."

Beanie spoke up. "Wha dah agin? Maginatin?"

"Imagination. It's what you think—a piccha in yo head. What can your own smaat brain think up, that you want to draw and show the family tomorrow? So, everybody, right where you are, we gonna sit and think for five minutes. Brent, you tell us when five minutes are up. And then, we are gonna help you choose what project to do. All right now, staat thinkin."

After a few seconds, Sunny added, holding up a finger, "And, you can decide what song you want to sing while holding up your picture. Or what dance steps you want to show off with your project, your art. And you might even have a poem to share. Maybe? So, let's close our eyes and think."

As if hypnotized, the children did so.

———◆———

IN THE KITCHEN, LILLY WAS THANKING HER DAUGHTERS-IN-LAW FOR all they accomplished. "You young ladies can help in my kitchen anytime. Nellie, you get so much done, and with that baby wrapped across your chest."

Amanda agreed, "You got so much energy in yo lee body, Nellie!"

"I gah fuh be fas to keep up with my big girl, that Jancy." Amanda laughed while urging Nellie to sit with her infant. "Tank you, Manda, but I gah fuh run home to git clothes fuh Douglass and de chirren befo it get too late."

Flora June entered the kitchen on her way out the back door and heard Nellie's plans. "Come with me, cuz. We go to your house, then mine. Leave da beautiful baby heah and come on. You got our kids covered, ladies?"

Lilly jumped at the chance to hold her youngest grandchild. "Sho do!" Nellie was anxious as she surrendered her sleeping baby girl. "Let me just hold this pretty little thing." Smiling as she sat down, nestling the undisturbed baby in her arms, Lilly urged her daughter-in-law, "Go! You ain never without yo kids. Go on, take a walk in the rain with Florie."

With their exit, the new kitchen crew turned to finish what Nellie started—storing the leftovers and the freshly cooked seafood with its smoky flavor. "That smells too good," Callie said as she slouched against the counter. "Mek me fugit I jus eat."

"Sista, stand up to this work," Lilly playfully scolded. "Where do you put all de food you been eatin anyway."

———◆———

AT THE FIREPIT, LUCAS FOUND HIS SONS CLEANING UP. "TANK YA, boys! We all gonna eat good, even if de stohm get bad. Can you do one mo big ting befo we stop fuh today?" Knowing their father's question did not require their answer, they nodded as Lucas proceeded, "We gah fuh pull we boats out de wadda, in case de stohm tear up our dock." To their questioning looks, Lucas responded, "Gah fuh pull de two bateau an de big rowboat up on de bluff."

"You tink it be that bad?" asked Douglass, who seldom questioned his father. Abram's look of concern supported the question.

"Stohm been building fuh days and we jus now gettin some rain? Clouds in big circles travelin wid de east wind from ovah de ocean. Tell you what though, we wait and see what happen round noon, when high tide come. Den we know ifn we gah fuh move de boats. All right?"

Tired, but ready for one last task, Abram feigned disappointment, bumping into his brother. "Today or tomorrow, we ready. Daddy needs his boys' free labor, again."

"Ain no free labor!" Lucas protested.

Douglass imitated his father. "Daddy say, 'De boys get paid in de food dey chew, de house wey dey sleep, and de wisdom dey let me put in dey heads.' Dah so?"

Lucas nodded. "Dah so."

Collectively, they agreed to wait until morning to see whether to pull the boats onto land.

IN THE LIVING ROOM, THE CHILDREN'S THINKING TIME HAD ENDED. Sunny and Brent were leading quiet conversations with first one child and then another. Robert was diligently looking at his Penn School notebooks and writing his thoughts after a serious talk with Brent. The twins were following different paths; Beanie had turned toward the corner and, hunched over the pad in front of him, was drawing and writing; Bobby had decided to sing and was talking with Sunny about choices. Saxton was sitting still, appearing deep in thought. And Jancy was all energy, drawing and singing. She looked up only to ask if there was extra paper. When told yes, she worked a few more seconds and, after standing and taking a critical look at what she had drawn, stomped on it once. Finger on her lips, she looked up, then bent over to pick up the paper. She folded it in half, and then again, and again, until she could not make another fold. She smiled while trading it in for another sheet of paper and went back to work.

Woody began sketching almost immediately after the five-minute thinking period ended. As Sunny watched, a fully spread live oak tree appeared before her eyes. With only the biggest branches traced in so far, her pride grew and she couldn't wait any longer to comment on his work. "You plan to do anything else with that fine tree?"

"Well, you said you want to mek a family tree so me and my daddy...can I call him my daddy?" Sunny nodded, catching the lump in her throat just short of tears. "Well, you said me and my daddy can know bout all de family ifn we see a family tree. So, my project be mek a family tree."

"So, you gonna fill in those spaces between the branches?"

"Mm-hm. Gonna put all yo family in de tree."

"All yo family, too," Sunny reminded him as he returned to sketching, smiling.

Amanda, fresh from kitchen duty, offered to stay with the children, allowing Sunny and Brent a rare moment alone. Noting that Woody was well into his project, they walked up the stairs for a private hug and a moment of sharing their own imaginings while waiting for the family to reassemble.

Callie and Lilly laughed their way out of kitchen, placed a tray with small pieces of peach pie on a table near Amanda in the living room, and headed across the hall to the parlor. Both exhausted, they collapsed into armchairs set on either side of the large bay window overlooking the river. Talking quietly, both began to nod off, only to be startled by the kitchen door slamming shut behind Flora and Nellie as they returned from their short hike in the rain. Their long skirts beneath their dripping canvas ponchos were wet with bits of mud along the bottom edges. After leaving their muddy shoes near the door, wiping off their feet, and shedding the ponchos, they carried their large bundles of dry clothing into the hallway, ready to meet the needs of their children and the working men. Minutes later, Lucas and sons climbed the back steps to the kitchen, arriving wet and sweaty. Well trained by Lilly, they knew to clean up upon entry. Nellie and Lilly stood by to exchange filthy wet items for dry, clean ones.

When Abram entered the living room somewhat dry, he saw that Amanda was with a group of quiet children. He veered across the hall to the parlor and plopped into the big easy chair next to Sunny and Brent, who had settled comfortably on the couch.

"So, cousin..." Abram smiled at Sunny. "What's new?"

"I know you think you be a funny man," Sunny said, while Brent chuckled next to her. "You know me, Abram. My heart is so full. I got a strong supm inside that keeps me doin what has to be done." She looked over to Brent. "Abram is the same way as me. He's workin hard wid twenty families to hep em make a profit on Oakheart crops, while bein out in the field himself half the day."

"Half the day?" Abram asked.

"I said that since I know you workin at bein a minister, too."

Brent said, "That's a fine combination, Abram, nurturing seeds and souls."

Proudly, Abram responded, "You know, every piece of food we ate tonight that grew from de land, somebody in Oakheart community farmed it."

"That's great, for you, your family, and everybody else. I remember when I grew up out on St. Helena how large the harvests were. Seemed like almost year-round there's something ready to pick, right?" Abram nodded with Brent, who added, "I really wish I could be farmin or fishin instead of spending my days in an office."

Abram asked, "What's your job?"

"I work as a clerk for one of the warehouses near the Beaufort wharf. As I say, I'd rather do what you do out here, any day."

Douglass and Nellie slipped quietly into the room, followed by Lucas. He overheard Brent's last sentence and gave him a little extra look as he crossed the room to his corner chair near the window. As he sat, most eyes turned to him.

"De kids be happy, some wukin so haad, some already asleep. Maybe we be asleep too, befo long. Seem like disyuh stohm tryin to get staated—rain an wind gettin bigga. We wuk today tuh be ready fuh nex day. Dah wha dis fambly always do." Nodded agreement surrounded him. "When we get togedda, fus ting, we fix great food an nyam (eat) it up." Laughter quickly subsided. "Nex ting we do—we talk bout ting wha madda." No one looked interested in deep conversation; they had all earned the right to be very tired.

Lucas seemed independently motivated. "Sometime we talk bout our babies, and wha trial an tribulation dey got, en dey gib us. An sometime we talk bout wha de outside world bring to our door. We may be done wid a day o wuk, eatin wid our family and be ready to put down anodda night, an supm come knockin. We didn't aks fuh em, an we mos sure don deserve em, buh we gah fuh be ready fuh em when ih come."

Puzzled looks greeted Lucas. Sunny spoke first, "Wha ting be knockin at de door, Uncle Lucas?"

"Like, you memba, we talk bout when de man in chaage, de white man, say yo community can't collect money to educate yo chirren? Das de kind a trouble been brought to we door in dishyuh community."

Lucas looked intently at Brent, who responded uncertainly, "Yes, sir."

"You know, or maybe you don't know. When you wuk each day fuh yo fambly, an de man keep findin new ways tuh keep you down. Da kinda trouble keep comin to my neighbors' door. I heah my friends who aren't out on de wada talkin bout how dey havin mo trouble gettin wuk, less it be a labor job, or gettin very little pay an white people gettin a whole lot mo. Seem like people tink some jobs jus fuh colored people. You know?"

Again, Lucas looked toward Brent, who nodded again, saying, "Yes, sir."

"You do? You know bout da problem we be havin?"

"Well, not directly."

"No, spose not. I hear you talkin bout your job. How you get it? You tink yo daddy's name hep?" At that, Lilly moved over to stand next to Lucas.

However, Brent was engaged. "Honestly, that probably helped, but I had training and good experience."

"I respeck dah," Lucas conceded, "but don't you tink yo name hep you almos as much as your skin color?" Lilly reached down and squeezed his shoulder just hard enough to be visible.

"Probably so, yes, sir. You are right, there aren't any black people workin in the office."

Lucas nodded. "Mmmm-hmmm. We be a fortunate family, thanks be to Gawd. We able to wuk, and buy ting we need, and keep disyuh land. We know how to wuk haad and do so we whole lives. Some gave dey lives, like my brother, BB....You know bout my brudda, BB?"

Lilly could tell this was becoming more than a family chat. "Lucas, let's open the circle of our conversation a little wider to everyone."

"Oh, I'm helpin open de family to a wider world."

"Yes, sir, you are." Brent continued, "And Sunny has told me the awful story of how her uncle died."

Lucas looked away across the room while gusty wind-driven rain started beating more intensely against the house.

Callie tried to address the awkwardness in the room. "You see, Brent, I been lovin Sunny all huh life, and she's my heart. And you, meanin not to offend, I just found it in my heart to think of you in a positive way, afta yeahs of...not doin so. I'm just adjustin..."

"We all adjustin, Mama," Sunny reasoned. "Ain you always been de one teachin, 'We got to adjust ourselves to the reality'?"

Brent spoke softly. "Sir," and he looked around the room, "everyone, I know how hard it must be to have me here. Sunny and I talked about how soon I should visit. I heard from Sunny what reactions might be." Brent took a deep breath and decided to proceed. "I don't know that I'm able to defend things white people have done to colored people over the years, and especially now. I'm pressed to account for what I have done. I want everybody to know how deeply sorry I am for things I said, and things my family said to threaten Sunny, or her mother. Miss Callie, you know how I feel. I would never want to harm this beautiful family. If I could take it back, I would. Now, I am trying to live a righteous life and earn your forgiveness."

Lucas leaned forward, his eyes still searching, his face showing displeasure. Sunny spoke first. "Uncle Lucas, I have received and accepted Brent's apology for the past, for what happened, and yet he still apologizes to me. And we keep changin in good ways by talkin to each other."

Brent placed his arm around Sunny. "I feel that I, that we, have been given another chance."

Callie said, "I just think that we all change a little every day. We be in a process of becoming a new mix. We blend many pasts, the colors of our skin, our hair, our talents, our opinions. We all learnin and growin and tryin to figure life out together. Right, Lilly?"

Lilly nodded, but before she could respond, Lucas persisted. "I appreciate what you say, Callie. I jus need fuh Brent to unnerstan, since you cause dis famly, my fambly, so much pain, it haad tuh tek wha you say fuh true." Lucas tried to peer into Brent's soul through his eyes. "You unnnerstan dah?"

"I do understand, sir. I do. That mix that you talk about, Miss Callie, I think I am an example of it, especially with the changes I've gone through. Now, I think I see the world more...fairly. I may not see it as you do. How could I? I'm not in your skin. But I try to understand the truth of things. Sir, I tell you I'm one of only a few white men in Beaufort who voted for Robert Smalls when he ran for office."

"Is that so? Tell me a lee mo." Lucas was confident there would be few reasons for his support of Smalls.

"Well, I didn't know much about him but the bad things my parents told me. Since I been on my own the last ten years, I been readin more. I even read the South Carolina Constitution, sayin that there should be education for all the children. I agree with that, and I found out that started in 1868, mostly due to Robert Smalls. Then I learned about the vote, and how white men are doin things to take away the vote from black men. That's wrong. I believe Mista Smalls was right again in 1868 when he led the change to the Constitution so everbody, all men, have the right to vote. I wish I coulda told my daddy about this before."

Lucas was astounded. He could not speak and didn't want to interrupt. "You wanna say supm mo?"

"Naw, sir. It's just that it took some learnin for me to see that colored people love their family just like white folks, and that colored people have good ideas, too. Mista Smalls helped me see that. Now, when I see him in town, still workin as customs collector for Beaufort, after all he's been doin for so long, I have to say I admire him. Doesn't matter what color he is, I'm real impressed by him."

Lucas turned to see who else was hearing this testimony. His gaze lingered on Sunny, with slightly raised eyebrows, as if to say, "Is this fuh true?"

Sunny seemed to sense the question and shrugged. "For a couple years now, he's been tellin me facts bout Robert Smalls that I never knew."

Lucas turned back to Brent. Slowly and deliberately, he said, "Fus, we happy to have Sunny's boy; nex, we happy to meet Woody's daddy;

now, Sunny, we happy tuh see yo new fambly." Sunny looked on for about three seconds before rushing to Lucas with both arms flying around his neck, knocking him back in his chair. Shortly, they opened their embrace, each one extending an arm to Brent, who joined them without hesitation.

"You know," Lilly said, as if a revelation had struck her, "seein this makes me think of a word I been hearin a lot more in the last ten yeahs or so. I hear Brent, how he feels, the way he talks with us, I can feel his goodness. And the word that comes to mind, especially after what happened the last ten or fifteen yeahs, is redemption. Not in the religious way really, but in a personal way."

Callie said, "By his own actions, and through his religious commitment, he is atoning for his past and has come to a new beginning. He is being redeemed."

Lucas said, "But das not de way I heah folks talkin bout Redeemahs (Redeemers) these days."

"Who you mean? White folks?" Lilly asked.

"Oh, yes. Now, de word redemption means de old planta class coming back to claim dey right to control us again. Like dey neba lost de wah and we neba won our freedom."

Flora said, "Sunny, memba de ladies talkin bout states' rights? Dey said dey glad de Redeemahs are in chaage agin."

"You right, Florie. And they said it while tellin us how nice our pies was."

"As if we didn't know enough or care about what they said."

Lilly shook her head. "Well, I'm sorry I mentioned it. It seemed like such a nice word. The way I meant redemption about Brent was him doing his best to make up for past mistakes."

Lucas managed a laugh. "Well, ain exactly what de Redeemahs in Sout Calina be doin now. Dey findin new ways to mek old mistakes." He quickly added, "Brent, I ain talkin bout you now."

"I know, sir, thank you."

"We got to use our history to move forward in a good way, seems to me," Callie said with all the best summarizing optimism she could muster.

To which Lucas responded, "I gonna use de history of my body dis day to move me to my bed—tomorrow we can talk bout de future. We gonna have a busy day, family, so I say you all gah fuh git yo rest. Abram, would you say a prayer for us."

Abram nodded and closed his eyes. "We all got to say 'tank ya' this evenin, dear Gawd, fuh givin our growin family a chance to come togedda. And not jus to come togedda in body to share a meal or some laughta, but to come togedda in spirit da reaches out to say I see we come from different places, but I see we so much de same. Through our good history and our bad, tank ya, Jedus, fuh bein heah tuh hep us see da our family bond is strong, and da a strong family bond can extend to all yo people. Tank ya fa hepin us learn to trust dah when we allow de family bond to come togedda wid yo grace, we do right, and we all be fine. Tonight, wid a stohm comin on us, we hold each odda jus as you hold us, in lovin arms and under yo watchful gaze. We ask yo blessin on our family, as we prepare fuh anodda day, in which we know we are in your care. Amen."

The family maintained the solemnity that Abram provided as they rose. The quiet mood thus created was aided by the fact that the children had fallen asleep under blankets on the floor of the living room, as Amanda rested on the couch above them. Quietly, Brent and Sunny were embraced by everyone before Brent lifted Woody to carry him up to their bedroom for the night.

Chapter 12

Saturday evening, August 26, 1893

Before Lucas steered everyone off to bed on Saturday evening, he saw his family grow and strengthen as they prepared for the challenges ahead. Perhaps he knew that the storm swirling toward them from the Atlantic Ocean would soon interrupt such normal life events as a good night's sleep. Like any ship captain in a storm, his experience and knowledge pressed him to prepare for the physical threat to property. At the same time, and more importantly, Lucas's fear for the safety of his loved ones, especially the children, kept his mind engaged even when his body begged for rest.

Abram and Amanda, with their boys, returned to their temporary bedroom in the library, which, located on the northwest corner of the downstairs, was usually the quietest room in the house. Upstairs, Sunny and her new family nestled together in her bedroom, where they slept, oblivious to the growing storm. There were two smaller second-floor rooms at the back of the house. When Flora June was in Beaufort, her twins slept in Abram's "growing-up" room, on two old beds—this night she shared the room. Douglass and his family settled into the spare room on pallets, after they relocated the boxes and folders with Callie's letters that Lilly had spread out in search for family history. Callie decided, after Lilly's invitation to share the bedroom with her brother and sister-in-law, that there was ample space for the small mattress Lilly insisted that Callie use instead of her makeshift pallet.

Steadily increasing wind began rattling the east-facing windows shortly after midnight. When the rain, which came in thickening downpours, relented for minutes at a time, it was possible to hear the pounding crash of large waves on nearby beaches. Then you could hear the old wooden structure creak and shudder from the pressure of much stronger gusts, followed by another round of rain that would drown out all other sound.

Callie was resting comfortably but sleeping lightly when she noticed her brother rise following a powerful whoosh of wind and rain. From her mattress near the door, she feigned sleep while watching Lucas look out the front window. After he left the room and soundlessly walked downstairs, Callie followed him.

"Brudda man," she whispered when she found him in the living room where the children had worked on their projects just hours before. Callie leaned into him as he put an arm around her shoulder, both peering through the front window.

"Can't see nuttin. What you lookin to see?"

"You ready fuh some worriation, sista?"

"You think this storm gonna keep getting bigger?"

"De longa I feel it comin dis way, de bigga I tink it gonna be. I be mos sure de bromedda slidin some mo tonight. Sorry to say we fixin tuh have ourselves a rough day."

"I'm hopin...," Callie started and stopped. "For the children, let's try to keep some fun in the day, if we have to be inside."

"Callie, darlin," Lucas said, smiling through a serious look, "we do bes we can fuh we chirren, but, dis stohm mos likely be bigga den wha ebba plans we mek."

After looking out at nothing visible but the rainwater racing down the windowpane, Callie agreed. "Lucas, tell me what to do and when and I'll be right there makin it happen."

Talking in a lower voice, Lucas added, "Now that's what I like, a little obedience from me oomen." As Callie feigned a frown, Lucas lowered his voice further, "Could you tell that to Lilly, please, so she don't boss me roun too much?" And, laughing, they clasped hands.

Callie said, "Let's get back upstairs and get some rest. Lilly be wonderin."

"Lilly know." Lucas looked outside. "Times like dis I be thinkin a lot. I'm goin down tuh de dock and see wha we need fuh do. Memba? I gah fuh see roun de nex ben in de riba. Gah fuh see wha I can see."

"I love you, brudda. Thank you for worryin for us all. I'm goin to sleep in wid Lilly until you get back. Be careful. That dock be real slippery tonight."

Others also found the night storm too disturbing to sleep, much less to stay in bed. Douglass went downstairs to check the windows for leaks, peering out to see tall pine trees swaying in occasional lightning flashes. Nellie had followed him, the thrashing of the wind masking her quiet steps. When she brought her small arms up to his chest from behind, he was startled, yet comforted. Nellie knew his worries needed her presence. They stood close, anxiously listening to the sheets of wind-driven rain pounding the old house. After a few moments sheltered in the alcove, Douglass and Nellie started up the stairs to join their sleeping children when they were startled by the sound of wind rushing through the open kitchen door. Douglass heard the familiar sounds of his father's return in the night and quitetly said, "Go to bed, Nellie. I want to see wha Daddy's doin." Lucas left his dripping oilskin jacket and muddy boots in the back hall and, quickly drying himself, had started shedding most of his clothes when he heard Douglass say, "Daddy, what's it like out dere? We need fuh do supm?"

"Not now, son. Try to get some res. Dis day comin gonna be too long." Lucas wearily climbed up to the bedroom. He had just stood into sustained northeast winds and felt the stinging pellets of rain. Not knowing the scope of challenge awaiting his family, he slid into bed next to Lilly, finding her presence an instant sedative for his tired body though not his anxious spirit.

Sunday morning, August 27, 1893

THROUGH THE NIGHT, PERIODS OF LIGHT RAIN MIXED WITH DOWN-pours, all driven by longer and stronger gusts, as measured by more sustained rattling of the east-facing windows. The storm's erratic intensity somehow became background noise that allowed most family members to sleep. Despite nature's assertive displays, even Lucas stayed down until just before first light. Lilly joined him in the kitchen, while Callie stayed behind and crawled into their bed, taking advantage of the cloud cover to deny the realities of this particular Sunday morning. She watched the dimly lit water patterns on the window and, smiling slightly, fell into a restless sleep.

Not an hour later, one of the tallest pine trees in the yard cracked and crashed down next to the house—almost everyone woke up. During the torrents of rainfall that followed, family members joined Lilly in the kitchen to eat a simple breakfast made from last night's leftovers and fruit. Conversation was terse as they drifted into the living room where the east windows shook almost constantly against the persistent wind. Though early morning, it was still so dark that rare lightning strikes illuminated everything, allowing Callie to see the tops of trees being buffeted outside the second-floor window. She came downstairs quickly, noticing that Sunny, Brent, and Woody had not yet stirred. The Sargent family adults sat at the dining room table, barely noticing the food they consumed as their eyes and thoughts were transfixed on the storm outside.

On hearing Lucas say that the rain would likely last all day, Lilly again urged that they make the day as normal as possible for the children. Callie repeated her hope for the same, to which Lucas responded, "I'm wishin fuh dah too—" A forceful wind blast stopped him and shook the house. "Feel dah? We do bes we can wid dis day."

"Thank you, Lucas," Lilly took over as if authorized. "After the children get up and eat, we gonna set up for the day in the parlor, away from these leaky windows. See heah." She pointed beneath two of the east-side windows where early light revealed water running down the wall. "So, we gonna have a little bit of family time mixed with a little church time on this Sunday morning." Driving rain thundered against the windows again, prompting Lilly to add, "Great God willing." The sound and fury of the roiling storm drove the children from their beds to the reassuring embraces of their parents. Jancy skittered down the stairs and across the floor to jump into her daddy's strong fisherman's arms.

Still upstairs, Sunny sat up from her sleep with her son and his father, urgency and alarm in her voice. "Oh, I wish I moved my paintings in from the shed." Brent blinked awake, looking outside at strands of Spanish moss whipping from outstretched live oak limbs in spite of the rain pouring down at a sharp angle. He interrupted Sunny's hugging and grooming of their son only to say that he would go find a way to protect her paintings and dashed out the door. On the way out through the kitchen, he greeted Lilly before asking if the extra tarpaulins under the house were available to wrap up Sunny's paintings. Her tentative nod sent Brent out and down the steps into the elements.

While Brent was on his mission, Sunny and Woody agreed that they were hungry and headed straight down to the kitchen. Woody's appetite had recovered fully from his journey, judging by the amount of food on his plate. It only took a few minutes for the children to fill up on biscuits and jam, fish, shrimp, and the last bit of Aunt Callie's pork stew.

Lucas asked his sons to join him in the front corner of the living room. "Boys, I ain gonna tek time wid it now, but I gonna be watchin de tide dis monin." Looking out the window, all three strained to get a clear view of the river with whitecaps starting to splash onto their dock. "Not yet high tide, so we gah fuh wait an see."

"I tink we be all right today, Daddy," Douglass counseled.

"Well, son, ain noontime tide got me worried. Ifn de stohm keep windin up on top o us, I worry bout wha be happenin roun midnight."

Abram, deferential to both father and brother in matters of the sea, asked, "How high you talkin bout?"

"We know bedda afta noon time. Afta high tide round midnight, we be pickin up fish in de yaad unda de full moon." They laughed lightly at what they hoped was a joke before Lucas urged them back to Lilly's Sunday service. "Let's jine de folks an gib tanks."

Different branches of the family had begun to settle in the parlor. Douglass got down on the floor with Jancy as she put final touches on her special project. Saxton was distraught, however, and nothing Abram or Amanda or even big brother Robert could say would console him as he clutched an object between his hands. Flora June had divided her attention, as usual, between the twins. Bobby finished his drawing of a building, and Beanie was writing the last line of text on white paper with fairly legible handwriting.

Sunny was delighted to see the next generation at work when she and Woody came into the parlor. Brent joined them after cleaning up from his wet and muddy work and putting on the change of clothes he brought with him. Woody hugged his parents and immediately took his sketch off to a corner of the room, where he began working intensely, occasionally looking over his shoulder at his new family. "My goodness, Flora June, look what we started yesterday. You chirren are too wonderful!"

"You young people ready to share your work with the family?" Lilly had the spirit and could contain it no longer. "All right, people, whatever age you are. We are up, and we are fed, and we are heah on a Sunday for our own homegrown family service. Make a joyful noise." They did and would have gone on, but Lilly raised her tambourine in rhythm, singing. "This little light of mine, I'm gonna let it shine..." And all joined in, even the young ones, so well known was this song through the islands, with each verse ending, "Let it shine, let it shine, let it shine."

Lilly began to move. First, she stopped in front of Callie, who understood that it was her turn to sing the first line in the repetitive song. Callie sang, "Comin back home to you, I'm gonna let it shine," and they all joined in. Then Douglass, smiling at Jancy, sang, "Raisin up my chirren, I'm gonna let it shine." When Lilly stopped in front of her husband, Lucas stood and belted out, "Takin off my wet clothes, I'm gonna let it shine," while shaking his backside back into his chair, to laughter all around. Lilly stepped over to Jancy, who popped up with her verse, "Mekin Woody's gif, I'm gonna let it shine." Thereafter, every child took a chance to sing a verse, ending with little Saxton, muttering, "Holdin Woody's gif, I gonna leh ih shine." Finally, Woody raised his hand and sang out, "Bein wid my famly, I'm gonna let it shine." Sunny had a chance to add a verse, but her emotions caught her words, and she couldn't get a sound out. Brent decided not to show off the singing voice he did not have. So, Lilly slowed the singing to a final chorus of "This little light of mine, I'm gonna let it shine. Let it shine! Let it shine! Let it shine!"

Shaking her tambourine gently until its sound faded, Lilly began, "That's a fine start for us today." Another wind blast made all eyes look over to the living room, where the windows continued to leak water into the house. "Thank you, dear God, we know of your power." Closing her eyes and elevating her voice, "I have such gratitude deep inside me for my family and for our time together, even in this storm, especially in this storm. We are grateful for a chance to draw close together, to have this house over our heads, and to live another day." As she lifted her eyes from prayerfulness, she saw Lucas pacing in the east room, watchful, on alert. "Sunny, can we see our children's projects now?"

Jumping to the moment, as was her style, Sunny spoke proudly. "We have de bes chirren in de whole worl in dis family. When we ask em to be safe and quiet yesterday, they were, and when we ask em to work hard on their projects, they did. They are here to share with you. Who wants to go first?"

Jancy, ever ready, popped up, holding her picture. "I be so happy to see cousin Woody sittin in de bateau, I had to mek a picture." Proudly, she held her work high for everyone to see the little boy face that looked like Woody, sitting in the bow of a boat, many little heads behind him, all with smiles. Then she gave it to her Aunt Sunny.

"Beautiful, Jancy," Sunny was quick to say, "and I loved that moment when you all met Woody in the bateau, and now I have a picture. Thank you for this."

"Tank you," Jancy said, bowing, "you fah too kind." And she plopped down, smiling broadly.

"Who's next? I see the twins have the same smile and are ready to go."

Usually more shy, Beanie and Bobby stood, keeping their proud grins as they said, "We love the Penn School song."

"So, Beanie wrote it down," said Bobby.

"...and Bobby made a picture of our schoolhouse. He's going to lead you singin."

Bobby continued, "You old people know de song, since you went to Penn School long time befo us. We sing dis in school all de time. If you don't know it, de tune is jus like anodda song, 'Londonderry Air.'"

After announcing the song title, pronouncing each syllable distinctly and correctly as learned in his Penn class, Bobby began with a beautiful, high-pitched voice, singing:

> *O dear Penn School,* the light of our fair island,
> A beacon light of hope for far and near,
> We love thy groves of pine and stately live-oaks,
> Thy furrowed fields of corn and homestead dear!
>
> (Chorus) Oh Island Blessed, God's hand is laid upon thee,
> Oh Dear Penn School, God guide thy upward way,
> And on that rough and rugged road to Heaven,
> May we all help bring in the glad, the brighter day!
>
> In golden marshes smiling in the sunlight,
> In winding creeks that open to the sea
> We learn the joy of an outflowing service
> To God, our own fair island, and to thee!

The family had been listening at first, then started humming with Bobby, and enthusiastically joined him on the chorus the second time through as Beanie held up his printed lyrics for all to see.

> (Chorus) Oh Island Blessed, God's hand is laid upon thee,
> Oh Dear Penn School, God guide thy upward way,
> And on that rough and rugged road to Heaven,
> May we all help bring in the glad, the brighter day!

When they finished, everyone stood and clapped for one another, for Penn School, and especially for the twins.

Callie was so enthused. "Boys, that was beautiful! I could feel how you love your school. You be proud, Florie!"

Robert remained standing after clapping for his cousins and said, "Woody, now that you heard that song, this a good time to give you my Penn notebook from last year with my notes from rithmetic, an spellin, an writin. And, here is an empty notbook ready for you to use. See?" Robert had written "WOODY" on the inside cover.

Woody beamed and said, "Robert, thank you!"

"Wait!" Everyone turned to the high-pitched sound to see Saxton getting up off the floor, still clutching something in his two hands. "I didn't draw nuttin." Pausing, uncertain, Saxton walked toward his new cousin and abruptly thrust his gift toward Woody. "My daddy mek de boat fuh me. You wanna hab it?"

Woody held the little bateau in one hand, allowing Saxton to hold it another moment, and whispered "thank you" in his ear. Then Woody kneeled to give a big hug to the little boy.

When Saxton sat down, Woody stood, smiling, "Is it my turn?" Woody took Lilly's smile as a signal and held up his paper—a detailed drawing of a full live oak tree, and in it, small drawings of the children grouped with their parents. "My mama heah," pointing to Sunny, "she say I could learn family names bedda if I saw a family tree. Then she say she don't have one. So, I made a family tree."

The family showered praise on Woody and all the children as their projects were passed around. Sunny embraced Brent and then knelt in front of their son. "You are so kind and creative. You make your daddy and me proud."

Lilly, seeing Sunny's blossoming motherhood and ever mindful of the power of a moment, asked, "Sunny, this has been a special week for you. Would you give us the message this mornin?"

"Oh, Aunt Lilly. I don't—"

"Just from your heart, ain no right or wrong."

Silently, Callie looked on, beaming.

Sunny brought her hands to her face and then joined them, prayerfully. "I am so thankful. To God; to fate; to my best friend, Brent; to my family; to my mama. Thankful that my son is here now and is such a special young man."

The family responded as if in church "Mmmm-hmmm."

"Sho is."

"Praise God."

Sunny went on. "I'm havin all these feelins I didn't know it was possible to have. Now I can see and feel the world in a whole different way. Can't explain it. Part of me seemed missin befo. But more than that, now that I have my boy, I feel my place is right here in this world, and I fit in with everything else, the stars and the moon and even dishyuh bad weather."

Above the words of admiration for Sunny from her family, Callie added, "Go on, Sunny Day."

"I didn't know I was askin a question, but I found my ansa wid my son." She turned toward Brent. "And his father. I had to find my family; my son had to find his mama and daddy."

Heads nodded all around. "We feel you, Sunny," Abram said. "So glad."

Sunny continued, "One more thing I'm feelin, just in these first two days as a mother—we all part of the universe, and we all have a say how the world be. Even bedda, as parents, we get to share it wid we chirren and help em grow." Hugging Woody close as they sat on the floor together, "I jus want to be the mother my boy needs."

Callie responded, "I got no doubt about that."

"Thank you, Mama."

Lilly interrupted with some hand-clapping. "My dear niece, your story jus make me wanna sing out. Song from these islands seems right, right now.

> Michael rowed the boat ashore, Alleluia.
> Michael rowed the boat ashore, Alleluia."

Sunny jumped up to sing to her son:

> "Woody rode the boat ashore, Alleluia.
> Woody rode de boat ashore, Alleluia."

Then Callie joined her to sing, with tears coming down her cheeks:

> "Woody's mama not waitin no more, Alleluia.
> Woody's mama not waitin no more, Alleluia."

Lilly reached for her tambourine and sped up the cadence, repeating each of the three lyrics. Her feet started stomping in rhythm, and she sang the verses out with the family repeating them back to her. As she began moving around the room, family members rose to dance, following her around in a circle. She only slowed to a close after seeing Lucas, who had not joined the family shout, staring out the front window. Lilly shook her tambourine to bring the moment back down.

"Praise God. We are a blessed family!" Lilly paused to catch her breath. "I tank you fuh makin our home a worship space dis mornin. Abram, could you say a closin prayer?"

"Take us forward, dear Gawd, knowin we done prepared ourselves as best we can. We know we ain aksin to be by your side unless we done our fair share to be ready, and sweet Jedus, we tink we done done it, an den done done it again."

Prayerfully, the family responded with "Yes!"

"Tell it."

"Go on."

And Abram did. "And yet we do go on, keep on keepin on, when winds of misfortune flow around us, we stand against it and shelter together. When seas are rough and storm-tossed, we steady each other gainst de risin tides, for we know that we are all in de same boat, risin or fallin togedda, knowin we done done wha we could do to live humble, good lives of service, in your name. Amen?"

"Amen."

———————◆———————

Lucas, who had returned from his anxious pacing in the hall-way, looked at Lilly somberly, asking, "Please tell de chirren to keep all de toys and supplies in de parlor so that we big folk can meet across de hall." He brought out the rocking horse he made for his grands. Lilly looked on, worried at first that everyone would want it at once. The children all deferred to Woody and then began to share time peacefully—it seemed Woody's presence had brought them to a new level of kindness.

Callie sat on the floor to officiate an intense game of pick-up-sticks between Robert and his father. Abram had long claimed magic powers that allowed him to be able to remove any stick without moving another, and his son was determined to match and defeat that excellence.

Jancy was studying the new "family tree" and identifying family members in Woody's art. To Woody's delight, she was correct almost every time. Jancy asked, "Would you do another drawing of me? I look too little."

Woody said, "Yep, but I make a big one, not one fuh de tree."

After considering her options, Jancy beamed. "Good. I'll smile, but only a little bit."

Overhearing, Nellie said, "Daughter, you bes smile pretty fuh yo cousin ifn he draw yo piccha." Whereupon, Jancy smiled broadly and held the pose while Woody began his work.

"Yes indeed, Miss Jancy." Callie added, "When an artist wants to draw you, you pose."

Douglass used his loud whisper to tell Abram, Nellie, and Sunny, "Daddy wants to meet. He say de children are being so good, nobody needs to stay with em."

"Shush!" Callie said. "You are right though. They aren't even looking for trouble."

Nellie nodded. "I tink dey be good to each odda an to us."

They joined the other adults in the living room, where water had started to pool below the windows. Until then, their interactions with the children had helped deflect their own storm-induced tensions. Perhaps the children intuitively muted their behavior in response to the disorderly weather outside. Whatever the cause, their quiet and contented play helped Lucas bring the focus to the tasks at hand.

"I jus step out de front door, an I gah fuh lean into de wind to walk across de porch. Dint have tuh do dah las night. Today, ain like day befo when we saw a few gaps in de clouds." Looking to Callie, "Ain no blue sky, sista." Hesitating, nervous, Lucas stepped toward the window and, looking out, continued, "I gah fuh say, my lovin fambly, supm you may already know. We who lib neah wada know de wada can give us all food fuh life. But it can be mean and skrong, and eben tek life away."

Lilly moved close to him as Lucas looked somberly at his sons, their wives, Flora June, Sunny, and Brent. "Sometime we gah fuh be at we bes to git on de odda side of a tough day. Dis be one of de times. I saw de high tide jus now roun noontime. De waves be startin to lift wood from de dock and chasin up the bluff. Now we in de aftanoon. De tide sposed to be goin out now but wada ain goin down."

"What you sayin, Lucas?" Lilly pressed into him.

"Dis stohm gonna blow wada in from de ocean, and I spec de wada to stay up through dis aftanoon. We see bout dah. So, wha worry me, when de full tide come at midnight, dey be wada gettin near de top of de bluff,

I'm mos sure." This stirred the family to pose many questions which Lucas answered by saying, "We don know wha dis stohm gonna do, but we bedda respek it. So, we gah some mo wuk fuh do while de chirren play."

"Wha you need from us?" Callie hugged her brother quickly to calm him, and herself.

"We gah fuh sto our food in de best possible way fuh de long term and so we can get to it. We stack it in de kitchen, I spose. You all know bes. Anyting you can do tuh keep we food good fuh a long time, ifn we need it. You all figyuh it out. I just say let's get to it."

Lucas turned to Douglass and Abram. "I need my boys tuh hep me pull de boats all de way up onto duh bluff. We gah fuh bring em up on land, an tie em to trees on de west side of de house. Look like the wind gonna keep comin easterly, an if de wada come up, it gonna flow da way, cross de land from Chowan Creek out into de marsh. Gonna be haad wuk in dis wind an rain."

"Daddy, you really tink it be so rough we gah fuh haul our boats out?" Too late, Abram realized it would not help to ask.

"Come on out yuh." Lucas called from the front hall, throwing them their oilskin jackets and hats as they neared the door. "It's time we got our minds right about gettin out in dis rain an wind. Get your boots on, too. Neba know wha ting dis storm stir up."

After they had fastened their jackets and tied on their hats, Douglass and Abram followed their father out, heads down to deflect water from their faces. They confronted a drenching rain on the roof-less front porch. Wind gusts plastered their oilskins to their bodies as they stood, momentarily transfixed by the wind-whipped mass of churning seawater they had previously known as Chowan Creek. With water pouring off their hats, they squinted into sheets of rain and shielded their eyes to see what Lucas had described to be true. Water levels after noon's high tide had not subsided and remained well above a normal high tide.

"Abram an me gonna get de two small bateau up on de bluff. Douglass, befo you hep us wid de big rowboat, I need you tuh tie us some extra special rope lines."

"Wha you wan, Daddy?"

Lucas shouted instructions through the howling winds, instructions he didn't want those inside to hear. "I need you to mek a safety line from de front porch post—see de piller?" He pointed beneath where they stood. "Tek it across de yard to de tree-boats an tie it off on dah tree. Den, climb de low branches and tek knotted lines up into de boats. If you can do it, tie odda tight lines between de high boats and den down to de bottom one."

"Daddy? Wha you sayin?" Abram's look of doubt became fearful. "You tink we be bedda off in de tree-boats den in de house?"

"We gah fuh be prepared." Lucas smiled. "Memba wha God told James and John. De right hand of God fuh dem wha prepare demselves."

"Daddy? You sho?"

"Douglass, son, not sho of nuttin dis day, cept we gah fuh mek it possible fuh my fambly tuh be alive afta de stohm pass. De odda ting I mos sure bout is de high tide tonight gonna be at least ten feet higher than da wada is now." Looks of heightened concern reflected his sons' deepened understanding as Lucas said, "So, ifn de house ain safe, den we might need to come to de tree-boats. Gah fuh hab rope to hep us ifn dere be mo wind an wada." His sons' eyes widened as they faced him, away from the piercing rain pelting their backs.

"Douglass, you drill a drain hole in da new bateau?"

"Naw, Daddy."

"Well, you may need to bail de wada out or punch a hole sometime today."

"You didn't secure it to the tree limbs either, like you did wid de high boats, right?"

"Naw. I figuh it so heavy ain nuttin gonna move it off de branches."

"Nuttin cept maybe wada." Lucas popped both his sons in their guts and growled, "Let's get to wuk."

Relentless, powerful gusts threatened to knock the men over as they worked. Salt spray from the stirred and swollen creek mixed with nearly horizontal rain to diminish visibility. After less than an hour's work, Lucas and Abram had pulled the two boats out and tied them to large oaks on the western edge of the front yard. Douglass was still securing ropes to the live oak trees, standing on a low branch in the blinding rain.

Lucas struggled to keep his balance as he climbed the front porch steps, every movement challenged now by gale force winds. He stepped inside, barely able to close the front door behind him, just as Brent passed by from the living room, carrying buckets, trying in vain to keep up with the leaks coming down the walls and through window casings. "Need help there, sir?" Brent asked with genuine concern.

"Yes, but finish wha you doin an come on out. We gonna pull yo boat up on de bluff next. But when we pull de big boat, we gonna need you, too."

"Thank you!" Surprised, Brent remembered to say, "And yes, I'll be right there. Sir, before you go, is there a place for Sunny's paintings inside? I put them in the storage space under the house wrapped in old sails and canvas I found, but that may not be good in high water."

Lucas looked at him intensely, as if the question was an intrusion, but his countenance lightened slowly as he said, "Sho. Dey probbly fit in de closet under de stairs, right back there." Pointing down the hall to the back of the house, he asked, "You love Sunny, fuh true, don't you?"

"Yes, sir."

"You be a good man, Brent."

Brent continued mopping up water under leaking windows for a few more minutes before heading down the kitchen steps to retrieve

Sunny's paintings. Lilly offered him a spare poncho that was hanging by the door, which Brent received with a smile, saying, "Thank you, ma'am, I left my slicker in my boat." He hurried down the steps, wrapped several paintings together, and brought them up to the closet that had recently been emptied of the extra bedding used for house guests. After four more trips, he had relocated all Sunny's paintings. Keeping his promise to Lucas, he hurried back outside and down to the dock for some real work.

Scanning the yard from the porch, Brent was glad to see that his boat had already been pulled up on the bluff. He was even more impressed to see the rope work that Douglass had completed, leading from the bottom of the front porch steps across the yard to the live oak trees, with knotted ropes strung above and between the tree-boats. When crossing the yard toward the dock, a wind gust almost knocked Brent over. He looked in awe at the conditions bearing down on the property, situated as it was at the convergence of two rivers in flood. Looking back at the house, he was relieved to see that those behind its comforting walls remained insulated from the escalating sounds and force of the storm.

With no time for idle observation, Brent arrived at the edge of the bluff just when Lucas and sons were ready to haul their twenty-six-foot rowboat up into the yard. Waves already covered the dock and were breaking at the base of the embankment even though the tide was supposed to be receding throughout the afternoon. Footing was muddy at best, and yet, through will and determination, Douglass and Brent pushed up from the muck below, struggling mightily to gain secure footing sufficient to support the weight on their shoulders while Abram and Lucas pulled the bow rope from the top of the bluff. They were barely able to hear the count from Lucas over the low roar of the wind. "One, two, three, HEAVE!" The rowboat lurched up the last angled feet of the slope and leveled off in the yard.

With that momentum, Lucas shouted, "Give me a few more pulls, boys!" The four of them pushed and pulled it across the yard close to a large oak, where Douglass tied it securely. He looked up as he finished with a satisfied smile that turned to laughter when he saw Brent's face, plastered with black mud and streaked with rain.

"Man, you got to decide." His hilarity was barely audible. "What color you be?" Since Brent had not yet seen the humor in his own face, Douglass added, "Brudda, you need a mirror to show you that, right now, you look blacker than me." With that, he reached into the nearest pooled water with cupped hands and splashed his new friend full in the face with it. "Heah, and heah come some mo." Brent finally laughed and felt the inclusion, working hard to remain standing in gale force, wind-driven rain. Douglass urged, his hand on Brent's shoulder, "Let's git yo boat tied up an git inside."

They splashed through puddles on their way to the back steps and arrived together outside the kitchen door. First Nellie and then Amanda greeted them and, through muffled amusement, extended towels while urging the men to clean themselves up. Their clothing was completely mud-spattered, to match Brent's face, and clearly, whatever protective oilskin gear Douglass had worn was not sufficient for the task. Amanda suggested, laughing out loud, "You boys both oughta go down into de yaad and let de rain clean yo mess."

Brent grinned at Douglass. "Why not?" Douglass kicked off his boots, as did Brent, and they raced down the steps, shed their shirts, and splashed around like ten-year-olds. Douglass hollered as he ran and slid headfirst into a big puddle. Then he sat up and asked Nellie, "We gah mo clothes fuh Brent?"

Nellie answered, "Yes," while Amanda shook her head and laughed out loud, "Dem boys been out in de stohm too long."

No sooner had they come back in and received dry jeans and shirts than Abram and Lucas arrived, looking only slightly better than the first shift of muddy, wet workers. Lilly took over and performed the same magic on this pair. Soon, the exhausted men had settled in the parlor, where food was brought to them.

With a few minor squabbles through the day, the children, who had been so well behaved and engaged with their own business, remained that way, despite the return of adults to the room. Somehow, the combination of inspiring projects, entertaining games, food, and a new cousin was the right blend of entertainment for indoor, rainy-day play.

Nellie and Amanda insisted that Callie and Lilly take off their aprons and join the family in the parlor. They ushered Sunny and Flora June out of the kitchen, too, though that was neither easily done nor sustained. Amanda said, "Go be with your boys!" Nellie picked up a broom and moved toward them in mock attack, despite having baby Nichelle cuddled in the blanket tied across her chest.

A little later, when Nellie came out with dessert for the family, her infant continued sleeping peacefully. Sunny, now keenly aware of motherly behavior, commented, "That is such a nice thing for you and Nichelle, the way you carry her."

"I jus always feel bedda when I got my baby neah me like dis."

Douglass explained, "When Nellie birthed Jancy, de midwife say it bes to carry de baby in front. I like it too, so, we figuh how to tie up a blanket."

Nellie looked at her husband and squeezed his hand. "Douglass tie de bes knots in de blanket, even bedda now wid baby Nichelle."

Lilly whooped and called out, "Baby-carry-sack designed by my son, Frederick Douglass Sargent."

Brent, still feeling the kindred relationship with Douglass from their muddy work, sat down next to him on the couch. "That is a fine name. How did you get it?"

"How did I get my name? Mama, you tell it better than me."

Lilly did not hesitate, standing, holding her head high, and speaking distinctly, as any orator would. She said, "These words were spoken by Frederick Douglass in 1857, before we be free from slavery: 'If there is no struggle there is no progress. Those who profess to favor freedom and yet deprecate agitation are men who want crops without plowing up the ground; they want rain without thunder and lightning. They want the ocean without the awful roar of its many waters.'"

Silence followed Lilly's recitation. Only the relentless whine of wind and rain lashing the house were heard before Douglass spoke: "And das how I got my name. See how much my mama like what Frederick Douglass say?" As if to emphasize the point, distant thunder rumbled through the house. "And Daddy chose 'Sargent' for our fambly name in honor of BB's service wid de Fus Sout Calina Volunteers."

Lucas added, "I memba BB, and you, Callie, and me, we all were agitated bout keepin Massa's name. No, we ain gonna do dah. Callie claimed her daddy's name, Hewitt, and I said to Lilly, let's mek our family name be Sargent."

Robert, who had drifted into the parlor to hear the adult stories, stood and raised his hand. "Scuse me, Grandmama Lilly, would you say again what 'agitation' mean?"

"It's when you do what you have to do to stand up for what's right."

"When you stand up and fight fuh yo right fuh supm?" Robert asked thoughtfully.

"That's right."

"Supm like...chocolate?" Answering Lilly's shaking head, Robert pursued his justice. "Memba, last Sunday grampa say da ifn we get de right ansa to his questions, we get chocolate?"

Lilly turned to Lucas with a "Well?" expression on her face and the words forming on her lips. The children, previously well focused on their own efforts, heard Robert say "chocolate" and were immediately alert to the pending chocolate question.

Lucas got up quickly, considering his age and the day's activity. "Oh, you too smaat, young man. Whose son you be? You my grandson?" He grabbed hold of Robert in a faux menacing way that turned into a full, giggling bear hug. "I tell you wha I do. I give you and yo cousins a chance to earn even mo chocolate." He saw his potential audience growing, and Lucas baited them. "Who be wantin to earn mo chocolate?" Robert looked on, slightly pained that his logical question had been turned into another contest, but he loved to play his grandfather's games, and so he raised his hand, too. Brent did likewise, but Sunny gently pulled his hand down, squeezed it lovingly, and held it tightly between them.

Lucas seemed to leave his worries behind. "All right then, jus a few questions dis gray day. Anyone who get one right git as much chocolate as yo grandmama lets you have." Lilly shook her head, questioning her husband's methods. "Aunt Callie, you still gah some chocolates in that Whitman's box from Washington?" Lucas gave a lingering, mischievous look to Lilly as he put a loving arm around Robert. "And, you chirren can thank Robert for this opportunity."

"Thank-yous" arose from the chorus of small voices.

"Now, first question. We all know that Robert Smalls stole the boat, named the *Planta*, from the Confederates up in Charleston during the wah, right?"

Robert said, "1862!"

Lucas continued, "And we know it happened in 1862. The two-part question is: How much did de govmint pay Robert Smalls fuh stealin de boat and givin it to de United States Navy? An, nex question, wha yeah did Mista Smalls git paid his money?"

To Robert's consternation, he knew neither answer, and his grandfather knew that he did not and was subjecting his grandson to another kind of test. "Nobody know?" Lucas waited while Brent bent over to whisper in his son's ear.

Woody stood with his hand up. "Five thousand dollahs!"

Then Brent quickly whispered to Jancy.

She popped up, screeching as if to compete with the wind, "1890!"

Lucas smiled at Brent's way of participating. "All right now. Dis question different from de oddas. No, it ain bout wha Robert Smalls do long ago. Question is, wha job he do today? And who put him in de job? Thas anodda two paht question. I'll jus wait."

Adults around the room thought they knew and wanted to say something. Brent had broken the unwritten rule—the questions were for the children—but he did so fairly. This question hung out there a long time until Lucas finally called out Callie's name. "Sista, do I see yo arm standin up in the air?"

"Well, family, I just happened to be in Washington in 1889 when...," and Callie hesitated, clearing her throat slightly, "when our dear friend and leader, Robert Smalls, was named to be the customs collector for the Port of Beaufort. And he was appointed to this position by the President of the United States, Benjamin Harrison." With that, Callie received cheers and applause on behalf of Robert Smalls.

"Final question, and dis one be tougha den all de oddas." The children came closer, and most of the parents leaned forward in their chairs. "A great American hero just completed service in Washington, DC. Afta hepin many injuhed an needful people, dis person finally come back home tuh her fambly."

Robert jumped up, shouting, "Aunt Callie! Aunt Callie!"

Lucas pointed at him and said, "You be right."

The ordeal made worthwhile by his final answer, Robert felt vindicated as he collected double earnings, two pieces of chocolate. Jancy and Woody each received a big piece. Callie said, "For me getting my answer right, let's make sure all the children get a piece of chocolate. Today, you all have been nice to each other and to us big people who had hard work to do. Thank you for being so smart and helping out today."

Enjoying the excitement of the children, Lucas asked, "Feel good to be smaat, don't it?"

"Doesn't it," Lilly corrected.

"Yes it does," Lucas answered. "I say 'yes' cause, mos of my life, Lilly been agitatin to mek me mo book-smaat—mo smaat bout de worl." Laughing, "Lilly even staat me readin an writin mo."

"Do you like it, Grampa?" Beanie asked.

"Yeah, I do, little man. But I tell you a secret. I like fishin bedda."

Suddenly, Brent stood up and explained that he had forgotten something. He returned seconds later with a cloth draped over an object that appeared to be an artist's canvas. Sunny sat up when she saw it. "Sunny, if it's all right with you, when I brought your paintings into the house today, I found this one, not yet framed, facing against the wall. You know what it is, I can see. You want to share it now?" Sunny nodded. Brent lifted the cloth from the one-foot-by-two-foot painting. Clearly depicted, with both figures illuminated by sunlight through the parlor window, was Lilly standing over Lucas as he sat in the comfort of his favorite chair, reading a book.

Lucas could not mask his pleasure. "My, my. Sunny. That is real! So see, chirren, de piccha prove wha agitatin can do." Reaching for Lilly's hand, then bending to kiss it, Lucas continued, "This teacher lady mek me like readin so much that a great artist wanted to paint our picture."

"This painting shows my life, too." Sunny received an embrace from her mother and then swung her around to face the family, arm-in-arm, and continued, "only with me, it was my mama hangin over me, askin questions. If we was down yuh or in Washington, she was always saying, 'Sunny, wha book you readin? Sunny, wha you done fuh improve yoself today? Sunny, who you hep have a bedda day today?'"

"And then what did I say sometimes?" Callie asked.

"Whenevah I do supm good to get ready fuh my future, you say, 'Sunny, you give me a hug in my head!'"

After a deep, distant rumble of thunder, the house began to shudder as more fervent wind wailed around it, causing everyone to draw closer. They looked to the west through parlor windows at nearby trees bending to the will of ever stronger rushes of air through their bobbing limbs. The late afternoon sky darkened as though the sun had already set.

Sunny moved closer to her uncle and asked, "Unca Lucas, it gettin so dark so early wid deese big clouds comin down so low—it mek me tink of de big horned owl we watch. Memba?" Sunny spread her arms and took a few smooth steps into open space. "Afta sun go down, we watch him glide off a branch, big ole wings spread wide, coverin ovah anyting it want to catch. Memba, uncle?" Lucas nodded enough to let Sunny ask, "We ain bout to git covah ovah, are we?"

"No, we ain, Sunny, naw, we ain let it happen." Lucas pulled Sunny to him and gave her a firm, reassuring hug, never disclosing his doubt.

"How you protect us all deese yeahs? Das how I want fuh protect Woody and Brent." Barely able to hold back tears, Sunny admitted, "I don't know how."

"You do bes you can, Sunny girl; bes you can be good enuf." Releasing Sunny, Lucas turned his attention to Callie. "Hey, sista, you be so smaat and connected up in Washinton. Didn you tell me bout de Weather Bureau of the United States bein staated back in 1870? Mo den twenty yeahs pass?"

"That's right."

"Dey job supposed to be to give people de wud bout real big stohms comin dis way?"

"That's right, brudda."

"Dey didn't tell you bout dis stohm though?" Lucas began to smile, finally.

"No, brudda, dey didn't tell me bout a big storm comin heah."

"Well, good den, we gonna be all right."

This comforting conversation was followed by a deafening roar of wind louder than had been heard all day. Lucas maintained his calm and redirected the attention of his favorite audience, his family. "Hey now. We been in one of deese stohm befo. Twenty yeah ago, we stay right in dishyuh house. Is it still standin? It standin. Fa true."

Then Lucas sat more upright in his chair. "I tell you anodda gran story. We had a stohm less than ten yeahs pass. It was so bad that a big boat sank just right out heah off Bay Point in the big wada." Lucas pointed southeast toward the Atlantic Ocean and continued, "A brave pilot captain named Von Harten swam out tru de wind and wave tuh bring a line out an save de crew of de boat. United States Govmint gib him a gold medal for savin lives." Lucas looked around the room to his family. "We all gonna do our bes tonight, wuking fuh gold medals just like Capn Von Harten. Right?"

CRACK!

This crack did not come from lightning, but from the tallest pine tree east of the house snapping at the twenty-foot level. Immediately, the upper forty feet of branches crashed through the back roof into one of the second-floor bedrooms. An immediate screech of air swooped down the stairs, swirling through each room.

Flora June jumped. "Hey, wah dah be—chirren screamin?" She quickly scanned the room; all the children were present and being held by their parents.

Lucas pulled Lilly to the corner of the room. "You know de wind comin through yuh gonna tear de house up."

"Rainwater comin in already. Ebbyting gonna get soak."

Lucas gripped Lilly firmly by her shoulders. "We be lucky if de roof stay on de house."

They stopped talking to listen, all eyes focused up. "That's some wood pullin apart, Daddy!" Abram shouted.

"It's always creakin," Lilly countered, desperate to be right.

"Nebba like this," Lucas said. Everyone startled as a window crashed into the upstairs bedroom with jangling sounds that made all eyes turn to Lucas for reassurance. He remained calm while speaking louder to be heard over the shrill air racing through the house. "Abram, see bout da window. Douglass, git down de front steps an tell me wha you see in de yaad and on de wada."

Abram came back from the second floor as another east-facing bedroom window blew into the house, glass shattering down the stairwell behind him. "Two windows out, Daddy. Winds workin haad on de roof an de walls."

More gusts of wet wind whipped downstairs around the huddled family. Lucas reasoned with his loved ones, "We cain't be trapped in yuh ifn de house comin down."

Douglass came through the front door and lost his grip on the doorknob. Pulling it shut took his best effort, and when he succeeded, he reported, "Wada is ovah de bank, staatin to come on de yaad." He shouted as the door blew open again, "De wind is rough, Daddy!"

"Can you walk in it?"

"It worse den befo. We can walk in it usin de rope an holdin de chirren tight."

Lilly and Callie confronted Lucas with questions. "Can we stay here in the west rooms downstairs?"

"You talkin about takin us outside?"

"Wha bout de chirren?"

"Where will we go?"

"My wife, my sista, we facin de wus possible ting. Our house ain safe. We ain gonna wait til it hurt us or de chirren. We gah boats that will stay in trees that will stay on the ground. De live oaks ain goin nowhere. We be mo safe in de boats in de trees dan in de house or, Gawd forbid, in de wada."

Both women were exasperated, and yet they understood his answer. Lilly locked eyes with Lucas, grasped his neck with one hand, and touched his cheek with the other, reluctant to let him go.

Callie spoke up, "Jus like I told you, brudda, I do wha you say do."

Lucas wasted no time after Callie requested orders. "Douglass, go with Abram and his family, and Lilly, you go, too. Cross de yard, follow de rope Douglass tied out tuh de oak trees wid de boats. Get Abram up in de top boat usin de pulley, an bring em all up. Come back yuh, Douglass, an den get yo fambly in de nex boat. All you, put on any oil-skin jackets we got, and tie some hats on de babies. Ladies, tie yo skirts up so dey don trip yo feet. Any odda ting we can do fuh be safe?"

"Use de knotted ropes ifn de pulley stops," Douglass yelled to Abram and his family, to reinforce their confidence and his own.

Sunny and Florie rushed to the kitchen and came back with food that had been stuffed into pouches. "Food fuh de top boat!"

"Daddy, you sho bout dis?" Abram knew the answer but had to feel his father's certitude. They embraced, and Lucas reached for Amanda after Lilly and Callie had hugged her.

"Let's act right fuh de chirren now. Each of you talk wid yo fambly. Let's move befo de wind and wada come up mo." He looked up as they heard the roof start to rip from the east-side wall. "Abram!" Lucas shouted above the roaring wind. "We caint stay. Ain safe."

Lucas threw his arm around his eldest son and gave a light shove. "Git yo fambly settled down in the top boat. Den run de pulley to hep em git in de nex one. We send em out when you show you ready. Git on wid it!"

Lucas watched Abram's group go down the front steps to the yard, where Douglass made sure his mother, brother, and Amanda held the rope and that the Robert had a firm grip on his mother and the rope. Saxton was tightly secured under his father's coat. They moved laboriously as one across the yard, where wind-driven waves were starting to break at the top of the bluff, sending water surging up the slight incline toward the house. Under the boat tree, where water was almost knee-deep, Abram sat on the bosun's chair gripping the knotted rope Douglass had installed earlier in the day. Douglass worked the pulley rope as Abram helped share the load by pulling himself up with his hands. Buffeted by the wind, it was a slow trip up. Upon arrival at the ten-foot level, Abram flung his legs over the gunnels and spilled into the boat. He grabbed the knotted rope flailing above and pulled himself into a stable position.

Next, Douglass lifted Robert into the chair, and the pulley system worked again. Abram tucked his oldest son into the stern, the area most sheltered from the gale. Below, Douglass had to tie a screaming Saxton onto the chair before he could be hoisted safely. Lilly went up next, showing expertise in chair-sitting from her practice only days before, even being able to swing her legs into the boat enough for Abram to grip her hands and help her slide in easily next to Robert. Finally, Amanda rode the chair up smoothly until the pulley jammed just below the branch the bateau rested on. Miraculously, she could reach her husband's fully extended arm and put a foot on the closest supporting branch, allowing Abram to lift her onto the edge of the boat. Lilly leaned out and helped muscle one of Amanda's legs up and into the boat, and the rest of her followed.

The old oak branches continued to sway somewhat in the relentless wind, but nearer the trunk, they gave just a little with the added weight. Abram looked over to shout at Douglass on the ground below, "We okay! Git yo family. Git Aunt Callie and Daddy, ebbybody, quick now!"

When Douglass came back to the house, he was adamant. "Daddy, I'm tekin you an Aunt Callie nex, along wid Sunny, Brent, and Woody to be in the middle boat."

Lucas looked out at the water starting to encircle the land on which the house sat, pulsing in repeated waves, racing to see which could advance the farthest. Lucas started to argue, but Douglass said emphatically, "You know I'm right. I can tek care of de ropes, de boats, an de people bedda from bein in de low boat. Time to go befo de wada git too high."

Lucas clasped his son's hand, smiling broadly. "You smaat and crazy like me." He turned back to the family. "Callie and Sunny, Brent and Woody, let's go."

Douglass shouted, "Daddy, tek my wife and baby wid you now. Befo you go up to de middle boat, put Nellie an Nichelle in de low boat. I come behind wid Florie an huh boys."

Sunny and Brent opened the front door as a great sound of ripping lumber overhead made everyone duck. More wind howled down from above. Sunny gathered Woody between her and Brent, saying, "We ready now. We goin to de boat eight feet up. We can do it!" Down the steps into the last gray light of dusk they went, waiting at the bottom for Callie, Nellie, and Lucas.

"Grab the rope line!" Douglass shouted after them and then turned to his wife. "Yo turn, Nellie. My daddy tek you an de baby down to de low boat. Jancy an me comin right behind wid Florie and de boys." Douglass held Nellie and their baby tightly as they moved down the steps to the rope line, joining together with Sunny and Brent. Getting blown off balance on his way back up the steps, Douglass shouted, "Nellie, hold tight to Sunny—don leh de wind tek huh."

Lucas hugged his son and took a final read of his barometer on the way out of the house, arm-in-arm with Callie. "Sista, I don't know bout yo Washington machine. Check it once a day—ain neba seen a readin dis low."

Callie tried to match his calm with understatement. "Brudda, may be a storm out there."

Lucas gently grabbed Callie's arm and hand. "It's our time. We got a rope to help us find our way, ifn de wada be too deep an swirly. Let's go."

Callie latched onto the rope when she got down to ground level and shared it with Lucas as they joined the waiting group of Sunny, Brent, Woody, Nellie, and baby Nichelle. To make progress across the yard, they had to lean into the wind. Within feet of the steps, they were walking in saltwater, and by the time they arrived at the boats, it was rising above their knees.

Lucas lifted Nellie and her swaddled infant into the low boat, placing them in the most sheltered corner on a bench above the rainwater that had pooled in the bottom. Lucas took Woody from Brent so that he could lift Sunny high enough for her to shimmy farther up the knotted rope by herself and swing into the boat that rested on branches eight feet off the ground. With the stabilizing assistance of the knotted rope, Lucas stepped from one large, rain-slicked branch to another before grabbing the gunnels and hauling himself aboard—decades of rowing, self-sufficiency, and pride combined with adrenalin to make him ready for the challenge. With Brent's help from below, Callie pulled herself up with the knotted rope, close enough for Lucas and Sunny to grab her wrists and pull. In spite of their soaked and slippery arms, hands, and feet, they lifted Callie with surprising ease, causing her and her handlers to tumble back into the boat. On any other day, their injuries to forearms, shinbones, and backs would have been important, but not this time. All three scrambled to reach for Woody as Sunny and Lucas each caught one of Woody's arms as his father boosted him up—Woody seemed to fly up into the boat. Mother and grandmother quickly enfolded him in their comforting arms, and then Callie held onto him as Sunny stood to help Brent. An agile man, Brent made his way up easily, standing and holding on to nearby branches for a brief, shouted conversation with the passengers in the top boat. When he finally sat down in the boat, his weary arms encircled Sunny and his son, while Lucas reached behind Callie to pat Brent on the shoulder.

Douglass, with his precious Jancy clinging to his neck, ushered Flora and the twins down the same rope line, now with water ankle-deep near the house. Together, their cluster leaned into powerful winds and slogged through shallow waves, with all hands but Jancy's holding the rope. When they arrived at the low boat, Douglass peeled Jancy's arms from around his neck and passed her to Nellie. Next, he lifted Bobby and Beanie in and made Flora June a step with his hands to help her board safely. Wearily, Douglass dragged himself into the boat and pulled out the buckets wedged under the bench. Handing one to Flora and keeping the other, they quickly began the endless task of bailing rain water from the bateau.

Suddenly, they heard more voices. Sloshing through the yard, Douglass saw his cousin Maybelle and her family. "Thank Gawd, you all are heah. Our house done fill wid wada. You got room fuh my baby and my man?" After tucking Jancy into the bow and telling her to stay still, Douglass helped lift them into the boat.

Now the entire family had safely reached a destination that they never intended. From the tree boats, they squinted back through the downpour to see that most of the roof on the east side of the big house had been ripped away. As the storm grew in intensity with downpours increasing, the fact that Douglass never drilled holes in the low boat became more ominous. Callie and Lucas looked down to see the deluge continue to fill it, despite the balers' best efforts. Their condition worsened when, suddenly, the boat shifted slightly. Douglass shouted, "The waves be risin up under us!" Again, the boat lifted and set down abruptly.

Douglass made a father's decision. He picked Jancy up from her spot in the bow and lifted her toward the middle boat. He screamed, "Daddy, get my baby! Get Jancy!" He stood, one foot on the gunnel and one on a bench, but he could not reach out far enough to get her across the four-foot diagonal gap between the boats. In a desperate effort to protect his child from harm, Douglass moved his foot from the bench up onto a slick oak branch. Lucas had just reached down to grab her arm when a terrified Jancy shouted, "Mama...Mama...Mama!" Still pushing his daughter up by her legs and feet as Lucas pulled Jancy to safety, Douglass teetered. Nellie stood and was able to steady him, but a great push of water suddenly jarred the boat. Nellie lost her balance, and her arms flailed in an attempt to regain it. The soaked blanket tied around her torso opened just enough for little Nichelle to pop out and plunge into the turbulent water below, now at least three feet deep. Without hesitation, Nellie shrieked and jumped in after her. Both were swept out of sight by the raging water. Douglass tumbled down into the boat. He did not see Nellie—Flora June pointed over the side, a horrified expression on her face. Douglass scrambled from side to side, scanning the roiling waves that surrounded them, and shouting his wife's name, before collapsing in the bateau.

Through the relentless rain and screeching wind, Lucas and Callie witnessed the family tragedy below as it was illuminated by distant lightning flashes. Sunny and Brent did not see Douglass lose his Nellie, nor did those in the upper boat, as it was positioned almost directly over their sightline to the lowest boat.

"I feel helpless!" Callie shouted. "What can we do?"

Lucas leaned into her ear. "It too rough to try to get de oddas up yuh. We lucky to have huh." Gesturing to Jancy now held tightly by Sunny, "We blessed my boy lifted huh up to us."

Above the din of the storm, they heard more fearful shouts from the family below. Choppy, lifting waves jostled the low boat, moving it up and slamming it down again and again. Then, when the boat lifted and jerked wildly into a tree branch, the force of the angled crash launched one of the twins into the night. Before anyone could react to that terrible loss, a bigger swell lifted the boat completely from the fork in which it was nestled and carried it over the bracing branches and out onto the swirling waters. Anguished screams were audible for only a short time, as Lucas watched the boat still afloat, being jostled and pushed by angry currents across the yard toward the marsh beyond. Only, there was no marsh visible, just an enraged sea.

Lucas, enveloped in grief, sank into the boat, Callie holding him up so she could lean into him for shared emotional and physical support. Brent, deeply shaken from their expressions of grief, sat up and looked below. With two terrified children desperately clinging to her, Sunny did not see what had occurred, but from Brent's shocked demeanor as he slid back down beside her, she assumed the worst.

Lucas moaned, "My Gawd, how much mo. We been through so much. We done done wha you tol we fuh do."

Callie tried and failed to stand up. She faced the torrent and wailed, "This ain fair!" Shaking a futile fist, she sank down again next to her brother. Shrieking winds drowned their shouts. Water rose up under their boat. Threat filled the darkness. "How much worse can it be, Lawd?"

"It be bedda soon," Lucas mumbled to her and to himself. "Fuh true."

Callie could barely get words out into her brother's ear. "Tide still risin?"

Epilogue

DECEMBER 1895

IT IS TWO YEARS AFTER THE STORM, AND I HAVE FINISHED WRITING my book. Even though the daily work of healing our people was exhausting, I had to take time almost every day to write. When I finished, I showed it to Lilly, of course, and to Sunny. They both thought I had done a good job describing my life and my work and my family through the years, but they said I had to add one more chapter to bring things up to date.

They said I had to write more about how the 1893 cyclone brought misery to us and somehow made us forget our troubles with our white brothers, but not for long. Whether our adversary has been bad storms trying to drown us or white folk trying to keep our race down, we struggle on. Knowing how important it is to tell the stories of the American people, I decided Lilly and Sunny were right, and I just finished writing the last chapter.

Callie Hewitt

Sunday night, August 27, 1893, was more terrifying than anything I could ever have imagined. In trying to tell about it, I can't do justice to how rough that time was—the cyclone drowned five members of my family. I never been so scared, never been so sad, never been so without hope. The cyclone took members of my family. Water rising has no mercy. Screaming wind don't care if you are praying or if babies are crying. I tell you, the children weren't the only ones what cried and soiled themselves before that storm pass by. It don't matter though. We were just glad to be alive.

All night, the wind howled at us—the strongest and loudest came around midnight, right at the high tide. We clung to one another and pressed down on the hard, wet floor of the boat. I never been so glad to be held so tight by my brother. Somehow, I had sweet Jancy in my arms and kept a hand on Sunny. Woody was squeezed between his mama and daddy, with Brent takin the worst of the wind and rain on his back through the night. While the nonstop, terrifying sound of the roaring wind got worse and worse, the water continued to rise, and the waves started crashing just below our boat even though it was eight feet off the ground. That big old trunk of the oak tree near the edge of the bluff stood staunchly. Its upper branches bowed and swayed and slapped at us in the boats underneath. The stronger limbs cradling our vessels in place created sanctuaries which, if the waters kept rising, would have become our death traps.

About an hour after the wind slacked a little, though the sound of it still scared me, the waters stopped splashing on the underside of the boat. Lucas said that's when he knew we had gone past the midnight high tide. I started crying, realizing we would live, and realizing how many folk died that night.

Before I tell you about my loved ones in the lowest boat, let me tell you about Lilly and Abram and Amanda and their boys. They had the same fright we did. Their boat, the top one, was higher and well out of the water, so they felt the wind and the movement of the branches more than we did. And the wooden braces holding it to the tree loosened sometime during the worst of the storm when one of the support branches cracked, making their boat shift down at an angle—Abram said later, he thought they would be dumped into the angry sea. They were most sure it would not stay up through the night, but it did. Later, they laughed that, in spite of their fright, the new angle of their perch allowed them to see better at first light just when the wicked wind started to slow.

For hours, my eyes saw nothing, they were so tightly clenched. Fear takes on many shapes in the human body. From the moment I watched that lower boat be swept away, taking my loved ones off in the swirling water, my stomach knotted and loosened so that I was real sick and real scared at the same time.

The thing about being in the most drenching rain ever, you can only get so wet. Even though the rain drops stabbed my skin with pain, they constantly washed me and drained out through holes that Lucas had made in the bottom of our boat. Somehow, I was reassured that when I expired that night, I would at least be clean.

Lord, have mercy on those thousands of souls who died on our islands. Most were drowned in the most hellish terror, and their bodies were found on the banks of these once lovely creeks and rivers, mixed in with the mud, debris, and animal carcasses that washed up on shores everywhere. Many families never made it out of their cabins, sheltered together as water filled their homes with death.

It was only after the cyclone passed that we learned the destructive winds were blowing at more than one hundred miles an hour across our islands at the worst of it. By first light, winds dropped down to about half that—in the middle boat, we were finally able to talk to one another. We called out for Lilly above us. She began checking on everybody, hollering out our names. Their boat was almost exactly above where the low boat had been, so they didn't know it got swept away in the night. After we answered back to her as loud as we could, we heard her call those who were down below. First "Douglass!" then "Flora June!"... over and over, she called their names. No one answered. Lilly started singing, "This little light of mine." At first, I thought she was crazy, but she was trying to lift us all up. We joined her for a little, but then we stopped singing, some of us crying. There wasn't any light shining for us, with storm clouds still swirling overhead. That great horned owl Sunny talked about, well, his wings covered us like prey.

After Lilly's sad calls for family went unanswered, and the winds were still so strong, we did not move for the next few hours. It's possible that some of us slept from sheer exhaustion. By mid-morning, we started to see the first hint of light breaking through a blanket of clouds down to the south. By then, Lilly had managed to look over the edge of her boat and, not seeing the low bateau or any of its occupants, began a forlorn sobbing such as I had never heard from her. After she finally cried herself out and settled down, we all stayed still and sad for another hour or so. Finally, with the gales subsiding and the creek water out of the yard for the first time, Lucas and Abram called back and forth and decided it was time to leave the tree-boats.

One by one, we climbed down, the men holding on to the branches with one arm and helping the rest of us grab the knotted ropes to climb from the boats and down to the ground. Some of us were more successful than others using the knotted rope, but we all welcomed the help and got down to the soggy ground safely. Stiff, yet weak and wobbly from the long hours cramped in the boats, we tried to rush toward one another—to touch, to embrace, to hold one another up. Realizing the number of our family members missing, we dragged ourselves dejectedly from the creek bank to the house, where the front porch steps used to be. We looked up at the big house that stood without its second floor and only a jumble of partial rooms left on the first. We sat, exhausted, immobilized, disconsolate.

In the midst of that despair, I have to tell you of the best surprise we got the day after the storm. For the longest time, we remained sitting in front of the house, listening to nothing but the swirling wind. Then, uncertain at first, we thought we heard voices from out on the swollen salt marsh. What do we see but a bateau with a big, strong man rowing through the choppy water, coming right toward us with a steady southwest wind at his back.

Flora June did not tell anyone that she was going to have her new man friend come to visit Oakheart on the day of the storm. He promised Flora that he would get there no matter what, to prove his good intentions to her. But he never arrived on Sunday. Turns out, as bad as that storm was, he tried to make it to Oakheart when the wind and high water forced his boat into some woods along the creek, so he tied on to a big old oak tree.

Late Monday morning, after the wind subsided enough, he started rowing again when he heard voices nearby. Rowing toward the sound and calling out, he came upon the Oakheart bateau, lodged in shrubs where floodwaters had pushed it the night before.

Lucas and I stood to get a better view of this man rowing so hard and, praise God, he had more people sitting down in his boat. Suddenly, one jumped up. We heard Flora June's big voice booming, "Who dere, Oakheart? Unca Lucas, Sunny, Lilly?"

There is no way to describe the joy. As the man rowed closer, we saw Flora and Beanie sitting up in the bow, and Douglass slouched in the back. Where were the others? There was no Bobby with his mama and twin brother, no Nellie holding her baby, no Maybelle, her infant, or her man. We had hoped and prayed so hard, and finding Douglass, Florie, Bobby, and Ed was an answer to our prayers.

Flora June's friend, Ed, rowed up near to the top of the bluff and threw the bowline to Abram in the yard. Ed climbed out of the bateau, lifted Flora June and her boy out, and helped them climb up the last few feet of the embankment into Lucas's open arms. Douglass was clutching a wet blanket when Ed helped him from the boat—but it wasn't the one Nellie had the night before. We wondered if Douglass was in his right mind, and then we saw the blanket move. It was the kick of a baby. Douglass told us that, somehow, before Maybelle was thrown from the boat, she must have tucked her child up under the wooden bench in such a way it stayed put, until he yowled and Douglass discovered him. Fuh true, God works in mysterious ways. We surrounded our new survivors—they lived when we thought they had died. We hugged, and we cried anew as we realized the depth of our losses.

Jancy lifted her head from her grandmother's shoulder, and for the first time—after twenty hours of terrified screaming or inconsolable whimpering—screeched, "Daddy!" She jumped into her father's arms just as Flora June took the swaddled, soaked infant from him. Father and daughter clung to each other, sobbing. Little Jancy cried for her mama often during the next year and didn't want to let her daddy out of sight.

Douglass has not been the same since the storm. He knew his Nellie's last two acts before she vanished were to support him while he passed Jancy to the middle boat and to jump in the water to save their baby. He never found them, and he has never forgiven himself. In so many ways, he is like his father. Lucas was just as inconsolable after the death of our brother, BB, thirty years ago.

Douglass committed to caring for Maybelle's child with Flora June's promise of help. Jancy wanted to hold him and feed him, too. Lucas said that the baby boy resembled his Grandpa BB, and I agreed with my brother. Then and there, "Lil BB" became the darling of the family and never lacked love and attention. I think he gave us hope for the future.

Flora June said she had a good hold on both her boys when a large wave lifted the bateau from its cradle of low-slung oak branches. As their boat began its wild, terrible ride, it suddenly lurched, and to keep her balance, she had to loosen her grip on one of the boys—Bobby was hurled into the raging water. She could not save Bobby without losing Beanie. Even now, you know from her far-off gaze that she is thinking about her Bobby. Perhaps her pain is lessening now that Ed has moved onto the island to share Flora June's life.

Cousins Sunny and Flora June have grown even closer than they were before the storm. I see my daughter being like me—at her strongest when she can help others to a better day. Sunny supported Flora June in many ways, especially by being the best possible aunt to Beanie as he learned to live without his twin. Fortunately, Woody and Beanie have become constant companions, doing schoolwork, completing home tasks, and, whenever they can, fishing together on the dock.

Brent had to work many extra hours helping his employer clean up the office downtown on Bay Street, and working on his own home, and helping his neighbors take care of their properties, just like we did at Oakheart. He wanted Sunny and Woody to stay with him in town sometimes, but Sunny and he both understood that Beaufort was not ready for a couple that looked like them. So, Brent began spending as much time as he could at Oakheart—he and Sunny have started a garden.

One day, when we were all exhausted from the endless, depressing work, Brent brought out several of Sunny's paintings from the still-standing hall closet where they were stored for safe keeping. You can't imagine how much this simple gesture lifted Sunny's spirits. The whole family saw her eyes light up and her proud, humble smile return. Certainly, her heartfelt artwork helped the family bridge the gap from the tragic days in our past to a more hopeful future.

After we got over the first shock of our losses, the family pulled together about as well as we could. There was too much to do, too many people in need. I had to be doing something every day until I got too tired. At first, it was finding out how our people fared in the storm. We lost a third of the nearly one hundred people living in the Oakheart community, five from our own family. I helped set some broken bones and give basic medical care with next to no supplies. We tried to find safe places for folk to live and helped rebuild their houses, if anything was left of them. We shared our food, of course, as long as it lasted. But within a couple weeks, we all started getting hungry. Our storehouses were flooded, and our fields, saturated with salt water, were not going to grow anything any time soon. Animal carcasses were spread out over the fields and in the water along with our people. These islands were the face of despair, a true hell on earth. Those that survived had to deal with all manner of sickness but with little, if any, access to medicines.

Because Lucas made sure our boats were tied up before the storm in a way to float with the waves and wind, we recovered them all except the tree-boat that took our family members away. Even those boats that filled with rainwater and sank, tied up in our yard, were back in service once they dried out. So, Lucas and Douglass were busy from dayclean to sunset each day, rowing here and there for every purpose, mostly trying to find sustenance for us and ferry people where they needed to go. Of course, there are always fish in the sea and people on the move. Our men were able to learn the news of the islands, which was never very good. We heard that on one night soon after the storm, many homeless folks had taken refuge in Darrah Hall, the big building on The Green near Penn School. It was so sad...somebody trying to cook food started a fire and burned Darrah to the ground.

We were blessed that, although the second floor of our house was completely torn up, the first floor survived the rush of water beneath it, the crush of branches from above it, and the rain and wind that passed through it. We lived on right there, day by day fixing it up to the point that the first floor is finally comfortable, even though crowded. At the same time, Abram, Douglass, and some of our neighbors have been building new homes on their land, too. You hear hammers all day long and into the evening.

There is no end to the number of folk who continue to seek Abram's calm, ministerial manner to ease their troubled spirits. People felt they had no choice but to keep their faith in their God, as they had during their days in slavery. Just when we were feeling most overwhelmed by the problems we faced, almost as in answer to thousands of prayers, we started getting help from outside.

I was so relieved and pleased when I saw Clara Barton had come back to these islands. During the Freedom War, she helped us, and here she was again, thirty years later. It was Laura Towne and Clara Barton who had gotten me started helping injured soldiers and thought I was quite good at it, so they had sent me to Washington to learn more nursing skills.

About ten years before the storm, Clara Barton started a group called the American Red Cross, and the 1893 storm was the first time the Red Cross ever tried to provide disaster relief following a cyclone. It distributed food and clothing and other needed supplies. Missus Barton also helped people organize to dig ditches all over the islands—to use rainwater to wash away the salt that the flood left on our fields. When she decided to move the Red Cross distribution operation away from Beaufort and across the river to Ladies Island, the people came back to the islands to work. Lucas and his boys had all the ferrying work they could do when they weren't trying to rebuild houses and tend to their families. Clara Barton praised us island people for how hard we worked to make our land and houses and fields right again. At the same time, she earned our deep respect for her efforts to give us a chance to take care of ourselves.

While I always try to maintain a generous spirit and not speak poorly of anyone, I must tell you what the state governor, Ben Tillman, said after the storm. In comparison with Clara Barton's praise of the islanders' hard work to recover, Tillman said: "The people have the fish of the sea there to prevent them from starving. I hope, too, that someone will make them go to work at once and plant turnips on the island. I do not want any abuse of charity."

Needless to say, Mister Tillman did not know our people well. We did get a sad chance to educate him once, just last month, but I will say more about that man later.

On a much happier note, back in the war, when I really got to know my cousin Will, he and I met the man who wrote a report to President Lincoln about how to help the newly freed people of our islands. His name was Edward Pierce, and he told Will to let him know if he could ever help the people of St. Helena Island. Pierce was a man of his word. In 1883, he gave eight hundred books to our island library. After the cyclone, Will learned that he was studying for a law degree at Claflin University in Orangeburg, so, upon Will's request, Mister Pierce made a handsome contribution to the relief fund.

About the time Clara Barton arrived on the scene with her American Red Cross, my cousin Will floated in on a small steam ship that he had hired. It was packed tight with construction materials, lumber, food, medicine, farming equipment, and seed. Will joined Nathan Gates and a paid crew to build a whole new house where his old one had been. After he lived there for a short time, Will decided to return to Maryland and you know what he did? He gave me the house. I told him that I would live in it and take good care of it, but because he had purchased the land and built the house, it would always be his—just like the land we freedmen bought during the war will always belong to us and our families. I started living there just this past year, and let me tell you how much I love that deck Will and Nathan made. On a perfect day, I have hosted some fine family gatherings on it.

That reminds me to mention that Nathan Gates has been a true gift to our family and the people of Oakheart. Before and after the storm, he worked so hard to make Will's house stronger, and he has been willing to help anybody at Oakheart with any project. Will and Nathan joined Lucas and his boys to rebuild our dock. This new one is smaller, but it has two levels, with the higher dock for bigger boats and a nice low dock that floats with the rise and fall of the tide. It makes it easy for even old bodies like mine to slide off into a small bateau.

Being out on the river on my own reminds me of what Lucas told the people in 1863 when he helped Harriet Tubman take hundreds of people from plantation slavery to freedom down the Combahee River to Beaufort. He told them on that boat, "It ain bout jus bein free—it bout how you use yo freedom." Now, when the water is calm and the tide is still, I can row out on my own in the most peaceful way and let my mind go anywhere I want. That's a new kind of freedom I'm just beginning to learn about.

Speaking of peace on the river, I hope I will not seem small of mind or of an ungracious spirit, but I also have to report on the family across the river that lived in some conflict with Lucas and his family. That too-long-a-Confederate man who demeaned my brother and threatened our safety with his weapons, well, his dock all washed away, and both floors of their house were destroyed. I take no satisfaction in these facts, as I have empathy for all people, but I have to get respect from someone to keep giving that person my respect. I especially liked the friendly young man who came back to make amends to Lucas for the rudeness of his family. Oh, I should add that the young man's nasty uncle was the only member of that family to perish in the storm.

The only thing my brother ever did wrong, in the eyes of that Confederate man, was to make himself a success. Even though Lucas worked hard his whole life, paid all his debts, and treated people right, that man still stood in his face—on his own dock, on his own property, in front of his own family. That man believed he had a right to threaten Lucas and this family and take away our peace of mind.

Why? Some people think they are better than others due to the color of their skin. Maybe the flood waters taking that man away is a higher power trying to tell us all something important. That's all I can say about that man.

And now, let me tell you more about Ben Tillman, another white man who could not be comfortable with a successful black man. As South Carolina governor, he has the power to harm my people right now—and he is doing so.

Tillman had a plan that he and the Redshirts started executing just as soon as they got rid of the United States troops in 1876. These newly "elected" leaders of South Carolina took control again—old Confederates acting like they won the war. They terrorized my people all through this state. Tillman said he was doing this to us because we are dark-skinned people, and he was damn proud of what he was doing. Please pardon my colorful language.

Five years ago, in 1890, he said he was going to return whites to power and find ways to ignore the Fifteenth Amendment to the Constitution, the one that guaranteed, "The right of citizens of the United States to vote shall not be denied or abridged by the United States or by any state on account of race, color, or previous condition of servitude." I think the Constitution describes itself better than I can. And one thing you know about old Ben Tillman, what he says about being bad to black people, he means. So, just this year, he said he wanted a new statewide convention to change the South Carolina constitution to take the right to vote away from black men that was granted to them by both the state and the national constitutions.

It was not enough for Ben Tillman that the numbers of dark men voting in South Carolina went down from about eighty thousand in 1868 to about ten thousand last year because of all the brutal acts committed against us around election time. No, they wanted to take away the right to vote officially, legally, so-called.

With the tide running that strong against us, the 1895 South Carolina Constitutional Convention began. In 1868, more than half of the convention delegates were dark-skinned people, but we freed-men were only six of the convention attendees this year. Of course, it was a preordained conclusion that we would lose the right to vote and that the freedoms won through the Union victory in the war would be snatched away as if all those men died for nothing.

We dark people may have survived a great cyclone, but another storm, this one made by white men, is drowning my people in every way except with water. It's true that my people have been through the storm, and not just that awful night two years ago when many of us lost our lives and property. We also have been through the storm of race hatred, time and again. It seems we come out stronger in spirit and determination after every one.

Our folks may not be richest in terms of money, but we have our land, our water, our faith, and our family, and we been through more hard time than a people should have to endure. It's like Robert Smalls said just last month at the constitutional convention, when he was fighting in vain to keep our voting rights: "My race needs no special defense, for the past history of them in this country proves them to be the equal of any people anywhere. All they need is an equal chance in the battle of life."

Oh, yes, all his life Mister Robert Smalls was brave enough to tell the truth. I know what he said to be true, from my life, and I especially know it from the lives of the colored men I saw fight and die during the war. I know they carried the load just like my brothers, BB and Lucas, with a dignity equal to any man.

So, it took me a while to write this story. Sometimes there are more important things to do than write about your life—you got to live it. Yes, I have to help others. I have to be the best grandmama, mama, and aunt I can be—partly, by telling them all these stories so their generation will know from what roots they grow. Speaking of which, did I tell you that last month Sunny birthed a new grandbaby girl for me to love? Her name is Dawn. I can see, even though she is young, that she likes my stories. Just like I have been asking her cousins and her brother and her mother, I will be asking her, "Now, Dawn, what you gonna do today to help make things better?"

I have finished telling you my story, dear readers. I have to ask. What stories can you tell, and what stories from others will you listen to, so that people who are called black and people who are called white can understand one another better? More important, what can you do to make things better for everyone, especially all of our children?

GULLAH GLOSSARY

ack – act
afta – after
agin – again
aks – ask
ancha – anchor
ansa – answer
anodda – another
aw – or

bedda – better
beengah – was going to
bidness – business
big wada – Atlantic Ocean
bol – bold
bret – breath
buckra – white person(s)

cah em – carry it
captcha – captured
chirrun – children
crack my teet – smile
creachah – creatures
cuz – because

daak – dark
dah – that
das – that's
deh- there
dey – their
didn – didn't
dishyuh – this here
dohn – don't
duh – are
dut – dirt

e – it
ebba – ever
ebby – every
ebbybody – everybody
ebbyday – everyday
eben – even
em – them
eyeschuh – oyster

faah – far
fait – faith
fayah – fair
feebah – fever
figyuh – figure
fine – find
foat – fort
follah – follow
fuh – for/to
fuhgit – forget
fus – first

gah fuh – got to
gi – give
gon – going
guh – am going
gwine – going

haad – hard
haats – hearts
hafta – have to
hahm – harm
haid – head
han – hand(s)
heaby – heavy
hep – help
hih – his
holla – holler
hongry hongry – very hungry
huh – her
huhsef – herself
huht – hurt

injuh – injured
ifn – if

jus – just

kine – kind
kyan – can't
kyetch – catch

laan – learn
layda – latter
lee – little
lef – leave
leh – let
leh em – let them
lessn – unless

maak – mark
malasse – molasses
maash – marsh
madda – matter
memba – remember
memry – memory
moanful – mournful

needah – neither
nuf – enough

mek – make
memba – remember
mine – mind
monin – morning

neba – never
needuh – neither
nyam – eat

odda – other
ooman – woman
oona – you

oudda – out of
ovah – over

path – part
pass – died
piccha – picture
planta – planter
pose – supposed
propaty – property

quaat – quart

regla – regular
ribah – river
ris – risk
roun – around

scaid – scared
scape – escape
sef – self
sence – since
shawt – short
shaya – share
sho nuf – sure enough
shree – three
skrange – strange
skrent – strength
skroke – stroke
skrong – strong
slabe – slave
smaat – smart

smaates – smartest

smaats – smarts

soljuhs – soldiers

speck – expect

splain – explain

spose – supposed

staat – start

stan – stand

sto – store

stubbin – stubborn

suffa – suffer

supm – something

sutla – sutler

swimp – shrimp

tarectly – directly

tas – tasks

tass – task

tawd – toward

tief – thieve

togedda – together

tru – through

trute – truth

tuh – to

tuhday – today

wada – water

wah – war

wedda – whether

wen – when

wey – where

whaaf – wharf

wort – worth

wud – word

wuk – work

CHRONOLOGY OF ACTUAL
EVENTS REFERENCED WITH
QUOTES AND SOURCES

1861–1865   **"The Port Royal Experiment**...was in effect
a dress rehearsal for Reconstruction acted out
on the stage neatly defined by the Sea Islands
of South Carolina....Here the first troops were
recruited among the late slaves and put to the
test of battle; the first extensive schools for
[freedmen] got under way and the assault on il-
literacy began; abandoned land was confiscated
and freedmen took precarious title; the wage
system received several trials and freedmen ex-
perimented with strikes and bargaining; political rallies and local politics first opened up an
exciting range of experience....The Port Royal
Experiment became not only a proving ground
for the freedmen, but also a training and re-
cruiting ground for personnel of the postwar
Reconstruction." (Rose, 1964)

May 1862   The United States Army trained and armed formerly enslaved black men as a new regiment,
the **First South Carolina Volunteers**. "I
cannot praise General David Hunter too high-

ly, for he was the first man to arm the black man, in the beginning of 1862." (Romero 1988)

May 13, 1862   **Robert Smalls and others stole the *Planter*.** "Robert Smalls, a native of Beaufort and the islands, the pilot of a steamship called the *Planter*,...quietly secreted his family and a few chosen associates aboard his master's vessel and in the faint dawn of Tuesday morning, the thirteenth of May, stole out of Charleston Harbor, bound for Port Royal." (Rose 1964)

August 1862   **Robert Smalls met with President Lincoln.** "Smalls told the President that former slaves were anxious, able and badly needed to protect the Union Occupied regions of the South from Rebel raiders. Lincoln gave permission to enlist 5,000 black men in the Union army, shattering the color barrier that had kept blacks out of military service." (Kennedy 2011)

September 1862   "**Dr. Jonathan Letterman** may not be as well known as General Ulysses S. Grant, but he played just as important a role in winning the Civil War for the Union. Known as the 'Father of Modern Battlefield Medicine,' Letterman's work saved thousands of soldiers from dying horrible deaths on the battlefield.... [He] started the very first Ambulance Corps, training men to act as stretcher bearers and operate wagons to pick up the wounded and bring them to field dressing stations. He also instituted the concept of triage for treatment of the casualties." (American Battlefield Trust Accessed 2018)

January 1, 1863

The Emancipation Proclamation was issued by President Lincoln. "Though limited to 'areas of the Confederacy outside Union control'...by decreeing the freedom of the bulk of the nation's black population, well over 3 million men, women, and children, the proclamation sounded the death knell of slavery throughout the country, and profoundly changed the character of the Civil War. Transforming a war of armies into a conflict of societies, it ensured that Union victory would produce a social revolution within the South." (Foner and Mahoney 1995)

May 1864

Battles of the Wilderness (May 5–7, 1864); Spotsylvania (May 8–20, 1864). (National Park Service, Wilderness 2018)

July 9, 1864

"During the summer of 1864, the Confederacy carried out a bold plan to turn the tide of the Civil War in their favor. They planned to capture Washington, DC, and influence the election of 1864. On July 9, however, Federal soldiers outnumbered three to one, fought gallantly along the banks of the Monocacy River in an effort to buy time for Union reinforcement to arrive in Washington, DC." (National Park Service, Monocacy 2017)

January 1865

Penn School, founded in 1862 and functioning from the old Brick Church during its first two years, moved into its own building as 1865 began. "A gift from the Freedmen's Aid Society of Pennsylvania, the three-room frame building arrived in already-built sections. This building, one of the first prefabricated structures in American history, was put into service as the first real schoolhouse in the South designed for the instruction of former slaves." (Burton 2014)

February 1865

Charleston abandoned and First South Carolina Volunteers enters. "On February 28, 1865, the remainder of the regiment were ordered to Charleston, as there were signs of the rebels evacuating that city....The mayor of Charleston readily surrendered it to Lt. Colonel A. G. Bennett of the Twenty-first US Colored Troops, who promised the assistance of the black men to the stricken people. The irony of this scene—the freed slaves now coming as victorious soldiers to the aid of the defeated, their old masters, makes one of the most poignant stories of the Civil War." (Romero 1988)

March 4, 1865

Lincoln's second inaugural address concluded: "Fondly do we hope, fervently do we pray, that this mighty scourge of war may speedily pass away. Yet, if God wills that it continue until all the wealth piled by the bondsman's two hundred and fifty years of unrequited toil shall be sunk, and until every drop of blood drawn with the lash shall be paid by another drawn with the sword, as was said three thousand years ago, so still it must be said 'the judgments of the Lord are true and righteous altogether. With malice toward none, with charity for all, with firmness in the right as God gives us to see the right, let us strive on to finish the work we are in, to bind up the nation's wounds, to care for him who shall have borne the battle and for his widow and his orphan, to do all which may achieve and cherish a just and lasting peace among ourselves and with all nations." (Lincoln 1865)

April 14, 1865 **President Abraham Lincoln was assassinated.** "On the island here they are inconsolable and will not believe he is dead. In the church this morning they prayed for him as wounded but still alive, and said that he was their Savior—that Christ saved them from sin, and he from 'Secesh.'" (Holland 2007).

May–June 1865 **General Lew Wallace** served on the military commission for the trials of the Lincoln assassination conspirators. On August 21, 1865, he was appointed to preside over the military investigation of Henry Wirz, a Confederate commandant of the Andersonville prison camp. (Wikipedia 2018)

May 23–24, 1865 There were no black regiments in the **Union victory parade** in Washington at (Civil) war's end. (Kreitner 2015)

1865 "No longer under the control of the US Army, Contraband Hospital, now known as **Freedmen's Hospital**, became in 1865 an official part of the Bureau of Refugees, Freedmen, and Abandoned Lands popularly known as the Freedmen's Bureau." (Newmark 2018)

March 3, 1865 "Congress passed, and Lincoln signed, a bill creating the **Freedmen's Bureau**, an agency empowered to protect the legal rights of the former slaves, provide them with education and medical care, oversee labor contracts between emancipated blacks and their employers, and lease land to black families." (Foner and Mahoney 1995)

December 6, 1865 The **Thirteenth Amendment to the Constitution** states that "Neither slavery nor involuntary servitude, except as a punishment for crime whereof the party shall have been duly convicted, shall exist within the United States." www.loc.gov/rr/program/bib/our-docs/13th-amendment.html

February 9, 1866   **The First South Carolina Volunteers mustered out, by order of Lt. Colonel C. T. Trowbridge.** "The hour is at hand when we must separate forever, and nothing can take from us the pride we feel, when we look upon the history of the 'First South Carolina Volunteers,' the first black regiment that ever bore arms in defense of freedom on the continent of America." (Romero 2007)

March 3, 1865   **The Freedman's Bank** was chartered by Congress in 1865 following efforts "to establish a 'benevolent' banking institution that would provide African American soldiers with a secure place to save their money and at the same time encourage 'thrift and industry' in the African American community....In 1864, for example, Gen. Rufus Saxton created the Military Savings Bank at Beaufort South Carolina, eventually known as the South Carolina Freedmen's Savings Bank, to secure the deposits of African American soldiers." (Washington 1997)

December 1, 1865   **"General Ulysses Grant** traveled through the South Carolina lowcountry from Charleston to Hilton Head to Savannah. Grant commented during this tour 'that the racial attitudes of the former Confederates could not be changed in a day' and that the freedmen would require protection and care from the Freedmen's Bureau agents 'for a few years.'" (Wise and Rowland 2015)

April 9, 1866

The Civil Rights Act of 1866 stated: "That all persons born in the United States...are hereby declared to be citizens of the United States; and such citizens, of every race and color, without regard to any previous condition of slavery of involuntary servitude,...shall have the same right in every State and Territory in the United States, to make and enforce contracts, to sue, be parties, and give evidence, to inherit, purchase, lease, sell, hold, and convey real and personal property, and to full and equal benefit of all laws...as is enjoyed by white citizens..." 1866 Civil Rights Act, 14 Stat. 27030, April 9, 1866 AD. https://en.wikipedia.org/wiki/Civil_Rights_Act_of_1866

May 12, 1867

At a mass meeting of Republican citizens on St. Helena Island, SC, "One black man said he wanted no white men on their platform, but he was taken to task by all the other speakers, who disclaimed all such feelings. It was funny to hear the arguments from the other side—such as, 'What difference does skin make, my bredren. I would stand side by side a white man if he acted right. We mustn't be prejuduid against their color.' 'If dere skins is white, dey may have principle.' 'Come, my friends, we mustn't judge a man according to his color, but according to his acts.'" (Holland 2007)

July 9, 1868   <u>**The Fourteenth Amendment**</u> **to the Constitution** was ratified, granting citizenship to "all persons born or naturalized in the United States," which included former slaves recently freed. In addition, it forbids states from denying any person "life, liberty or property, without due process of law" or to "deny to any person within its jurisdiction the equal protection of the laws." www.loc.gov/rr/program/bib/ourdocs/14thamendment.html

July 9, 1868   **Robert Smalls,** "as a delegate to South Carolina constitutional convention, introduced and won support for compulsory education for all children between the ages of seven and fourteen, the schools 'to be opened without charge to all classes of the people.'" (Burton 2014)

October 30, 1868   **Violence against African American voting participation.** "They say that fears are entertained of Mr. Tomlinson's safety—no one knows where he is....The colored Senator from South Carolina was shot down a day or two ago." (Holland 2007)

"White Democrats in South Carolina, a minority in the state, were not content to win elections fairly. They ushered in a reign of terror, and no action, no matter how heinous, went untried in the effort to eliminate African American voting power. One effective tactic was to murder those who voted or held office. Seven state legislators were murdered between 1868 and 1876." Burton, *Penn*, 38.

1869

General Robert E. Lee counseled Southerners, "I think it wiser not to eep open the sores of war, but to follow the example of those nations who endeavored to obliterate the marks of civil strife, and to commit to oblivion the feelings it engendered." Robert E. Lee commented "when asked to attend a meeting to commemorate Civil War monuments." (Fellman 2003)

February 3, 1870

The Fifteenth Amendment to the Constitution stated that the "'right of citizens of the United States to vote shall not be denied or abridged by the United States or by any state on account of race, color, or previous condition of servitude.'" www.loc.gov/rr/program/bib/ourdocs/15thamendment.html

October 1871

President Grant sends US troops into nine upstate counties in South Carolina to stop Ku Klux Klan lawlessness and violence. "The legal offensive of 1871, culminating in the use of troops to root out the South

Carolina Klan, represented a dramatic departure for the Grant administration....Judged by the percentage of Klansmen actually indicted and convicted, the fruits of 'enforcement' seem small indeed, a few hundred men among thousands guilty of heinous crimes. But in terms of its larger purposes—restoring order, reinvigorating the morale of Southern Republicans, and enabling blacks to exercise their rights as citizens—the policy proved a success." (Foner 2014)

1874

The Freedman's Bank failed. "The closure of the Freedman's Bank devastated the African American community. An idea that began as a well-meaning experiment in philanthropy had turned into an economic nightmare for tens of thousands African Americans who had entrusted their hard-earned money to the bank. Contrary to what many of its depositors were led to believe, the bank's assets were not protected by the federal government. Perhaps more far-reaching than the immediate loss of their tiny deposits, was the deadening effect the bank's closure had on many of the depositors' hopes and dreams for a bright future." *https:// www.archives.gov/publications/prologue/1997/ summer/freedmans-savings-and-trust.html*

May 1875

DeTreville v. Smalls, **court decision on land title held by freedmen.** "Thomas, whom I sent to a meeting Robert Small(s) had called yesterday, to see what it was about, came back joyfully saying that one Yankee lawyer, Mr. Corbin, had got the better of eight rebel lawyers, and that the lands were safe. The newspaper confirmed the news in a telegram from Charleston." (Holland 2007)

"The decisive case in these disputes over land titles was *DeTreville v. Smalls*, which was finally settled by the US Supreme Court in 1878. This case upheld ex-slave and war hero Robert Small's title to a Beaufort home formerly owned by South Carolina lieutenant governor Richard DeTreville." (Wise and Rowland 2015)

1876 election

Democrat wins popular vote; Republican wins electoral college vote and becomes president. "In the national election of 1876, the Electoral College chose the Republican Rutherford B. Hayes over the Democrat Samuel Tilden, but the deal making that gave Hayes the presidency included the end of political Reconstruction, meaning that the nation was no longer willing to enforce voting rights, or any civil rights, for African Americans." (Burton 2014)

Subsequent "negotiations produced results inescapable by February 1877: [Republican] Hayes's inauguration and an end to Reconstruction. By this time, everyone understood that Hayes would adopt a new Southern policy....Wrote the chairman of the Kansas Republican state committee on February 22: 'I think the policy of the new administration will be to conciliate the white men of the South.'" (Foner 2014)

July 15, 1877

South Carolina denies localities right to tax for education. "Our little island has been expressing itself. We met as usual on the legal day for the district school meeting, June 30th, but we could not vote to levy any school tax, because the Democratic legislature had forbidden it....[T]he people here are the taxpayers, there being on the island five thousand blacks and not fifty whites, twelve hundred and eight black children of age to attend school, and only seven white children, and because the few white people here are as anxious for schools as the blacks, and as willing to pay the tax voted at these meetings. This is to be published in the newspapers and will show not only the injustice done in forbidding people's providing for the public schools adequately,—and as handsomely as they please—but also that the St. Helena folks are awake to their rights." (Holland 2007)

1874 to 1888

Robert Smalls served five terms in the US House of Representatives. "An escaped slave and a Civil War hero, Robert Smalls served five terms in the US House [from 1875 to 1887]...Smalls endured violent elections and a short jail term to achieve internal improvements for coastal South Carolina and to fight for his black constituents in the face of growing disfranchisement."

Smalls escaped the Democratic tsunami that swept South Carolina local elections [in 1876]. Polling places were spared much of the Red Shirt violence, primarily because Governor Chamberlain requested federal troops to stand guard....Defending himself in the final session of the 44th Congress, Smalls called Election Day in South Carolina 'a carnival of bloodshed and violence.'" US history.house.gov/People/Detail/21764

See US House of Representatives, Robert Smalls Biography, introduction.

October 7, 1877	**"Robert Smalls has been arrested.** They have two objects in this. One is to prevent his taking his seat in the approaching Congress, and the other to bring odium upon him and give his opponent in the contested seat a better chance." (Holland 2007)
November 6, 1878	"On Saturday I went to a Republican meeting at the church. Robert Smalls told of his mobbing at Gillisonville. He was announced to speak there, and when ten o'clock—the hour—came, he was on the spot and with him about forty men. The stand was in front

of a store in the street, and men and women were coming up the street to attend the meeting, when eight hundred red-shirt men, led by colonels, generals, and many leading men of the state, came dashing into the town, giving the 'real rebel yell,' the newspaper said....Then the leader, Colonel somebody, came up and demanded half-time. Robert S. said there would be no meeting. Then they said he *should* have a meeting and *should* speak. He refused to say a word at a Democratic meeting, and as there was no Republican one, he said he would not speak at all." (Holland 2007)

November 10, 1878 **"Robert Smalls was defeated**, and the people are greatly grieved about it, and are not reconciled." (Holland 2007)

August 25, 1885 "That day a near hurricane brushed the coast. Five pilot boats were caught offshore in the storm and all were sunk. Fourteen crewmen were drowned....But for the heroism of the pilot captain, W.H. Von Harten, who swam through the raging surf off Bay Point to bring a life line to the stricken pilot boat of Captain John O'Brien, the loss of life in 1885 would have been greater...and Von Harten was given a gold medal for lifesaving by the US government." (Wise and Rowland 2015)

1889   **Robert Smalls appointed collector at the Port of Beaufort.** "Republican President Benjamin Harrison appointed him the collector at the port of Beaufort. He held the post until Republicans lost the White House in 1892. Smalls regained the appointment in 1898 from Republican President William McKinley. Over time, his duties as collector became more onerous in the face of racism and segregation in Beaufort. He was forced to step down in 1913 after the White House again transferred to a Democrat." US history.house.gov/People/Detail/21764

See US House of Representatives, Robert Smalls, Biography.

1890   **Congress approves $5,000 payment to Robert Smalls for the *Planter.*** "The US Government never fully compensated Smalls for the value of the *Planter* as a reward for its capture [he received $1,400 in 1863]. During the next 30 years, black Members of Congress sought compensation for Smalls equal to the value of the ship. The House finally approved a measure...on May 18, 1900, during the 56th Congress (1899–1901). [While the original request was] that Smalls receive $20,000, the Committee on War Claims, however, reduced the amount to $5,000." US history.house.gov/People/Detail/21764

August 27, 1893   *"The Great Sea Island Storm of 1893* is a heartbreaking tale. As many as 2,000 people, maybe more, were killed in the hurricane that hit coastal Georgia and walloped South Carolina with winds up to 120 miles per hour and a ten- to twelve-foot storm surge. Another 1,000 may have died afterward from injury, dehydration, starvation, and illness." (Marscher 2003)

1895   **South Carolina Constitutional Convention revoked voting rights granted in the 1868 constitution.** Robert Smalls spoke in opposition: "My race needs no special defense, for the past history of them in this country proves them to be equal of any people anywhere," Smalls asserted. "All they need is an equal chance in the battle of life." US history. house.gov/People/Detail/21764

See US House of Representatives, Robert Smalls Biography.

BIBLIOGRAPHY

American Battlefield Trust. "Civil War Biography Jonathan Letterman."
    Accessed July 26, 2018. https://www.battlefields.org/learn/
    biographies/jonathan-letterman.

Bartleby .

Burton, Orville Vernon with Wilbur Cross. *Penn Center: A History
    Preserved.* Athens, GA: University of Georgia Press, 2014.

Clinton, Catherine. *Harriet Tubman: The Road to Freedom.* New York:
    Back Books/Little Brown and Company, 2004.

Conner, T.D. *Homemade Thunder: War on the South Coast, 1861–1865.*
    Savannah, GA: Writeplace Press, 2004.

Cross, Wilber. *Gullah Culture in America.* Winston-Salem, NC: John F.
    Blair, 2012.

Daise, Ronald. *Gullah Branches, West African Roots.* Orangeburg, SC:
    Sandlapper Publishing, 2007.

Downs, Jim. *Sick from Freedom.* New York: Oxford University Press,
    2012.

Edgar, Walter. *South Carolina – A History.* Columbia, SC: University of
    South Carolina Press, 1998.

Elliott, William. *Carolina Sports by Land and Water.* Charleston, SC:
    Burges and James, 1846.

Faust, Drew Gilpin. *Mothers of Invention: Women of the Slaveholding
    South in the American Civil War.* New York: Vintage Books,
    1996.

Fellman, Michael. *The Making of Robert E. Lee.* Baltimore: Johns
    Hopkins University Press, 2003.

Foner, Eric. *Reconstruction: America's Unfinished Revolution 1863–1877.*

New York: Harper Collins, 2014.

Foner, Eric, and Olivia Mahoney. *America's Reconstruction: People and Politics After the Civil War.* New York: HarperCollins Publishers, 1995.

Fraser, Jr, Walter J. *Lowcountry Hurricanes Three Centuries of Storms at Sea and Ashore.* Athens, GA: University of Georgia Press, 2006.

Furgurson, Ernest B. *Freedom Rising: Washington in the Civil War.* New York: Vintage Books, 2005.

Garrison, Webb. *The Encyclopedia of Civil War Usage: An Illustrated Compendium of the Everyday Language of Soldiers and Civilians.* Nashville, TN: Cumberland House Publishing, 2001.

Glen, Isabella C. *Life on St. Helena Island.* New York: Carlton Press, 1980.

Grim, David Bruce. *Swift Currents.* Bloomington, IN: iUniverse LLC, 2014.

Helsley, Alexia Jones. *Beaufort, South Carolina: A History.* Charleston, SC: The History Press, 2005.

Higginson, Thomas Wentworth. *Army Life in a Black Regiment.* New York: W.W. Norton & Company, 1969.

Holland, Rupert Sargent, ed. *Letters and Diary of Laura M. Towne.* Salem, MA: Higginson Book Company, 2007.

Hurmence, Belinda. *Before Freedom, When I Just Can Remember.* Winston-Salem, NC: John F. Blair, 1989.

Kennedy, Robert F., *Robert Smalls, The Boat Thief.* Collingdale, PA: Diane Publishing, 2011.

Kozak, Ginnie. *Eve of Emancipation: The Occupation of Beaufort and the Sea Islands by Union Troops.* Beaufort, SC: Portsmouth House Press, 1995.

Kreitner, Richard. "Victory Parade 150 Years in the Making." *The Nation.* May 11, 2015. https://www.thenation.com/article/

victory-parade-150-years-in-the-making/

Lamson, Peggy. *The Glorious Failure: Black Congressman Robert Brown Elliott and the Reconstruction in South Carolina*. New York: The Norton Library, 1973.

Lander, Jr, Ernest McPherson. *South Carolina: The Palmetto State*. Chicago: Childrens Press, 1970.

Lincoln, Abraham. Second Inaugural Address. March 4, 1865. www. bartleby.com/124/pres32.html.

Marscher, William and Fran. *The Great Sea Island Storm of 1893*. Macon, GA: Mercer University Press, 2003.

McDaniel, Rick. *An Irresistible History of Southern Food*. Charleston, SC: The History Press, 2011.

McFeely, William S. *Yankee Stepfather: General O. O. Howard and the Freedmen*. New York: W. W. Norton & Company, 1968.

McPherson, James M. *The Negro's Civil War: How American Negroes Felt and Acted During the War for the Union*. New York: Vintage Books, 1965.

Mitchell, Patricia B. *Plantation Row Slave Cabin Cooking: The Roots of Soul Food*. Chatham, VA: Patricia B. Mitchell, 1998.

National Park Service. Wilderness cites of Civil War in Spotsylvania and Orange Counties, Virginia. https://www.nps.gov/abpp/ battles/va046.htm.

National Park Service. Monacacy National Battlefield site in Civil War. https://www.nps.gov/hfc/pdf/ip/2010-02-22-MONO-FinalDocument.pdf.

Newmark, Jill. "Contraband Hospital, 1862–1863: Health Care for First Freedpeople." *BlackPast*. Accessed May 30, 2018. www. blackpast.org.

Rhyne, Nancy. *Before and After Freedom: Lowcountry Folklore and Narratives*. Charleston, SC: The History Press, 2005.

Robinson, Sallie Ann. *Cooking the Gullah Way Morning, Noon, & Night*.

Chapel Hill, NC: The University of North Carolina Press, 2007.

Romero, Patricia, ed. *A Black Woman's Civil War Memoirs*. New York: Markus Wiener Publishing, 1988.

Rose, Willie Lee. *Rehearsal for Reconstruction: The Port Royal Experiment*. Athens, GA: University of Georgia Press, 1964.

Rubillo, Tom. *Hurricane Destruction in South Carolina: Hell and High Water.* Charleston, SC: The History Press, 2006.

Segars, J.H. *Andersonville: The Southern Perspective*. Gretna, LA: Pelican Publishing Company, 2001.

Taylor, Taylor.

Washington, Reginald. "The Freedman's Svings and Trust Company and African American Genealogical Research, 1997. https://www.archives.gov/publicatons/prologue/1997/summer/freedmans-savings-and-trust.html

Wikipedia. "Lew Wallace." Last modified May 29, 2018 *https://*:wikipedia.org/wiki/Lew_Wallace

Wise, Stephen R., and Rowland, Lawrence S. with Gerhard Spieler. *Rebellion, Reconstruction, and Redemption, 1861–1893, The History of Beaufort County, South Carolina, Volume 2*. Columbia, SC: University of South Carolina Press, 2015.

AUTHOR NOTE

THE SIGNIFICANCE OF THE RECONSTRUCTION ERA IN AMERICAN HIS-tory is not well understood today. That is unfortunate for our country because many of our lingering, festering racial tensions arise from this period when enslavement of people by race ended and we had a chance to take positive steps toward reconciliation.

There was remarkable progress toward racial justice during the 1860s and 1870s, until Reconstruction ended. Then, through inattention, racism, and cold calculation, racial inequities between United States citizens grew over the next century. We, as a people of many colors, have been unable to settle our racial discomfort.

To heal our wounds from once being a slave nation requires empathy for those who have been victimized by racial hatred, and even for their progeny. This book, *Still a Rising Tide*, and its prequel, *Swift Currents*, attempt to share the joys and sorrows of this journey toward justice from the perspective of those who have been lifted up by its promise and held back by its cruelties. It asks the reader to imagine the challenges and disappointments inherent in the transition from enslavement to freedom for people of color.

We all may not agree on the causes and solutions for our racial strife. It seems to me that we as Americans, who speak proudly of our heritage, should also be able at least to give our empathy to those persons who suffered under slavery, and their descendants. They have borne a deeply unfair burden during the first four hundred years of American racism.

When will our racial animus end? Can we, I wonder, join together to *Still a Rising Tide*?